Sweet Sleep

KIM CORMACK

Mythomedia Press 2754 10th Ave

V9Y2N9 Port Alberni BC

ACKNOWLEDGEMENTS

To my wonderful children, Jenna and Cameron. Thank you for giving me strength in the moments when I felt like I had none left. You are the reason I get up every morning and push myself forward. May you always believe in magic and never stop fighting life's dragons. Always believe in the impossible.

To Mom, Dad and Nana Scott. You are my support system. Love you always and forever.

To Carol for your endless hours of support and friendship.

To Leanne and Haley for the hours upon hours of editing fun xo You ladies rock!

To my friends, for always giving me a reason to laugh and for always providing me with such awesome comic material. You endlessly listen to the inner workings of my mind and not one of you has asked me to stop talking about this series...yet. I love you all more than a few typed words at the beginning of a book can say.

WARNING

The information contained within this book is not intended for mere mortals. Reading this may inadvertently trigger a Correction. If you have shown great bravery during your demise, you may be given a second chance at life by one of the Guardians of the in-between. For your soul's protection until your 18th year, you must join one of three Clans of immortals living on earth. *You are totally still reading this, aren't you? You are such a badass I'm impressed. You'll fit in great.*

A LETTER TO MY READERS

This series started out as a nightmare and turned into a dream. It kept me moving forward during a time when it would have been so easy to give up.

Thank you for joining me on this incredible journey towards my own Enlightenment. Every mountain you climb makes you stronger. Every struggle gives you wisdom. You have the strength to deal with anything life throws at you. We are strong. We are durable. We are all immortal. I hope to keep you happy with these characters and this series for many years to come.

Kim Cormack XO

PROLOGUE

In every lifetime, there is a moment, so clear, so profoundly unique that it stands out against billions of other moments. Pay attention, it may contain something that defines you in the future.

"Are you certain she's the one?" Lily whispered.

Frost replied, "Pretty sure, she even looks like Freja. How old do you think she is? Four, maybe five?"

A duplicate of the child ungracefully plopped onto the grass beside her twin. Grey commented, "This is an unexpected glitch. What does this mean? How is this possible?"

They were mirror images of each other. Frost replied, "It's not."

Lily whispered, "This complicates things."

One of the freckle-faced twins noticed the Ankh watching. She sprang to her feet, raced over to the fence and stood on her tippy toes. Grinning, she stuck her chubby fingers through the rungs of the fence, squeaking, "Do you want to play?"

Lily gushed, "Aren't you the most adorable thing in the

whole wide world."

"What's your name, delightful creature?" Grey asked with an Aussie accent.

"I'm not a thing or a creature, I'm a kid. My name is Kayn, that's my sister Chloe," she pointed a tiny finger adorned with messy sparkle nail polish at her twin.

The scrappy child at the fence radiated joy and the blissful innocence of childhood. There was sand on her lovely frilly white dress, grass in her hair and a frog sticker on her cheek. Her twin was glaring. Clearly, Chloe was not going to be the one abducted by a stranger. Frost was standing there beaming like a fool, so captivated by the scrappy child standing in front of him that he couldn't even speak.

"You guys look like movie stars." Kayn gushed, and then turned her attention to her hand, "I have nail polish on, see?" she exclaimed, her eyes gleaming with pride as she displayed her wiggling fingers for the rest to see.

"Lovely," Lily appraised.

A little boy with a mess of dark curls came running up to the fence. Glaring at the group, he grabbed Kayn's arm, leaned in and whispered in her ear, "Chloe says you're not supposed to talk to strangers."

The little girl stated, "Chloe's not the boss of me." Grasping the fence, she stuck her face against it with her upturned nose sticking through to the other side.

Blown away by the feisty, spirited child, Frost touched one of the little girl's dainty fingers through the fence. Marvelling at the vibrant intensity of the innocence shining behind the chain link barrier, the immortal whispered under his breath, "It's important you become strong," touching the tip of her nose with his finger.

The Beginning

1

THE MOMENTS BEFORE SHE SLEEPS

The humming of Kayn's blood as it coursed through her veins seemed to sing along to the steady, almost tribal beat of her feet pounding rhythmically into dirt. She resembled a flaxen-haired angel attempting to outrun a cloud with a veil of earth flowing behind her for a moment or two longer than it should with not a whisper of wind in the afternoon air. A smile spread across her lips. Her heart was overflowing with too much joy to be contained beneath a serious competitive demeanour.

In a moment of clarity, she noticed Kevin wasn't sitting in the grass watching her train. She pictured him rushing to his locker and fumbling with the lock while attempting to keep the facade going. She wasn't stupid. She knew he didn't enjoy watching her run. There was a method to his madness. Her best friend was madly in love with her twin sister. He'd been addicted to the mere sight of her since kindergarten. To anyone else this would make no sense but Kayn understood. She was Kevin's friend. Chloe was his fantasy. In her vision of why he was late, he was caught in a swarm of students squishing through the doorway into the gym, shoved against the wall and his books fell out of his backpack. After collecting his papers, he zipped up his bag, continuing his quest to be in the presence of her twin, the unattainable Chloe Brighton. Out of the corner of her eye, she saw Kevin racing up the hill. He unceremoniously plopped himself in the grass next to her school bag and things were as they should be.

As she rounded the corner, Kevin was fiddling with his cell. *He was timing her.* She flashed past in a cloud of dust. Lean and freckled, with tanning spray sparkles glittering in the sun, Kayn imagined she looked quite magical at the beginning of a run, but by the end, she would always end up looking like she'd spent her afternoon rolling in dirt, instead of running on it. They smiled at each other through the haze. With the warmth of the sun's rays whispering on her skin, she rounded a corner kicking up another cloud to outrun as electricity surged through her. Adrenaline rippled a winding path beneath her flesh, igniting her soul and setting it afire with insurmountable pleasure like she'd been given an anointment of power. She hit the straight stretch in transcendent euphoria, baptized by the sweat trickling down her forehead. Alive in a way only a runner could comprehend, every nerve ending was humming, *"Faster, Kayn. Go faster."* Born to push limits, runners were a breed of their own. "Don't Call Me Baby," was cranked in her ears. Powerful and strong, she kept pace with the beat.

Listening to his music, plucking grass, Kevin glanced up as she approached, overzealously waving with a charming toothy grin. *He'd done this since kindergarten.* Shaking her head, she slowed her pace. Her heart thumped wildly in defiance to her walking feet as she licked salty lips and wiped the sweat off her brow, drying her hands on her shorts. Noticing the streaks, she knew there was dirt on her forehead. Grassy scent signalled his arrival, and as she turned, his grin told her she was right about the dirt, but he was too busy cheering to mention it. *You'd think she'd just won the Olympics or something equally spectacular. The sight of him cheering with no sound to the music in her ears was more than a little adorable.* Kayn yanked out one of her earbuds.

"Holy crap!" Kevin yelled in her face. "That's your best time this year! You are going to kick butt at the finals next month!"

"My earbuds are out. I can hear you," Kayn hinted, smiling.

"Oh, you think you're pretty cool because you're fast. Well, young lady, plenty of people are fast, but how many people can do this?" Kevin ribbed, doing a dance involving a twirl and a running man, laughing at her mortification.

"Please stop," Kayn sighed, surveying the surrounding area for witnesses. *She was the socially awkward version. She was fine with that but always did her best to avoid Chloe's friends after a run when she was in desperate need of a shower. She preferred to skip the week of snarky comments in the hall.* She took off as he jogged to keep up with her athletic strides. *He was giving her a weird look. He'd often told her she resembled an Amazonian sized forest nymph. She knew it was probably because she was tall and didn't care if she was covered in dirt. She had never been sure if his observation was meant as a compliment.*

Kevin was the most adorable child but when puberty hit, so did a crazy amount of acne. She'd been way taller since seventh grade. *Their mothers hadn't anticipated this complication while plotting their nuptials when they were seven. She thought he was adorable. His skin was clearing up a bit. Her affliction was different, she was invisible. To her, this was a good thing. It was her preference to blend into the crowd.*

"You are awesome. I'm not saying that to butter you up, so you'll put a good word in with your sister," Kevin bantered with a grin.

She loved him to death, but she'd been letting him down easy for a decade. Slowing to a casual stroll, Kayn put an arm around him, teasing, "My sister is way too advanced for you."

"Right, that's what you say to all the guys stalking your twin," he countered, grinning at her creative way of calling Chloe slutty.

Choking on a laugh, Kayn sparred, "I was forced to come up with one token line to use for everyone. It's a time saver."

Feigning distaste, he flirtatiously responded, "I can't believe after all these years, I'm merely a number to you."

His flirtation attempt was cute. She might have been flattered if he meant it. Giving Kevin a friendly pat on the shoulder, Kayn said, "Do yourself a favour, take a hint. She's not right for you." She slapped his butt. He yelped, jumping away. "At least have the decency to warn me if you find yourself wanting to wear my sister as a skin coat so I can get you help," she teased. *He shot her a dirty look.* Grinning, she taunted, "How hard can it be to arrange an intervention in your honour? Let's try to avoid the padded cell." Kayn winked, waiting for his comeback.

"You should have your own comedy show," he commented.

"It'd be hilarious if it wasn't the truth," Kayn challenged. *Chloe was the polished version of her. Always the picture of perfection, her twin was stylish, popular, and described with flowery words like captivating, stunning, and provocative. Kayn was blandly characterized as cute, funny, and a good runner. They didn't hang out in the same crowd. Kayn had no crowd. It was just her and Kevin. The only boys who'd shown interest were after her sister. Being less sophisticated, Kayn would fall for their games, thinking foolish thoughts like, maybe this time he likes me? They'd chat on the phone, and just as her heart fluttered with romantic possibilities, they'd make their intentions clear by calling her a friend and asking about her sister. Friends was an uncomplicated word, she had despised from a young age because of Chloe. It felt like the wind from a breath that would blow out every candle of hope she'd kept lit inside of her heart her whole life to date.*

She'd be lying if she claimed this constantly repeating scenario hadn't bred resentment, but she never let it show. Not once had she freaked out at Chloe for stealing her imaginary boyfriends or for being morally bankrupt. Her twin didn't adhere to the same ethical codes as everyone else. Kayn had this thing called a conscience, which included guilt and a voice in head repeating, don't do it until she chose to listen. She was certain Chloe's inner voice urged, do it because there was no need for sentiment or morality in Chloe's mind.

The self-contained universe revolving around her was simply amazing. One could stand with mouth agape for hours listening to stories of mini catastrophes her womb mate caused. It was like she was protected in a snow globe with life's chaos merely surrounding her. Occasionally someone stirred up the water, but it swirled around her like everything else did, never touching her or causing her to lose a second of control. She was unaffected by the world, unwavering through life's currents. Believing her alluring sibling had mystical powers, Kayn couldn't be angry. Chloe had always been enticing like there was catnip for men on her. *They were in the same womb for nine months. How all the game ended up in one baby was a mystery.* Kevin's opinion was the only one she valued. They'd joke about her sister's voodoo magic, but as soon as Chloe was within a ten-foot radius, even he couldn't tell you his name. She stopped walking and looked back. *It felt like she was being watched.* Kayn shivered as an icy breeze passed through her, fluttered through the grass, carried on up the hill and stirred up the dust on the track. *A random cold spot on a sweltering day was strange. She overworked herself today.* Noticing the motionless trees surrounding the track, she turned her attention back to Kevin to hush the nagging voice in her mind, repeating, *something's wrong.*

"Someone walk over your grave?" Kevin whispered in her ear, breaking the silence.

Kayn smiled at Grandma Winnie's quote. *She always said that if someone shivered in her presence. If you sneezed, it was a ghost passing through you. If she was called out for shivering, her retort was, I'm not dead, Granny. The elderly woman's response was usually something wise and ominous like, if only you knew how irrelevant that word is.* Kevin's grandmother seemed to have a direct line to the spirit world, and nearly all their chats were more than a wee bit creepy. She was a quirky, warm, witty woman who treasured her from day one. Kayn was a faithful member of team Granny. Unlike the rest of the planet, she saw through her sister. She'd gasp for oxygen, whenever Chloe was nearby, pretending she couldn't breathe while making foul stench related comments, believable enough to cause her twin to smell her own armpits. Being void of respect for her elders, and pretty much everyone else, Chloe would refer to her as a crazy old bat or a witch, then Granny Winnie would call Chloe out on an evil deed like she'd read her mind.

The clear blue-sky altered to a powder of fast-moving clouds. *Strange weather.* Her pulse raced. The potent scent of grass and pine needles from the trees lining the far side of the track made her eyes water as amplified grass rustled underfoot. *Maybe it was a flu?* Snapping back to reality as Kevin's feet came into sight, she raised her brows and pointed out his untied sneakers. As he tied his shoes, Kayn commented like she was reading his obituary, "Kevin Smith was a wonderful boy, so smart and good looking but a little clumsy. Had he only tied his shoes, he wouldn't have fallen down the stairs and impaled himself on a janitor's broom. Remember kids. Tie your shoes. Safety first."

"Have I told you lately that you're an asshole?" he jousted as she finished taunting him.

She didn't have a comeback, just a nasty case of the heebie-jeebies. The hairs on the back of her neck prickled. Kayn glanced behind her and then from side to side, unable to shake the unnerving feeling something was coming. There was a hollow ache in her chest and a sensation that lingered each time she swallowed.

Leaning in, Kevin whispered, "Your sketchy behaviour this afternoon is beginning to creep me out."

His warm breath made her shiver, and she had the strangest urge to kiss him square on the lips. *It must be low blood sugar?* She replied, "Just overtired, I guess," glancing back again.

"Stop looking behind us, you're freaking me out!" Kevin laughed, hip checking her.

Shaking her head, Kayn giggled, "I don't know what's wrong with me today."

Twirling in a circle, Kevin announced, "Nobody is stalking you I swear."

"I know," Kayn answered, "Maybe I'm coming down with something?"

"We should be more worried about your creepy behaviour causing you a nasty case of whiplash," Kevin chuckled, flinging his arm around her, giving her a buddy squeeze as they walked. "You should go have a shower. You are sweaty and nasty. What do you do, cover yourself in honey before you go for a run?" Chuckling, smelling his hands, he groaned, "Ewww, that's not honey."

"There you go talking dirty, literally," Kayn sparred. "All of this talk about toxins and waste is so hot."

"What was your boyfriends' name again?" Kevin taunted.

"What's your invisible girlfriend's name again?" Kayn asked, winking.

"Her name is Chloe. She just doesn't know it yet," he teased.

Ugh, he couldn't help himself. Constant talk of her sister irritated her to no end. It was his easy smackdown in a comedy standoff. "What's the difference between you and a stalker?" Kayn responded sweetly.

He sighed, "Do tell, wise and mighty stalking connoisseur."

"It's whether or not you're wearing my sister's stolen thong underwear right now," Kayn declared, trying to peek down his shorts.

"Hey, hey, simmer down. I'll yell rape, I'm going commando. Pulling my shorts off isn't a great idea," he laughed, fending her off.

"Like you could handle me," Kayn chuckled, cringing with pain, shifting her backpack to her other shoulder. *It had twenty pounds of books in it. She couldn't memorize her locker combination. She was horrible with numbers. That was her excuse. The real reason being, she'd be obliged to speak to the vapid girls that hung out around by her locker. She liked to be left alone in her own little world.*

Grabbing her heavy bag, Kevin remarked, "Hey, I'll have you know I've been going commando since my first wedgie in fifth grade. If they grab for underwear and don't find any, they back right off."

Giggling, Kayn countered, "I don't doubt that for a second."

"You learn lots of nifty things to help you manoeuvre through geekdom unscathed if you're crafty, you know," he toyed as they continued walking.

He was carrying both bags trying to be a gentleman, it was adorable. She knew how heavy hers was. Smiling, Kayn snatched her backpack back. *These moments always made her wonder if they'd ever be something more. Would he ever make a move? She wasn't sure he had any. If he tried something, she'd probably assume it was a joke.* He caught her staring and winked. *What was she thinking? She must be hormonal.*

Nudging her, Kevin questioned, "Why is Chloe being into me so impossible to you?"

Wincing, Kayn scolded, "Stop talking about Chloe, I'm sick of it."

Placing a finger over pursed lips, he whispered, "You know not to speak of her voodoo powers."

She grinned. *It was the truth. The phrase, Chloe has a boyfriend was easily comparable to cursing out loud in the Brighton household. Her sister ran like she was on fire from every boy she dated. Seemingly normal guys would lose their marbles. The fear of losing her made their sanity unfold like a reversal of an origami swan. It would start with a vehicle outside of the house in the middle of the night and escalate. Once Chloe grew annoyed by their obsessive behaviour, they'd break up, and no matter how wonderful they were, things always went dark. It wasn't just those she dated. Random guys would break into the house and steal objects belonging to her. After a couple trips the police station, where full-grown men were fawning all over her, her parents understood what she'd always known, Voodoo Powers. The last thing she needed was to be caught gossiping by one of Chloe's minions.* "The last guy she broke up with went crazy. Let's talk about something else," she replied. They looked at each other, giggling. A stinging slap on her rear made Kayn jump.

"Hi dorks! How's social purgatory?" Chloe baited, grinning.

Her infamous moderately evil twin was gracing them with her presence, good times. Chloe acknowledged Kevin's presence with a glance. He turned ten shades of red. *Pathetic.* Kayn shook her head.

Putting her arm around her, Chloe grimaced, shoving her away, saying, "Ewww, yuck, you are sweaty. Listen, backstabbing witch with a B, I don't feel good. I'm heading home, do you need a ride?" She finished the sentence with a show-stopping smile.

It was like her sister's life was an endless beauty pageant. She was always prepared for a picture. Her show pony sister was sarcastic ninety-nine percent of the time so Kayn rarely took her insults seriously, "I'm all good. I'm going for a shower, then to Kevin's for dinner."

Kissing her cheek, Chloe grimaced, whispering, "Yes, go have that shower." She dramatically sighed, "I'm grounded again for no reason."

"Shocking," Kevin mumbled, rolling his eyes.

Her sister purposely got grounded to have a forced break from her social responsibilities. If medals were doled out in the Olympics for groundings achieved in a three-year period, she would have a gold medal.

"Bye Kevy," Chloe sang, flouncing off.

"Voodoo powers," Kevin whispered, watching her go.

"I heard that you little stinker," Chloe sparred, laughing.

As they strolled away, Kayn teased, "I bet when you thought of sexy couple nicknames, little stinker wasn't one of them." *She couldn't help it. She was on a roll.* He socked her arm.

Kayn spun around, accusing, "I can't believe you'd do that," rubbing her arm, pretending to be upset.

"I didn't hurt you, did I?" Kevin whispered right away.

Her serious expression crumbled into a grin. She chuckled, "No hitting women," smoking his arm twice as hard.

"What woman? I don't see one," he slammed, pretending to search, rubbing his arm. He chuckled, "Oh, you mean you."

"I'll butt you out like a cigarette little man!" Kayn jousted, making a fist. Kevin glared at her. *Oh, no. He had that expression. It was all fun and games until she made one too many short jokes.*

"I'm not little," he declared, stomping off.

"Vertically challenged?" Kayn provoked, pursuing him. *She was digging her own grave. He could argue for hours.*

"I only look short to an Amazonian like you," he countered.

"Touché," Kayn admitted, suppressing laughter. *He had to stop.*

"I'm still growing," he bantered. "I may be the hottest guy in this town in a few years."

If his voice kept cracking, she was going to lose it. They walked into the fitness centre. "I'll see you in fifteen minutes, sexy," Kayn seduced. Grinning, she shoved on the door to the changeroom.

"Quit mocking me, Amazonian!" Kevin shouted dramatically.

His retort echoed off concrete and tile as she took off her shoes. The cool flooring soothed her aching feet. She dropped her runners. As they landed on the tile, it echoed and repeated like someone dropped another pair. Kayn stripped and gazed at her reflection. She tugged out her ponytail, and damp ringlets fell down her bare shoulders. She tilted her head, posing seductively. *He was having a coffee ogling the girl's swim team. There was no need to rush. He was fine. Maybe, she should start wearing makeup to school? She could look just like Chloe if she wanted to.* Kayn plastered a giant pageant smile on her face and scrunched up her nose. *She enjoyed being dorky and weird. It would take far too much effort to pull off her sister's level of perfection. She didn't need to be perfect. She would wither and fade if she had to live her life under a microscope. She let her strange roam free.* Her stomach cramped. She winced and glanced back at her reflection on her way to the shower. The conversation with her sister flashed through her memory. *She'd had sympathy pains before when her twin wasn't feeling well. Chloe was sick today. That's all this was.* She turned on the water and stood under the spray, smiling as it relaxed her weary muscles. Lathering herself with scented pump soap, she hummed her favourite running song. She was singing when the door opened. *Awkward.* Silently rinsing off, Kayn stepped out of the shower and towel-dried her hair. *Nobody was in the change room. Weird?* She passed by the mirror, wondering if her sister ever wanted to be more like her. *That was crazy. Only five minutes older, Chloe had always acted like those minutes were years. Maybe, it was skills-wise? It would be nice if someone asked her on a date before she was eighty. With no voodoo powers to speak of, all she ever felt around boys was awkward. She was different with Kevin. Having feelings for him would not be a great move friendship-wise. There it was again, that ominous word, friends.* With moisture from her hair trailing a river down her spine as she dressed, Kayn's thoughts kept drawing her back to confusing romantic feelings for her best friend. *What was with her inner dialogue today?* Hoping Kevin hadn't reached the point of being frustrated waiting, she grabbed her bag and shoved open the door. He was sitting on the railing, looking up at the sky with his mouth open. Wandering over, she teased, "Trying to catch flies?"

"Always," Kevin sparred with quick wit and a dimpled grin.

"What are we looking at?" Kayn asked, gazing up, mimicking his open-mouthed awe.

"Come on, I'll show you," Kevin laughed, taking her hand as they strolled to the field.

She'd lived this moment a thousand times. Kevin sprawled in the grass, and she did the same. "Oh, wow. I get it. Look at how fast the clouds are moving. Maybe there's a storm coming?" Kayn whispered, observing the sky from her spot in the plush cushion of greenery. A sharp pain seared through her core. She grabbed her stomach. Sucking a deep breath in, she gasped, "What the hell was that?"

"You okay, Brighton?" Kevin said as he sat up and reached for her.

Kayn winced again as she doubled over, her insides afire with strange, penetrating pain. Kevin placed his hand on her midriff, and the pain disappeared as quickly as it began.

He looked at her, saying, "I bet you need a big glass of water and something to eat?"

She shook off the feeling she was missing something and got up. *She forgot lunch. She was just dehydrated and hungry.* With the pain gone, she replied, "Yeah, that's probably it."

"You skipped lunch again, didn't you?" Kevin scolded with a disapproving look.

Smiling, she admitted, "Guilty as charged." *There was a simple explanation for the pain. She was practicing at lunchtime, she forgot to eat.* Shivers crawled up her spine and she felt the urge to look behind her. Concerned, she spun around, trying to shake off the strange sensation plaguing her all afternoon. Her internal dialogue was still whispering, *be careful.* She shook off the anxiety. *It's just low blood sugar or the heat.* As they strolled home, they stopped by the turn off to Lakeshore Drive. *The last horror move they watched took place at a lake. It was probably a mix of a bunch of things. Low blood sugar, heat exhaustion, and recalling a horror movie was enough to make anyone feel a bit wonky.* She laughed at her overactive imagination.

Yanking a handful of grass from the earth, Kevin inhaled its fragrance and declared, "Just what I thought."

"What's that?" Kayn enquired, knowing he was about to make a joke about the movie.

"It's hillbilly urine, we'd better get our tasty selves' home," he announced with dramatic flair. Kevin ominously pointed in the direction of his house, proving he had no acting chops.

"Let's get out of here geek," Kayn sighed, shaking her head.

Grinning, he posed like he was at the start line of a race, provoking, "It's got to be close to five, I bet dinner's already on the table."

Eyeing up the competition before simultaneously grinning, they sprinted through the field before the trails. *They'd been doing this ritual race home since they were allowed out of their yards as children.* Kevin was a sneaky opponent because there was no possible way to beat her in a race without trickery involved. He shoved her, and she fell with a thud into the grass. "Cheater!" She hollered after him as he ran away, cackling. Sprawling dramatically in the grass, she gave him a head start before scrambling to her feet and beginning her pursuit. On his tail even with his rule stretching, she slowed her pace. *It was good for him to win sometimes.* Vaulting over the fence, Kevin beat her, raucously cheering with his arms raised. *He'd never won graciously. She'd take one for the team to see him this happy.* As he opened the door, delicious aroma wafted out.

Greeting her with an enormous loving bear hug, Mrs. Smith raised her brows, scolding, "You two are covered in grass. Brush yourselves off outside and go wash your hands. Make it quick. We're all at the table ready to eat."

Wiping each other off outside, they raced for the bathroom. *This time he legitimately beat her.* When Kevin came out, he gave her a playful shove as he passed. She checked herself out in the mirror and giggled while picking grass out of her hair. *How wrong must it look when two teenagers of the opposite sex show up for dinner covered in grass? Well, anyone else. For them, platonic wrestling was normal. If her dad caught them wrestling on her bed, he wouldn't flinch.* After washing her hands, Kayn wandered into the dining room and sat at her usual spot. *Kevin's family mirrored her own. They were always cracking jokes and chatting loudly about their day.* She loved everything about the Smith house, from the mismatched frames filled with family photos in the dining room to the outdated green shag carpet in the den. The ambiance was completed by a cozy couch with two peacefully lounging felines. Granny sat at the head of the table. Her wispy white hair was even more wildly untamed than usual. She'd always been able to envision Kevin's grandmother as a younger woman because of the black and white picture of her in the hall. Beautiful didn't encompass Granny in her youth, for she had been enchanting with crimson curls and exquisitely structured cheekbones. There was strength of spirit in her eyes. Physically as frail as a fawn, she wasn't the picture of pin-up perfection, but had an unexplainable quality that made you curious. She was a girl with many secrets. The chapters were written in the creases of her smile.

Famished, Kayn devoured her meal and reached for another bun. *Granny Winnie had been staring at her for fifteen minutes. It didn't look like she'd blinked. She hadn't touched her meal. Was she alright? Usually talking everyone's ears off, she hadn't spoken a word.* Smiling, Kayn enquired, "How was your day, Granny?"

Granny Winnie said, "You know something's amiss, don't you?" Her eyes widened. She covered her mouth like she'd said something naughty.

Granny was always saying ominous things. This wasn't even the creepiest thing this week. Kayn took a bite of her bun, unsure of how to respond.

"Kayn had cramps. She forgot to eat lunch," Kevin answered for her.

Kevin's mom reprimanded, "You are going to make yourself sick, honey. You need to eat properly!"

"Perhaps," Granny Winnie replied, glanced down at her plate.

Granny looked ill today. It felt like she had more to say. Feeling eyes on her, Kayn peered up.

With unmasked sadness, Granny warned, "Always listen to your instincts, child. They are never wrong."

She'd been saying that for years, so she brushed it off.

After dinner, they hung out in Kevin's room until his mom came in to tell her it was nearly eight. *She didn't really want to go home, but they'd reached the age where boy-girl sleepovers were frowned upon.* As Kayn was preparing to leave, Granny made her way over, embraced her so tightly she couldn't breathe, and whispered in her ear, "You survive this night. You fight hard."

There would be at least a three-hour-long conversation about spiritual things if she asked her to explain what she meant. She didn't have the mental steam left inside of her to go through the motions today. Kayn excused herself and went to the bathroom. She called home and it went straight to voicemail. *Chloe was probably on the phone. Heaven forbid she had a crisis and needed to talk to her parents. Chloe had a cell, but she was always grounded from it. They allowed her to talk on the landline for hours, which meant nobody else could get through.* She tried her mom's cell, knowing she was going to be a few minutes late and left a message when there was no answer. She shoved her phone back in her pocket and tip-toed down the hall to Kevin's room. *She had time for a prank to liven up his evening.*

When she reappeared, Kevin's mom handed her a bag of eggs for her family from the chickens in their backyard. His dad offered to drive her because it was already dark. The drive was uneventful. The same old muted dusk scenery flashed by her window. As they pulled up in front of her house, she leaned across the seat and thanked Kevin's dad with a hug. She opened the door and took a deep breath. *The air smelled like wet cherry blossoms. It must have been raining while they were eating dinner.* She stepped out of the car into a puddle and twisted her ankle. *Of course.* With a soaked foot, eggs, and school bag in hand, she hobbled up the driveway towards the front door. She lived in a wooded, somewhat isolated area. Normally she would have darted from Kevin's dad's car into the house, but her ankle stung each time she put pressure on it. As she came closer, she noticed the door was partially open. *It was a little windy out and quite normal for the door to be unlocked. Maybe it was left ajar and opened by the wind?* She heard tires on gravel and turned just in time to see Kevin's father driving away. Kayn felt off, apprehensive as she made her way up the gravel driveway to the door that seemed to have a life of its own, shifting from cracked to closed with the breeze. She dug out her phone to look at the time. *Quarter after eight. She was fifteen minutes late.* The door moved again. She shook her head and laughed. *This was obviously a prank. They'd left the door open, and entrance lights off to freak her out. Chloe was probably hiding around the corner. Practical jokes were a daily occurrence in their household.* Slivers of light from the moon flashed through branches as they swayed in the wind and for a moment it felt like they were waving her away. *She was being silly.* She shoved her cell into her pants, accidentally pocket dialling Kevin.

"I'm home!" Kayn yelled, kicking off her shoes and dropping her backpack. She flicked on the light and nothing happened. *The power wasn't out. The lights were on upstairs when she walked up the driveway. It's just a burnt-out lightbulb.* She massaged her ankle. *Great, there goes the track meet.* Kayn tried to take off her wet socks. A stab of pain from her freshly twisted ankle caused her to place a hand on the wall while attempting to balance. Her hand slid off as she struggled to tug off a sopping wet sock. "Kevin's mom gave us eggs," she called out, realising she was alone. *Where would they go at this hour? Her mind sorted through scenarios. Something wasn't right.* "Mom... Dad?" She said, answered by silence. She went to close the door and felt something wet. A faint sliver of light was streaming through the doorway. She stepped into it and held out her hand. Her palm was covered in blood. *Whose blood was this?* Paralyzed by fear, adrenaline coursed through her like thousands of tiny spiders running on the surface of her skin. A dark figure loomed at the end of the hall. *Who was that?* She gingerly stepped backwards.

In a primal shrill pitch, Chloe shrieked, "Run Kayn!"

With survival instinct on fire, Kayn fled with the bag of eggs. Rattled, she ran with no rhyme or reason, slipping in wet grass. Scrambling forward, she sprinted for the trails, pitching the bag to slow her attacker. Fuelled by panic-induced impulse, she burst through overgrowth, ignoring pain as blackberry brambles tore her flesh, running with everything inside of her as twigs snapped behind her. Rounding a corner, she slipped in mud, skidding not falling, losing her half-second lead with her heart thudding wildly as athletic legs propelled her body through winding trails. Rocks on the path brutalised her bare feet as sharp, reaching branches and twigs slashed her limbs.

'You have to run faster, Kayn! Run faster!' Her sister's voice screeched in her terror-driven mind. *He was inhumanly fast.* Lights from the neighbour's house peeked through the trees. *She was going to make it. She was almost there. Almost to safety, just over the creek.* Her feet hit the wooden bridge as the darkness pursuing her kept pace, panting. *Almost there. She was going to make it.* About to burst through the bushes, she felt the elation of victory as something hot was driven into her back. Her eyes widened in terror as his knife seared a molten trail of agony. He muffled her cries as she sunk to her knees in disbelief and crushed her larynx with python strong arms so she couldn't scream. At the brink of strangulation, he revived her with his tortuous blade. *Why was this happening?* Propping her up to see salvation she wouldn't be granted, she saw someone in patio lights through the trees. *Help me. See me. I'm right here.* Kayn's mind begged as he knifed her. *He's killing me. Please,* her soul pled. Her vision blurred with tears as blood sputtered from her lips. The competing rhythms of their hearts and his rapid breathing made her stomach churn with revulsion. His quiet laughter echoed in her mind as blood soaked through her clothes, trickling down her arms. *She was going to die.* He released her, whispering in a language she didn't understand. She slumped forward and tried grasping the ground with her fingertips, but no matter how hard she struggled from within the confines of her mind, she couldn't move. A soothing voice in her mind, whispered, *sleep, it's time to go to sleep.* As she closed her eyes, she heard Grandma Winnie's final words to her, 'You survive. You fight hard.' She screamed from within, clawing at the soil, forcing herself up to her knees. There was a blinding explosion of pain across her face. The lights flickered and went out. *In the woods lay a bleeding angel in all her glory. Her arms posed gracefully above her head, her hair soaked in the mud, blood, and feces in which she lay. Dying, fading into the other realm, her form was christened by rain, as the trees wept upon her for the brutality she'd endured.*

Kayn awoke in frigid darkness to the fragrance of damp moss, tree sap and the sweet metallic taste of the blood in her mouth. Images from her childhood flickered through her mind as pain recycled in waves until it dulled to become a tolerable numbness. *She was so cold. Where was she?* Her body involuntarily shuddered as her mind fed slivers of the inhuman savagery she'd suffered until she understood where she was and how she'd come to be dying in the forest all alone. *Maybe if she kept her eyes closed, he'd believe she was gone? She could slip away peacefully and become one with the forest.* Soothing raindrops tapped on the branches above her. *Maybe, he was gone?* She opened her eyes and imagined the lush green branches of the cedar trees above as giant arms, capable of offering her protection from the elements. At first the image was nurturing and beautiful, but the trees came to life. They cackled and mocked, "You're going to die, you silly bitch," as they waved their branches to the haunting sound of rattling raindrops and the howling of the wind. Kayn's consciousness snapped back to reality. *She'd lost a lot of blood. None of this was real.*

The forest floor was alive with a dancing mist that seemed to add a thickness to the tapping raindrops. Writhing in the mud as her essence moistened the ground beneath her, Kayn willed her body to move. Her fingers clawed at the soil until she was spent. She lay still like a half-dead animal waiting to be finished off by a hunter. With her eyes gazing to the heavens, she watched a stream of light from the moon that made it through the cover of rain clouds and branches. *It felt like she was breathing through a pinched straw.* She concentrated on each breath. *In and out, a little air.* The glimmer of light vanished, leaving only cold, isolating darkness and the flickering of blurry, confusing images. *Help me.* The only answer to her soul's plea was the crackling of rain. What vision she had clouded with tears as excruciating pain returned and she screamed from within the confines of her mind. As the wave of agony passed, she sensed his presence and tried to focus through the glossy film of her tears. His dark shadow ominously loomed as it had in the hallway, watching her. *Please. No more.* She willed herself to grasp at the moist cold earth with her fingers, but she was unable to move. *Her body was nothing more than a broken shell. How cruel for her mind to desire life at this point.* As his form loomed above, she thought, *why are you doing this?* Involuntarily shuddering, she realised she was exposed to the elements. *Why was she naked?* Her eyes filled with tears. *Why was this happening?*

The dark mass of her violator knelt and leaned in. She smelled his putrid breath as it moistened her face. There was an electrical current between Kayn and the man in the dark. Every hair stood on end as he ran a finger over an exposed breast, disclosing, "You were never to be born, this situation had to be corrected."

His knife glinted in moonlight as he raised it above her chest. *Yes. Let it be over.* She closed her eyes as he sliced into her flesh and opened them with acceptance. *She felt no more pain.* She stared into his eyes as hers filled with tears.

With a voice thick with emotion, he declared, "From this life unto the next."

He carved a symbol above her heart. She lay limp in his arms, conscious of what was happening, as he cradled her like a baby, rocking her broken violated flesh, stroking her blood-soaked hair, sobbing as though he were repentant for how he'd tortured her.

As her vision flickered one last time, the man was gone, and in his place was her mother. Her eyes were filled with so much love it released her from pain and fear as it had when she was a child. Safe in her mother's arms, she was at peace. *Mommy*, her heart sang, *you're here to save me*. The warmth of her mother's love enveloped her tortured soul. She gazed into her mother's eyes as she lovingly caressed her face, singing a song she'd sung to her every night when she was small. *Sleep, sweet sleep till the morning. Just dream away and close your eyes. My love, you'll be safe until the morning. Sleeping in my arms, all through the night. Although bad dreams come to scare you. My love will scare them all away. My heart...*

The lights flickered, the pain went away, and her mother was holding her, singing, "Sleep, sweet sleep."

The Beginning

2

CONNECTED

Connected: To be joined or linked together. Having the parts or elements logically linked together presenting a thoroughly connected view of the problem.

Kevin stood at the window waving as his father's car pulled out of their driveway as he'd done for nearly a dozen years, picking at the blue weathered window frame. He got a sliver under his nail, cursing, "Son of a..." He dug the shard out with his teeth. Blood seeped, he stuck his finger in his mouth and sucked on it. "Works better than a Band-Aid," he commented, checking for witnesses. *Every time he talked to himself, someone always appeared out of nowhere and made a smart-ass remark. No, he was alone in his room. It was time to relax.* Sprawling on his bed, with his arms behind his neck, he spotted the alterations Kayn made to the sexy poster of Megan Fox above his bed. *Funny. His shenanigan loving friend had given her a jiffy marker moustache. That's why she was laughing so hard when she came back from the bathroom. It was a stroke of evil genius on her part.* He stared at his ceiling, shaking his head. *She was so weird.*

The day he met the Brighton twins always stood out in his

memory as truly magical. He was playing in the park with his mother and brother a few days before kindergarten started. A woman gave him a flower and told him a story about it. When she was finished, she'd pointed at identical girls and suggested he tell them about the flower. He remembered walking over. They were quietly watching bumblebees. Intrigued by their unusual behaviour, he joined them. Before they left, he put a flower in Kayn's shoe.

In school, the twins wore matching sundresses. They looked like tiny blonde angels with freckles and glistening shiny ringlets. The Brighton twins weren't cute identical, they were disturbingly similar. They'd simultaneously respond to questions and often even be thirsty or need to go to the washroom at the same time. He recalled his kindergarten teacher's frustration with their in-sync questions and answers. No matter how hard she tried to socialise the twins, they'd just play together like no other children were even in the room. Different in some ways, Chloe never had a hair out of place. Kayn was all grins, grass stains and mud. He smiled at the friendly one a lot because Kayn smiled back and wondered if she still had a flower in her shoe. He knew he'd have to find a way to become her sister's friend if he wanted to play with Kayn, so he decided to win over, Chloe Brighton.

His quest began at lunchtime that day. The Brighton twins were lying in the field intently watching a patch of clovers. Kevin walked over and sat with them, asking, "What are you doing?"

Glaring, Kayn whispered, "Shhh, you will scare them away. We are petting bees."

Even at the tender age of five, he knew petting bees was a crazy idea. "Bees sting, it hurts a lot. Believe me, I know," Kevin whispered.

"My daddy says they won't sting us if we're gentle with them," Kayn whispered back.

He watched the twins petting bees for his entire lunch hour waiting for one of them to be stung, so he could say, I told you so. He was impressed when it was time to go inside, neither twin had been wounded. He'd been so quiet, they decided he'd be a suitable addition to their duo. Chloe hadn't acknowledged his presence that first day, but the next, it was her who asked if he'd like to come to watch bees. They did this all the way through that year and for many after.

One-year he bought Kayn a stuffed bee for her birthday. She still had it on her bed even after she found out she was allergic to bees. She swelled up like a balloon. It was a scary day. She still loved bees from afar and with an EpiPen in her fanny pack. Her parents forced her to wear that fanny pack every day because being allergic to bees was a life or death thing. When questioned about whether she had an allergy to bees like her twin, Chloe would reply, "A bee wouldn't dare sting me." He'd believed that statement as fact the first time she said it. They were eight years old, but he'd wager her voodoo powers worked on bees as well as boys. Kevin grinned as he realised the mission of that second day never ended. *It had been well over ten years, and he was still on a mission to win over, Chloe Brighton.* Kevin lay on his bed, listening to the hum of a vehicle as it faded into silence. *For some reason, he was feeling anxious tonight.* Someone knocked on his door.

Standing there, leaning against his door frame, smiling in her all-knowing manner, his mother said, "Do you want to know what I think?"

His mom was sweet to her core, the sound of her voice always put him at ease. With a funny look, he teased, "Not really, but I bet you're going to tell me anyway."

His mom marched over, gave him a playful swat for being a smart ass and questioned, "Is it possible you're pining over the wrong sister?"

"I guess anything's possible," Kevin replied, smiling.

Rolling her eyes, she urged, "Just think about it. Which one do you really want to spend time with?" Kissing his forehead, she ruffled his hair and left, shutting the door softly behind her.

The door slammed downstairs. *Great, the Hulk was home.* His older brother Clay came thundering up the stairs. It was like his testosterone level made him incapable of even the simple act of climbing stairs without announcing his all-powerful presence. His older brother was a muscle-bound meathead of astounding proportions. *Please, don't come in my room.* He wasn't a fan of the inevitable sock in the stomach he'd receive for calling his older brother out. It was difficult to keep his lips sealed when he had a great slam teetering on the tip of his tongue. *It was a sibling thing.* Clay was working for a mechanic in town, saving for college. He was also best friends with the twin's older brother, Matt. His bestie was in university with a football scholarship. Kevin's bedroom door swung open without a polite knock. *Here we go.*

"I need to use the cord for your iPod. I'm going to the gym later, I forgot to juice mine up." Clay blurted, digging through the cords around Kevin's computer.

Raising his brows, Kevin commented, "What if I said no? Presumptuous much?"

Clay shook his head, questioning, "Did you seriously just say presumptuous much to me? You need to start hanging out with dudes." Walking to the door, he stopped and added, "No more big words. It's painfully dorky. You're my brother. You should be making out with chicks on a Friday night."

Squinting at his brother, Kevin thought, *if I looked like a Greek god instead of a vertically challenged dwarf, maybe I would. Kayn's slam from earlier stung. Oh no, she called him vertically challenged. Someone else had called him a dwarf.* Scrunching his face, he glared at his buff stallion of a sibling. *It was genetically unfair.* At one time his brother had been built just like him, but after finding a reverence for the gym and football, he achieved Greek god status and never looked back. Kevin's phone rang.

Grinning, Kevin teased, "Well, wouldn't you know it. There's a chick right now."

"Kayn doesn't count," Clay chuckled. Noticing the poster on the ceiling, he exclaimed, "You are a creepy little dude."

Ignoring him, Kevin took off, answering her call, "Thanks for pimping out my poster." With knowledge of her usual foibles, he jogged down the stairs, teasing, "Did you forget your bag?" *She wasn't talking.* He stopped halfway down. *It was the infamous pocket dial.* Hoping for juice on Chloe, he kept listening. His cell squealed like there was interference. Just as he was about to hang up, Chloe shrieked in an ungodly pitch for Kayn to run. He froze as the colour drained from his face. Clay came down the stairs with his iPod cord in hand. Kevin grabbed his brother's arm, urging, "We have to get over there." *He had to get to Kayn. Chloe's desperate scream was playing on a spine-chilling loop in his mind.*

The brothers ran out the door, jumped into the car and peeled out of the driveway, passing their father coming home from dropping Kayn off at the end of the block. Frantically honking, signalling for him to follow, their father swerved a U-turn.

Chloe's inhuman screaming was still ringing in his ears like a sick recording, driving his desperation to reach Kayn. The phone was by his ear. There was a lot of crunching, sloshing, swishing, then silence. *He couldn't hang up. He knew she needed him.* They raced down the gravel road to her house with desperation constricting his heart. The idea of someone hurting her was too much to bear. His mind raced through worst-case scenarios. His dad caught up as they pulled over in front of Kayn's house and got out.

His father shouted, "What in the hell is going on?"

Choking on adrenaline, knowing there wasn't time to explain, Kevin sprinted up the path with Clay, forcing their father to follow. The veil of trees blocked the glow of the moon, making it difficult to determine where the path was. Slowing, so his dad could catch up, Kevin explained, "Chloe was screaming on the phone for Kayn to run."

"Stop!" his dad hollered with authority reserved for danger.

He couldn't. Clay seized his arm, preventing him from pushing past his father.

"We don't know what we're walking into," his dad asserted. Blocking the path to the door, he commanded, "Stay behind me, I'm going in first."

Danger was in the air, making his skin crawl. *It was too quiet.* "I have to get in there," Kevin asserted, wrestling free of Clay's grasp.

Grabbing Kevin, his dad calmly stated, "I know, son. We are just going to exercise caution, that's all. Stay behind me."

The ominous feeling came to chilling fruition as they walked through the pitch-black doorway. His father attempted to flick on the light. *It didn't work. Was the bulb burnt out?*

In darkness, his brother stated, "The lights were on upstairs."

"I know," his father replied, reaching up to tighten the bulb.

A student manually loosened each bulb in the school. He always checked to see if they'd been loosened now. The light flickered on revealing a morbid display of blood spatter on the walls. *This wasn't happening.* Tears clouded Kevin's eyes. *This was his second home.* Thick drag marks lead to the hall closet. Covering his hand with his sleeve, his dad opened the door. *It's not Kayn, it's not her,* Kevin repeated in his mind. *It can't be.*

The opened door revealed the lifeless body of Kayn's mother. Claire Brighton's eyes were wide open, staring off in the distance. His father looked back and shook his head.

"Don't touch anything. It's unlikely someone capable of that left witnesses," his dad decreed. On autopilot from his younger years as a medic, the soldier took over. He stepped away to call 911.

In shock, Kevin stared at the gruesome scene with eyes glued on Claire's open, glassy stare. *All that had been Kayn's mother was gone. This was nothing more than the vacant case she came in. Spiritual clarity amidst the macabre.* Kevin's brain sparked with thoughts of Kayn. *Find her. She needs you.* The Smith brothers slipped down the hall. Kevin reached up and twisted the bulb as his father had in the entrance.

His dad shouted, "Don't touch anything! You're destroying evidence! Go back outside!"

They left the light alone but continued down the hall, ignoring his order. *They couldn't wait for police.* Kevin's mind kept repeating, *Kayn is alive. Find her.* He turned on the light in the kitchen. *It was normal.* The boys snuck back down the hall and slipped past their dad on the phone. Their father had closed the closet to shield them from the horrors within. *It was too late for that.* Kevin raced upstairs, knowing his brother was behind him. The upstairs hall was lit up, displaying a path of morbid bloody footprints leading to the twin's bedroom. They cautiously made their way by family portraits, now serving as an eerie reminder of what used to be. Approaching sirens brought Kevin's shock numbed mind back a touch. A vision of Mrs. Brighton's corpse distorted his view of the hall, he blinked it away.

His father's voice called out, "The police are here! Get back down here!"

Kevin brushed a crusty red footprint with his shoe. He bent and touched it with his finger. *It was dry.* The voice in his head whispered, *find her.*

His father's voice bellowed, "I have to stay down here to let them know you boys are upstairs! Once they see this blood, they might shoot us first and ask questions later!"

The doorknob to the twin's room was caked in blood and left slightly ajar. Kevin stiffened, preparing himself. Elbowing him out of the way, Clay shoved the door open from the upper left corner. The beds were still made. Bloody footprints led to the adjoining bathroom like ghoulish breadcrumbs. Kevin's stomach clenched. *The scent in the air reminded him of a handful of pennies.* Edging by his older brother, he opened the bathroom door with his foot and staggered backwards, choking on bile as it spurted out through his fingers. *No. It's not her.* Kevin manoeuvred past his heaving sibling. Pre-emptively covering his mouth, he stepped into the bathroom and slipped, landing on his hands and knees. Blood covered the white tile. His hands were submerged in it. Grasping what he'd slipped on, his lungs constricted. *He couldn't breathe.* Unable to inhale the smallest amount of air. His vision wavered as his mind fought to stop him from seeing what could never be unseen. *Don't... You don't want to see it.* He looked up from his blood-soaked hands. It was one of the twins. He crawled through her essence, blinded by tears. She was naked in the fetal position, her grotesquely swollen, severely beaten face was unrecognisable. Her blood and brain matter were sprayed on the shower curtains and walls. *No, no. This can't be real.* Taking in the ruthless macabre display, he reached out to touch her. Her wheat coloured locks were matted with blood, the eye closest to the floor was missing. Her remaining eye stared into oblivion just as her mother's had. Her fingers were clawed, and her arms reaching out as though she'd been willing her body to crawl away from the brutality she'd succumbed to. The towel rack had been ripped off the wall, it lay just out of her grasp on the blood-soaked tile. *Had it been used in her torture or had she ripped it off the wall to use in her defence?* Covering his mouth with the crook of his arm to stop a wave of nausea, Kevin inched closer until he was kneeling before her body, tranquillized by shock as an unfamiliar voice kept repeating, *this is not Kayn. This is not Kayn. You must find her.* He felt an eerie inner calm, it was like he'd stepped away from himself. He heard the rustling of officers, the voices, and cries of despair, but he was detached from it. *This is not Kayn, you must find her,* a voice kept repeating the mesmerizing mantra. A hand clutched his shoulder. A voice was repeating his name, it was of no consequence, coming from far away. His mind repeated the words, *this is not Kayn. Find her. She can still be saved. Snap out of it.*

"Kevin, snap out of it!" His dad shouted, dragging him away from the body and out of the bathroom.

When he saw the carpet beneath him, he started to come back to reality. The reasons why this could not be Kayn filtered through Kevin's mind as he scrambled to his feet. His father pulled him into his arms. Allowing himself a moment of serenity hearing the steady beat of his heart, he tried to ground himself. "It isn't Kayn," Kevin whispered against his father's chest. His father held him tighter. Once again, he spoke, "It isn't her, Kayn had a shower after track."

His father consoled, "It looks like a home invasion. You need to prepare yourself."

Aware of the accumulation of officer's, ambulance attendants and first responders moving around, still in shock, Kevin heard his brother speaking to someone, "Matt's at school. We were texting earlier. He was going to a party tonight. I just texted him again and told him to call me back. I also called and said it was an emergency."

His inner voice asserted, *find her, she's alive.* Kevin struggled out of his father's arms, so he could make it known, "Kayn had a shower before we left the school. That's Chloe in there. It's not Kayn. We need to find her." He tried manoeuvring by officers blocking the door, they wouldn't allow him to pass. *He'd seen enough C.S.I to know they were trying to protect the integrity of the crime scene. What did that matter? His DNA was everywhere in this house.*

His father whispered, "Son, they're searching the house for the other bodies, even if it isn't her, chances are…"

"No," Kevin blurted, shaking his head in denial. "No." *He couldn't listen to unhopeful words, not now. Not when every nerve ending in his body was vibrating with the knowledge that she was alive.* To prove his point, Kevin addressed the lady taking pictures of Chloe's body in the washroom, "Chloe has a crescent shaped birthmark behind her left ear. Kayn has one on her right." Kevin marched over, puffed himself up in front of the officers blocking the door, insisting, "Kayn's fast, she's a runner. If anyone could get away, it would be her. She would have found somewhere to hide. I know her hiding spots. You have to let me out of here."

Touching his shoulder, Clay squeezed it, whispering, "Kevin, you don't want to be the one that finds her."

They were in no hurry because they thought they were looking for bodies now. They were counting bodies, and there were two unaccounted for.

He knew she was alive with every part of his being. Kevin looked back at his father and brother, saying, "You all know how fast she is. She would run with everything she had. She would run!" Kevin spun around and attempted to burst through the blockade of men, struggling as they restrained him.

Shoving through the crowd, Officer Jenkins came to his aid, ordering, "Hands off. I know these people, he's a good kid." Friends with Kayn's father since high school, Jenkins piped in, "Son, if she's in this house, we'll find her."

"I can find her faster," Kevin stated.

An officer in the hall announced, "We found Stan in the

carport. Looks like he didn't even make it into the house after he arrived home from work."

Officer Jenkin's face lost its colour as he numbly disclosed, "We're still missing one of the twins."

A young officer addressed Kevin, "We all know there's been a history of issues with men and Chloe Brighton. Has she broken up with anyone recently? They were identical, do you think it's possible Kayn was mistaken for her sister and abducted?"

Kevin's heart sank as he responded, "No, Kayn was nothing like her." *They thought a Chloe stalker went nuts and massacred the entire family.* Looking directly into Jenkins' eyes, Kevin pled, "I know Kayn's alive. You have to let me look for her, she's not dead."

Taking Kevin's desperate pleas to heart, Jenkins stepped aside and motioned for the others to let him pass, declaring, "There's nothing to lose at this point. Take the lead, kid. Find her."

The voice in his head prompted, *there's still time, find her.*

Jenkins began rallying the troops, "We still have a missing girl, it's possible she's found somewhere to hide. The kid is her best friend, he may have insight. She could be in shock or wounded. Let's find her."

Kevin descended the stairs, knowing she wasn't in the house. *She would have tried to run.* He stepped outside following the pull of intuition and walked around the side of the house into the backyard. An officer tossed off the panel to the crawl space beneath the house. *She wasn't in there. The spiders would have been a deterrent.* Kevin called out, "She's not in there, you're wasting time!" *Kayn could run. She could run fast.* He glanced at the opening to the trail, spotting something white in the grass and sprinted over knowing what it was. *It was the plastic bag with eggs his mom gave her.* "She's in the trails!" Kevin shouted as his heart cheered. *She got away. She knew these trails. It was possible, that's all that mattered. She was alive.* Enveloped in incapacitating darkness as the search party entered the overgrown bike trails, Kevin dug through his pockets for his phone to use the flashlight. He paused midstride and peered down at the cell in his hand. *I can't believe I'm this stupid.* Kevin grabbed an officer to get his attention, explaining, "She pocket dialled me. That's how we knew they were in trouble."

The officer got everyone's attention. The crowd hushed. The woods were pitch black with shadowed outlines of trees and stumps. They couldn't see two feet in front of their faces, but maybe they'd hear her phone. *She would have called him by now if she escaped. No, he needed hope. Kayn was alive.* He dialled her number in dead silence, pressing the speakerphone setting on his phone. Her ringtone, as an eerie muffled melody through the misty trails. They made their way towards the ring. Holding his phone, it went to voice mail on speakerphone like she'd answered his call, "Hello, Hello, I can't hear you. It's a bad connection." Everyone was silent as the message continued, "Ha-ha, got you. I can't get to the phone right now. Leave a message." *He'd forgotten about that message.* Everybody was frozen in place as the hope in their hearts dissolved when they realised it was only a recording. *That joke message had been hilarious the first time he'd fallen for it and started talking. It was horrible now.*

Officer Jenkins piped up, "Walk slowly and cautiously people. We need to find that phone. There should be a blinking message light. Look for flashing light. If her mailbox isn't full, we'll be able to call a few more times before it goes directly to voicemail."

There was no point in trying to call. Her inbox was always full. The next unanswered call would go straight to her voicemail.

The trails were onyx with an eerie lacing of mist lingering just above the forest floor. Even with their makeshift flashlights, they might walk by her. Walking the path through memory,

Kevin felt the absence of the voice in his head. *It wasn't urging him on anymore. Maybe she'd dropped the phone as she escaped?* Seeing a faint glimmer through dense foliage, Kevin gingerly made his way towards it using the message light indicating the missed call as a lighthouse beacon to guide him through the mist.

"It's over there," someone yelled.

"Kayn, can you hear us! Kayn!" The mix of voices shouted.

Picking up Kayn's phone, Kevin stared at it. *Come on, Brighton. Where are you?* Defeated, Kevin passed her cell to Jenkins as the rest continued scouring the bushes.

A man's voice yelled, "Hey, what's going on? Can I help?"

"We're looking for a missing girl!" Jenkins hollered.

Kevin made his way through the foliage towards the voice. With a backyard adjoining the trails, he couldn't have missed the sirens of every cop car in town.

The man pushed his way through the bushes at the back of his property to see the excitement in the trails. "Oh my God," he choked, "Over here, she's over here!"

Kevin frantically forced through the bushes at the back of the property until he saw the man standing solemnly before a bloody naked body in the fetal position at his feet. *It was more than he could bear.* Immobilized by grief as everyone shoved by. The violence of the night spun around him. He dropped to his knees trying to catch his breath. *She isn't dead. She can't be gone*, his mind repeated like he could make it true if he believed it. An emergency team rushed by. Never overly religious, Kevin closed his eyes, praying, "Don't take her away from me. Please, I'll do anything."

Someone yelled, "We have a pulse! We have a pulse!"

Joyous tears filled Kevin's eyes. "Thank you," he whispered, looking up through dark branches to the heavens. Watching in elation, he followed the paramedics out of the forest. Standing beside his father and brother as they put Kayn into the back of the ambulance, desperately fighting to keep her alive. *When they announced there was a pulse, Kevin was overcome by a sense of peace. He couldn't explain it, but every cell in his body knew that she'd survive. Kayn would fight her way back because she was the strongest person he'd ever met.*

3

CLEANSED IN CHLOE'S BLOOD

*K*evin looked at his brother. Clay kept staring at his phone. *He needed to go to Matt. It would be horrible to hear this news from a random stranger.* His brother had been leaving cryptic messages and texts for over an hour. *They all knew, Matt. He'd left his cell at his dorm, so he wouldn't lose it, partying. He was blind hammered.*

"I'll go get Matt," Clay stated.

As the ambulance sped away, Kevin replied, "Yes, he has to come home." The Smith brothers blankly watched ambulance lights fade into the night.

Clay squeezed his shoulder, assuring, "She'll be okay."

More ambulances pulled up with no lights or sirens. The brothers stood there as two attendants, and a lady in a suit made their way to the house. A black SUV pulled up, four people with suits got out and quickly walked up the hill after them. *They'd be bringing the bodies out soon. He didn't want to be here. He needed to get to the hospital. Where was his dad?*

Clay asserted, "I'm not sure I want to see this. We should leave. I need to get to Matt. You need to get to the hospital."

For once, he was in tune with his brother. Emotionally spent, Kevin felt his sibling grasp his shoulder. Kevin glanced at his brother, anxiously staring at his cell. They heard their father's voice and saw him coming. *Everyone knew each other in this small northern town. This would rock it to its core.*

"The police are done with us for tonight," His dad confirmed. Touching Kevin's shoulder, he suggested, "We should leave."

Meeting his father's eyes, Kevin stated, "Someone has to be there for Kayn."

"We're going to the hospital. Mom's bringing you something to wear," his father answered.

Kevin glanced down at his pants and shirt. *He was covered in blood, and not just a few drops.* A vision of Chloe flashed through his mind. Her hands frozen in time, clawing at the bathroom floor.

"I'm leaving. I need to get to Matt before the police do," Clay announced as they unceremoniously parted and left in separate vehicles.

Kevin had never seen his father look this way. His eyes were vacuous, he was speaking in fragments. He was thin threading it. He chose to do nothing, say nothing, concentrating on breathing. A deep breath in and a breath out as they travelled in mentally vacant calm. *Why wasn't he crying?* Flashes of savagely brutalised bodies entered his mind. Each time they materialized, something shut them down. He gazed out the window at the scenery, he'd passed a thousand times, travelling between their houses. *Everything would be different. The family picture in the upstairs hall would be nothing more than a heart-wrenching gut punch. He'd never enter the Brighton house and walk by that closet without seeing*

Kayn's mother's lifeless glassy eyes. They arrived at the hospital with nothing to say. There would be no consoling words of acceptance for they'd been set adrift in numbness. A mortal's mind was built to shut itself down during immense pain or when the grief is too extreme. Thoughts were nothing but torture. Following his father on autopilot, cloaked in the mental silence of shock, they approached the sliding doors. He remembered to breathe. The doors slid open. Unable to reign in the horror, his mother burst into tears. Her grief brought him back a touch.

With her eyes a steady stream, his mom whispered, "Kevin, you need to come with me. You can't sit in the lobby like this."

He followed her gaze to his crimson stained clothes. *Chloe's blood was all over him.* Hospital staff rushed to his aid. Kevin raised his hands, numbly explaining, "It's not my blood." His mother manoeuvred him through the gathering crowd of stunned staff. He heard his father saying, "We came from the Brighton house." His mother handed him a bag with clothes in it and accompanied him down the hall.

A lady he recognized as someone his mom was friendly with sweetly assured his mother, "I've got it from here, honey." She pushed open a door into a private room. Directing Kevin inside, she asked, "Is there anything you need?"

Looking into her eyes, he answered, "I just need to know how she's doing?"

The nurse gave him a towel and replied, "We're not equipped to treat her injuries here. Once they have her stabilised, she'll be airlifted to Vancouver."

It felt like someone let a burst of oxygen into the room as he took in her words, questioning, "She's still alive?"

The nurse affirmed "They're working on her. Have a shower, clean yourself up. I'll let you know if anything changes." Smiling, she closed the door.

Seeing his reflection in the mirror, Kevin gripped the sink, sobbing. *This wasn't real. It didn't happen.* Raising his eyes back to his reflection, his pants and shirt were drenched in blood. It was smeared on his face and clumped in his hair. He recalled falling in it. He must have wiped his hands on his face. *It was Chloe's blood.* His mind snapped back to reality. *Chloe's blood.* He tore off his soiled clothing and got into the stall. *He couldn't breathe.* Turning on the water, he stepped under the powerful stream. Water pummelled his skin. Gazing at his feet as red tinted water circled the drain, he reached out to grab shampoo, soap, and a scrub brush. Turning up the heat until it was scalding, he lathered and scrubbed until his flesh was enflamed. Sitting on the bench with tears streaming down his face, he scrubbed his toenails. *It wouldn't matter how much scalding water he rinsed his skin with, this night couldn't be washed off. Chloe's blood was never going to wash off. He could still hear her screaming in his head.* Getting out, Kevin looked at his reflection again. His skin had been scrubbed raw. After putting on clean clothing and untainted shoes, he leaned against the vanity dizzy from the heat of the shower. He gapped out staring at the soiled pile of clothing on the floor. *He didn't want those clothes. He needed every scrap of that blood-soaked material to be burned, even the shoes.* Putting everything in the plastic bag, he tossed it into the trash. Kevin paused at the door, knowing when he left the bathroom, he'd have to face the weight of everyone's concern. *He needed to focus on Kayn. Everything was going to be all right if she survived. He had to believe she would.* He walked out, bumping into the nurse coming to check on him. He cautiously enquired, "Is she still alive?"

"Yes, she's still alive," the nurse answered, smiling.

The weight on his heart lifted. Tears of relief formed in his eyes, following the nurse back to where his parents were waiting. *He knew there were things the nurse wasn't allowed to say. They weren't Kayn's next of kin. They may not be blood relatives, but they were the best she was going to get until her brother arrived.*

With open arms, his mother soothed, "I wish I could erase everything you had to see tonight, honey."

With intense spiritual defeat, Kevin walked into her embrace. Her chest heaved with rhythmic sobs of empathy. With his head on her shoulder, he allowed tears to moisten his eyes, calming as he listened to the soothing rhythm of his mother's heart. It seemed to whisper, *it's okay, everything is going to be okay. I have you and I love you.*

His father joined their hug, sobbing, "I used to walk her to the door and make sure someone was home for her. I dropped her off with a maniac in the house and left her there. I drove away. I didn't even wait to see if she made it inside. I'll never be able to forgive myself, this is my fault."

"They aren't children anymore," his mom whispered against his hair as they clung together.

The dam inside his soul opened, releasing a flood of tears. *Their innocence had been lost in the worst possible way. They would never be children again.* The Smith family clung to each other until their strength was renewed.

Hours passed, each minute inching by took twenty. Sensing someone, Kevin peered up from his ancient magazine A nurse told them Kayn would be in surgery for the rest of the night. She suggested they go home to get some rest. They looked at each other. There was no way they could leave knowing they were almost all Kayn had left. She was fighting for her life. They had to stand in solidarity.

"We're staying here," his mother affirmed, her voice unwavering.

They sat on leather benches, thumbing through endless old magazines. No one forcing small talk or even attempting to speak. They took turns travelling to the vending machines for snacks and the nurses checked in occasionally. Nobody noticed as four strangers arrived at the cusp of dawn. No one except Kevin. He'd seen them outside by the sliding door. He'd almost cracked a smile as one began cursing because the doors were locked. They didn't seem to notice the buzzer. They had to call someone to let them in. He watched the teens as they strolled around the side of the building past windows. *They weren't from around here. There was only one high school. They must be college students camping, or hitchhikers?* Tossing his magazine on the table, Kevin headed to the washroom. When he turned the corner, a redhead was standing in front of the door. Unaccustomed to talking to girls, he contemplated going to a different bathroom.

She smiled sweetly, saying, "She's in my class. I just heard, it's so horrible." Sobbing, she threw herself into his arms.

Awkwardly standing there with a hot redhead hugging him, fake crying into his shoulder, Kevin patted her back with no idea what to do. *No, she wasn't in Kayn's classes. He would have noticed this girl. He didn't want to be rude, but he had no idea who she was. He was starting to feel funny. Her hands were unusually hot. What in the hell?* Everything spun, he passed out cold in the hallway.

He awoke to nurses lifting him onto a gurney. His parents were there. *Ouch, who pinched his arm? What was that needle for? He felt fantastic.* As he slipped in and out of the foggy haze, he heard Chloe's voice whisper, "Thank you."

4

THE DEVASTATION OF MATTHEW BRIGHTON

*M*att opened his eyes and groaned as his ringtone went off for the eight millionth time. He threw a pillow in the direction of the phone.

His roommate Ryan murmured, "I'm going to smother you the next time that effing phone rings."

Chuckling into his pillow, Matt mumbled, "That won't stop her from calling."

His roommate snapped, "Great, that psycho woke me up. I have to go take a piss."

"Good to know," Matt mumbled, trying to smother himself with his pillow as his phone rang again. "Get rid of it, I'm going to lose my shit," Matt slurred into his pillow, but Ryan wasn't in the room to hear him complain.

His dorm mate hollered from the bathroom down the hall, "What the fu... My front tooth's chipped."

Someone from another room yelled, "Nobody cares!"

Staggering back into their room, Ryan crawled onto Matt's bed to show him his tooth. *His breath smelled like cinnamon crap.*

Fireball shots! They'd been drinking cinnamon whisky all night. Matt hid under his pillow, teasing, "I'll scream if you try anything."

Always the comedian, Ryan stumbled back to his own bed, chuckling, "You would have loved it."

He could actually hear his headache. Did he have his teeth? Running his tongue over his teeth, made him gag. His mouth was filled with chalky paste. *Another night lost to the blackening effects of Fireball whisky. Clearly, he forgot to guzzle his usual amount of water before passing out.* He opened an eye to see if there was any on his nightstand. *None.* He was feeling rough, he wasn't going down the hall to get some. *What did they have in the mini fridge?* He glanced at it. *No, too far away.* He'd drooled all over his pillow, so he rolled onto the dry one, inhaling sweet-scented perfume. *Had he slept with someone last night? He must have. Nice.* Matt stretched his toned, bronzed arms, hearing one crack. He peaked over to look on the floor to see if his nameless booty call had left anything behind. *When did I have the time to have sex? Oh yeah, I brought her home after my morning class. We came back here and partied. Ryan chipped his tooth opening a beer. They'd started drinking in the afternoon, yesterday.*

Matthew Brighton's life was a responsibility free party. Easy on the eyes with a full ride scholarship, he was a great friend but a shitty boyfriend. *Relationships had never been his thing. He'd dumped his girlfriend via text before sleeping with somebody else. He wasn't a cheater. He'd been ignoring his phone all night. Why wouldn't she just give up and go away? This was probably why all his exes venomously despised him. He must have been too drunk to figure out how to turn off the ringer.* Gazing across the dorm, his friend was feeling equally brutal. His phone went off again. *She's effing stone, cold, insane.*

"Matt, I'm going to shove that phone up your ass to muffle the sound," Ryan warned.

Matt chuckled, "No means no, Ryan."

His roommate launched an empty beer can, it missed him by a hair and hit the wall on the other side of his bed with a ting. Matt got up, staggering around in search of his phone. He was about to turn the power off when it rang. Staring at it grimacing, he thought, *Oh, what the hell. I'll be a frigging man.* His roommate was rifling random things from the nightstand. He yelled, "All right, I got it." He flirtatiously slurred, "Matt's love palace, Matt speaking."

Clay curtly stated, "I'm downstairs. Kick her out, I'm coming up."

He'd expected a pissed off ex, but it was his best friend. Weird timing for a visit. Far too bombed to notice he was naked. Matt valiantly attempted to balance on his wobbly legs, slurring, "No, no, don't you get up Ryan. I'll get the door." Glancing at the clock on the wall, he groaned, "What in the hell is that douche bag doing here at four o'clock in the effing morning?" Ryan moaned, pulling the covers over his head. Cupping a hand in front his mouth, Matt exhaled. *Welcome to the jungle. He couldn't even stand the smell of his own breath.* Matt flopped on his bed. Opening his nightstand, he ate toothpaste, giggling. *Now, he'd smell like minty cinnamon poop.* He heard footsteps in the hall. *That was fast.* He launched himself to his feet. Staggering over, Matt opened the door before Clay had a chance to knock. Hanging onto the doorframe as the floor moved beneath his feet, naked Matt slurred, "It's four o'clock in the effing morning, Shithead."

Exhaling, Clay sighed, "Lovely, you're friggin' wasted. Put on shorts, Bro. Do you usually answer your door naked?"

Ryan chuckled from his bed, "Only if it's you."

Stumbling back over, Matt sat on his bed, reaching for shorts on the floor. He tugged them on, grimacing. *These weren't his shorts. Gross.* Clutching his pounding head, he questioned, "Why are you here at four in the morning?"

"You didn't answer your phone. Damn it, Matt. You need to be sober," Clay confessed, strolling over.

"You'd have to call before noon," Ryan teased, from beneath his covers.

Matt chuckled, "Scratch that, I was already having sex with a stranger by noon."

Ryan rolled over, mumbling, "Don't be a tool, her name was Laura."

Tossing an empty can at his roommate, Matt sparred, "What was the other one's name?"

Lifting his lip, Ryan asked, "I chipped a tooth. How did I do this?"

Rifling a Kleenex box at his roommate's face, Matt laughed, "You chipped your tooth opening a beer."

Frustrated, Clay explained, "Buddy, something happened. We need to sober you up."

Pissing himself laughing, Matt teased, "Did Timmy fall in the well, Lassie? Spit it out." *Clay's eyes didn't register the joke. That was funny.*

Grabbing a shirt from Matt's drawer, Clay tossed it at him, directing, "Splash water on your face. I have to get you home." He walked over to the counter, picked up a cold Tim Horton's coffee, sniffed it, and put it in the microwave.

Weird? Why was Clay microwaving coffee for him in the middle of the night? His eyes were full of tears. He'd never seen his friend cry before. Not once. Not even when they were kids. The microwave beeped. Clay tried to pass him the cup. Matt waved him away, knowing if he drank it, he'd puke.

Clay ordered, "Don't mess with me. I will force you to drink this coffee. This has been the worst night of my life, it's about to become the worst night of yours. I wish I could leave you drunk and pretend this didn't happen, but I can't. The police are going to be here any minute."

"What? Just say it," Matt questioned as his Fireball whisky-soaked mind began battling its way back. *Police, did he do something?*

Tearing up, Clay disclosed, "I wanted to talk to you before the police did, that's why I'm here."

Matt's mind reeled through possible scenarios. *Police... What did he do?*

"It's your family," Clay's words tightened in his throat.

What? "What about them?" Matt whispered, instantly sober. He took the coffee from his friend, and chugged it, prompting, "Was there an accident? Is someone hurt?"

"They're dead," Clay whispered with tears in his eyes.

"This is a prank," Matt replied, willing a smile to appear on Clay's sombre tear streamed face.

Looking him dead in the eyes, Clay repeated the words that would shatter his world, "Your family is dead. I have to take you home, Matty."

Stumbling backwards, Matt sat on his bed. *He called him Matty. Only his sisters called him Matty. No, they couldn't be dead, they weren't.* "You're joking," Matt stated, like he could change reality with force of will. *No way. No.*

"They were trying to save Kayn when I left," Clay explained. "She made it to the hospital. I'm here to take you to her."

Ryan was sitting up staring at him with a stricken expression. *No, no.* Deafening silence was only broken by the humming light above his head. Adrenaline kicked in and Matt found the ability to speak, "Was it a car accident?"

Solemnly, Clay explained, "The police think it was a home invasion."

Home invasion. No, things like that didn't happen where they live. Stunned, Matt looked over Clay's shoulder at the picture of his beautiful sisters on his desk. His world stopped moving.

"I was sure the police would beat me to you," Clay quietly

said, trying to touch his shoulder. Matt recoiled from his friend's attempt to console him. He shook his head, grimacing. *This can't be real. This wasn't really happening.* He heard the hollow click of footsteps in the hallway, followed by the jangling of keys. Matt stared at the door, thinking, *No, don't you dare come here. Don't come to my door. If you come to my room, it's real.* There were three loud knocks. Matt couldn't swallow. *It was real.*

Making his way to the door, Clay glanced back at him before opening it, saying, "One of us has to answer."

Matt rose to his feet feeling like he was on his way to lay his neck on a guillotine, knowing this was the end of his life. With steady legs, he walked over to stand beside his best friend. The door opened, revealing the school's counsellors and someone else he didn't recognize. *It wasn't the police but that didn't matter. The truth was in their eyes.*

A counsellor with a consoling voice said, "Mr. Brighton, you need to get dressed and come with us. It's better if we talk about this in the office."

Matt solemnly replied, "Give me a minute, I'll be right down."

"Take all the time you need," the man responded, retreating down the hall.

Blankly, Matt remained in the doorway with his mind reeling from his best friend's words. *His family had been murdered in a home invasion. They were gone. His mother wouldn't want him reeking like alcohol when he spoke to the police.* Walking back in, Matt grabbed his shower bag off the dresser. *He was supposed to come home this weekend because it was her birthday. He had an opportunity to sleep with someone, so he partied instead. He didn't think it would matter if he drove home the next day. He was still planning to come home for her birthday dinner on Saturday night, but she would never know that. It mattered. He'd let her down. She had no Saturday.*

Clay touched his friend's shoulder, urging, "Forget about the shower, nobody will care."

Solemnly, Matt answered, "My mom would have cared." *He'd spoken her name in the past tense for the first time.* His heart ached. Tears blurred his vision, he blinked them away. *She would want him to be clean and smell nice.* His shocked mind was only capable of spurts of rational thought. Holding a hand up, Matt gestured that he needed a moment. Maintaining composure long enough to get into the bathroom, he closed the door. Collapsing in front of the toilet with tears burning in his eyes, his chest heaved as his body purged itself of alcohol. No amount of vomiting would dull the devastation and guilt sickening his brain. *He'd let her down. He should have been at home tonight.* He could almost hear his mother's voice speaking softly, giving him instructions. *She would have told him to try and calm down. Then, she would have told him to think about what he needed to do next.* He turned on the cold water and let it run. Matthew Brighton had been a hyper child. His mom had repeated those words on countless occasions. *Calm down, think about what you need to do next.* As Matt stepped into the shower, ice-cold water pummelled his skin. He couldn't fathom the idea that he would never hear those words from his mother's lips again. The freezing water brought him back to the here and now. As his brain defogged, he knew what mattered. *He had to get to Kayn. She was still alive. He wasn't sure what he'd do if he lost her too.* Closing his eyes as icy water rushed at his face, he prayed for his sister. *He would hold onto the sound of Kayn's laughter and the innocence of her smile. He'd focus on her. She needed him. He had to keep it together.* Dashing back into the room, Matt put his clothes on.

Catching his attention, Clay suggested, "Grab clothes to take with you. You can't go home."

Matt frantically tossed clothing into his backpack. He thought about bringing the picture from his desk. *They had lots of pictures at home.* Confused thoughts raced through his mind. *Why couldn't he go home?* Reaching for the picture, Matt asked, "Why can't I go home?"

Clay dodged the question, saying, "Listen, don't worry about packing anything else, you can wear my clothes."

His house was a crime scene. Tears flooded his eyes, Matt choked out, "Thanks for coming to get me." As they embraced, Matt stifled a sob. *He had to be strong.* Stepping away, he stated, "I don't have time for counsellors, I need to be with my sister."

His roommate Ryan answered, "You go to Kayn. I'll tell them where you went, just go."

Matt squeezed his roommate's shoulder in appreciation and they dashed down the hallway into the stairwell out through the courtyard to where Clay parked. Speeding away from campus onto the highway, they were pulled over.

Rolling his eyes, Clay complained, "Crap, we don't have time for this."

An officer they recognized peered into their window, saying, "We suspected you boys weren't going to wait around to speak to a counsellor. Follow us. We'll get you back to town faster."

As relief spread across his face, Clay stammered, "Thanks."

Escorted with wailing sirens and whirling lights, they arrived in half the time it would've taken. Jumping out, Matt sprinted to the entrance of the hospital with Clay right behind him. With a whoosh of automatic doors, Matt's eyes met Clay's parent's with unspoken gratitude.

Escorting Matt to another area of the hospital, the nurse by his side warned, "Prepare yourself for what you're about to see, your sister has been to hell and back. The helicopter just arrived. She's being airlifted to Vancouver. You have a few minutes to say..."

He finished her sentence in his mind. *Goodbye. They don't*

think she's going to make it. Looking through the window into the room, Matt asked, "Am I allowed in there?"

The nurse answered by holding the door open. Matt walked past her and made his way to his ailing sibling's bedside. Clasping a hand over his mouth as he got a good look. Tears clouded his vision as the violence she'd endured sunk in like a weight on his heart crushing his resolve to stay strong. Taking his sister's hand, he noticed the machine was breathing for her. She was on life support, covered in tape, needles and tubing. Her disfigured face was, twice its size, partially concealed by bandages. *Who would do this? For what?* He felt the urge to check the birthmark but let it pass. The monitor beeped slowly. With each beep, a voice in his head whispered, *you should have come home. You could have saved us. How could you let this happen, Matthew?* His eyes blurred with tears as guilt swallowed ration. *I should have been there. I could've stopped this. They wouldn't be dead. My baby sister wouldn't be... dying. This was happening.* His soul ached with every beep of the life-sustaining machine. *He'd let them all down. He couldn't lose her too.* A river of devastation was flowing down his cheeks as he lovingly caressed her lifeless hand. There was not a sign of life, not a twitch of a finger or a movement that wasn't being created by the machines that kept her breathing. *What had someone done to his baby sister?* He heard a noise and glanced back at the door. *They were waiting to take her away. They didn't think she was going to live. He could see it on their faces. He had to say something. He couldn't let them take her without saying anything.* Kissing her hand, he whispered, "It's Matty, I'm here. I'm with you. You're not alone. Please don't go. You need to fight. They need to take you now. I'll be with you as soon as I can. Don't leave me. You can't go. I need you here. Please don't go." The nurse touched his shoulder. *It was time. He was being forced to leave her first, but what if he couldn't? They were gone. Everyone he loved. They were all dead. What if he never saw her again? He couldn't breathe.* Panicking, gasping for breath, Matt sunk to his knees internally pleading, *take me instead. Please, I'll do anything you want. I'll be a better man. I'll be better.* They were gently helping him up. *No, I'm not done. I can't go. I can't ask Kayn to have the strength to stay with me and then leave her first.* Matt reached for his sister sobbing, "No, no, I can't leave her," as they maneuvered him to the door. He could taste the salt on his lips as he blinked tears away so he could see his sister one last time.

The nurse whispered, "They need to get her to Vancouver. It's her best chance. We're wasting time."

Defeated, by logic, Matthew Brighton noticed the lack of dry eyes in the room. A nurse escorted him out into the hallway and walked him over to stand against the wall. Everything happened quickly. Attendants rushed past with his sibling on a gurney, running alongside of it with tubes, bags, and a monitor. They disappeared at the end of the hall. *This wasn't goodbye. He had to believe it.*

The nurse assured, "I have faith she'll survive. If your faith is in short supply, I have enough for both of us."

Matt fell into the wise stranger's arms but was only granted a moment of solitude before seeing his father's friend Jenkins walking towards him. A minute later Matthew was being led to the morgue to identify the bodies of his family. *Jenkins asked if he was ready. How could you ever be ready to identify the bodies of your family? They'd been murdered. It was something that happened to other people. To people in movies or T.V shows. In those shows, when they took a family member to identify the bodies, he'd always thought it wasn't fair. It wasn't, and it was happening to him right now.* The elevator closed, humming Matt's descent into hell. It paused and the doors slowly opened. It was cold and sterile in the basement as he stepped out. The rest of the hospital had pictures on the walls and a vastly different feel. There was no need for pretty pictures in a place that only housed the dead. Knowing it was

Jenkin's duty to do this didn't make it easier to stomach. There were no large signs in hell, no colourful arrows pointing the way, just a plaque on the morgue's door. His father's best friend paused before shoving on the door and greeting a man in a lab coat by shaking his hand. Squeezing Matt's shoulder, they took the final steps into hell together. Without ceremony, the morgue tech opened a metal drawer, slid it all the way out and lifted the blanket revealing his dad's body like ripping off a band-aid. *He'd never seen a dead person before.* His father was an empty void with a partially open mouth. *He was as hollow as Matthew felt. Someone had taken everything he loved, lit it on fire and he'd been sent to sift through the ashes. That's all this was. He was sifting through ashes.* In shock, his mind took him to a better place. He was supposed to be sitting by the campfire roasting wieners with his dad. A precocious child, he was trying to catch the ashes floating in the air. That was how he found out that you can't hold onto something once it's nothing but ash. It disintegrates with the slightest touch and floats away on the gentlest breeze. He recalled rubbing his hands together and being amazed when the black soot staining his palms disappeared. It was magic to the seven-year-old version of Matt. *He knew different now. The adult version of Matt knew that ashes became nothing. This was what they were in the end, absolutely nothing.* His heart felt like a solid mass in his chest as he stared at what was left of his father. *He'd been the most hilarious, loving, example of what it was to be a dad. Until this moment, he hadn't understood how lucky he was to have him in his life. He'd never appreciated him like he should have. Someone had beaten him to death like he was nothing. He would never get to know that Matt had always wanted to be just like him. He'd never get to say the words.*

The tech prompted, "Is there anything you want to say?"

Matt understood, he needed to go through the motions. He hadn't said anything aloud because he understood that his father was gone. Feeling the warmth of Jenkins' hand on his shoulder, Matt whispered, "I should have come home this weekend. I just always do the wrong thing. I don't know why I do the things I do. I'm sorry I let you down. I was coming home on Saturday for mom's birthday. I didn't forget. Kayn is alive. I'm going to take care of her. I know I've never been the good person that you wanted me to be, but I know that I have what it takes to grow into that person someday, because I was raised by you. I couldn't have asked for a better father. I always knew you loved me. I hope you knew how much I loved you. I should've said the words to you more often." His voice cracked with emotion as he struggled to continue, with a raw whisper, he promised, "I'm going to try to be a better man." Finished with his final goodbye, he looked at Jenkins.

In tears, Jenkins took a step closer and spoke next, "I'll keep Matt and Kayn safe. I'm going to find the bastard that did this to your family. I miss you already, my friend."

Numb, Matt watched as his father's body was covered up and slid back into the drawer. He looked at Jenkins and said, "Thank you for coming with me."

Jenkins nodded, answering, "I've known your parents since high school. I loved your father like a brother. They were there for me through my daughter's death and the divorce. Your family has been my family for many years. I'm still here for you, Matt. I know it's what your parents wanted. You need to know, whatever happens, I'm still here for you kids."

As they embraced, Matt understood he wasn't alone. *He would have to quit school and get a job so he could take care of Kayn. He wasn't a child anymore, he couldn't go on pretending he was. It was time to change.*

Jenkins forewarned, "Your mother's body is worse than your father's."

The tech pulled out the next drawer. Matt would have

known this was his mother's body even if he hadn't been warned. *She'd always smelled of Sunflowers perfume. He'd never been able to smell that sweet fragrance without his mother's smiling face crossing his mind and now, he'd never smell it without her absence breaking his heart. In life, Claire Brighton had curly shoulder length auburn hair and an infectious laugh. She was funny and kind. She was his safe harbour, his happy place and number one fan.* The tech removed the sheet, and in one act, he ripped away the veil of reality. Her lifeless eyes stared into the distance, beyond him. Her lips were parted too. *Did souls leave our body in a final breath through parted lips?* There was no animation in her face, all that remained was a violated shell resembling her and a whisper in the air of the torturous delicate scent she always wore. His heart ached with the knowledge that he'd never feel the warmth of her embrace again. Caressing his mother's icy cheek, he leaned over and lovingly kissed her forehead. *She was gone. She was really gone.* Lost in the flood of tears, blurring his vision, he choked out, "Mom, I'm so sorry. I should have been there. I was still coming home for your birthday. I didn't forget." He touched her hair, staring at his mother's lifeless body. *The woman with the most beautiful sounding laughter in the world had moved on.* He prayed she'd never stop laughing, and when she smiled, it would always be with the same all-encompassing joy. *His mother's laughter would follow him for the rest of his days.* Matthew Brighton crumbled, sobbing as he lay his head on material draped over his mother's chest. Closing his eyes, he inhaled her scent. He wanted to hear her heart beating, but knew it would never beat again, the thought shattered his into a million pieces. He felt Jenkins' hand on his shoulder and the warmth of the living, brought him back to reality. Matthew moved away so Jenkins could have a chance to say, goodbye.

Leaning forward, Jenkins lovingly kissed his mother's cheek, vowing, "I'm going to take care of them, Claire. I'm so sorry this happened to you. I can't imagine anyone ever wanting to hurt the gentlest soul I've ever met. Be at peace, sweet girl. I promise to keep them safe."

The tech covered up his mother's body and slid it back into the drawer. He looked at him and whispered, "Mr. Brighton, I wish you didn't have to see this but legally a family member needs to identify the body."

Jenkins turned to face the mortician, whispering, "This can't be unseen."

None of this could. He wasn't going to be able to take much more but he needed to be certain it was Chloe and there was only one way to do that. He had to see her. He had to know it was her without a shadow of a doubt. Matt nodded his consent. The sheet was lifted off her body. He burst into tears, covering his mouth. *He was going to be sick. One of her eyes was missing. She'd been brutalised to the point where she was almost unrecognizable. Why? What kind of monster would do this?* Matt stepped closer and looked behind her left ear. Once he saw the crescent birthmark, he was certain. He sunk to the cold cement floor, choking out, "It's Chloe. Cover her up. I can't do this anymore." Covering his eyes, Matt rocked as he wept. *He'd let them down, and now, they were all dead. He couldn't fathom the horror of his sister's final moments.* She'd been beaten so badly she was missing an eye and her face was crushed. The coroner hadn't had the time to clean her up. *Her throat had been slit. Who knew what horrors were hidden beneath the blanket?* He thought about Kayn. *Would she be horrifically disfigured? Was she missing an eye? How would Kayn survive this savage of a beating? Who would she be when she woke up? How could you ever be the same person?* He wasn't going to be the same person after seeing it. Swaying back and forth, he sobbed, "I should have come home. I could have changed this. I could have saved them." Matt's heart began to race. He was finding it difficult to breathe.

Sitting next to him on the floor, Jenkins whispered, "You would be dead too. If you came home last night, you'd be in this morgue. I'd be here identifying you. That's all you would have changed. Kayn would have woken up to your nightmare."

Matt quietly replied, "You can't know that."

While meeting his gaze, Jenkins clarified, "They were dead by early evening. You would have walked into that house like it was a normal day and you'd be dead. Initially, we thought it was a home invasion but the length of time between the deaths in the house and Kayn's assault makes it personal. The assailant waited for her. We know she was dropped off around eight pm. It looks like she tried to get away. She almost made it out of the trails. That's where we found her. Your sister's fighting for her life and she only has someone to come home to because fate kept you away from that house last night."

They sat in silence as the tech stood quietly by the door. *He hadn't gone to afternoon classes but would have if an incredibly hot girl hadn't accosted him and practically thrown herself at him. He would've been home around the same time as Kayn. Maybe, he could have distracted the killer long enough for her to get away?* Once Matt felt like he'd been sitting long enough internally obsessing over the details, they left the morgue and numbly rode the elevator back up to the lobby. Stepping out with Jenkins at his side, Matt made eye contact with Clay's mom and walked into Lillian Smith's open arms.

She stroked his hair, whispering, "It's okay sweetheart, I have you. You never have to see anything like that again."

Crumbling into a childlike state in the warmth of her maternal sanctuary, listening to the rhythm of her heart as she consoled him. His chest heaved, imagining her heartbeat was his mother's. *How desperately he'd wanted to hear her heartbeat when he'd placed his ear against his deceased mother's chest.* She kept him safe in her embrace until his tears were spent and all he had left were trembling sighs. He whispered aloud the word repeating in his mind, "Why?" *He needed to know. He wanted to run around the hospital screaming it at the top of his lungs.*

"We may never know," she soothed, rocking back and forth.

He would never be held in his mother's arms again. He didn't want to let go. "Did you see what they did to my sisters?" Matt numbly asked, stepping away.

Putting his arms around him, Clay's father affirmed, "Son, you're staying at our house. There's going to be a lot to deal with, we're going to help you."

Kevin was missing. "Where's Kevin?" Matt asked without letting go.

"My brother's in a bed down the hall," Clay answered.

Turning to his friend, Matt said, "He wasn't at our house, was he?"

"They had to sedate him," Clay replied. "He's having a mental vacation."

Matt blankly mumbled, "That sounds nice." *He was light-headed.* Lillian walked him to a bench, excused herself and left him with the others. Jenkins went to ask for updates. He just sat there watching people coming in and out of the door in slow motion.

A while later, Mrs. Smith reappeared with a doctor. He asked him to come to his office for a few minutes, Matt obliged. *He had nothing else to do. Nowhere to go. Everyone was gone. All gone. The cases they came in were downstairs, but they weren't there.* The physician led him to his office, directing him to take a seat. Matt sat down, blankly looked around. *Motivational posters. A glass jar full of candy. No cotton balls. Why didn't he have cotton balls? He shouldn't be here. He should be dead too. They were lucky they were gone.* The doctor cleared his throat. Matt peered up. He was sitting in a chair smugly observing. *He wanted to throat punch him for smiling.*

The physician enquired, "How are you feeling?"

He was feeling unusually hostile about the ignorance of that question. He spitefully muttered, "Someone slaughtered my entire family, how in the hell do you think I feel?"

"I understand. You're angry. Rage is a fight or flight response to stress. Your brain is trying to process great loss. Anger isn't the most beneficial emotion to go with in this situation, it can lead to rash decisions," he said, jotting down notes.

Matt coldly bantered, "What would you suggest I feel? Should I have a friggin' party? A giant bloody celebration for the demise of everyone I love. What in the hell is wrong with you?" He got up intending to storm out, but he was unsteady on his feet. His headache was brutal. Matt dropped back into the chair, clutching his head. *It was about to explode. It felt like he was being stabbed between the eyes.* A memory of his mother's voice surfaced instructing him to breathe. *She's gone. She would be upset he was acting like this.* He teared up, apologising, "I'm sorry. I don't know why I said that. I'm not like this. I swear, I'm not. My head is killing me."

The doctor got up, pulled a machine to Matt's side and said, "You have just lived through what will likely be the worst day of your life. You smell like you had too much to drink last night. Wait here, I've got something to for that." Reappearing with an electrolyte drink, he handed it to Matt. "Here, this will help. I'm going to check your blood pressure while I lecture you on the importance of sleep."

After a few tests Matt decided the doctor was an alright guy and sheepishly followed him back to Clay's mom.

The Doctor addressed Lillian, "Matthew has prescriptions, it will be a difficult month. Stress induced raised blood pressure is normal, but it being this high at his age makes me uncomfortable. I'd like to see him in a week." He gave Matt a pat on the back but spoke to Lillian, "I explained to young Matthew here that he needs lots of sleep, it's unwise to go more than a night without in his situation. We'd like to keep him thinking rationally. Best case scenario, his sister has a long road to recovery. He needs to be strong for her so let's get him through this." The Doctor gave Mrs. Smith a few pills in a bottle and whispered, "This is a light sedative. It should be good until you can get the prescriptions filled tomorrow." He gave a pill to Matt and told him to place it under his tongue.

Too mentally exhausted to argue, Matt did what he was told. His stomach grumbled. He looked at the clock on the wall. It was late afternoon the next day. His head was probably pounding because he hadn't eaten since yesterday. Truth be told, he didn't care if he ever ate again. *His mother's first line of defence for a headache was five glasses of water. The doctor had given him a drink. That made sense.*

Like she'd read his mind, Clay's mom passing him a can of orange juice, saying, "Let's go home. We'll call and check on Kayn as soon as we get there."

Clay's father placed his arm around him and led Matt out into the fresh air. *It was raining. It suited the moment.* Water pelted his face. *In the evening shower, there came a strange sense of peace. Perhaps it was the calming effect of the drug. It felt nice. He didn't care. He didn't care about anything. He felt wonderful. It was an emotionless stay of execution.* Matt startled as someone slammed the car door, giggling. The car started moving and now he was chuckling. *How did he get into the car? Was he magically transported here? Maybe, it was all a bad dream? When he woke up everything would be fine. He was fine. Everybody was fine. Everything would be fine.* Those were his last semi-rational thoughts as he succumbed to pharmaceutically enhanced calm, drifting off to sleep.

· · ·

MATT AWOKE THE NEXT MORNING IN A BED THAT WAS NOT HIS OWN and it came flooding back. He stumbled out into the kitchen with unthinkable visions in his mind. *Everything was not fine. It was real. It all happened, and nothing would ever be fine again.* He wept until he made himself sick, hugging the toilet and dry heaved with no food in his stomach. They gave him another pill and everything was fine again. *He survived that first week in that docile state of numb.*

While Matthew was having a mental vacation, Lillian arranged for someone to clean the house so it would look like the violence never happened. Jenkins was named the executor of his parent's will so he dealt with the bills and kept the empty Brighton house in order while Matt remained fine. Lillian and Jenkins went ahead with funeral preparations, after finding out Kayn would be in the hospital for months longer than antici-pated. Matt had moments of clarity each day before he began to melt down. It was only postponing the inevitable, but he took another pill, and then, he was nothing. *Being a numb unfeeling zombie was preferable to the agony he was languishing in.*

One day, Matt awoke knowing he'd been dreaming of his final words to his father. *He'd promised to be a good man.* He got out of bed and went downstairs with a clear mind. *It was time to be strong.* He did not cry that morning, knowing he had to find a way to pull himself together. *It was time to stop hiding from the truth.* One of his mother's favourite quotes had been, fake it till you make it. *He imagined he'd be living that way for a while.*

Matt and Kevin boarded the short flight to see Kayn. They arrived in Vancouver and took a cab to the hospital. His sister had been kept in a medically induced coma. When they heard the details of Kayn's injuries and how many surgeries she'd been through, it seemed impossible that she'd survived. *It was a mira-cle. He had never done anything worthy of a miracle.* They spent a couple of days by Kayn's side, sleeping in chairs in her room.

Kevin seemed bigger. Maybe he just looked more mature after everything he'd been through? Kevin had been sitting on the edge of the bed holding his sister's hand for hours. A thought popped into Matt's head. *Perhaps, this was Kevin's miracle.* Passing Kayn's bestfriend a coffee, he said, "We never talk about Chloe. Why do you think that is?"

Staring at the coffee, Kevin replied, "We found her. It's still too painful to think about."

That was understandable. They were trying to forget what they'd seen. He wished there was a way to forget what he'd seen. Matt casually sipped his piping hot coffee as he stated, "You had the biggest crush on Chloe."

Meeting Matt's gaze, Kevin confessed, "I can't shake the feeling that Chloe's still here. It feels like she's going to bust me talking about her and whip me with her jacket."

Kevin looked past him like someone came in the room. He turned, no one was there. Glaring, Matt teased, "You're officially freaking me out, Smith. What are you looking at?"

"It's not important," Kevin replied, caressing Kayn's hand. Smiling, he whispered, "It looks like she's lost in a beautiful dream."

"I hope she's someplace wonderful. I hope they all are," Matt answered, smiling.

Tucking Kayn's covers around her, Kevin assured, "They all are, I'm sure of it."

Matt tossed his empty cup in the garbage, teasing, "Except for Chloe, right? You feel like Chloe's still here."

Kevin didn't answer him, and he didn't blame him. That was an asshole move. He had to find a way to stop himself from saying whatever crossed his mind. He had to try to be a better man.

Kissing Kayn softly on her cheek, Kevin said, "Here isn't that bad."

"Saturday will be bad for me to go through all alone," Matt

replied. He took it back, "I'm sorry, that was a selfish thing to say."

Kevin smiled as he remarked, "You're not alone and you're just being honest. Kayn wouldn't want you to go through the funeral alone either."

Leaning over, Matt kissed his sister's unbandaged cheek and whispered, "We'll be back tomorrow."

After a few more days of vigil at Kayn's bedside, the boys returned home for the funeral. Feeling guilty, his sister wouldn't be able to be there to grieve and have closure, he also felt jealous. *He wanted to be able to check out again.* Matt had purpose by his ailing sister's side. She was all he had left. Still terrified he could lose her to a random complication, each time the phone rang his heart leapt and his stomach lurched.

5

THE EDGE OF THE ABYSS

On the day of the funeral, there was not a cloud in the sky as far as the eye could see. The family, always being the last to arrive at the service, pulled up at the church and snuck into a side door. Matthew stood there in his suit and tie gripping the paper, he'd painstakingly written his eulogy on. *He wasn't ready for this.* Just as panic tightened in his chest, he felt Jenkins' hand on his shoulder. The door opened and all eyes turned to them as they were escorted to their seats. The congregation was asked to rise, and everyone began singing a hymn. The sight of the large family portraits at the front made Matt feel such raw excruciating loss, he had to look down at the eulogy in his hand. He couldn't meet anyone's well-meaning smiles; *it was killing him.* He entertained the thought of abandoning his seat and bolting out of the church. *He'd jump on the first flight to Vancouver and be by Kayn's side while the rest of his world was laid to rest. I shouldn't be here. I should be dead too. My picture should be up there beside Chloe's. I'm just a selfish asshole. I was out drinking, while everyone I loved was brutally murdered. Why am I such a horrible person? How had two wonderful selfless people created a piece of shit like me?* Matt openly wept. *He didn't care who saw, all he felt was overwhelming guilt. The minister had been speaking for a while and he hadn't been listening.* He was halfway between a panic attack and a mental breakdown when Jenkins touched his arm, whispering, "It's your turn."

Staring at his piece of paper, Matt got up. Jenkins also rose and touched his shoulder for comfort. *He was sweating profusely. It was so hot in here. It was way too hot.*

Jenkins whispered words of assurance Matthew Brighton's heart had been longing for, "I'll go up there with you. You don't have to do this alone."

With tears streaming down his face, Matt understood Jenkins had no intention of leaving him alone in this world. He intended to stand beside him. *Those words meant more than he could express.* Walking up to the pulpit, Matt felt Jenkins' hand on his shoulder. It was such a simple gesture, but it gave him the ability to find the will to begin. Matt cleared his throat and looked up. For the first time, he saw how many people had come to pay their respects to his family. The church was at capacity, people were even standing outside by open doors. They were all waiting for him to speak. He looked down at the words he'd painstakingly written, tore the paper in half and spoke, "I spent a lot of time writing out what I was going to say today, but I know the best way to honour them is to speak from my heart. The world was a far better place with my family in it. The sound of my mother's laughter could fill an entire room with light and when she smiled, everyone around her couldn't help but smile back, because my mom was full of joy. She was the most loving person and it was a privilege to be her son. We were so lucky to have her as our mother." He'd choked out the last couple of words, tears flooded his eyes, grief flowed as a waterfall and he couldn't continue. He knew he had to, but he needed a moment to compose himself. He glanced at Jenkins.

Jenkins understood what he needed without words and took over, "Matthew's father was my best friend. He was funny and eternally optimistic. I'm going to share moments that stand out in my mind. On their wedding day, everything went wrong. We'd had the bachelor party the night before, which is never a good idea. My buddy was ill-equipped to deal with any drama that day and we were late to start." He looked at Matt as he continued speaking, "Your mother was incredibly beautiful, walking down the aisle to your father. I remember the look on his face. He was crazy in love with her. When they started their vows, I thought they both might be a little wacky. It was the strangest thing I'd ever heard. It wasn't until I had experience with love myself that I understood what they were saying to each other. Your father said, I can't promise I won't drive you crazy. I can't promise that there won't be hills on this rollercoaster. I can't promise you there won't be pieces of the track missing, but I promise to stay on this ride with you. I won't get off until the end. Your mother repeated his words." Jenkin's composed himself and continued, "This will make sense in a minute. Your parents went to the same high school, but they'd barely spoken to each other. We knew who Claire was, but we were in different friend groups. The fair was in town. We were waiting in a line to get on the rollercoaster and the operator paired the two of them up. The guy running the ride laughed and said, you look like you should be on this ride together. Your father fell in love with Claire the second he sat down beside her. We were walking home with a group of friends that night, when my friend looked at me and made the craziest declaration ever, I'm going to marry her someday." Clearing his throat, Jenkin's blinked away tears, persevering, "Through three children, they never lost their sense of humour about life. The whole family was magic. There was so much laughter in their home. They took me in when I lost my daughter and showed me that life was still worth living. Your father kept his word. He stayed with her on the ride until the end." Jenkins fared well until those last words and broke down.

Matt stepped back in, "The night I found out they died. I made a promise to my father that I would try to be a good man. All I needed was a few more minutes with him. I wanted to tell him, he'd been the best dad. The best example of what a father should be. I never got the chance to say those words. When you all go home tonight, say the words. Tell your family how much you love them. Say the words out loud. Don't just assume they know how you feel because if something happens, you will always wonder if they knew how you felt…" Matt couldn't go on, neither could Jenkins, they were both sobbing.

Kevin made his way up to the pulpit. He took his place and began to speak, "I remember Kayn's mom telling us about their wedding. She said the caterer didn't show up and the band didn't come. A friend had a karaoke machine and guests made their own music. They didn't let anything stop them. Their daughter Chloe was an equally unstoppable girl. Chloe was beautiful and she was so smart. Chloe Brighton was a force of nature, she was also my friend. I've been friends with the Brighton twins since kindergarten. I can still picture them as little girls, lying in a field watching bumblebees, braiding head-bands out of flowers and dancing around together wearing buttercup crowns. I remember thinking they looked like angels. Chloe always had big dreams. She was a fighter by spirit. I went to see Kayn in the hospital, it felt like Chloe was there with her somehow, watching over her. Maybe, it's because I know Chloe was actually stubborn enough to refuse to leave this place without her sister." Giggles erupted in the congregation of mourners.

The thought of his sister's feisty spirit being described in that way made Matt smile through his tears. *It was the truth.*

Kevin kept talking, "On the wall in their house there was a framed poem Kayn's mother wrote in high school. I read the words every time I walked past. *One kind word can guide a soul out of the darkness. A hug can show someone that good hearts still exist. Be the hand someone can hold onto while teetering on the edge of an abyss.* This was the Brighton family creed. This was who they were, and they will always be missed."

The Minister took over the service. Every person in the town had known or loved one of the Brighton family members. At the end of the funeral, there was a beautiful prayer for Kayn. A prayer she would return as beautiful and innocent of spirit as she had been, before that night. It was a heart-wrenching service.

Strolling out of the church with an arm around Matthew, Jenkin's promised, "Just in case I haven't made myself clear. I'm here for you. When Kayn gets home from the hospital invite me over for dinner, we'll talk about it. Your parents wouldn't want you to drop out. You should go back as soon as you can. The faster you get back to school the easier it will be to pick up where you left off."

Matt slowly shook his head, saying, "Kayn needs me, I have to keep her safe."

Jenkins assured, "Kayn's in a medically induced coma. You'll visit when you can. I'll visit when I can, and we'll try to get her moved back here as soon as possible. Your job is to go back to school. I will keep acting as executor. I'll pay bills and carry on doing the adult stuff. You just let me know when you feel ready to do it by yourself."

Jenkins winked at Matt, patting him on the shoulder and Matthew Brighton knew he still had family even if they weren't related by blood. *Jenkins and the Smith's had been there for him. They would be his family now. A new kind of family made of friends.*

6

THE LONG KISS GOODNIGHT

*D*ays turned to weeks, and weeks to months and still Kayn slept. They transported Kayn Brighton back to her hometown where she could be closer to what was left of her family. There she lay like an angel in sweet, uninterrupted slumber. An induced coma had given her body time to heal. Still, she slept, even after her doctor's attempted to awaken her.

She would have to wake up to the reality of what happened. Would she still be the same person, or would she live each day with memories of that horrific night scorched into her soul?

With Matt at school, Kevin was the one by her side each day, watching her dream. "Look at all these flowers you have, I bet you had no idea this many people loved you," Kevin said, sitting in the chair by her hospital bed. *He'd come to realise he was in love with her. Perhaps, he'd just needed to be faced with the thought of losing her to see things clearly.* He tucked a strand of hair behind her ear. He wanted to kiss her lips, to see if she'd awaken like sleeping beauty, but always stopped himself. He needed her to be present the first time his lips met hers in that way. Leaning in,

Kevin whispered in her ear, "I think I've always loved you." He dug around in his backpack, saying, "I have your iPod here with your favourite songs on it. I added some Rascal Flatts." He got up and placed the buds in her ears. "It was your mom's favourite group. It was always blaring in your house. I thought it might make you happy." Glancing at her heart monitor as it beeped rhythmically, Kevin willed the conversation to reach her wherever she was. He spent at least an hour with her daily, telling her about his day and how girls were hitting on him at school.

In the weeks after her attack, Kevin woke up to a slightly buffer version of himself each morning. He'd take his shirt off in front of the mirror, thinking, *what in the hell is going on?* He wasn't complaining, but it wasn't normal. He'd also had a growth spurt, shooting up a good three inches. His father always told him he was short until he was sixteen so that part could be explained. He'd started working out with his brother at the gym, so he had an explanation that seemed rational. He'd never thought he'd go out of his way to spend time with Clay, but in the aftermath of that night, they found the sense of brotherhood they'd been missing.

The police hadn't come close to catching her assailant, there wasn't one strange fingerprint at the crime scene. They had no leads and no suspects. A piece of him feared someone would show up to finish Kayn off. When he felt uneasy leaving her, he'd sleep in the chair beside her bed. *He was strong enough to protect her now. Nobody would ever be able to hurt her again.* Kevin stroked her hair. A plastic surgeon dealt with her injuries. Her face had healed without scars except for a thin one beneath her jawline. She had brain activity but there was a chance she had brain damage. They wouldn't know until sleeping beauty awakened. He squeezed her hand and whispered, "I'll be back tomorrow." He knew he might be talking to himself but didn't care. He'd started running and doing the things she loved because it made him feel closer to her. He listened to the same music. It felt like these minuscule things, kept them connected. He left hoping she was dreaming of peaceful things like catching bumblebees as a child, surrounded by music she loved.

Kevin couldn't wait to close his eyes each night for he'd been having beautiful dreams of them as children. They'd catch bees, climb trees, and look in nests but never touched the tiny blue eggs. It would always feel so real he'd wake up disappointed. In dreams, he could talk to her and feel whole, if only for a little while. They'd watch clouds guessing what they looked like. He'd pretend to be disgusted but was always secretly impressed when Kayn's ideas were dirty. Smiling, he plugged the earpieces into his ears and slipped off to sleep, hoping to see her in his dreams.

7

WHILE SHE LAY DREAMING

Dreaming: A succession of images, thoughts, or emotions passing through the mind during sleep.

*H*er hair was caressed, Kayn focused on her mother, yawned, and rubbed her eyes groggily. She was lying beside her sister. *They were young, maybe five or six years old.*

With blonde curls fanning out behind her, Chloe complained, "She's wrecking my story."

Scooping Kayn up into her arms, snuggling her, her mom consoled, "It's okay, sweetheart. It was just a bad dream."

She had a horrible dream but couldn't recall what it was about. It didn't matter. This felt wonderful. She loved snuggling with her mom. Inhaling her mom's perfume, Kayn stated, "I like this smell, it's a keeper."

"You're a keeper," her mom teased, tickling her.

Squiggling and squirming, giggling, joy flooded Kayn's being.

"People. Control yourselves. We are reading a story," Chloe crossly huffed.

"Oh, really," her mother giggled as she began tickling Chloe too.

All three were laughing, tickling each other when their father walked in and announced, "There was a story on the news today, a wild animal escaped from the zoo. It was last seen in our neighbourhood. Do you know what it was?" their dad said in his scariest voice.

"What was it?" the girls asked in unison intensely curious.

"It was a tickle monster," their dad yelled as he leapt on the bed, tackling all three.

They tickled each other until one of the little girls squealed, "I'm going to pee!"

The memories flickering through Kayn's brain were so real, it was like someone was changing the channel on a TV. Every so often, she'd hear a faint echo of a familiar voice, and music, there was always music. Blissfully unconcerned, as the scenery changed, Kayn lay peacefully in the grass by her twin watching bumblebees vaguely aware someone was missing. *They were fascinating creatures.* If she watched closely, she could see the pollen stuck to their tiny legs. "I don't ever want to leave here. Let's stay forever, Chloe." Kayn whispered to her sister.

"You can't stay here forever, Kayn. You have to go home soon," Chloe whispered back.

"I can't go without you," Kayn answered, mesmerised by a furry bumblebee.

"We can always be together. I can go back with you," Chloe whispered with a mischievous twinkle in her eyes.

"Where did mom and dad go?" Kayn enquired.

"They had to leave without us. It's okay, they are always close by," Chloe whispered like it was a secret.

"I'm so tired," Kayn mumbled, yawning, stretching her arms so high it felt like she was almost touching the clouds.

"Go to sleep," Chloe whispered, watching a bee with chubby pollen covered legs.

"But they might sting me when I'm sleeping. I'm allergic, remember?" Kayn replied as bees delicately danced from flower to flower.

Chloe whispered, "They can't hurt you. Nothing can hurt you here, Kayn."

Sprawling amongst flowers with blonde locks cushioning her head, fragrant cherry blossoms from surrounding trees soothed her senses as Kayn slipped into a peaceful slumber.

Feeling a tickle, Kayn woke with bees carpeting her entire body. *She wanted to scream.* Her father's words replayed in her mind, *be calm Kayn. Stay calm my sweetheart.* Her even and steady breathing continued as thousands of tiny feet tickled her face and body. *Was Chloe okay? Where was she?* She heard Chloe laughing.

A male voice she didn't recognize ridiculed, "They can't sting you for real, silly child."

Who was that?

"So hilarious," Chloe chuckled. "I bet you're freaking out. I asked them to land on you and they did, so cool."

Ask them to get off me. Afraid to move covered in bees, Kayn couldn't say the words. *This isn't funny, Chloe. I'm scared.*

Chloe let out an exasperated sigh, "Spoilsport, you never let me have any fun." Her twin commanded, "Bees, fly away."

Lifting off in unison, buzzing filled her ears as the swarm flew away. Furious, Kayn shouted, "They could have killed me! Why would you do that? How did you do that?"

"I've always been able to do it," Chloe boasted, smirking.

"You never told me you could," Kayn countered, amazed.

"You don't believe in hocus pocus, mumbo jumbo. Isn't that what you always say?" Chloe sparred saucily.

She'd never been a believer in mythical creatures or mystical things. "You could have shown me," Kayn replied while plucking a tiny purple flower from lush grass.

Gathering the courage, Chloe confessed, "About that, I did show you. I asked a bee to fly to a certain flower and it did. Then, I asked it to land on my arm because I wanted to touch it, and it did. I wasn't sure if it was just dumb luck, so I asked the bee to sting you and it did. You swelled up and almost died. How could I tell you after that happened?" After a pause, her twin disclosed, "I can't accidentally hurt you anymore."

Reality filtered in, Kayn whispered, "Are we dead? Is this heaven?"

Angrily, Chloe scolded, "I'm not allowed to talk about that."

"We aren't children anymore," Kayn divulged, noticing the strange multi-hued splotchy cerulean sky. Taking her twin's hand to prove she held no grudge, she persisted, "We're sixteen. In three months, we'll be seventeen. Where are we? What is this place?" Eight-year-old Chloe vanished. Rattled, Kayn stood up in the vast field of buttercups and clover. *She'd been abandoned.* She spun around, frantically searching for her sister. "Chloe, where are you? Please don't leave me here!" she hollered into the vast empty space. Confused as the buttercups, speckling the endless field vanished in the blink of an eye. She slowly turned, barefoot in lush, brilliant teal grass. *What is this place?* The temperature plummeted. Shivering with icy feet, Kayn looked down as a circle of snow appeared beneath her feet. *What was this?* The icy circle rapidly expanded until the field was covered in snow. *Her feet hurt.* Standing in snow barefoot was shockingly painful. With visible breath, she danced around trying to get out of the snow but there was nowhere to go. Wearing a childlike white sundress, shivering uncontrollably, she wrapped her arms around her chest. *This must be a nightmare. She was asleep and safe in her bed.*

Trying to use logic to make sense of how her surroundings

shifted from spring to the dead of winter, Kayn stopped moving for what felt like a second and snow was up to her knees, solidly packed around her. She struggled, frantically trying to move her limbs, but they wouldn't budge. The weight of the snow made even the smallest movement impossible. *She needed to wake up.* Sensing a presence, Kayn realised she wasn't alone. A dark figure was strolling towards her on the surface of the snow holding her captive. A tidal wave of terror swelled in the core of her being, causing her to attempt the unachievable feat of escape once again. *Who was that? She wasn't usually afraid of strangers.* By encasing her legs in snow rendering escape impossible this nightmare or place triggered something. As the figure approached, a rush of survival instinct shrieked at her to run. *Run! You need to get away! Run!* Adrenaline-induced terror surged through her, followed by a sense of déjà vu. *Struggling to move, it was impossible. She couldn't get away. She was trapped.* As the temperature continued its relentless descent, her hypothermic flesh felt like it was submerged in boiling water. She wailed in anguish as forming ice crushed her imprisoned limbs, shattering bones as it torturously solidified. *No, more. Help.* Tears froze where they trickled down her face. *Please. No more.* Her raspy voice crackled through the icy air, "Chloe, Chloe, help me, please." The menacing being crouched and commenced crawling. Panic-driven terror coursed through her as she writhed in agony, croaking, "Chloe, please." Clawing at ice as it crept stealthily towards her, she croaked, "What do you want?"

Athletic, agile like a dancer in form-fitting black spandex with peculiar movements like a cat hunting prey, it cocked his head and sat cross-legged. "I truly despise cleaning up after my sister's mistakes. Frankly, it's beginning to piss me off," he stated with unveiled sarcasm.

His quirky mannerisms reminded her of someone, she couldn't place. Numbed by shock, she noticed her bloody, jagged, savagely torn nails from clawing the ice.

Entertained by her frazzled state, he prodded, "You still don't remember anything, do you? Did you think I was someone else?" The man slinked closer, ordering, "Give me your hands."

Freezing, Kayn wrapped her arms around herself, hiding her hands. *She didn't trust him. For all she knew, he was planning to bite a finger off.*

"For heaven's sake, I was just being polite. It's not like you have a choice," the dark being held his hands out. Against Kayn's will, her hands moved out in front of her. "You seem confused, there's no need to be. It's in your best interest to do as I say," he stated. With an almost trustworthy smile, he hovered his hands over hers without touching her flesh.

The pain vanished, and her hands were healed. *What was he?*

"Has anyone ever accused you of being a tad overdramatic?" he remarked, grinning.

"No," Kayn responded, viewing her healed hands, amazed.

"A woman of few words, I like it." he commented, smiling in a way that made her feel at ease.

Kayn was still looking at her hands, trying to process her surroundings. *Was this heaven or hell?*

He answered like she'd spoken the words aloud, "Have you ever waited at a doctor's office for your turn? It's kind of like that."

"So, I'm dead?" Kayn stated, staring into the being's eyes.

"I bet you've been accused of jumping to conclusions before," he teased like he was speaking to a child. "Are you still cold?"

"I'm up to my knees in ice," Kayn answered, shivering.

"No, you're not," he answered, shaking his head.

Peering down at healed legs in warm water, stunning purple

and orange starfish were scattered around her. Kayn wiggled her toes as a crab scurried over, smiling because it tickled. *Were those tiny diamonds mixed with grains of sand beneath her feet?* She jumped as orbs of light startled her, flashing past. "What is this place?" Kayn whispered, with water caressing her legs.

The dark man said, "Fancy a closer look?" He ran his hand through the water, creating ripples as they moved, turning into waves travelling in each direction, growing larger as they headed away, leaving them on a circle of dry sand. Exposed to the sun, the grains shone like stars beneath her feet. Getting down on her knees to have a closer look, Kayn ran her fingers through the luxurious sparkling silky sand. *They are diamonds*, she thought, as she scooped up a handful.

A memory surfaced like watching a movie starring people she'd loved. She was an infant in the sand on a beach with Chloe. Their mother was talking about something in her hand with curls flowing in a summer breeze. She looked like an angel. Matty was running around with their tanned young father, flying a colourful kite. Her sister kept trying to pick up the sand only to have it slip through her chubby fingers. Each time Chloe cried, she sobbed out of empathy.

Snapping back to reality, Kayn looked at leftover sand from a handful that slipped through her fingers while lost in memories. *It seemed fitting. Her hand was the hourglass. There were only a few grains left so she held onto them tightly, just in case.* The man was smiling like he'd also seen her beautiful memories. Kayn looked around, the circle of sand they'd been standing on was now a vast beach with only a hint of blue in the distance in every direction. Her bare feet were toasty warm. Sitting there, she wiggled her toes in silky sand, smiling because it felt incredible.

Grinning, he commented, "I'd better get rid of that water altogether. Being hit by a forty-foot wave will wreck your day."

Moving his hands through the air, the scenery became one large beach as far as the eye could see. He sat with her in the sand.

Had her white lacy dress grown with her in size? Was she still a child? She peered at her chest. *No, I'm a teenager. This was completely insane.*

"I prefer sanity challenged," the being answered her private thoughts. Gazing into her eyes, he questioned, "You have pretty eyes. Do men come on to you a lot?"

No, never. They come on to my sister though. Cross-legged, the cheeky man put his hand over his mouth like he was trying to stop himself from saying more. *It felt like he was collecting data for a science project.*

The wiry being responded like she'd spoken aloud, "Well, they'll only be hitting on you now, won't they?"

"I doubt that," Kayn answered with disbelief.

"She's dead, you're not. Get with the program," he coldly answered, getting up.

"Chloe's really dead?" Kayn whispered, standing as the words sunk in like a weight in her chest. Her eyes glistened with tears as she choked out, "I just saw her."

Checking for witnesses, the devious being rubbed salt in her wound, revealing, "They're all dead. Your mother, father, and your feisty twin. Overkill if you ask me, gruesome stuff."

She was going to vomit. It didn't make sense. This place, the things she'd seen, it had to be a nightmare. What if it wasn't? Shuddering between sobs, Kayn paced, repeating, "No, no, no." *It can't be real.*

"Yes, yes, yes," he musically tormented, revelling in her grief. With a blatant distaste for humanity, he sighed, "Mortals, always so needy and emotional."

This was happening. They'd all been murdered, even her. Why else would she be here? Her families smiling faces flashed through her memory. Why? The mass that was her heart ached until it fragmented into pieces just like he'd ripped it from her chest, thrown it on the floor and crushed it underfoot. Hyperventilating as grief demolished her universe, she paced.

After allowing her a well-deserved breakdown, he cleared his throat. She looked at him through a veil of tears as he assured, "Your body is still alive."

"Why am I here then?" Kayn asked the being, appearing to have a touch of empathy.

Removing all doubt, he was horrible, he taunted, "You're sort of dying if that makes you feel better for surviving that depraved bloodbath. You should have seen the disgusting entrails, missing eyeballs, blood was everywhere. Throats were slit, people were disembowelled it was hideous." Kayn fainted.

She awoke to the scent of grass and a familiar female voice, scolding, "You, my brother, are an asshole."

"She only freaked out because she thought a shell was coming to finish her off," he chuckled.

"As I said, you're an asshole. You should have left her to me," the female reprimanded. "You always treat traumatized ones like they're ants under a magnifying glass in the sun. You should be ashamed of yourself."

Motionless, Kayn pretended she was still unconscious.

The female's voice assured, "It's okay child, we know you're awake."

Squinting in the blinding sunlight, Kayn sat up. The grass was full of buttercups and scattered orange flowers. One of the delicate flowers magically fluttered away. *The field was full of monarch butterflies, thousands of them.* Her heart soared as all at once, they took off in flight. She rose to her feet, taking in the awe-inspiring sight. As butterflies flitted the sky above, she noticed the dazzling radiance was a beam of light attaching the glorious lady in white to the swirling cobalt sky. Awestruck, she stared at the woman whose being exuded royalty. Overwhelmed by emotions, it felt like she should be kneeling.

Sensing Kayn's hesitation to speak, the lady in the light spoke first, "My dear, you aren't supposed to be here."

Still afraid to speak, Kayn thought, *Is this heaven? Are you God?*

The man in black started giggling.

"I'm not God," she whispered, as though Kayn were a child who had said something adorable. She gave her a warm, maternal smile.

Exposed in a way she'd never experienced, it felt like this woman was looking directly into her soul. "Who are you?" Kayn asked, sensing her gentle nature.

The lady in the light introduced herself, "My name is Azariah, I'm a benefactor of chances and giver of choices, but I have a small predicament as far as you're concerned, Kayn." She paused the conversation for a second before continuing her explanation, "I can step towards you or away. That part is my choice, but once I take you into my arms you will go one of three places and that will be determined by you."

Trying to pay attention, Kayn could hear a Rascal Flatts' song playing in the distance. She turned towards the music. *She loved this song. It was one of her mother's favourites. It was always playing in the car. They'd all sing along to it, even Matty.*

The woman in white continued, "There are a few things you should know about your unusual situation before making any decisions."

The song in the distance changed to, "Don't Call Me Baby." *It was her running song.* Kayn felt warmth and an unbelievable sense of calm as the lady began telling her a story, "Your parents were told it was impossible for them to conceive so they adopted your older brother Matthew."

Her parents never told them Matt was adopted.

The angelic being continued speaking, "Driving home from a shift at the hospital, your mother, Claire saw a pregnant woman in distress. She pulled over to help. Savagely beaten, Freja pled with her to go. She told Claire the people after her would kill anyone who interfered, but your mother refused to leave. She waved down a passing truck, they called for an ambulance. Freja knew the Third-Tier would never allow her to give birth. They had her for breaking immortal law. She escaped with one goal, to save her unborn child's soul. As Claire tended to her wounds, she confessed, she'd recently miscarried and vowed to stay with her so she wouldn't be alone. As fate would have it, Freja's ability was to be a giver of new life. Knowing she'd be entombed, and the life thriving within her destroyed, Freja felt her child move within her for the last time, as she willed the unborn soul to switch wombs. Your mother found out she was pregnant the next month. Something unexpected occurred, the egg separated, creating identical twins bound by Freja's ability, unable to leave this realm but as one. You became somewhat of an experiment for those of us who knew the situation. One soul shared between two bodies." She paused, waiting for questions. Kayn was silent, so the luminescent being continued, "Now, new souls can grow. This is the purpose of humanity. Are you following this, child?"

It felt like being told a fairy tale that couldn't possibly be true. Had she just asked her a question? "I think so," Kayn quietly replied. *The need for tangible sense kept her silent as she pieced together what she'd been told. Was she really one of those babies? What did that mean?* The angelic lady stepped closer, trailed by luminescent light. Recalling what she said about a step towards her or away, Kayn smiled. *That was two steps towards her.*

"Only three of us know what Freja did that night. If you understood how difficult it was to keep this quiet for all these years, you wouldn't be grinning," the immortal scolded.

"Sorry," Kayn apologized, afraid the divine being would step away.

"Without wisdom the proper choice can be difficult to see," the lady in light asserted, continuing, "Souls grow each lifetime from newborn to adult, just as bodies do. In your case, one soul split between two embryos. This was both a miracle and a tragedy. We checked in on you as children, hoping neither would have an ability and you'd slip through the cracks. Unfortunately, as Chloe aged, she discovered her abilities and began using them recklessly. You had no powers to speak of just natural athletic talent. For your sake, we'd hoped we could keep you girls concealed, but as time went on, we knew it would be impossible. Your twin's morality and conscience were severely lacking. She started to control men without setting them free, causing multiple lifepaths to veer off course. She was detected by Third-Tier Oracles, scheduling your family line for Correction. They wait until after your sixteenth year, so you have the ability to fight back."

This was ten levels of crazy but strangely plausible.

"Under Third-Tier law, any soul who alters a lifepath has committed an offence punishable by Correction. This sentenced your family line to death. Your older brother is alive because he isn't genetically related to you girls and he wasn't home. We don't think they know the details, only that a soul slipped through with gifts. Genetic lines with abilities must be Corrected to prevent evolution, for gods are no longer gods if mortals are their equals."

The lady in the light continued the tale with a warning, "Now, here is where the complication lies. Your souls are meant to be one and they've grown while apart. Each half, almost as strong as a full soul but bound together. Your sister is deceased. You are hanging on somewhere between life and death. You cannot leave without understanding, if you chose to return, Chloe will follow you back. Her soul must merge with yours. The strongest soul often will be the dominant one. There's a chance you may lose who you've become in the process."

It felt like she was listening to a story and her character had no chance.

Smiling at her inner-dialogue, Azariah continued, "There are three Clans of immortals on earth. If you choose to return, they will come to provide you with protection and training. If you survive until your eighteenth year, you become sealed to your Clan."

As the song ended in the background, Kayn thought of how running made her feel. *Not once in sixteen years had she ever won a battle of dominance with her twin.* Her mind raced through all the information she'd been given and settled on love. *She would have given her life for her sister in a heartbeat.* Kayn was lost in selfless thought, as the lady in the light took steps closer. Kayn looked up without fear in her voice, saying, "Yes, Chloe can join with me because I love her and I would have given my life for hers, if I'd had the choice."

Standing in regal brilliance, the angelic entity touched her shoulder, whispering, "One more warning, when people return from this place the ability to see the deceased may be triggered. On the mortal plain, your sister will appear as her last earthly image. You may fear her, and she may be angry with you. Dark things will be drawn to the light of the newly Corrected. You must join with the first Clan that comes, for you will not survive on your own. Do you understand?"

"I do," Kayn solemnly vowed, thinking about her brother. *Matt was all alone. She understood things would never be the same. She just wanted to go home.* The lady in the light took a final step and opened her arms. As they embraced, the warmth of uncon-ditional love enveloped her being. She closed her eyes, light exploded around her, it felt like she was moving. She took a deep breath and opened them.

KEVIN'S LIPS PARTED IN SHOCK. Tears of joy began streaming down his cheeks as he said, "It's okay. You're in the hospital. It's okay Kayn." He ran to the door and yelled loudly, "She's awake!"

8

SLEEPING BEAUTY AWAKENS

here was she? There was so much white.

Kevin began yelling, "She's awake! She's awake!"

Where am I? Squinting in bright light, Kayn tried turning her head. *It wasn't cooperating.* Her limbs were heavy and her muscles uncooperative as she made a feeble attempt to get up. *Well, that wasn't going to happen. She'd start smaller.* Kayn moved her fingers, even that took effort and concentration. Her eyes focused on Kevin. *Kevin? He looked bigger and older. Perhaps, her eyesight was as foggy as her mind?*

"Please, don't try to move. Wait until the doctor gets here. You need to calm down," Kevin asserted.

He embraced her and began stroking the side of her face, whispering about how much he missed her and how scared they all were. *What was he talking about?* "What happened to you?" Kayn said, but her voice was barely audible. *She was in a hospital room. There were so many flowers.* In rushed celebrating hospital staff. They gathered at the foot of her bed in awe. *This was getting weird.*

Smiling, a doctor announced, "Welcome back Miss Brighton. Can you tell me your name?"

"If you're my doctor shouldn't you already know my name?" Kayn sparred with a raspy voice.

Joyously laughing, Kevin covered his mouth and continued giggling.

"Just a few questions and I'll be satisfied," the doctor with silver-speckled hair patiently stated.

"Kayn Brighton," she replied with a strange look as she took note of everyone's fascinated expressions. *Did she bump her head?*

"What's the last thing you remember doing?" Her physician questioned.

Flashes of running around the track with the sun beating down on her, followed by a quick image of dinner at Kevin's house. Megan Fox with a moustache? It didn't make much sense. She whispered the only thing that did, "I was running."

The vibe in the room became strained as the doctor probed, "Where were you running?"

"The track. I was on the track," Kayn stated what should have been obvious. *Where else would she be running?* Relief crossed everyone's faces. She hesitantly enquired, "Why am I here? Did something happen?" She met Kevin's eyes, knowing he couldn't lie to save his life. *He was visibly disturbed. Was that fear in his eyes? What was he afraid of?*

The doctor placed a hand on her shoulder, gave it a squeeze, and said, "Welcome back Sleeping Beauty."

"Back from where?" Kayn whispered, confused. She noticed the absence of her family. *Why aren't they here?*

A nurse brought her a drink with a straw and sweetly enquired, "Would you like a sip of water? How does your throat feel? You haven't spoken in a while Sleeping Beauty."

Sleeping Beauty? This was concerning. Nodding, Kayn sipped from the straw the nurse held against her lips. *She was exhausted. It felt like she needed a nap. She wasn't a napper.*

The nurse corrected herself, "Sorry, old habits, you've been asleep for a while sweet pea. I should start using your name."

Agitated, Kevin stammered, "I'll be right back."

She followed his departure with her eyes. *Why were the police outside her door?* She watched Kevin arguing with the officers until her eyelids grew heavy and she drifted off to sleep. When she awoke, Kevin was sitting on the edge of her bed, caressing her face lovingly. She brushed his hand away in an uncoordinated movement, whispering, "Dude, this mushy stuff is creeping me out."

Grinning at her, he replied, "Point taken."

She couldn't peel her eyes away from him. *How much time had passed? He seemed bigger. His skin cleared up.* A mix of confusion and attraction gathered in the pit of her stomach.

"Do you remember what happened after you left my house?" Kevin asked cautiously, giving her a moment to scroll back in her mind.

She'd gone for a run, she had stomach cramps. She remembered that much. It popped into her head. *She went to Kevin's place for dinner. He was waving from his bedroom window. There was nothing after that. Did they get in an accident on the way home?* Kayn whispered, "I remember leaving your house. I saw you wave from your window. Did we get in an accident?"

Tearing up, Kevin hugged her and whispered in her ear, "It wasn't an accident."

What's with the hugging? Staring at him, she stated, "You look different."

"You've been in a coma for almost seven months," he replied.

Kayn shook her head in disbelief. *Seven months, that's ridiculous.* There was drama outside of her door. She looked up and noticed the police were still there. She recognized Jenkins. He appeared to be involved in a heated discussion. *She'd never seen him angry, not once.*

"Seven months," she repeated, processing it. Her mind spun through fragmented memories. Kayn felt the absence of her family but sensed she'd regret asking the question teetering precariously on the tip of her tongue. Ignoring self-preservation, she looked into Kevin's eyes and asked, "How come my parents aren't here?" Her subconscious whispered, *you don't want to know.* An officer pushed past the doctor into the room.

With clear disapproval, her physician stated, "I'd like it on record, this isn't an appropriate time to talk to my patient."

The officer insisted, "Security may be an issue. Once news of her recovery hits the papers, her safety could be compromised. We need to speak to her."

Safety, security. She was uncomfortable with those words. Ignoring everyone else, Kayn looked directly at Kevin and restated her question, "Where are my parents?" Her mind was scrolling through what she could recall, it was mostly images of Chloe. "Where's my sister?" Kevin's eyes filled with tears again. *Why weren't they here? Mom? Dad? Chloe? No, no, she had to go home.* Kayn tried, pulling adhesive monitors off her chest but her fine motor skills weren't cooperating. *She had to get out of here, now, right this second.*

Kevin held her, pleading, "Honey, you can't stand up. You need to be calm. Please Kayn, I can't lose you again."

Lose me? Honey?

He held her in his arms, whispering, "I wish there was a way to keep you from knowing this, but there isn't."

Understanding she wasn't strong enough to get out of bed, she whispered, "What happened? Just tell me."

Her best friend whispered against her hair, "This is going to be difficult to hear, prepare yourself. I'm not going anywhere tonight. I will be right outside your door. I'll be here when you're ready to talk about this."

Kevin turned to look back at her as an officer politely ushered him out. *He was already crying. This wasn't good.* Her eyes teared in preparation for what was to come. Kevin was watching her through the window. *The look in his eyes told her everything she needed to know. This was going to be bad.* Kayn wanted to sink into her mattress and disappear but willing her hospital bed to become quicksand would be pointless. She couldn't tear her eyes away from Kevin. *She knew what each of his expressions meant. He was afraid. Not just frightened, scared to death.* She silently prepared herself for the worst as she looked down at the white bedding that covered her legs. *If she didn't look back up, maybe they wouldn't be able to say the words. The words she knew were coming. She wanted her mom.*

An officer she'd never met introduced himself as Officer James Brandon. Her heart palpitated a wildly erratic rhythm. *No, don't say the words. Don't you say it.* Kayn took a deep breath as he informed her of the brutal nature of her family's demise. *Murdered?* Trembling, she absorbed the information. *It was too much to take. Her tough exterior wasn't real, it was an act, she was as fragile as glass and her spirit shattered into a million misshapen shards.* Her eyes rolled back as she passed out. She managed to find a way to disappear, if only for a little while.

THE DOCTOR CAME OUT OF her room and the noise in the hallway ceased. He updated the family friends, "It went as expected, it was too much for her to handle. She's resting." He smiled kindly at the Smith family as he left and made his way down the hall. The whole police station had accumulated near the nurses' station. They'd all been at the Brighton house that horrible night and it changed everyone's way of life. They'd all assumed they were safe in this sleepy town where locking doors was never common practice. Since Kayn's return they'd been checking in, hoping her survival would bring back peace of mind and clear the air, frigid and thick with fear of the unknown.

As word spread of Kayn's recovery a new dread arose. What if her awakening brought the person responsible for this brutal massacre back to town? There had been many theories created by the rumour mill. Maybe, it was a drifter just passing through, or perhaps a resident whose evil had been lying dormant for all these months. Would the fear of being identified ignite their murderous impulses? Would there be more death? The residents of this town had believed they were safe but that false sense of security had now been exposed as nothing more than a mirage. The locals had gone nutty, turning on friends and relatives. Anyone that couldn't account for that chunk of time became a suspect.

Kevin's mom whispered, "The police are afraid the killer will try again, aren't they?"

"I'm staying here tonight; don't even try to stop me," Kevin stated firmly.

"We wouldn't dare," his father replied as the hustle and bustle of the hallway returned to normal with the clicking of footsteps and ringing of phones.

"She's lucky to have you looking out for her," Kevin's mother whispered and winked.

They Smith's spent a few hours chatting outside of her room drinking coffee, waiting for Kayn's brother to arrive. Jenkins had no plans to leave either. He pulled up a chair and sat in the hall outside of her door.

When Matt arrived, he burst out of the elevator with a smile so animated and joyous it caused everyone's emotions to surface. He jogged up and hugged Kevin without a thought about being cool or manly. In the last seven months Matt had gone through changes too.

"I bet she's sleeping now, isn't she?" Matt enquired. He gazed down the darkened hall and added, "My roommate's waiting in the lobby. They wouldn't allow him up here. It's past visiting hours." Noticing Jenkins sitting on a chair outside Kayn's door, wearing his uniform, Matt asked, "Is this an official thing or are you here as family?"

"Police protection," Jenkins replied. "Kayn's recovery hits the papers tomorrow morning."

The grin on Matt's face was replaced with an expression of worry that jolted everyone's heart.

"Do they think there's something to be concerned about?" Matt probed.

Standing up, Jenkins answered, "Nobody knows. Better safe than sorry. If the person who killed your family thinks Kayn can identify them, she may be in danger."

"I'll go down to the lobby to give Ryan my keys, so he'll have somewhere to stay. I want to be here when she wakes up," Matt explained. He turned and walked back down the dimly lit hall to the elevator. The dark hallway was peaceful at night with only a steady buzzing and muffled voices. Nothing seemed ominous or dangerous. They had all been dreaming about her waking up for so long, they'd never considered how much safer she was asleep.

KAYN AWOKE TO SUNSHINE STREAMING through the blinds. She

wanted to go outside so she could feel the warmth of the sun on her skin. Her brother and Kevin were fast asleep in chairs by her bed. What she'd been told about her family flooded her mind. She closed her eyes and willed the pain away. *It still felt like a lie.* She watched her brother dream for a while. *He'd dealt with their loss alone. He didn't need her to freshen the wound. He'd been strong for her, she planned to do the same for him.* With a raspy, "Morning Matty," Kayn let him know she was awake. Matt woke up confused, *he'd obviously forgotten where he was.*

He got up and stumbled over with sleepy Jell-O legs, hugged her tightly, and exclaimed, "You have no idea how incredible it feels to have you back.

She needed to lighten the mood. Kayn complained, "Ouch, ouch, that hurts."

"Oh no, I'm so sorry?" Matt apologised, releasing her.

"I'm joking. I'm fine," Kayn chuckled quietly.

Kevin woke up, mumbling, "Yes, she's all good Matt and as you can tell, still completely full of shit."

Laughing, Matt shook his head, hugging her again. He pulled away and cautiously asked, "They told you?"

With a weighted throat and survival instinct numbed brain, she responded mechanically, "When they let me out, I'd like to see where they're buried." She focused on the rays of light on her sheets. *Only time would reinforce the wall, she was building around her heart regarding the topic of her family. Matt already built his emotionless fortress. He'd had seven months to reinforce walls and learn how to shut down intrusive thoughts. There was no healthy way to process the brutal information she'd been forced to swallow. She imagined it was all just a matter of compartmentalization.* A crack formed in her foundation, but she held back her tears, certain her heart would ache like this each time they crossed her mind. Even from this vantage point, she knew it was her dad's friend on the other side of the glass barrier. *He wasn't buff or intimidating looking. He was like her dad. He had an aura of peaceful-ness that made her feel at ease.* Jenkins turned and waved. *He must have felt her watching. Yes, she felt better knowing he was close by.*

"You're not getting out of here for a while. There's a fair amount of rehabilitation ahead of you. Well, and the whole pesky security issue," Kevin explained. He also waved at Jenkins who waved and smiled back.

"Which one of you wants to tell me the dirty details? I need to know what happened to me," Kayn asked as she felt her face thoroughly. *Did she look the same? It felt okay but she didn't feel the same.* "Kevin, can you find me a mirror?" she prompted.

"You look beautiful, there aren't even any noticeable scars," Matt responded.

She wanted to see her reflection to pretend it was Chloe. It wasn't vanity. She just needed to see her twin, even if it wasn't real. It felt like she'd lost a limb. It was a continuous sense something was missing.

9

LEARNING TO LISTEN

K nuckles rapped on her door. The doctor stuck his head in, saying, "Good morning, Sleeping Beauty.

He asked the boys to leave for a minute so he could check her out with some privacy and they both hesitated. *They knew she wanted to know what happened to her.*

The doctor grinned and teased, "She'll be fine for a couple of minutes. Go grab yourselves a coffee." He pulled the curtains closed.

"Let's get this catheter out first. We'll try to get you standing today." The doctor pressed the buzzer and called a nurse in to help. Opening the front of her gown, he said, "You shouldn't have any pain."

Watching as he ran his fingers over visible ridged scars on her chest and abdomen, Kayn met her physician's eyes, asserting, "What happened to me."

Mechanically, he disclosed the gruesome details, "You were found in the trails behind your house. You were naked, but there was no evidence of sexual assault. You'd been stabbed twelve times and severely beaten. A symbol was carved on your chest. Your jaw and nose were broken, it's a miracle they saved your eye. We stabilised you and airlifted you out. In Vancouver, you had many reconstructive and reparative surgeries. You are healing at an amazing rate." His hand covered his mouth as he thought, *what in the hell is wrong with me?*

Kayn knit her brow. *Had she just heard the doctor's thoughts?*

The nurse was visibly shocked at the physician's robotic blunt narrative. He leaned against the side of the bed, confused. He shook his head a couple of times before regaining his composure.

Looking at the nurse, Kayn questioned, "Is there anything else?"

In a calming tone, the nurse added, "Most of your scars will disappear altogether, those that remain wear proudly as a symbol for what you've overcome. I have faith you're strong enough to do that Kayn." The nurse thought, *what in the hell has gotten into me?*

She heard every unspoken word. This was getting weird. The nurse's words of wisdom vetoed the harshness of the doctor's words.

Dr. Cambridge glanced at the nurse and proclaimed, "That is the most profound thing, I've ever heard you say."

"Thanks," she replied, thinking, *no idea where that came from.*

"Well, it was beautiful," the Doctor acknowledged. He thought, *you probably just saved my ass.*

It felt like she'd done something to them to make them say way more than they intended. Was she doing this or was her groggy coma mind playing tricks on her? Her mortified caregivers excused themselves and sheepishly left her room. *Well, that was awkward.* Her stomach grumbled. She looked up at the bags of liquid hanging by her bed. *I see, I've been on a liquid diet. Some-*

body needs to feed me, I'm starving. A nurse appeared with a tray containing chicken consommé, soda crackers, and Jell-O. *That could have been a coincidence.* Kayn scowled, and said, "Tell me this isn't breakfast, I'm so hungry." She glared at that bag dangling beside her and sighed, "Have I really been living off that for seven months?"

The nurse smiled at her and replied, "Baby steps, it's been a long time since you've digested solid food."

Her brother wandered back in, drinking a steaming cup of coffee, "Hey princess, how's breakfast?"

"You are such a jerk," Kayn mumbled as she glared at her bowl of clear soup and Jell-O. Stealthily motioning her brother closer, she whispered, "Grab me a coffee."

"Don't you dare!" the nurse scolded, with a comical scowl. She pushed her water with a straw closer, shot her the fakest smile in the universe and asked, "Would you like some help eating?"

She liked this nurse. Strained politeness always made her smile. It was a skill she admired. She recalled her mother's words, *a summer job in customer service would do you girls a world of good. Her mother was gone.* A wave of overwhelming grief snuck up and silently gutted her. *She'd never be there to reprimand her for her smart-assed remarks again. She was gone. They all were.* She blinked her tears away and swallowed the lump in her throat. *Logic had to prevail if she wanted to get out of this bed. She couldn't allow the harsh reality of her life to destroy her. She'd pretend her family was on vacation somewhere beautiful. Avoiding the truth would work for a while. She had to deal with her physical limitations and that would never happen if she sat here wallowing in self-pity. She'd cry when she was healed.* She'd moved her arms with no problem earlier, but her fingers were a different story. She fumbled, trying to pick up her spoon with uncooperative digits until she was boiling chicken consume with her mind frustrated.

The nurse was watching her stubbornness. "I can do it," Kayn stammered. The nurse smiled as she puttered around the room. Her brother was zoned out drinking coffee and didn't notice her struggling. He finally clued in and without saying a word, he scooped a spoonful of cold consommé into her mouth. *She despised feeling weak, she was an athlete.* He kept feeding her until the unappetizing entrée was gone.

The prickly nurse poked her head into the room, teasing, "That straw on your tray was for drinking the soup."

Kayn politely replied, "Thank you, I guess I'll know for next time." *Touché food lord. Her mother would have been so proud. The coast was clear.* She leaned over and whispered, "Matty, is there ice-cream in those vending machines?" Matt grinned, he knew she was intentionally pushing the nurse's buttons.

The nurse stuck her head through the door, promising, "After dinner, I'll get you some myself, if you don't throw up those crackers."

She'd been given a symbolic fig leaf. Kayn smiled as she countered, "I can't exactly run to the bathroom."

The nurse strolled back in, placed a small styrofoam container on her lap and said, "Just in case you need it." She gave her a look that read, *I'm being nice, but you are super high maintenance.*

Kayn looked at the tiny container. *Has anyone in the history of humanity ever puked up that small of an amount? It looked like it would only hold a serving of fries. She'd need like ten of those. She must have imagined those mind-controlling abilities because they weren't working now.*

Weeks passed uneventfully, with no attempts on her life, just many small victories, leading to larger ones. Kayn was doing surprisingly well physically. Emotionally, she hadn't dealt with a thing. She'd simply avoided any thoughts that led to tears. In the wee hours, dreams fed her fragments of her Sweet Sleep.

Strange images flickered through her mind. Visions of joyously running through an endless field of buttercups with her sister, hearing the musical buzzing of bees. Movie reels of brightly coloured starfish and orbs of light as they sped past her toes in the water. It wasn't only good memories that followed her back to the land of the living, the torturous agony of legs solidified into ice and the blinding panic of the unknown came along for the ride. She had magical visions of a lady standing in a beam of glorious light and a mysterious slender man crept in from time to time. She wasn't sure what any of these images meant but had the impression she'd understand when she was ready.

After a month, Kayn pretty much felt like herself again. She'd been rather badass in physio, regaining full use of her body in record time. During each psychiatric consult, she went through the motions without a speck of negativity, knowing anything she revealed would make her sound insane. Since the department concluded her assailant must have been a drifter passing through, the officers outside her door were there voluntarily.

Tomorrow was the day. It was finally time for her to go home. Her brother would be home for the weekend. She was excited to go home to feel close to the family, she'd lost. The tentative plan was that Jenkins would stay there each week while Matt was at school. She was seventeen and her brother was twenty, everyone thought it would be best to leave them be. Kevin's family assured her they set up a bedroom at their house just in case. *In case she couldn't handle staying in the house where her family was slaughtered.* Kevin's visits were her favourite part of each day. He kept leaving stones on her windowsill saying they were gifts from his grandmother. Granny Winnie had always been a believer in the energy they held. The rose quartz was there to help her heal. Knowing his grandmother, the others were used to ward off evil. *She'd experi-*

enced true evil. *She'd been a victim of darkness.* Kayn had never believed in his grandmother's tales. She'd listened and even professed to believe but hadn't. She could now profess without a shadow of a doubt, that she'd become a true believer in magic. She'd been seeing and hearing things in the hallways at night. A giggling little girl running up and down the halls. A child nobody else could hear. She had the unmistakable feeling she was being watched. *It wasn't a sense something ominous was watching. Just a feeling someone important was close by.*

Kayn swung her legs over the side of her bed and went to the bathroom. She looked at her reflection in the mirror and imagined she was seeing her sister. *This always made her feel better.* She could almost hear Chloe's well-timed snide remarks as they passed in the hallway while getting ready for school. *This is crazy. Why am I continuing to torture myself? She's gone. Chloe is dead. It was easy to bring herself back to reality looking at the scars from that night.* Kayn lifted her nightgown in front of the mirror staring critically at her body. It was strange to look at the scars, wondering what happened. It felt like staring at a stranger's body. Detached, her forefinger traced a pronounced scar. *This one would never go away.* She trailed her finger again. Her memory flickered and took the journey into her darkest night. A cold, damp place surrounded by trees, the fragrance of moss and cedar after the rain. She felt stripped of dignity. Searing, burning pain made her cry out in agony and double over in tears. Trembling, she knew she'd regained a memory from that night. With her arms wrapped tightly around herself, she regained her composure. *She was in the hospital.* "It's not real," she repeated under her breath. As she stood up, her sister Chloe's bloody brutalised image was where her own reflection should be.

Her twin's remaining eye smouldered with vengeful distaste.

With venomous fury in her wraithlike crackling voice, Chloe's manifestation commanded, "Stop!"

Startled by her sister's apparition, she jumped away from the macabre mangled version of her twin. *Chloe was angry. It was Chloe. She was here.* Summoning the strength of unconditional love, Kayn swallowed her fear and stepped closer to her sister's ghastly Spector. With the agony of loss in her eyes, she confessed, "I miss you so much. What am I going to do without you?" Tears streamed down her face as she placed her palm against the mirror. Chloe raised her hand to meet Kayn's from the other side. As their hands met on the reflective glass, it felt like they were touching. A burst of euphoria enveloped Kayn's entire body. Their joined hands were glowing with white light and it felt wonderful at first. Chloe smiled in a way that made her uneasy. She couldn't remove her hand, it was stuck. Chloe's face contorted into a twisted evil smirk, as she gleefully cackled. Kayn squirmed with quiet desperation as she fought to get away. The white light turned orange and began to burn. *It was hurting her.* Chloe was smiling as though her pain pleased her a great deal. Her hand was glowing crimson; it felt like her skin was ablaze. Kayn started pleading for Chloe to let her go, screaming for help. Someone began ramming the other side of the door. Light exploded throughout the room, blinding her and then, went out.

She was shaken back to reality by nurse Penny, with whom she had a rather comical love-hate relationship. Confused, Kayn sat up. *She must have blacked out.* She helped her up maternally stroked Kayn's hair, triggering a vision of being cradled in her mother's arms and a flash of the moon through swaying branches. *Images that didn't make sense without context flickered through her mind. A swinging front door. A cars lights driving away. Her sister screaming for her to run. Intense pain, so much pain. She was being fed parts of an intricate puzzle with too many pieces missing to make sense of the big picture.* Her eyes widened as she whispered, "I'm starting to remember." She was still in her arms when the doctor walked in.

Jenkins had only left his post long enough to grab coffee. There was panic in his eyes, but he managed to calmly say, "Did you see the face of the person who hurt you?"

There was only one issue in her guilt-ridden mind. "I saw Chloe in the mirror. Did I see her being killed? Did I run away and leave her there?" Kayn asked, desperate to understand her twin's rage.

Jenkins responded with the fatherly tone she'd grown to depend on, "There was some confusion. Kevin said he went to your house because you'd pocket dialled him. He heard Chloe screaming for you to run but we determined your sister had been dead for hours at the time of your attack."

"I remember hearing her screaming for me to run but the context of the memories is mixed up," Kayn explained.

"A part of me was hoping you'd never remember anything so you could live out the rest of your life without ever having to relive the pain of that night, even if it meant we'd never know what happened," Jenkins confessed, giving her hand a reassuring squeeze.

"I'm not sure you should go home tomorrow," her physician stated, "I'm concerned about the psychological stress of being in that house."

She knew it was imperative to regain the missing pieces of the puzzle but she couldn't explain why. Kayn assured, "I'm not worried. For my own safety, I need to remember. I want to go home and sleep in my own bed."

Looking at the doctor, Jenkins promised, "I'm coming home with her. If she's not adjusting, we'll deal with it." He gave her hand a pat, got up and strolled over to chat with the doctor privately. He called out, "I'll be back later."

She was so glad he was on her side. He would have been a great father if he'd had the chance. She knew the story. Jenkins' wife left him after their four-year-old daughter Katy drowned in the swimming pool. He'd lived with them for a while afterwards. That's why he stepped in to help so quickly. *Katy and Kayn, their names were so close. Katy would have been the same age as her now. He hadn't been able to help his daughter, but he could help her.*

Strange things had been happening since she woke up. She didn't feel like switching to a padded room, so she kept it to herself, explaining the creepy weirdness away as brain trauma. One night she'd been listening to giggles and child's feet running up and down the hall for hours, when a little girl ran into her room. Exhausted, she looked her dead in the eyes and scolded, "It's the middle of the night, go to sleep." She realised the little girl looked like Katy after she left but convinced herself it was just an old memory replaying in a broken mind and went back to sleep. *It was Chloe in the mirror today, that was an irrefutable fact. Her perspective had changed drastically, and now, anything felt possible.*

After dinner, Jenkins came back to keep her company. They spoke about her doctor's concerns and she made it crystal clear that she needed to go home. He asked if she wanted him to stay for her last night. It was easy to see protecting her had given him purpose outside of work and a sense of family. *She needed him too. He'd given her the parental security she'd lost.* "I'm sure I'll be fine," Kayn assured, secretly wanting him to stay.

He sat in the chair, saying, "I'll just stay for a while." Jenkins grabbed the remote. She watched whatever he wanted enjoying the company. In no time at all, he was out cold. Kayn fell asleep soon after and awoke in the wee hours of the morning with a grin, listening to giggles and the pitter-patter of feet running up and down the hall. This time when Katy came into her room, she smiled and didn't shoo her away. *She was beginning to see the big picture.* Katy climbed up on Jenkins lap. Kayn rolled over and closed her eyes. *Maybe one day she'd tell Jenkins his daughter never really left his side.*

The morning of her release, her nemesis slash favourite nurse brought her a tub of ice-cream so decadent it was called, Twisted. It was chocolate chip cookie dough and brownie batter. She was touched, Penny remembered their first spat over ice-cream.

She'd been academically advanced since elementary school so even though she'd missed a significant chunk of time, all she had to do was catch up on a list of assignments and take exams to re-join her classmates. In a few weeks, she'd be back in the grind of regular life. *To be honest, it felt great doing something normal. She could almost forget the noise in her head. The voices she shouldn't be able to hear. The things she shouldn't be able to see. The feelings she had for her best friend.* Kevin's mom gave her an open-ended invitation to stay at their house whenever she needed girl time. *She was touched, but instinct told her she couldn't, not even for a night. She was a murderer's loose end. What happened to her family could happen to the Smith's if the killer returned and she was there. She couldn't take the chance. There was less guilt involved, knowing Jenkins put himself in harm's way for his job. He knew how to handle himself in dangerous situations. She needed to do that too. She had to start running as soon as possible to regain the sense of strength and control she had before a stranger destroyed her world. She'd been given a second chance and sensed she knew why. It was right on the tip of her tongue. The plot holes in her memory were frustrating.*

When Jenkins arrived to take her home, she attempted to walk out using her functional legs but was told it was hospital policy to be wheeled out. So, Jenkins made it fun by racing her down the hall into the elevator at full speed, laughing. Outside of the hospital, she stood in the sunshine, took a deep breath of fresh air, and felt her life coming back each time she exhaled.

Matt pulled up in the car, followed by Kevin's parents and Clay. Jenkins opened the door. She slid into the car next to her brother and turned to Kevin. *He was trying to look happy. What was going on with him?* Everyone was stressed as they departed the hospital. She could hear Kevin's thoughts, loud and clear. *He was nervous. He hadn't been back to her house since that night. Officer Jenkins and her brother were wondering if the house would trigger more memories.* She was agitated. *Everybody's internal dialogue was getting to be a bit much.* She glanced back at Kevin, assuring, "You don't have to come in, I'll understand."

Kevin snapped out of his pity party, answering, "No, I'm fine."

He wasn't fine. He was terrified but in best friend mode. He was going to suck it up. It occurred to her that everyone had a version of that stressed smile on their face. *The one that meant, I'm smiling on the outside.* Passing recognisable scenery, it wasn't the same anymore. *Nothing was.* So, she kept her gaze fixed on her brother until the car stopped. Excited to be home, Kayn got out and looked at the upstairs windows. *She wanted to see if the lights were on but wasn't sure why.* She sauntered up the hill to the house she'd grown up in, oblivious to anything but happy childhood memories. She hadn't been given details on where bodies were found. It was a planned decision, made between the police department and the Smith family, knowing the Brighton kids had no hope of ever selling the house to anyone with full disclosure of what happened within its walls. She strolled through the door into a brightly lit foyer. *They'd decorated.* There was a sign, saying, 'Welcome Home Kayn.' She noticed something new on the wall and questioned, "What's that?"

"It's a battery powered push light, if there's a power outage solar plugs will light up outlets," Kevin's dad rationalised.

"Safety measures," Matt explained. "There's also a security

system. The downstairs windows are armed and there's a panic button on each floor."

She may be in danger. Their paranoia was understandable. Without responding, Kayn went to the kitchen. She spied colourful stones on the windowsill. *That was the fragrance in the air. Granny Winnie had been burning sage to clear the house of all things dark and twisty.* Kevin's mother was placing trays of sandwiches on the table in the kitchen. *Chloe provoked her daily at that table. One of her mother's speeches about how special it was to be a twin replayed in her mind. She needed to be alone.* She thanked Kevin's mom and escaped before she could respond. Everyone was chatting in the den. She slipped past her well-wisher's unseen, dashed up the stairs, walked by the family pictures without looking and froze at her partially open bedroom door. She pushed past the uneasy feeling and went in. *Their ridiculous sibling bickering flooded her mind. The countless nights in side by side beds, talking about their hopes and dreams for the future.* She numbly stood there. *This room was an echo of who they were. Chloe had no future. The empty bed beside hers would be a constant reminder.* Kayn wandered over to Chloe's dresser, picked up her perfume and sprayed her comforter. *She'd pretend she was still sleeping beside her until it hurt less. It would work until she opened her eyes.* She squirted some in the air and walked through the fragrant mist. *She'd never liked this perfume but did now. Weird.* Kayn ran a fingertip across her sister's dresser. *This needs to be dusted.* She went into the bathroom and grabbed a hand towel. *Was that a new towel rack?* She opened the drawer, grabbed a lipstick from her sister's makeup case and applied some to her lips in the mirror. It looked good. So, she put on blush and eye shadow. Her sister's live image was staring back at her. She pressed her hand against the glass, willing there to be a hot shock or signal her sister was still with her. She wiped Chloe's makeup off. *If she walked downstairs like this, it would freak everyone out.* Removing her ponytail, hair flowed in golden ringlets down her back. *She'd wear her hair down in tribute. It felt like someone was watching her.* She turned back to the mirror and saw only her reflection. Shaking her head at herself for being paranoid, Kayn left the washroom and startled when she saw Kevin standing in the doorway, grinning. *She didn't hear him come in.* "You scared the crap out of me," she accused, nervously catching her breath. Lights flickered as the air became icy cold. She turned away from Kevin, feeling a presence. As she exhaled, her breath was visible. Her heart began thudding wildly. *She was dizzy.* The room shifted around her and the lights went out.

10

A DOOR IS OPENED

Kevin went upstairs to check on Kayn. It took a moment to regain his composure after smelling Chloe's perfume and seeing her in the bathroom where they'd discovered her body. There was an air of sensuality in her mannerisms, as she gazed at her reflection. He'd been relieved when she took off the makeup. "It's so cold I can see my own breath. Jenkins must have turned the heat off. You're going to land yourself right back in the hospital with a nasty case of hypothermia," Kevin taunted. He went to turn the heat up, but it was already. *Weird.* He turned it off and on again, as Kayn dusted Chloe's dresser and smoothed down her deceased twin's comforter. "We should go downstairs and have lunch. I heard there's even a cake down there." Kevin baited as he watched her get down on her hands and knees to straighten out the fluffy pink rug beside Chloe's bed.

"Cake...I hope it's cheesecake," Kayn sighed as she stood up.

"You mean rice crispy cake? That's your favourite. You hate cheesecake?" Kevin responded with a strange look.

"I'll be right down. There's just one more thing I have to do," Kayn declared while dusting her dresser. Scrunching her nose, she examined the cloth, mumbling, "So, gross."

Since when did Kayn care about being tidy? Her side of the room was usually strewn with clothes. Chloe was the anal-retentive one. He snuck up behind her, planning to playfully guide her back to her company. *Ouch.* There was a quick zap followed by a rush of warmth. "You shocked me," he laughed nervously, peering down to see if she had plastic soled slippers. *She was wearing florescent cartoon cat socks.* Kevin grinned at her wacky choice of footwear. *Chloe wouldn't be caught dead in those.* He winced at his inner dialogue. *It was probably quite normal for someone dealing with an identical twin's death to emulate certain aspects of their behaviour.* He motioned with his finger for Kayn to follow and sweetly urged, "Eat cheesecake if that's what you feel like."

THERE WAS A FLASH OF light in the dark sea of nothing. Had she dozed off? She'd never woken up from a nap to find herself standing in the doorway of her room before. Was sleepwalking while napping even a thing? She shrugged it off. Kevin motioned for her to follow and told her she could have cheesecake. *She didn't like cheesecake.* She went with him, confused. *Who randomly falls asleep with a houseful of guests?*

They had a wonderful visit, sharing stories. When it was time for guests to leave, she walked them out. Her brother stood in the doorway as they said goodbye, hugging everyone. When it was only Kevin left, Matt excused himself and went inside.

The sky was beginning to darken, a light breeze tousled her hair as she inhaled the pleasurable scent. *Kevin Smith was wearing sexy cologne. Sometimes it felt like she'd woken up in a parallel universe.* She noticed the definition of his muscles through his form-fitting shirt. *He must have been working out like crazy while she was in that coma. He was hot now and it was messing with her mind. It was like he'd grown up without her.*

"I should get going. Everyone's waiting in the car," he said.

She caught herself staring at his lips. Leaning in, Kayn boldly smelled his neck, complimenting, "I like that scent. What is it?"

He grinned and answered, "It's a new one. It's called scared shitless. Have you heard of it?"

There he was. Grinning, Kayn teased, "It suits you." *It was sexy.* She hadn't pulled away after smelling his aftershave. *She had the craziest urge to kiss him.*

Gazing into her eyes, he whispered, "Glad you like it."

Time stood still as his lips moved closer. The wind went from light breeze to gust of an impending storm, whooshing hair into her mouth. She puffed her cheeks and blew it out. *Sexy moment over.*

"I should get down there before they start honking," Kevin chuckled. He dashed down the hill, yelling, "I'll text you later."

He was watching her from the rear window of the car as they drove away. She waved and grinned. *Nothing says I want you to kiss me like a puffy-cheeked blowfish impersonation.* She shook her head at herself as she closed the door and made her way down the hall to the kitchen. Jenkins and Matt were sitting on stools at the island drinking coffee. *They'd already cleaned everything up and made a fresh pot. Impressive.*

Jenkins got up and announced, "I'm going to do a perimeter check and lock up." He grabbed his coffee to go, a flashlight from the counter and strolled out of the kitchen leaving the siblings alone together.

"We've got this security stuff covered. There's nothing to be concerned about, just enjoy being back in your own bed," Matt said, casually sipping coffee as he flipped through the local paper.

"I can see that," Kayn teased. She grabbed a glass, poured herself some orange juice and leaned against the counter as she drank it. *Nice.* The headline on Matt's paper was, Survivor of Brutal Massacre Goes Home. *Guess she wasn't going to be flying under the radar.* She refilled her glass, saying, "Do me a favour, get rid of that paper. I'd like to avoid that headline at breakfast."

He flipped over the paper and growled, "Seriously, printing this story is like daring someone to come back and finish the job." Mortified, Matt looked up, apologising, "Sometimes, I'm so stupid it's ridiculous."

He wasn't wrong. She saw Jenkins' flashlight bobbing in the dark yard out the kitchen window and announced, "I'm off to bed." She wandered out into the hall with her glass of juice in hand. A piece of paper came flying at her. *Jenkins didn't close the door properly.* She placed her drink on the bookshelf and went to close it. Her heart clenched. She froze mid-step too terrified to move as the wind gusted rain sideways down the hall at her. Her mind flickered through memories she'd already recovered. She stopped herself from calling out for Matt. *What if she was being ridiculous? The headline made her paranoid.* Once again, she attempted to walk to the open door, but a burst of irrational panic kept her feet firmly in place. Exhaling, she cautiously stepped forward as tears formed in her eyes. Her head started humming. *What was this?* The door shifted in the wind. Inhaling the scent of fresh rainfall, she listened to gently tapping drops trickling through branches of ornamental bushes outside. With the next gust of raindrops and wind, the clouds in her mind cleared to a vision of Kevin's dad driving away from her house. As she started walking up the hill, she noticed the front door was slightly ajar. Kayn's memory fed her breadcrumbs as it allowed her to reach the door and go inside. *Her ankle hurt. Her feet were wet. She'd tried to turn on the light, it was burnt out. There was something on her hand.* She recalled the sight of her bloody palm in a ray of light, followed by the sensation of millions of spider legs scurrying across her skin.

"Close the door. Everything's getting wet," Matt complained.

His voice was far off in the distance, but she became aware of his presence.

Directly behind her, Matt asked, "Are you alright?"

She couldn't answer, lost in returning memories, blood, there was blood. She heard Chloe screaming for her to run. *There was a shadow at the end of the hall.* She backed out of the doorway and ran. *Someone was chasing her.* She tossed the grocery bag of eggs behind her before running into the woods. Sprinting through trails driven by fear, the visions stopped. *What happened next? She had to go into those trails.* Jenkins appeared at the door. *She needed to know.* Bolting past Jenkins in stocking feet, the wind whistled as Kayn sprinted across the backyard towards the opening of the trails.

"Where are you going?" Matt shouted, pursuing her.

Slipping, Kayn got up covered in mud and continued to run. *She had to know everything.* She sprinted into freshly cleared trails. Hearing the steady crunching of footsteps chasing her, she was jolted back to that night. She raced over the bridge and down the winding path. *She saw a light through the trees. She was going to be okay. She was almost there.* At the precise moment she believed herself free, she felt the excruciating heat of a blade penetrating her back and crumbled to her knees on the forest floor.

113

WITH TEARS STREAMING DOWN THEIR faces, they watched Kayn relive that fated night. In a trance-like state, she dropped to her knees with terror-filled eyes. Being strangled and stabbed with nobody there, her body crumbled inwards. She was clawing at the earth with tears in her eyes as an invisible entity savaged her. "I can't watch this anymore," Matt wept, gutted. He tried to go to her.

Grabbing his arm, Jenkins asserted, "No, this isn't about you. She may still be in danger."

Matt covered his tear blurred eyes, unable to witness to the depravities done to his sibling. Jenkins spoke his name. Matt removed his hands, knowing he had to remain present. Kayn's face contorted in anguish as she writhed in the dirt. Wiping away his tears, Matt pled, "No more. We have to stop this."

"I want to stop it too, but she wants to remember," Jenkins replied.

Her torture appeared to be over. Kayn was in the fetal position on a bed of moist earth, humming a song. As they made their way closer, the wind whistling through the trees sounded like it was humming along to the haunting lullaby. Colour drained from Matt's face as he realised, "Mom used to sing that to us." He sobbed, "Enough, that's it." Choking back tears, Matt scooped Kayn into his arms and carried his drenched, shivering sibling back to the house. Emotionally drained and soaked to the bone, they stepped back through the open front door and closed it.

KAYN BRIGHTON HAD A DREAM that night, it included bumble-bees and impossible situations. There were frightening images only remotely plausible in someone's most terrifying nightmares. In the midst of these horrors, were flashes of splendour and bliss. Visions of magical places, so intoxicatingly beautiful they took her breath away. *The lady in the light had granted her a second chance at life.* Able to recall every moment, she understood her twin wasn't lost to her. *They'd never been normal girls. Kayn had always known life's simple pleasures held the greatest joy. Chloe was the opposite side of the coin, tossed into the air for sport by immortals. She would show them what their little human experiment was capable of.*

Kayn opened her eyes to rays of sunlight streaming through her window. *The sunlight blinded her. She felt purified by its rays. She had been in the dark for so long and in so many ways.* She'd awakened to a new day, understanding what her future held. *Matt was sleeping in Chloe's bed. She'd been changed into pyjamas. She recalled that night, but her emotions were dulled like it happened to someone else.* Tiptoeing away from her sleeping brother, Kayn snuck to the bathroom. Soundlessly closing the door, she took a gander at her frazzled self. "Chloe," she whispered, willing her sister to answer. *Maybe, it needed to be just like last time?* She slipped her top off and stood before the mirror, looking at her scars. She ran her finger across one as she gazed at her reflection hoping to see her sister. *No Chloe.* Deciding to get into the shower, she turned the knob and water came out freezing cold. *Nobody had touched this shower in months.* She allowed it to run before stepping under the spray and closed her eyes as the water pelted her skin. When she was done, she reached for a towel from the rack. It shocked her. She yanked her hand away rubbing wounded digits, cursing. Only moderately intrigued by the zap, she continued her preparations for the day. Drying her hair while staring at her reflection, she felt attractive. *She should go to the high school to pick up her work. She didn't feel like being invisible today.* Expertly applying her twin's makeup, Kayn gazed in the mirror. *That's much better, she'd see Chloe every time she passed a mirror.*

When she wandered back into her room, her brother was gone. *She must have been in the bathroom for a long time.* The enticing aroma of coffee and bacon travelled up the stairs. Spraying a touch of Chloe's perfume on herself, she inhaled the delightful fragrance and gracefully made her way down the hall, descending the stairs feeling like everything was amplified, even the sun's rays filtering through the sheer curtains felt glorious. The carpet caressed her feet as she pranced to the kitchen with her hair floating behind her like a runway model. Her brother and Jenkins began choking on their breakfast. *Weird?* Matt sent a text. Nonchalantly, Kayn enquired, "Who are you texting?"

Peering up, Matt replied, "Kevin."

Morbidly fascinated, they watched Kayn searching through cupboards while eating bacon, dancing around the room.

"Are you feeling alright this morning?" Matt asked, sipping coffee.

"I'm fantastic," she sang, shooting a toothy pageant smile at her brother, flipping her hair with a devious glint in her eyes.

"I think I might be going crazy," Matt mumbled, downing the rest of his coffee.

Composing himself, Jenkins probed, "What exactly do you remember about last night?"

"Absolutely everything," Kayn disclosed, pouring herself a cup of java. As she added sweetener, she didn't normally use, Kayn preened, "Yum, I love bacon, thanks Matty."

Puzzled by her Chloe-esque behaviour, Matt questioned again, "Are you certain you're feeling alright... Kayn?"

"I'm extra wonderful," she decreed. *What's with these two?* She squeezed her brother's shoulder affectionately as she flounced by and Matt's confusion heightened.

"Do you know who killed your family?" Jenkins asked out of the blue.

She far too casually answered, "I couldn't make out his face. It was too dark. He was heavy set and he smelled awful. I'd know who he was if I ran into him again."

"Are you suggesting you could tell who he was by his scent?" Jenkins probed.

Rolling her eyes, Kayn countered, "I'm saying, I have a feeling my sister saw him. So, between what I smelled and what she saw, I should be able to identify him."

Confused, Matt clarified, "Chloe's dead. I was at her funeral."

This wasn't the right timing for this conversation. She'd have to give it to them in small doses, so they'd see it as irrefutable fact and not merely a fictitious tale from a grieving somewhat nutty coma girl. She pictured how the conversation would go. *Hey guys, due to an immortal mishap, I share a soul with my twin and our spirits must become one.* She giggled because even in her mind, it sounded insane. They looked at each other, simultaneously thinking she'd gone crazy. Kayn answered like they'd been spoken aloud, "I heard that, and for the record, I'm not crazy. You guys are just going to have to trust me. I'm going for a run to the high school later. I need to get back into a routine, I'd like to figure out my schedule."

"I'm not sure that's a good idea today, Kayn," Jenkins replied aloud, then thought, *because you've gone batshit crazy, being out in public isn't a good idea.*

"I'm not batshit crazy, Jenkins," Kayn sparred, awaiting his reaction. When he didn't play along, she referenced her in-between tormenter, "I prefer to think of it as sanity challenged." She shot him a charming pageant grin. A knock followed by a doorbell ring abruptly ceased their conversation. She went to answer the door.

Peering over his paper, Jenkins said, "I should answer the door until we know it's safe."

"Kevin's knocked on that door the same way since we were kids. Kayn's perfectly safe, don't get your panties in a twist," she stated, flouncing away, leaving them in the kitchen.

"Did your sister just talk about herself in the third person?" Jenkins whispered from behind his newspaper.

"I believe she did. Personally, I'm contemplating the idea of going back to bed and pretending that last night and this morning didn't happen," Matt sighed as he got up to rinse off his dish.

Kayn opened the door. Kevin's jaw dropped when he saw her. *Oh, get a grip it's just makeup.* She flirted, "Good morning handsome." With all the guts in the world, she boldly kissed him, enjoying his shock as their lips parted.

"What was that for?" he stammered, standing in the doorway.

"Just for being you, sweetie" she toyed, seductively. *He'd been flirting with her since she woke up, why was he freaking out over a peck on the lips? Perhaps she misread his intentions? Maybe he just wanted to be friends?* "The boys are in the kitchen," she disclosed. She had the urge to smack his butt as he walked away, so she did.

He jumped, placed his hand over his behind and asked, "Are you feeling alright this morning?"

She nodded and replied, "I feel amazing, Kevy." They parted ways, Kevin walked to the kitchen and she went upstairs. *She needed to lie down and rest her eyes. She was so tired.* She wandered down the hall to her room and flopped down on Chloe's bed instead of her own. She was out cold in a matter of minutes.

As Kevin entered the kitchen, he confessed, "She just kissed me and smacked my ass. What in the hell is going on?"

Raising his coffee mug, Jenkins saluted him, saying, "Your guess is as good as mine."

"This is why I asked you to come over. She woke up like this," Matt explained, pouring Kevin a coffee. "Would you like Baileys, instead of creamer? That's what we're having."

They were offering to spike his drink and Jenkins was a police officer. It must have been an epically strange morning.

Glaring at Matt, Jenkins scolded, "Don't offer the minor alcohol. What's wrong with you?"

For a second there he thought they'd both lost it. Kevin grinned and questioned, "Why is she acting like a horned-up version of Chloe? Did something happen between last night and this morning?"

Matt finished his coffee and replied, "Did something happen? That's an understatement and a half. She remembered everything last night. When she woke up this morning, she came downstairs as Chloe, switched to Kayn, and then back to Chloe again."

Jenkins blankly stared into his empty coffee cup, mumbling, "Apparently, she can hear what we're thinking now too."

"I'll go check on her," Kevin assured. Concerned, he briskly made his way down the hall and up the stairs. *It felt like his duty to protect her. He'd been by her side for so many months waiting for her to come back. He felt guilty for not being here when her memories surfaced.* Passing the photos in the hall, Kevin had a split second flash of bloody footprints on the carpet. *Would he ever be able to walk down this hallway without having flashbacks from that night?*

He paused outside her bedroom and peered in. *She was out cold, sleeping in Chloe's bed. Maybe it made her feel closer to her sister?* He snuck in and sat on the bed, imagining it was Chloe. *She was still alive, and she'd been the one to kiss him at the door. For years he'd dreamt of nothing more than that. She'd been the star of every one of his prepubescent fantasies. He'd be sitting on her bed just like this, she'd look into his eyes and he'd just know she wanted him back.* He touched Kayn's hair, grinning. *If this were really Chloe, she'd wake up and call him a dirty pervert right now.* He caressed her silky hair running one of her ringlets through his fingertips feeling strangely drawn to her. *Snap out of it, man,* he thought.

Opening her eyes, Kayn pouted and baited, "I saw you wipe my kiss off your lips earlier."

Before he could stammer out an apology, she slid a hand through his hair and aggressively pulled his lips to hers. With an intoxicating mix of guilt, shame, and arousal, he succumbed to her seduction. As her tongue darted against his, he lost all self-control, passionately kissing her back until every nerve ending in his body was wildly exposed and raw. Her hands began searching under his shirt, he shivered as they met with his flesh. *He heard footsteps on the stairs.*

"Hey! You guys okay up there?" Matt hollered.

Abruptly pulling away, Kevin yelled back with his voice a couple octaves higher, "I'll be right down!" It took him a minute to regain his composure as need for her pulsed through his body. He touched his swollen lips and when he looked back, she'd rolled over and gone back to sleep like nothing happened. *Could Kayn be possessed by her twin? He'd been seeing strange things and knew anything spiritual was feasible. He needed to stop staring at her and get off the bed but the pull to stay was so powerful it felt impossible to move. Chloe had always made him feel like he wasn't in control of his actions.* He touched his lips again as his body hummed with desire. *He had to think clearly. He wasn't going to be able to do that if he kept sitting here willing her to wake up and rock his world again, but he couldn't exactly go downstairs in his condition.* He went into the bathroom, looked at his reflection in the mirror and saw Kayn sleeping peacefully in the background. *He felt guilty for kissing her while reliving old fantasies.* Kevin splashed cold water on his face. When he opened his eyes and looked in the mirror, the brutalised bloody version of Chloe was sitting on the edge of the bed watching Kayn sleep. He spun around but there was nobody there. He turned back to the mirror. Chloe looked up from her sleeping sister, met his gaze in the reflection, and placed a finger to her lips, signalling for him to be quiet. With adrenaline rippling through him, he spun around, but she'd vanished. He looked between his legs. *Problem solved. Apparently, fear trumps being turned on.* Kevin strolled over to where he'd seen Chloe and waved his hands in the air. *There was nothing there.* He left Kayn to her dreams and snuck out. *He'd always wanted their first kiss to be incredible and it was amazing. He wished he was sure she wasn't being possessed by her dead sister at the time.* Racing downstairs, Kevin bumped into Kayn's brother.

"What took you so long?" Matt questioned, "I thought you were just checking on her?"

Hesitating, Kevin answered, "I'll tell you if you promise not to hit me."

"You didn't have time for anything I'd beat you up for," Matt teased, giving Kevin a playful brotherly shove.

"She kissed me, it sure seemed like Chloe," Kevin cautiously replied.

Shoving him again, this time not so lightly, Matt scolded, "What are you thinking? She's clearly not herself today. Chloe's dead. We buried her."

Kevin stammered, "I know, it's just the way she kissed me. Kayn would never kiss me like that."

"What do you mean?" Matt probed, glaring.

He felt guilty enough without Matt's protective reaction. It felt like he'd taken advantage of his best friend in a weakened state. "She kissed me with experience. Porn star experience," Kevin explained the best he could, but when Matt's expression changed to anger, he knew he'd only made it worse.

"Let me get this straight before I deck you. Are you calling my dead sister a porn star?" Matt came at him.

Defensively stepping backwards, Kevin replied, "No! I'm just saying there's a difference between your sister's skill levels with the opposite sex."

Matt scowled as Kevin valiantly tried to save the conversation, "Kayn's only been kissed a few times in elementary school. That kiss was from someone who knew what they were doing." The Neanderthal in Matt wasn't capable of hearing what he was trying to say. "We should call her doctor or maybe a priest?" Kevin cautiously suggested.

"Why? Do you want to marry her first? Because I'm all for that," Matt teased making it obvious he'd been messing with him. With a shit-eating grin, Matt roughly patted Kevin's shoulder and snickered, "You must name your first born after me."

Relief spread across Kevin's face. He bluntly decreed, "Either she's mentally ill, in need of a psychiatrist, or possessed and in need of a priest." *It was obvious Matt thought he was full of shit.*

With not so thinly veiled sarcasm, Matt clarified, "So, you're going with Kayn would only kiss you if she were possessed by Chloe? What do you expect me to say? Why Kevin that sounds like a perfectly reasonable explanation, I'll find a priest that's willing to do an exorcism because Kayn's a better kisser than you thought she'd be. Maybe, she's kissed a bunch of guys and didn't tell you?"

Rolling his eyes at Matt, Kevin said, "We've spent almost every day together since we were in Kindergarten. She doesn't even speak to other guys. You texted me saying she was acting like Chloe, I'm agreeing with you."

Their voices were getting a little loud as they debated. Matt whispered, "Listen, she remembered everything last night. It was horrible. She's traumatized, and from what I witnessed, she's entitled to a breakdown." He paused before quietly asking, "What would you have me do? Put her back in the hospital? I finally have her home after almost a year. She's all I have left."

"I'm not saying she needs to be in the hospital. I'm suggesting she may require a different kind of help," Kevin whispered back.

Matt stared blankly at Kevin, knowing where he was going, yet not wanting to say it aloud.

"What if she's possessed? I saw something strange in the bathroom mirror," Kevin reasoned with no humour involved.

Officer Jenkins walked into the room adding his piece with perfectly timed sarcasm, "Why don't we try calling her doctor first and save the exorcisms for another day."

KAYN BRIGHTON AWOKE FROM A sexually charged dream with someone knocking on her bedroom door. *Why was she sleeping in Chloe's bed?* Clearing her throat, she said, "Come in." She felt the heat of embarrassment rise in her cheeks as Kevin entered her room. *It felt like the details of her naughty dream were written in neon, flashing across her forehead.*

He strolled over and sat on her bed, enquiring, "How are you feeling?"

Attraction enthusiastically tugged at her insides. Tingly, Kayn shifted away from his gravitational pull. *Am I really this shallow? I'm not remotely attracted to him for all these years, then he works out, gets a little hot and I want to roll over with my legs in the air.*

"Just a wild guess, you don't remember kissing me, do you?" Kevin probed, running his hand down the length of her arm.

Warm shivers rippled over the path his hand travelled. Her memory brought her back to the sexually charged kiss they'd shared. Her cheeks turned crimson as she realised the naughty dream was mortifyingly real. "I remember," Kayn admitted.

Confusion registered on Kevin's face as he whispered, "I was sure..." He paused mid-sentence. Gazing into her eyes, he asked, "Do you mind?"

Her heart palpitated as he did to her what she'd done to him in a dream. He ran his fingers through her hair and drew her close. Their lips met in a blend of molten electricity and urgency. Instinct took over as she rolled on top of him and slid her hands under his shirt, wanting to see what he looked like with his shirt off. Confused as he tried to pull away, Kayn whispered, "What's wrong?"

Caressing her face, Kevin groaned, "I don't want to take advantage of you."

Pinning his wrists to the bed, she teased, "Who is on top of whom right now?"

"You're on top of me," he replied, grinning.

Making her intentions crystal clear by seductively kissing him. Swept away, neither cared where they ended up in the end. There was a loud pound on the door, they jumped away from each other. Kevin fell with a thud onto the bedroom floor and ducked. He was hidden on the other side of the bed as Matt strode in. Flustered, with kiss swollen lips, Kayn laughed, "You scared the crap out of me."

"I thought Kevin came up here to get you?" Matt interrogated from the doorway without entering her room.

"He's not up here anymore," Kayn replied calmly. *Usually, she couldn't lie to save her life. Her voice was a few octaves higher when she wasn't telling the truth.*

Knowing her tell, her brother believed her. Suspiciously, Matt commented, "Weird. Maybe he went for a walk?" Leaving, he turned back, teasing, "Or he's hiding under your bed."

Kayn darted her eyes over to where he was hiding. Smiling, she announced, "He's not hiding under the bed today." *It wasn't a lie. Not really. He was beside it not under it.* Kevin pressed himself against the floor beside the bed, silently laughing.

Pausing in the doorway, her brother disclosed, "Your doctor thought it would be a good idea if you spoke to the counsellor after everything that happened last night."

Suspecting he was waiting for her to get angry or deny she needed help, she answered, "Okay, that's probably a good idea." *The sooner Matt left her room the better.*

Smiling, Matt admitted, "Good, I already agreed. He's coming over. Come downstairs and have lunch first. We saved you bacon from breakfast. You've been asleep for hours. I'll make you a B.LT."

"I'll be right down. I just need to freshen up," she hinted for him to leave. Kayn smiled as she slid off her bed and strolled to the bathroom, leaving her brother standing in the doorway. In the reflection of the mirror, she saw Matt looking under the bed. *Oh shit!* There was a loud crash downstairs, Matt left cursing. She heard Chloe's voice in her mind, '*you owe me one. You little slut, I didn't know you had it in you. Kevin isn't looking half bad, I understand.*'

Emerging frazzled, Kevin got up, chuckling, "That was close. Good thing I moved. I'd better go out your window." He was climbing out as her brother walked outside to look for him. He dove back in, laughing.

Kayn giggled as he checked to see if the coast was clear so he could sneak out her bedroom window as he had a million times before. *This time it wasn't innocent.* He waved before crawling out.

Matt stuck his head in, announcing, "The doctor's here. It looks like you'll have to wait for lunch."

Turning back, Kayn replied, "I'm not hungry yet anyway." Her door shut again. She dashed to her window. Kevin was hanging from the lower level gutter

DANGLING THERE, KEVIN MADE EYE contact with Jenkins through the living room window. He mouthed, "Oh shit," as he dropped from the gutter.

Perplexed, Matt walked in and said, "Have you seen Kevin? I thought he was upstairs in Kayn's room, but he's not there."

"He's outside. I just saw him a minute ago," Jenkins answered truthfully, hiding behind his newspaper, silently giggling.

Knitting his brow, Matt grilled, "Are you laughing?"

"Nope," Jenkins snickered, tearing up.

Kevin walked in, saying, "Hey guys, what's up?" He plopped himself on the couch.

"Where were you?" Matt asked, glaring at him.

"I needed fresh air," Kevin casually replied, trying to keep a straight face because Jenkins was shaking behind his paper.

"What's so funny?" Matt growled, getting ticked off.

Pressing his lips together so he wouldn't giggle, Kevin looked down, avoiding eye contact with them, especially Jenkins.

"Do you think I'm a moron?" Matt interrogated. They lost it, laughing. He walked away, mumbling, under his breath.

KAYN WAS ALREADY SITTING AT the island in the kitchen chatting with the doctor when Matt came in. *Doctor Corning wanted to walk her through what happened. She was surprisingly fine with taking a return trip down the emotional rabbit hole.*

Doctor Corning enquired, "We're going for a walk in the trails. Do you want to come with us?"

"I'm not sure that's a great idea," Matt replied, protectively. "Jenkins already gave a statement to the police. Can't we just do the counselling and hit pause on the field trip for a few days?"

"I can't hide from this, it's already happened. I have to exhume the past, so I can learn how to deal with it," Kayn explained as she glanced at the doctor.

As Jenkins strolled in, he was filled in on the plan. "Nobody goes anywhere without me," he asserted.

Kayn walked her doctor through that night, detached like it happened to somebody else. *This was how she was dealing with it. Wrong or right it worked for her. She needed everyone to believe that she was okay. Nearly nine months had passed for everyone else, but not for her.* When they reached the place in the trails where her body was found, she abruptly stopped. *The area was a shrine.* Kayn read the notes, most were still legible after many months of island rain. *Her fated spot had become a memorial for her entire family.* She touched a picture of her mother in her younger years, glowing with promise. *The happiness in her eyes never dulled with time.* A picture of her dad in high school. *She'd never seen this picture of her father. He'd always been a strong, gentle soul. There was a hollow void in her where love used to be. She missed them so much. She'd resolved to live by her mother's wisdom, fake it till you make it.* She touched a picture of her mirror image. *She under-*

stood the complexity of their intertwined life paths now. It made sense as it was revealed. On some level, she'd already known it to be true. Tears blurred her vision, she blinked them away. *If she started blubbering, she'd trigger a pity party and she'd been denying break-down invites for a month.* A salty escapee fled down her cheek.

Unable to look at photos of oblivious smiles, she hung her head and stared at the soil beneath her feet. *In her final moments, she'd been cradled in her mother's arms. She remembered every detail.* The others silently gathered as she processed the madness. She heard Matt's thoughts. *He was still torturing himself for not coming home that night. He felt selfish, soiled and ruined. She wanted to tell him everything. What happened on that night had nothing to do with him.* Kayn fought the urge to run into her brother's arms. *He'd been carrying this burden. She wanted him to know she'd never blamed him. There was nothing he could have done. It was predestined. She'd said far too much this morning. She couldn't risk his safety. Her sister hadn't known using her gifts in public would make her bloodline a target. She kept her mouth shut even though it broke her heart to do so and allowed the urge to console her brother to pass.* She looked up. *They were genuinely concerned.* Kayn's gaze met her doctor's as she enquired, "Should I keep going?"

"We'll come back tomorrow, if it's too much," he sympathised.

"It'll always be too much. Let's just get it over with," Kayn admitted, opting to give only facts, leaving out magical things they wouldn't understand. After the tale was told, the emotionally exhausted group solemnly left the trails and walked out into the sunshine leaving behind shrines and memories of evil best left buried in the past.

11

LEAVING NORMAL

For weeks she'd been consumed by researching those claiming to have similar abilities while longing for a sign Chloe was still around, but she'd vanished. On the bright side, her body wasn't being highjacked by a Spector anymore, so her erratic behaviour stopped. She hadn't pounced on poor confused Kevin in weeks, and even though she had the urge to put on makeup, she didn't. Kayn spent most of her time catching up on semesters of missed schoolwork, listening to thoughts, and finding ingenious ways to deter Kevin's visits. *She'd complicated things by adding making out to their list of activities. She wanted to be with him so badly but wasn't sure she should.*

She fell asleep one night holding the plush bumblebee he'd given her when they were kids and something peculiar happened. She could see Kevin in his room and hear his thoughts, but the words echoed like they were coming from the end of a tunnel. It became a regular thing, she randomly checked in on him. He was thinking about sex far too often and his intimate daydreams weren't only of her. There was another girl, she was exquisitely beautiful with shiny flowing midnight tresses. She knew it was normal, but it stung. *A teenage boy probably looked at a desk and fantasized about making out on one.*

Eventually, Kayn discovered she didn't need the stuffed animal. If she relaxed, closed her eyes, and thought about Kevin, she'd just be there. He'd be sprawled on his bed, listening to music or playing guitar unaware. She looked this up online, it was called astral projection. *It was also stalking.* She grinned, as she thought of the conversation they'd have if she was forced to come clean. *There was no possible way to broach the subject without it sounding slightly disturbing and more than a wee bit creepy.* "Kevin, I've been watching you in bed and listening to your thoughts for weeks," she disclosed, playing out the conversation, in the mirror. *There was no possible way to make that sound less creepy.*

She found herself fixated on her ability, and as this obsession escalated, the urge to push it further was always in the back of her mind. *It felt dangerous, intoxicating and extremely addictive.* There was a primal urgency to unleash the energy building beneath the surface of her skin, and for the first time, everything became clear, the struggles of her twin's abilities had driven their relationship apart. *She'd resented her twin for shining like a diamond because she'd walked through life feeling like a stone. None of this was her fault. It had been the luck of the draw and she'd always thought she was the unlucky one.* Guilt crept in. *How much of her sister's pain had she ignored while drowning in jealousy? How many times had she tried to tell her? Had she come to her for help? She needed to know.* Kayn began the search for her sister's diary. It became her mission to learn more about her sister's feelings in the weeks and months prior to her murder. She looked under mattresses and in every box in the closet, needing to tie up loose ends in her heart. *She couldn't see Chloe hiding it somewhere difficult to get to in a teenage venting emergency.* Kayn recalled her sister's lengthy bathroom visits. *She'd always assumed she was texting friends or talking on the phone.*

Underneath the sink there was nothing out of the ordinary, just cleaners and feminine products. *Where would it be?* She opened drawers, finding only nail polish and makeup. In the linen closet, the towels were folded neatly. She scaled the top shelf, ran her arms under bedding and her fingertips brushed against something hard. *She'd found it!* Grasping the diary, she climbed down. *Her sister may have written every sneaky deed and evil thought in this diary. Should she be reading it? Did she really want to know her twin's deepest thoughts? Her sister's uncensored for kindness reflections on her day would be in these pages.* Kayn didn't want to taint her sister's memory but needed to know if she'd missed her emotional turmoil. *Maybe that was the reason her twin's spirit was so angry with her?* She sat on the counter and opened the diary. It was thick and pink, with words hastily scribbled on each page. On the first pages were little ditties like, *'life sucks. Kevin is so Kayn's little bitch.'* Kevin was always Chloe's little bitch. It still irked her even though she understood why. *Was her inability to see Chloe's pain the reason she made Kevin want her?* She flipped through endless dribble. The entries became longer and more in depth as the pages went on. It was as if Chloe started the diary on a whim and then realised the purpose behind having one. Kayn read on, realising that even though her sister appeared to have hundreds of friends, she was lonely. *She longed for true love and happiness just like everyone else.* Finally, she found what she was looking for. *How would she know if anyone truly loved her? Were there others like her?* Chloe wrote about feeling out of control. *She didn't know how to fix them once they were broken.* This was about the obsession after ending things. She'd filed multiple restraining orders. *All she had to do was decide she wanted someone, and they'd be hers. She'd realise they had no free will and didn't really love her, this made her feel hopeless.* She wrote about the guilt involved in cutting someone loose and having them lose their mind.

Her sister loved her. It had been difficult to see in those last years. All it would have taken to end her friendship with Kevin was for Chloe to tell him not to like her. Their friendship annoyed her. It made her jealous, but she'd never messed with it. She wrote about being purposely cruel to Kevin. *She wasn't being a bitch to hurt Kevin. It was so she didn't accidentally take him. She had nobody to trust with her secrets. She wanted to tell her sister but knew she wouldn't believe her.* Kayn teared up as she read the entries filled with loneliness and isolation. *She'd been covering her true feelings under cockiness and bravado. How had she felt so in tune with her sister in their younger years and never picked up on this?* Even though her twin wasn't alive, she climbed up and put her diary back where it belonged. Pausing in front of the mirror, Kayn whispered, "If you were here, I'd tell you how much I miss you. I'd want you to know that I'm so sorry I didn't see what was happening to you. To be honest, I was always jealous. You were being cruel to Kevin for me, weren't you?" *If the master plan was to join with her, where was she?*

Kayn discovered quit by accident she could move things with her mind if she concentrated hard enough while upset. She stepped on a fork barefoot and in her pain-induced fury, shot it across the kitchen floor. After that random discovery, she moved saltshakers, plates, and a phonebook. Her Jedi-esque mind powers failed her whenever she tried to move something larger. Long-term survival probably involved using these abilities. If something scary showed up right now, she only had enough juice to toss a fork at it. She knew there was a Clan coming to help her but didn't know what that meant. *Maybe they were all going to toss forks together?*

Most evenings were spent watching Jenkins pretend to read while thinking of his daughter. *Katy hadn't followed Jenkins home from the hospital. Maybe she'd moved on? Hearing thoughts was beneficial but heart breaking whenever she took a stroll through Jenkins' mind.* Time passed in the blink of an eye. She'd been talking to Kevin on the phone and texting but kept him at arm's length saying she was swamped with schoolwork. Visiting in person wasn't a pressing issue, she'd spent time with him every day, he just didn't know about it.

Finally, it was time for her to return to school. Throwing away preconceived notions about recovery time, her physician assured Matt she was well adjusted all things considered. Any quirky behaviour was explained away as grief or figuring out her place in the world without her family. Matt had a year to adjust to his new life. She only had a few months to adapt and deal with her grief. She was a marvel to the medical community, but only Kayn understood, her miracle came with a price she'd yet to pay. There was fine print at the bottom of her contract, soon she'd be forced to read it.

12

WHERE THE WILD THINGS ARE

*K*ayn awoke to the annoying crow of the alarm, set for the first time in nearly a year. The clock was a funny gift from Chloe, who'd always been a perky morning person. She'd loved watching her twitch and cringe with every obnoxious cock-a-doodle-doo. She needed to be left alone for at least twenty minutes in the morning. Any human contact before her first cup of coffee wasn't usually a bright idea. Chloe also bought her a coffee mug that read, *Duck and Cover.* A family joke aimed at Kayn's distaste for morning conversation. She smiled as she thought of Chloe's gift. *It would have been much funnier if everyone but her had a duck and cover mug.* She could picture her family gathered around the island in the kitchen, drinking coffee and teasing her lovingly. Her heart ached just a little for the list of things she'd never experience again.

Taking exams with everyone else this week was a longshot, she wasn't prepared. What would her reception be like? She despised being the centre of attention. Kayn imagined the whispers while walking down the hall and pulled the covers up over her head. *Maybe she could just hide here for the rest of her life?* She tossed her purple patterned comforter to the side and decided to get up. *She couldn't hide in her bed forever. Why not get it over with? There was no point in pretending it wasn't going to happen. The drama that came with being in high school was a certainty.* She put on makeup to draw from any residual self-confidence Chloe left behind when she'd hijacked her body. She tugged on a pair of jeans and sporty t-shirt thinking, *maybe I can just blend in.* Her nerves were screaming, *home-schooling. You want to keep home-schooling.* She grimaced and jogged down the stairs with her bag. Jenkins met her at the bottom with a travel cup of coffee and a piece of toast with peanut butter and jelly. *He looked nervous. That wasn't helpful.*

Jenkins grinned, urging, "Eat this. Kevin is showing up in five minutes to drive you."

"Thanks," Kayn answered with a smile. *She hadn't had peanut butter and jelly since she was a child.* She ate every bite in a flash and then dove into the bathroom to check her teeth for toast. She applied lipstick and summoned her twin, "Come on Chloe. Help a sister out." Not even a scary version of her appeared in the mirror to terrify her. She sighed and thought, *I guess I'm on my own. She hadn't seen Kevin since that kiss, it probably looked like she'd been avoiding him. She couldn't give him an explanation, fingers crossed he wouldn't ask for one.* There was a knock at the door, but it wasn't his usual knock. Kayn peered through the peephole. *It was him. He just keeps getting better looking.* She opened it, smiling.

"Hi stranger," Kevin teased as he strolled into the house.

They'd shared two amazing friendship altering kisses, then she'd ghosted him. What if he assumed that was the reason? Was this going to get weird?

"Is something funny?" Kevin asked, leaning in to kiss her. She moved, his lips landed on her nose.

Surprised, she had a comeback, "That was hot."

Skipping a second attempt, he laughed, "Grab your bag. We

still have time to stop for coffee on the way."

She wanted him to try again, but coffee sounded like a great alternative. Kayn followed him to his blue, beat up ancient Pontiac. *He had a car, this was so weird. She'd missed an important gap of time.* As they approached, she commented, "Love your ride. It's cute."

Kevin rolled his eyes and replied, "It's not much but it's mine. No payments." He winked at her.

Why had he rolled his eyes? Oh yes, she'd called his car cute. Even though he'd bulked up in size and was no longer short, cute was still his kryptonite.

"You also look cute today," he flirted.

She wasn't a fan of the word cute either, touché. She enquired, "Are you going to unlock the door or are we just going to stand here making cute jokes?"

Tilting his head, he boldly taunted, "Was that an accidental evasive manoeuvre or are you always going to duck when I try to kiss you?"

Enjoying the flirty standoff, she confessed, "Accidental." She held her breath as he leaned in and sweetly kissed her cheek while reaching behind her to open the door with the length of his body pressed intimately against hers. *His cologne was amazing.* He didn't move. Her pulse was racing. *Was he toying with her?*

Kevin whispered in her ear, "I can't open it if you stand there."

She was such a dork. She was in front of the door. Kayn awkwardly stepped out of the way. He opened it and she slid in. *She'd almost forgotten to breathe. This new version of Kevin had game.*

He slammed it. A second later, he got in the driver's side and chuckled, "Sorry about that. If you don't slam the door it swings open when I turn corners. I took it upon myself to assume you wanted to stay in the car."

Intrigued by their new dynamics, Kayn crossed her legs and bit her lip. *This was the smart assed Kevin she'd missed.* She winked and replied, "I guess only people who know how to tuck and roll get to ride shot gun."

Kevin hadn't started the car. He teased, "Or I could just make sure my passengers wear their seatbelts."

Funny. She quickly did up her belt. They drove in silence as she beat their attraction to death in her mind. *Chloe's first act while possessing her was to make out with Kevin. Awkwardly enough, she'd been aware of what was happening. She'd recalled every detail like it was a dream and just gone with it. Had he wanted to kiss her, or had he been enraptured by Chloe's presence? It was an exhilarating, sensational kiss with no ration or boundaries but was Kevin merely an addict in search of another fix? Boys were drawn to Chloe like fireflies to flames, unafraid of being consumed lost embers floating away in darkness. He'd gone after that flame and it had been incredible, but how awkward would it be if the next kiss was nowhere near the last? What if they'd both been lost in the magic of Chloe's ability? This is what it must have been like for Chloe, never knowing if anyone chose to love her.*

Glancing over, Kevin remarked, "Don't be nervous. It's only a few exams. You'll barely have time to be accosted in the hall by random strangers."

Not even close to what she was thinking about. Kayn smiled and replied, "I've got this."

With his hand on her knee, he said, "We've been over-thinking everything for far too long."

He took the words right out of her mind. She grinned, as they passed familiar scenery. *Everything looked the same, but it wasn't. Nothing was. It felt like she'd gone to sleep one night and woken up to a different life.*

Kevin cleared his throat, drawing her attention away from the blur of local sights and cautiously probed, "How do you really feel about going back to school? Aren't you even a little freaked out?" He glanced away from the road to gauge her response.

"Not at all, Smith. I'm looking forward to a glorious day of peopling," Kayn sarcastically jousted while digging through her purse looking for gum.

"Ha-ha funny, Brighton," Kevin chuckled. He handed her a piece of juicy fruit from his pocket.

Unwrapping it, she said, "I'm superwoman, mere mortals may not harm me." *Now, he couldn't accuse her of lying by omission. She'd say, on my first day back I told you I was superwoman. He'd smile and accept the insanity. She wasn't naive enough to believe it, but it was a nice thought.* With a grin, she patted her friend's arm, saying, "Kayn out."

"I see my sporty, slightly dorky friend has returned," Kevin teased. "Might I make a small suggestion? Always stop short of quoting Star Trek."

Since when? Oh, yes, he'd changed too. They approached the coffee shop, conveniently located across the street from the high school. *It was packed. They never used to come here. This was where the jocks and princesses bonded over lattes. Where Chloe used to hang out. Introverted her, wanted to wait in the car.* Kevin parked his beat-up Pontiac and jogged around to open her door. *She'd only been joking about that, but she liked it.* She sucked it up and followed him. They pushed through the swinging doors and humming whispers began. *She was the girl whose family had been murdered.* Her sister's minions were at their regular table. She was expecting hostility, but they came at her in a swarm of empathy and overzealous embraces. As her twin's besties released her, Kayn found her eyes drawn to a beautiful girl sitting in the corner. *The word beautiful couldn't even begin to do her justice. This girl was breathtaking. She'd seen her before. She wasn't a figment of Kevin's naughty imagination after all.* The most intimidating female she'd ever seen, barely acknowledged their presence. "Who is that?" Kayn whispered in Kevin's ear. She was miraculously stunning with midnight hair glistening in sunlight streaming through the window.

Kevin knew who she was talking about without even turning around. He whispered back, "Her name's Lily."

Cat-like teal eyes peered up to see what the fuss was about. *Those must be coloured contacts.* Lily made eye contact with her and smirked like she wasn't impressed. *Lily had a strange vibe. She felt important and a little dangerous.*

"Our new queen bee has a thing for me," Kevin preened, draping his arm over her shoulder. Kissing her hair like they were only pals, he enquired, "What do you want, Brighton?"

The feeling of floating through romantic territory was snuffed out by being publicly shoved back into the friend zone. Kayn sighed, "Surprise me." *The new girl seemed irritated. Was she jealous?* Kayn swallowed the urge to ask questions as Kevin passed her a coffee. *This day was destined be full of drama without adding more to the pile. As uneducated as she was in the romance department, she wasn't an idiot. She was moving ten steps ahead of herself. They'd kissed a few times.* Needing to lighten things up, she suggested, "I have to figure out where my tests are. Onward Smith, the concrete jungle awaits."

Pushing open the door with a hip, he sang, "My lady."

This was why dating your best friend wasn't a good idea. It was like starting on date five hundred. What were the rules? How was she supposed to act? Hell, she'd never even been out on a real first date.

He one arm hugged her as they crossed the road, declaring, "Go forth and conquer. Good luck on test number one." He kissed her hair again.

"You too," she replied. *What in the hell was with this hair kissing thing?*

Kayn attempted to slip down the main hallway unnoticed

but was repeatedly stopped for random hugs and condolences from people she'd never spoken to. While sitting through her tests, she realised how easy everything would be for her. Every decision, every test answer she could hear in a room full of internal dialogue. If she kept pace, she could check her answers with the majority to make sure she aced it. *Some people might call it cheating, but her thoughts were so jumbled with everyone else's, she had no choice but to listen.* When her test was completed, she sat there watching Kevin struggle. *Could she send answers through her thoughts without him freaking out? What question was he on?* Kayn focused on his thoughts through the jumble of everyone else's. *He was a quiet thinker. Nobody else was.* She touched the spot he'd kissed earlier and concentrated. *He was frustrated, reading the same question repeatedly. The answer is C. Kevin, listen to me, the answer is C.*

He looked back at her and thought, '*Was that Kayn? It couldn't be, she's sitting too far away. Someone else must have said it.*' He looked down at his paper and surmised, '*It looks right. I'll go with that.*'

He wasn't stuck anymore. Lily passed Kevin a note. He looked up, smiled, and slipped it into his pocket. *He looked flattered and curious. He wanted to read the note. She'd been asleep for nearly a year. Maybe her recovery interrupted something? He'd changed so much during her absence. There was a sexy confidence he didn't have before.* She wished he still had a scrawny body and took it back. *After everything he'd done for her, how could she wish him anything but happiness, even if that meant it would be with someone else.* She recited in her head, *it was only a kiss. Just a few mind-blowing kisses, that's all it was. He's your friend. It doesn't matter if you can see that girl coming a thousand miles away, it's his life.* Her gaze locked with Lily's. She winked at her. *That witch was messing with her on purpose.* The humming of muffled inner dialogue grew louder as adrenaline surged. Irrationally livid, she contemplated using her rage fuelled ability to smoke that bitch in the head with something. A female voice in her mind scolded, *'Don't you dare.'* Kayn spun around. *Lily didn't appear to be concerned about anything, she was reading. Was she losing her mind?* Instinct urged her to leave before she did something stupid. Kayn put her test on the teacher's desk and left, without even glancing back at Kevin. With her focus elsewhere, she bumped into a boy she'd known since elementary school. *Jesse was his first name. She didn't recall his last name.* Kayn stammered her apologies, as she darted past.

KEVIN WALKED OVER AND PLACED his test on the teacher's desk. Smiling, he left the room expecting to see Kayn waiting, but it was Lily instead looking insanely beautiful as always.

"So, did you read it?" she flirtatiously enquired as she kept walking until she was intimately close.

"Not yet," Kevin answered. *She was surprisingly easy to talk to.*

"I'll get that for you," Lily smiled, as she slipped her manicured fingers deep into Kevin's pocket.

"I can get it," he choked, squirming as she dug around.

"I've got it," she assured, smiling seductively as she unfolded it and passed it to him.

It was in another language. It looked Greek. Kevin asked, "Is this a poem?" Lily urged him to read it aloud. *The words were dark and ominous, not sexy in the least.* Somehow, he knew how to read it but had no idea what he'd said. He sighed, "Is this a joke? Are you filming me saying something messed up in another language for YouTube? I probably said, I love a good donkey show, didn't I?"

Leaning, Lily whispered in his ear, "You see dead people. Those words will help you create boundaries. They might come in handy someday."

How could she know that? Flustered, he grilled, "How do you know that?"

She spun around to walk away, glanced back, and probed, "Can you see the future yet?"

He shook his head and replied, "No, I can't. Who are you?"

Lily took a lighter out of her pocket and said, "A friend."

As she wandered away, she casually lit the note on fire and tossed it into a metal garbage can. He followed the hypnotizing sway of her hips with his eyes as she strutted away. *What just happened?* The fire alarm went off causing students to giggle, squeal, and scramble, exiting the school. She'd disappeared, it was like she'd evaporated into thin air halfway down the hall. Kevin raced to where he last saw her. *What in the hell?* He looked in each direction. *She was gone.* He gave his head a good shake. *Evaporating into thin air was impossible but so was seeing the dead.* Dumbfounded, he stood there as students funnelled past.

He was the only one left in the hallway as the principal came around the corner and directed, "Get to the meeting place."

DESPERATE TO BE RID OF the humming excess of noise, Kayn rushed down the hall. *It wasn't any better in the bathroom with the amplified buzzing of fluorescent lighting. Her emotions were all over the place, she'd overwhelmed her senses with information. It was time to pull herself together. He wasn't a dorky little guy anymore. Why wouldn't girls flirt with him? She couldn't be weaving skin coats in the corner every time a girl spoke to him.* Grinning at her hilarious inner commentary, she came around the corner just in time to witness him being publicly fondled by the hot girl from the coffee shop. *There was something about that girl that rubbed her the wrong way.* She observed the intimate exchange from afar. Lily strolled away, lit the note on fire, set off the fire alarm and disappeared from her line of sight. Kevin ran after her and she was forced to exit the building with the herd of students to the meeting place. *This hurt. Why hadn't he just told her? She would have been fine with it if he hadn't confused her with kisses and mushy stuff.*

Standing with a group of people, Kevin waved her over. *Five minutes ago, he was being fondled by a ridiculously hot girl.* She was torn between high fiving him and beating him senseless with her binder for being led around by his manly bits, so she pretended she didn't see him. *She wasn't sure why she'd expected more after how he'd been around Chloe.* Lily was surrounded by an adoring swarm of admirers. Instinct prodded her to see what was right in front of her face. *No way. Lily was like Chloe.* They were told it was safe to go back inside.

Everyone was already seated by the time she made it to her next class. *Of course, Lily was sitting beside Kevin. What was she up too? Why was she intentionally baiting her?* Kevin kept looking, smiling. *He was worried about her.* She smiled back, assuring him all was fine. *What was she going to say? Hey, I think the hot girl that hits on you all the time might be an immortal sent to protect me?* Lily kept giving her smug little smiles during the test, so she grabbed her books and moved to an empty desk closer to the front of the classroom. She was gathering up her things when she was smoked on the back of the head by a heavy textbook. She was stunned for a second before turning around and sputtering, "What in the hell?"

The puzzled boy sitting behind her, started apologising, "Oh God, I'm sorry. It must have slipped out of my hands."

Lily pageant grinned and winked at her. That psychotic Bitch! She brainwashed a guy to chuck a book at her. Oh, it's on. She was so done with this skank. Seething with fury, she glared at Lily's coffee until it exploded like a caffeine bomb.

Lily was laughing amidst the confusion as Kayn grabbed her books and fled. Her heart was beating so rapidly she could barely catch her breath. *She just publicly exploded a mean girl's coffee. A part of her was elated for nerd girls everywhere.* Reality smacked her down. *She'd just publicly used her ability because she was jealous. She wasn't in control of this at all. She had to get the hell out of here.* She sprinted down the hall and burst out of the main entrance into the group of jocks she usually avoided. *Crap. Do not see me. I'm not here.* She slinked by the hot guys congregated at the steps.

"Wait," Jesse called out as he mischievously snatched her arm to keep her from escaping and led her away. "Talk to me."

His flirtation intrigued her, so she willed herself to act normal. Confidently meeting his gaze, Kayn replied, "Long time no see." *He was her elementary school crush and the only boy she'd ever kissed, until Kevin.* The entire teams' heads were shaved but it worked for Jesse with those blue eyes. *He hadn't spoken a word to her in five years.*

Once they were out of earshot, he divulged, "I thought about you a lot but never had the guts to go see you because we hadn't spoken in so long."

Smiling, Kayn replied, "We're speaking to each other right now."

"Yes, we are. I just wanted you to know I was pulling for you the whole time. I'm sorry about your family," he disclosed, still holding her arm so she couldn't politely escape. Her former crush switched directions, "What's the deal with you and Smith? Are you together? Did I miss my opportunity?"

Really? Right now? "Honestly, it's been a confusing day," Kayn admitted, perplexed. *She'd stumbled into a parallel universe. It had to be an alternate reality because he'd never known she existed.*

"Join me for a coffee if you ever find yourself available," Jesse proposed. He let her go to wave at one of his impatient buddies. She watched in astonishment as he took out his cell phone and confessed, "Chloe gave me your number last year. I tried to talk to you at school a few times, but it felt like you were avoiding me."

She'd been avoiding him for years. She dove into many bushes.

He showed Kayn her name in his contacts with an XO beside it. "I wanted to ask you out a long time ago," Jesse revealed.

He'd liked her before all of this. He'd just given her a much-needed dose of reality. She smiled, wishing he'd asked her out a year ago when her life wasn't this complicated.

"I should get going but I'll text you, then you'll have my number," he promised, smiling flirtatiously.

"Sure," Kayn replied, feeling a mixed bag of emotions. He texted her as she walked away. *She wasn't invisible anymore. Maybe she never had been?* She glanced back, saying, "I have it." *She'd seen Kevin standing there in the doorway watching the conversation a minute ago. Where did he go? Maybe, he just went to the car?* She left Jesse standing there holding up his phone.

Her surprise admirer yelled after her, "I'll be waiting."

She was still giggling when she arrived at Kevin's car.

Kevin was comically banging his head on the steering wheel saying, "Stupid, stupid, stupid."

She rapped on the window. Kevin peered up as she teased, "If you're finished beating yourself up, can you still give me a ride home?"

"How was school?" Kevin blankly questioned looking at the steering wheel.

"Things have changed a lot since I left," she answered quietly.

13

FORGIVEN AND FORGOTTEN

*T*hey rode in detached uncomfortable silence, managing to make it all the way home without uttering a word to each other. *If they'd been walking home, they would be lying in the grass talking things out by now.*

"What are your plans?" Kevin asked, attempting to clear the air.

Maybe a few hours of normalcy would fix the uncomfortable mess otherwise known as her first day back at school? "Come for a run?" she offered.

"That actually sounds great," he sighed. Their eyes met and a hopeful spark ignited between the pair as they go out of the car.

"You can borrow shorts from Matty. I saw some in the folded clothes on his bed," she disclosed as they entered the house.

"Be right back," Kevin ditched his shoes and raced upstairs with a giant smile.

Kayn grabbed bottled waters from the kitchen, downed a glass of orange juice and darted into the laundry room. She stripped down, knowing she had shorts and a tank top in the dryer. She was down to thong underwear and nothing else when Kevin abruptly opened the door.

"Hey Kayn," was all he said before noticing her sparsely clothed state. He covered his eyes with both hands and with a mischievous grin, spread his fingers and peeked, getting a good look at her nearly naked.

"Kevin!" She shrilly scolded, "Get out of here! I'm changing!"

"I can see that. You look incredible," he countered, boldly removing his hands from his eyes and stepping closer. His gaze was drawn from her arms covering her breasts to the barely visible scars on her chest. He whispered, "You're perfect."

"I'm not," she replied covering her chest.

He intimately caressed the ridged scar above her heart that looked like a symbol and whispered, "What does it mean? Did you look it up?"

Her scars looked hideous, especially the creepy one carved above her heart. "No, I haven't," she answered, avoiding his eyes. *It was the truth. With everything, she'd explored online, she'd never looked up the meaning of the symbol. Perhaps, she really didn't want to know.*

"I'll wait outside," he offered. As Kevin turned to leave, he confessed, "You've always been beautiful to me."

As he gently shut the door, she whispered under her breath, "I feel the same way about you." She envisioned him leaning against the other side of the door. *They were going to be fine.*

They left through the kitchen out the patio doors. The trails loomed ominously in the distance beckoning her. *Challenge accepted.* Kayn sprinted towards the opening.

"Are you sure you want to run through there?" Kevin called after her, breathing heavily.

Kayn stopped so he could catch up. Grinning, she declared, "It's the fastest way to the track isn't it?" Her mind darted through foggy memories as she burst into the trails with an odd sense of rebirth. She heard every noise and made a mental log of every change in her surroundings. The trees blowing in the wind applauded her re-entry with the brisk rustling of their branches, even though her heart was staging a revolt pounding vigorously through the sparse material of her tank top. *She would have to keep running through these trails until she conquered the fear. She needed to feel powerful again.* Kevin was just a pace behind her. As the trail thinned, she realised they'd chosen the route that hadn't been cleared. She jogged through mossy branch strewn path, wincing at the sound of Kevin's repetitive steps behind her. The steady crunching of twigs stimulated a subconscious need to run faster. As she burst through the overgrowth a branch sliced her arm creating a visual pathway to the horrors she'd survived. The hairs on the back of her neck prickled. She fought against the instinct to panic as her bloody arm flashed by in her peripheral vision. She clenched her fists. *Woman up. It's only a scratch.* Even though she was doing her best to avoid overreacting, flashes of blood stood in front of her wall of strength and screamed. *She couldn't wimp out, it was time to slay fear with determination.* It was more than strength she sought, she yearned for the rush and longed to recapture the joy she'd lost to the depravity that failed to consume her. *He was keeping pace with her. Weird, it felt like she was running fast.* A wave of adrenaline fuelled her amplified senses. She heard musical crickets, chirping birds and could distinguish scents in the air. *Hearing thoughts was only the tip of the iceberg.* They passed the shrines for her family. She saw Chloe through the trees and silently thought, *I miss you.* They broke through the overgrowth into the yard behind her property. A man was on his back porch having a cigarette. He waved as they jogged up the side alley. They smiled, waving back. She was waiting for Kevin's commentary about being half dead, he was still jogging beside her as an equal. *It seemed impossible. I guess the same could be said of her recovery.* Instead of slowing as they hit the track, they both sped up. It quickly escalated into a competition as they sprinted around the track. Instinct urged her to show him up, but they were running impressively fast already, passing the track team like they were standing still.

The coach shouted, "Brighton! You still got it kid!" as they passed in a flash of limbs. He did a double take, cheering, "Smith! Way to go son! Wow!"

After completing another lap, they collapsed on the grass laughing. Sprawling on the lush greenery, Kayn mimicked the coach, "Way to go Smith! Wow!"

"Oh, it's on," he chuckled as the wrestling match began. He tickled her until she was out of breath, giggling, "Stop. Stop. I'm going to pee."

He ceased his tickles and teased, "You know, I'm into many things, but peeing isn't sexy."

They almost had a normal moment. The track team had gone inside. They were all alone. She gave him a playful shot in the stomach. He stopped himself from returning one. *He'd recently seen the scars and wasn't ready to take off the kid gloves.* Their eyes locked as she replied to his thoughts, "You won't hurt me."

Positioned on top of her, staring into her eyes, he whispered, "I would die before I let anyone hurt you again."

He seductively ran his thumb along her bottom lip. *She wanted him to kiss her.* She caressed his face and as their lips met, she allowed herself to believe she was just a girl and he was just a boy. Their G-Rated make out session went poof as tongues darted between parted lips and hands roamed beneath shirts. She arched her spine, succumbing to his pleasurable touches. *They were in a public place.* She whispered, "What are we doing?"

Nibbling on her ear, he toyed, "Whatever we want."

She believed him. She looked into his eyes and knew he loved her. *He didn't need to say the words. They'd always been said, through his actions and with the way he'd always been there for her. They'd always loved each other.* A voice in her mind whispered, *'Run, Kayn'.* She looked over his shoulder. *Something was falling from the sky. Move Kayn,'* the voice prompted. In a fluid movement, she rolled them away, launched him to his feet and ran, towing a confused Kevin thirty feet in seconds. There wasn't time for a breath before a gigantic blazing tree hit the field with such force, they were knocked off their feet. In the grass, choking and sputtering as the dust cleared, an enormous flaming tree was where they'd been making out.

"Holy shit," Kevin stammered seeing how close they'd come to being squished.

"You can say that again," she whispered, catching her breath as they got up.

"Holy shit," the gym teacher shouted as he raced up the hill, "You kids okay?"

Not really, she was reasonably certain a mythical being just tried to kill her. She felt sick to her stomach. Instinct was prodding her to keep moving. Briskly walking away, Kayn aggressively towed Kevin with her.

Forcefully planting his feet, Kevin asserted, "Hold on! Where did that tree come from?"

There was no logical explanation. Her mind reeled. *She'd pulled him out of the way too quickly. Would they Correct him now? What had she done?*

"How did you see that before it hit us?" Kevin questioned, visibly freaked out.

He wasn't coming with her until she explained, and she couldn't. It felt like a cruel joke. Her feelings were crystal clear, now that it didn't matter at all. She loved him. She loved him so much it hurt. He'd almost been killed. That tree was meant for her. What if there was another one coming? Kayn tugged his hand, pleading, "I have to get you inside." A shiver ran up her spine. Her stomach cramped. *It was a warning. She was beginning to understand.* She looked back just in time to see a second flaming tree flatten the gym teacher. Waves of guilt washed over her, watching the train wreck her presence created. *She'd killed the coach she adored by being here.* Stunned, Kevin gaped as traumatized inconsolable teens gathered. *She'd get him inside, and then, she'd stay away from him. It would kill her, but he'd be safe.* "We should go," Kayn urged, as she led her unwilling friend to the gymnasium. *She felt numb, emotionless, with her need to keep Kevin safe guiding her. They weren't going to kill thirty people just to kill her, but she could be wrong.* Sobs echoed as she forced her way through the horrified mob of teens. *Here it was, she'd caused the death of another human being. She knew it was the truth. She had to push him away so he wouldn't become collateral damage in this twisted immortal game. This new life was not her own. This was the fine print in the contract. She couldn't stay.* With eyes moistened by tears, she said, "You should stay away from me."

Blankly, Kevin met her gaze, asking, "What do you mean?"

"It's the only way you'll be safe. I can't keep myself alive if I'm worried about you, and your family all of the time," Kayn disclosed with unfiltered honesty.

"What in the hell are you talking about, Kayn? My family is safe," Kevin countered, confused.

He tried to touch her. She asserted, "Don't make it harder."

"Wait a minute, what's going on? You don't seriously think someone just tried to kill you with a tree? That's insane," he questioned, desperate to know why she was pulling away.

"You can't understand," Kayn whispered as she took a step back.

"What are you talking about, Brighton? You're not making sense," he replied, shaking his head as she continued to back away. "What could this possibly have to do with you?"

"I wish I could explain. I can't be with you, I'm sorry," Kayn apologised with her heart aching. She fled, forcefully shoving her way through the stunned crowd.

Kevin shouted after her, "Seriously? You're breaking up with me? We can't break up! We never got together!"

Her heart disintegrated into a million pieces as she walked away from his voice.

"I love you! I'm coming over later! We're talking about this!" Kevin yelled over the noise.

"You shouldn't," Kayn whispered back under her breath.

A blonde guy Kevin didn't know poked his arm and teased, "If you come over after they break up with you, that's how you get a restraining order put on your ass."

"She's my best friend, it's not like that," Kevin explained.

The stranger winked and sparred, "That's what they all say."

DUSK ARRIVED AS KAYN RAN HOME LIKE SHE COULD ESCAPE WHAT happened. *She couldn't elude the inevitable. A future without Kevin was certain. Her mind needed more time to wrap itself around the clause in the second chance she'd been given. She couldn't be more than friends with him. A Clan was going to come for her, she would have to leave. She didn't even know what that meant? What kind of help was she going to be able to offer anyone? Wow, she could move salt and pepper shakers around a table and explode someone's coffee, what was that going to accomplish?* Nausea slowed her pace to a jog. *Everything was about to change. Why rush it? She'd convinced herself she'd have plenty of time to say goodbye. She didn't.* Kayn quickened her pace. *No matter how fast she ran, she couldn't outrun fate. Something fated was predestined, so leaving was inevitable.* She stopped as she reached the winding unfinished gravel driveway that led to her door, needing a minute to compose herself. She felt a tickle on her forehead as sweat trickled from her hairline.

Wiping it away with her hand, she trudged up the path. Halfway there, she froze. *She should walk away from this house and never come back if there was even a chance her presence might hurt the people she loved. She'd thought she was dealing with mortal evils, not amped up immortals throwing flaming trees. It felt like tempting fate standing outside alone and motionless. Anything could snatch her up or toss a fiery tree at her. Maybe that would be better than a life without them?* A gust of wind burst through the trees, she could almost hear the sand in the hourglass of her life trickling through the branches. *The lady in the light told her a Clan would be coming for her. Help was coming. She wasn't going to be left alone.* Kayn continued her journey towards the front door, relieved to see it closed. *If a Clan was coming to protect her, they'd better hurry up.*

14

THE ARRIVAL OF CLAN ANKH

*I*n a rustic cabin on picturesque Sproat Lake about fifteen minutes from her house, a group of partially immortal beings met to discuss all things Kayn Brighton related.

Markus, a slight built man with dark features and kind eyes rose to speak before a long cedar table. Ankh's leader had a surprisingly deep voice. If one closed their eyes, they'd imagine him seven feet tall. He cleared his throat. Whispers hushed as he began, "Hayley from Seattle didn't survive her Correction, and as you all know, we lost Melody to Trinity at the beginning of the year. Sharon from Minnesota did not survive. Brantley from Arizona also didn't make it. We've had one survivor from this last group. Kayn from British Columbia is why we've gathered here today. After a lengthy recovery, she appears to be fully healed. It's time to step in and claim her. We have a couple of weeks' leeway before the other Clans arrive, a month at best, but Abaddon could show up anytime. You've been made aware of the special circumstances. We can't lose her. It's game time."

Lexy, a crimson-haired vision with a sultry hint of southern accent spoke first, "Once we've marked her and begun training, she'll be tracked by the Legion. The deceased twin had abilities, this kid can't fight her way out of a paper bag."

"She's Freja's offspring," Markus curtly replied.

"Come on, she's only half of a half of Freja's offspring. She isn't even a whole one, and she has obvious issues with authority, just like her mother. I have the coffee stains to prove it," Lily huffed. Her cell vibrated for the tenth time. She picked it up and smiled at the text.

With impeccable timing Frost wandered in, sat in the empty seat beside Lily and questioned, "How in the hell do you have service?"

Scowling, Markus, remarked, "Good of you to join us."

Frost grinned as he stretched and said, "No problem."

Fiery tempered Lexy glared at Frost, comically pointing out what ticked her off, "Number one, why are you not wearing a shirt?" She directed her next jab at Lily, "Number two, I swear with everything inside of me if that phone buzzes one more time, I'll be forced to shove it somewhere offering you the same irritation I get from hearing it all of the damn time." Her comic timing took out her Handler. Grey laughed and spit his gum on the table in front of her. Scrunching up her face, Lexy picked up the chewed wad and stuck it on his arm.

"Cute Lex," Grey chuckled, he popped it back into his mouth.

A pretty blonde named Arrianna sipped her wine and declared, "That's disgusting, Grey. Nobody wants to kiss someone who eats table gum."

Grey teased, "Is that an offer? I thought we weren't doing that anymore?"

Lily's phone vibrated again. Lexy stood up. "Don't get your

panties in a twist," Lily sighed. She turned off her phone and slid it across the table to Lexy, snuffing out the cause of the squabble.

Lexy brushed Grey's slightly unkempt hair out of his eyes. He placed his hand on her shoulder and whispered, "Mellow out my feisty friend. I'll have to retrieve the phone."

"Would that really be so bad?" Lexy sparred with a wink.

Leaning closer, Grey whispered, "Awe Lex, you're the best wingman ever."

Markus smacked the back of Grey's head and scolded, "I'm standing right behind you."

Turning around, Grey innocently said, "Didn't see you there, my bad."

Their frustrated leader shook his head, strolling over to stand at the head of the table. Whispers hushed as Markus addressed the group, "I need at least one of you to attempt to act your age. Fake it if you must. I need to feel there's a remote possibility at least one of you is capable of following orders."

Leaning over, Frost whispered in Lily's ear, "I bet frog sticker girl has less of a problem with authority than you do."

Giving the dark-featured sexy adonis a scathing look, Lily sparred, "Go put on a damn shirt."

Frost's eyes met Lily's as he mouthed, "You want me."

"Kiss my ass," Lily whispered with a smile.

"Name the time and place," he quietly flirted, returning her sultry smile. Lily's phone buzzed in front of Lexy. Frost offered, "I'll get it."

Markus slammed his fist on the table, angrily scolding, "Cut that crap out. I don't feel like being roofied by you two."

"What crap, Daddy?" Lily replied. Her innocent smile deceiving no one.

"Pat down your horns honey, they make your hair poufy," Lexy countered.

Pacing behind his daughter's chair, Markus lectured, "Lilarah, help me understand today's events. I'm assuming you know it's a bad idea to kill our only survivor for spilling your coffee." He stopped walking, waiting for her response. She didn't give him one. Clutching the back of her chair with every speck of patience left, Markus scolded, "I sent you in months ago to protect the girl and keep an eye on the Clairvoyant. You tried to murder the girl on her first day back to school. You killed an innocent gym teacher." He met Lily's defiance with fatherly disapproval.

"I wasn't trying to kill her. I was just messing with her a little," Lily answered, tapping on the table.

Markus spun Lily's seat, so she'd be forced to look him in the eyes, reprimanding, "How old are you? We aren't allowed to off mortals for no reason. We're liable to get into serious medieval shit for altering timelines."

Rolling her eyes, Lily explained, "He walked right under it. I blame it on movies. Mortals are desensitized from the shows they watch. I don't know about you, but when shit starts falling from the sky, I run away. I don't wander over there to get a better look."

"You've volunteered to be a member of Kayn's permanent detail. Freja's kid doesn't leave your sight until she's eighteen," Markus ordered with no room for objection.

"Grey, keep an eye on my daughter. Make sure there are no more unfortunate incidents," Markus commanded with a hand on Grey's shoulder.

Grey glanced back and replied, "No problem. I'll keep an eye on her." He winked at the raven-haired seductress.

Winking back, Lily flirted, "You know how much trouble I get into if I'm left unattended."

Sitting at the head of the table, their leader muttered, "You people are driving me to drink." In a beautifully timed move,

Grey slid a bottle of wine down the table and it stopped in front of Markus. As he picked up the bottle, their leader questioned, "Am I supposed to magically open this or use my teeth like one of you, dumbasses?"

Always having her Handler's back, Lexy strutted over to the fireplace. She came back with the poker and snatched the bottle of wine off the table. If one didn't know her, they'd assume she was going to jab the cork into the bottle with the fireplace poker. Instead, she swung her arm like batting practice and smashed the neck of the bottle off. Shards of glass exploded everywhere, and tiny droplets of wine covered everyone. Grinning, Lexy filled their leader's glass. Pulling out her chair, she sat, saying, "Avoid swallowing shards of glass, it might hurt on the way out."

Silently laughing, with a hand over his mouth, Grey reached for another bottle and slid it to Lexy, prodding, "Do it again." Everyone else was dead silent.

She laughed, everyone cautiously joined in. Lexy walked the line between sanity and insanity as though it were an invisible tightrope. It was always a horrible idea to wiggle her wire. She was the Clan's Dragon, which was a nice way of saying she was an immortal hitman with anger management issues. Nobody wanted to piss Lexy off. Grey and Arrianna could get away with almost anything. Forty years ago, they were in Kayn's position.

They'd gone into Immortal Testing together. She'd never hurt them.

Catching Frost's attention, Grey asked, "What about the boy? Is he viable?"

The devilishly gorgeous immortal answered, "He was easily tiered-up due to Psychic lineage. Did you see how much that kid filled out in seven months?"

"One, can only binge watch so many hours of Netflix, I've done research. His grandmother is Psychic. He can see dead people now," Lily disclosed.

Confused, Arrianna questioned, "How did we find out about this other kid?"

Trying to fish a shard of glass out of his wine, Markus opted out, explaining, "We suspected the boy had Psychic lineage after finding out he heard the dead twin during Kayn's Correction. Based on a hunch, Lexy gave him a jolt of energy that night. His interference may have triggered another Correction. We couldn't risk the Brighton girl being caught in the crossfire, so we kept an eye on the boy. We need Psychics, we've lost a lot of people this year. Not murdering her boyfriend might help us all become friends."

"You should avoid sleeping with him," Frost whispered in Lily's ear.

Glaring at Frost, Lily teased, "Back atcha, frog sticker girl fan. Will you be wearing clothes to school? It's hard to stay under the radar when you look like a thirst trap."

Their leader instructed, "Please, just this once, can you four do exactly what you've been told to do. No creative changes. No excuses. No messing around. No ego trips. No more accidental murder sprees. Just go pick up those two Second-Tier kids and brand them Ankh."

"No problem," Frost replied.

Their fearless leader sighed, "Right. No problem." Looking at Frost, Markus exclaimed, "You've been waiting a long time for this one. Go brand frog sticker girl. If you get the chance to mark them both, do it. We'll worry about explaining everything to the boy later."

"If he doesn't want to come?" Lexy enquired as she slid Lily's phone back to her.

Proud of her for giving the phone back, Grey squeezed Lexy's hand as he answered, "He is in love with her and he's her best friend. He'll come."

Markus stood up and announced, "We have no time to dick

around. If the boy doesn't come willingly, mark him Ankh and kill him. We can worry about becoming friends later. The girl will have to suck it up, better us than a Correction."

15

WELCOME TO CLAN ANKH

*F*lopping on her bed like an exasperated ragdoll, Kayn lay motionless wishing she could reverse the hands of time. There were a million seemingly insignificant moments that could have been altered today if she'd had the ability to do so. The guilt from her teacher's death was eating her alive but it was more than just one thing. *She was a danger to the people she loved. She'd always thought the person who killed her family was just a man. They could put alarms on houses and lights in hallways. Everyone would be protected, and she could go on living her life. She wasn't even going to graduate. She'd lost her life that fated night. Her departure was inevitable. How could she just leave with strangers?* She sobbed into her pillow, allowing herself the luxury of the mental breakdown the year owed her. *She should have trusted her instincts.* She'd woken up feeling wary, with a dozen reasons to stay home, but instead of listening to that inner voice, she left quiet solitude and entered the lion's den, otherwise known as high school.

She felt vulnerable. She hadn't understood the severity of her situ-

ation, blinded by the death of her family. She'd falsely believed if she concealed her abilities, she'd be reasonably safe for years. Perhaps, she just couldn't take another second of reality, so she pretended her life wasn't over. Watching, she rubbed her thumb and forefinger together. She wasn't supposed to be alive. This was only a skin suit. Her life was not her own. It had been given back to her for service in a Clan. She didn't even know what that meant. What Clan? Where were they? As in love with Kevin as she was, there were no choices left to make. There was only one way to guarantee his safety. She should have called him. She would have had these last weeks to hold onto in her memory. She could have kissed him a hundred times by now. She rolled over and stared at her ceiling. The gym teacher crossed her mind, she cried until her eyes were puffy and swollen.

When she'd cried herself out, she started obsessing over what she'd done. She'd publicly broken things off to keep him safe but now all she wanted was to be in his arms. She could check on him, it's not stalking if you're concerned for their safety. What if he wasn't alone? She recalled his comeback, we can't break up because we were never together. A glimmer of jealousy expanded until common sense was non-existent. The thought of him with someone else was a heart-wrenching possibility. She knew him better than anyone else, he made rash decisions when he was hurt. He was making out with Lily right now and she'd shoved him into her arms. If only she'd owned up to her feelings years ago when he was just her geeky, scrawny remarkably endearing friend. Why was everything so damned complicated now? Mentally exhausted, Kayn closed her eyes.

Her eyes were graced by the darkness as she looked at her window. How long had she been asleep? She glanced at the clock. It was flashing 4:00 p.m. She hadn't been home to accidentally unplug it at four. Her socks hit cushioned carpet as she wandered to her en-suite. A metallic scent made her hesitate before reaching for the doorknob. There was a fragrance she recognized. *Was that Chloe's perfume?* She shook her head at herself. *She must have sprayed it before she fell asleep. She always felt disoriented after an impromptu nap.* She opened the door, flicked on the light, and staggered backwards until she was flush against the bathroom wall. On the floor was Chloe's freshly brutalised body. She swallowed the lump of shock in her throat. It was like watching Chloe on a television screen; her sister's fingers twitching as she willed her nearly lifeless body to move. *It was a vision of her sister's final moments.* Kayn whispered, "Chloe," as she inched closer. A chill shivered up her spine, she shuddered as the air grew colder. *It didn't feel like they were alone.* It was chilly enough to see her breath pirouetting in front of her. *She'd heard many stories about visitors from the other side.* Granny's tales always included frigid temperatures when spirits were present. Since the incident in the hospital, she'd only seen Chloe out of the corner of her eye. She'd sensed her presence, thought she heard her voice and caught a glimpse of her in mirrors as she passed, but when she doubled back, it was always her reflection. *She'd seen her in the trails today. She'd been certain of it.* Her sister's fingers twitched as her breathing slowed. Something cuttingly cold passed through her. *It was a darkly clothed man.*

He leaned over Chloe's body and whispered, "You scratched me you little bitch. You're a fighter. You've proven to be a worthy adversary indeed." He stroked her sister's wet hair away from her bloody disfigured face and removed a concealed blade from his pocket. Leering over her with sweat glistening on his brow, he panted with anticipation while carving something into her flesh.

Tears fogged Kayn's vision as her twin shuddered and made eye contact. Sensing Chloe was trying to tell her something, she had to pay attention, even though every cell in her body was screaming at her to stop him from hurting her. *This had already happened. There was no way to stop it.*

He stroked her hair once more and creepily whispered, "Why don't you just die?"

Her mother's voice called out, "I'm home! You'd better be doing homework, Chloe!"

Mom. No. Shivers coursed through her being as tears flooded her vision.

The man who'd just mutilated her twin whispered, "Oh dear, mommy's home. I should go greet her at the door. Wherever are my manners?"

As the evil passed through her, Kayn gasped. It was as though the entity was the dead of winter. As soon as he left the room, Chloe began struggling again, willing her savaged body to save her mother. *She wasn't dead.* Kayn wanted to cheer, forgetting how it played out for a second. *She hadn't been able to save her mother. This must have been where they found Chloe's body.*

"Mom," her sister raspily croaked.

She was trying to warn her. She felt Chloe's desperation.

Her voice crackled, "Mom." Shuddering, Chloe soundlessly mouthed, "Mom."

Anxiety filled the air as her twin's internalised emotions pulsated through Kayn's being with such raw urgency it became impossible to separate reality from the vision. There was no way to disconnect from the horror as her twin's soul shrieked within her mind, '*Run! Mom! Please run!*' Kayn wanted to go to her mother but couldn't bring herself to leave. *She couldn't let her die alone again.* She heard a single, muffled scream from the landing and found solace in how quickly her mother was silenced. *She'd died fast. He hadn't come for her.* With thankful tears blurring her vision, Kayn sat down in her twin's blood. "I'm here honey," she whispered to her dying sister in the fetal position barely breathing. "I'm with you. You are not alone," Kayn consoled lovingly.

"It's going to be okay," she vowed. She sang to her nearly lifeless sister, "Sleep, sweet sleep till the morning. Just dream away and close your eyes. My love, you'll be safe until the morning. Sleeping in my arms all through the night. Although bad dreams come to scare you. My love will scare them all away. My heart..." She was too choked up to continue. Peace slipped across her twin's face and with a final shuddering breath, she was gone. Her remaining eye vacantly stared through her. *She was afraid to move for fear of breaking their fragile connection.*

Chloe's head ominously cranked, looked directly at her and creepily warned, "You're next, Run Kayn." Her entity turned to mist and evaporated.

Scrambling away, Kayn whipped around to check behind her, breathing a sigh of relief when nobody was there to kill her. With an uneasy feeling, she scanned the bathroom. *Was her sister talking about that day or right now?* Her legs felt like Jell-O as she got up. *How long was she sitting there?* Her bedroom door abruptly opened, and she leapt.

Matt stuck his head in and announced, "Twenty minutes until dinner."

Kayn scolded, "You scared the shit out of me." Giggling, Matt closed the door. *She didn't know he was home.* She felt a presence, turned and squealed. A hot guy wearing black silky shorts was lounging on her purple comforter.

"They were right, you are overdramatic," the half-naked dark-featured stranger teased as he got up and boldly strolled towards her.

"How did you get in here?" Kayn demanded as the living, breathing underwear model from a city billboard confidently approached. She backed down the hallway into the bathroom, prepared to slam the door in his face and lock it.

Holding up his hands, he chuckled, "Kayn, take a deep breath and calm yourself down. I'm from Clan Ankh. I've been looking forward to meeting you. I'm Frost. I know Freja. Your bio mom, or whatever you plan to call her."

He was from a Clan. It was surprisingly difficult to ignore the rules she'd grown up with. Even if it was a good half-naked stranger, surprising her in her bedroom. She'd agreed to this as the terms of her survival. She hadn't known they could appear out of thin air in her bedroom. She should say something. "Jack Frost?" Kayn teased, flinching. *That was weird, even for her.*

"Wow, she has a sense of humour. It's not like I haven't heard that one a million times," the uncomfortably sexy guy fired back.

She couldn't pry her eyes away from his chiselled abs and perfect everything, not even for the sake of being polite. *He smelled incredible.* With a deviously naughty grin, he continued to approach. She felt the colour rising in her cheeks. "Is it part of your job to show up half-naked?" Kayn enquired.

He winked and roguishly replied, "It is."

His presence turned her sex drive up ten notches. Of course, it is. She felt a disturbing absence of control as heat surged in the pit of her stomach. *He was like Chloe but a guy. She got it now, although it didn't help much.*

Enjoying her weakness to his mind-altering pheromones, he flirtatiously taunted, "I think it's time you became less interested in stalking that boy and more concerned with what I have to offer you."

Swallowing nervously, Kayn asked, "What's that?"

The half-naked Adonis inched closer. "Safety in numbers and training, what do you think I'm offering?" Frost toyed, oozing charisma.

Closing the bathroom door clearly wasn't an option. He'd over-power her and she'd let him. She wasn't frightened. It was quite the opposite. She felt dangerously alive.

First things first, don't be ridiculous get over here, you can't get away," Frost chuckled, summoning her.

Shit, she might as well. She followed him into her room.

"Open your hand." The roguish immortal commanded.

He placed a small bag of what felt like rocks in her palm. Kayn cheekily pointed out, "I've had the healing rock thing covered for years, my best friend's grandmother has a fetish."

"You didn't look, what if they're magic beans?" he provoked, intrigued by her weird comebacks.

"Magic beans didn't work out well for Jack in that unfortunate beanstalk incident, did they?" Kayn sparred, defiantly tossing the bag on her bed.

"You're quite the nerdy little smartass, aren't you?" Frost chuckled, shaking his head. He patiently held out his hand.

She stifled the urge to ask for a spanking. *Calm down. He has voodoo powers. He's like Chloe. You love Kevin*, she repeated in her mind, trying to keep her shit together.

Chuckling, Frost teased, "It doesn't matter how much you love that Kevin kid. Right now, the only thing that matters is that you play along. You've agreed to the contract."

He'd read her mind just like she'd been able to eavesdrop on people's thoughts. Could they all do this? With a touch of foreboding, she placed her hand in his unprepared for the surge of hedonistic pleasure that made her tingly everywhere. She yanked her hand away, saying, "Let me get this straight. You want to give me a bag of rocks and drug me by holding my hand. Assuming I'm not a complete moron, how about an explanation first?"

"You're entering a new existence where explanations will be few and far between. Sweetheart, life will be way easier if you just go with it," he coolly responded.

That was ignorant.

Grinning at her inner dialogue, the roguish immortal said,

"Those stones you tossed on the bed are for protection and healing. I bet your friend's grandma didn't tell you they come in handy when you're in need of privacy from a higher-level soul? Humour me, I'll give you more details later." Frost extended his hand, urging, "Take my hand frog sticker girl, this is getting old."

Confused, Kayn questioned, "Frog sticker girl?"

Frost winked and replied, "It's a long, adorable story. I'll tell it to you someday."

She was afraid but she wanted to trust him.

Frost's eyes softened as he responded to her thoughts, "You have to be marked Ankh. It'll be worth it, I promise. We're spiritually bound. If you're in danger, we'll protect you."

"I can't bind myself permanently to anyone at seventeen," Kayn stated with adult resolve.

Frost patiently clarified, "If I have to take you by force, you leave right now. If you do this willingly, you'll have more time."

Twenty minutes had to be up by now. What would happen if Matt came back upstairs?

Gazing into the immortal's eyes, Kayn asked, "Will it hurt?"

"Yes, but I swear it'll be worth it," Frost tenderly responded, extending his hand.

Hesitantly, Kayn took it, feeling the same intoxicating, carnal sensation he'd given her before. He roughly pressed his ring into her palm. "Son of a bitch!" she shouted as the symbol on the ring melted her flesh. *He'd branded her! Holy hell, it was excruciating.* Defensively holding her wounded hand, Kayn angrily hissed, "What, in, the hell!"

"I'm sorry, it had to be done," Frost apologised. He tugged off his white fingerless leather glove, showing her his brand to justify his actions. "The symbol of Ankh is our key to the in-between. It has been branded on your flesh and soul. One of those rocks in the bag you tossed on your bed is for protection while travelling in your mind, I thought that might interest you.

The Snowflake Obsidian is for foresight development. You know that feeling you get when something is about to go wrong?" Frost paused, asking, "Did you catch any of that?"

Kayn shot him the dirtiest look in her repertoire and accused, "I lost the ability to pay attention when you branded me."

He sighed, "Just let me get through the welcome to Ankh speech and you can go back to obsessing over your boyfriend. You can't just astral project wherever you want. Well, not if you'd like to come back and find your body in one piece. You need a spiritually safe zone."

Was that why Granny Winnie kept giving her stones?

"Probably," Frost responded to her inner dialogue. "Now that you're Ankh, you can't die. If you're killed your soul will remain in the in-between and be drawn back to your body when we heal you. Once you've reached the age of eighteen that mark is permanent, you'll do the Testing and earn a tomb."

Kayn raised her brows as she declared, "Feel free to quote me, I'm never sleeping in a tomb."

"Oh, you don't have to worry about falling asleep in one of our tombs," Frost chuckled.

Deafened by the stinging agony of melted flesh, she pursed her lips and gave it a cooling blow, but it only made it worse.

"Oh, quit being such a baby," Frost reprimanded as he reached for her hand.

"Seriously? Do you think I've been sniffing glue? Why would I give you my hand again? That hurt," Kayn said, offended he thought her that stupid.

"Sniffing glue?" Frost questioned, missing something in her sarcastic wit.

How about, I'm not crazy enough to give you my hand again. If you burn my hand once, shame on you. Burn me twice, shame on me.

"You have quite the active hamster wheel spinning between your ears, frog sticker girl," he teased, grinning.

Kayn glared at him, boiling rabbits with her eyes. *I'm in pain you douche.*

"Do you want me to heal that for you?" Frost asked with genuine tenderness.

Her instincts were telling her to trust him even though it made no sense to.

He held up his branded hand, instructing, "Place your symbol against mine."

What would it hurt now? She'd already let him brand her. She did it. It tingled, warmed up, then felt normal as he took his hand away. Kayn stared dumbfounded at her pain free healed palm.

"Better now, sweetie?" He flirted.

She nodded, fascinated. *He'd healed her. This was so crazy. All of it.* He cleared his throat and she peered up.

"Let me show you something cool," Frost said, pinching her.

She snapped, "Ouch! Not cool!" *What is wrong with this asshole? That was hard, she was bleeding.*

Smiling, he instructed, "Now, look at your palm."

Kayn looked at her hand. *It felt warm and her mark was glowing. Crazy.*

Showing her his hand was glowing too, he explained, "Once you're Enlightened, you'll get a ring just like this one."

"Do I get to burn unsuspecting people too?" Kayn cheekily sparred.

"You sure do frog sticker girl," Frost laughed.

He seemed proud of that condescending nickname. This wasn't even an act, he was a douche. Hoping he heard every word, she spoke, "This is a lot to take in."

Grinning, the immortal grew serious as he disclosed, "You had natural talent and likeable humility but no ability. We weren't allowed to stop the Correction, but we did what we could by amplifying the spirit world. Hearing your twin screaming for you to run gave you a few extra seconds. Freja's our friend, we wanted you to have a fighting chance. There was a glitch in our plan when your friend also heard Chloe scream."

Kevin. Kayn asked, "Is he in danger?"

Frost answered, "Truthfully, he might be. He interfered with a Correction."

Her heart sunk as she bargained, "He doesn't know. I haven't told him anything."

Frost did his best to explain, "Any mortal with a genetic predisposition to access unattainable portions of their brain can have a dormant ability triggered. When we left that door open, your sister was able to reach you and unfortunately him. Under immortal law any mortal that has knowledge of the immortal world must be Corrected, but any Second-Tier can be claimed by Clan. Knowing he must have Psychic ability, we took a chance and gave him a surge of energy from one of our Healers to see if we could make him viable enough to claim. You didn't find his dramatic physical changes strange?"

"Of course, but there was so much to take in when I woke up," she replied.

"Psychics are naturally occurring genetic mutations among the human population, sort of like evolution. Most Psychics know not to mess with fate and never with death," Frost responded.

Kevin's grandmother knew I was going to die and let me go home anyway. Kayn felt the ache of penetrating betrayal.

He whispered, "She knew if she stopped it, her family would be next. Nobody escapes their Correction. If you'd been paying attention, you would have seen the signs of your demise."

Kayn slowly shook her head in denial even though she knew he was speaking the truth.

"Think about it, you felt your sister being killed as you lay in the grass and blew it off as hunger pains even though you knew it was far too painful to be that. You had a sense of foreboding you chose to ignore as you walked towards the house. There should have been three, Kayn. When was the other one?" Frost questioned.

The wind blowing up the dust on the track when there had barely been a breeze. She'd even joked about someone walking over her grave.

Irritated, Frost apologised, "One second, love. I need to deal with this." He strode over to the window and flung it open. Kevin startled and slipped. Frost grabbed his arm as he dangled off the ledge, menacing, "Are you going to be a problem or an ally?"

"An ally! Definitely an ally!" Kevin vowed as the immortal yanked him through the window like a rag doll.

Stunned, Kayn implored, "Don't hurt him, Frost."

Winking, Frost stated, "I knew he was out there the whole time. I let him hear everything so I wouldn't have to explain it twice. Your grandma's a Psychic, Kayn's a Second-Tier. You're alive because you might be, do you need anything explained?"

"I think I got it. I'm good," Kevin quickly answered.

"Are you going to tell anyone, kid?" Frost grilled, staring through Kevin like he had a built-in lie detector.

"No, never. I wouldn't," Kevin stammered.

"Any questions?" Frost commented with dry annoyance.

"Where's your shirt?" Kevin teased.

"You two are perfect for each other," Frost sparred, struggling to hide a smile creeping to the corners of his lips even though he was trying to be intimidating. "It's your turn, kid," the immortal directed, smiling as Kevin willingly held out his hand. Taking it, Frost sighed, "How blindly we love when we're young and unscathed." He branded the symbol into Kevin's hand as he repeated Kayn's colourful words. "Welcome to Clan Ankh," Frost chuckled. "We'll be in touch, you kids have a lot to learn." Grinning as he twisted his ring around, Frost grabbed a couple fingerless gloves out of his pocket, tossed them on the bed, and stated, "Cover your symbols with these. Any other questions or are we good here?"

"Is someone still coming to kill me?" Kayn pressed as she looked at Kevin, her heart aching because he'd tied himself to her.

"Oh sweetheart, you can count on it," Frost blurted, coldly. Smirking, he announced, "On the bright side, if either of you are brutally murdered, we can bring you back. You're Ankh now, it's no big deal."

Right, brutally murdered, no big deal.

"Kev, you okay little buddy?" Frost gave him a brotherly pat on the shoulder.

"Just trying to absorb everything. It may take a minute, or a year or so," Kevin numbly responded.

"Well, my young friend, time is irrelevant. Does that help?" Frost countered with a grin and a supportive shoulder clasp.

"Not so much, but thanks for throwing that out there," Kevin mumbled shaking his head.

Frost grinned and replied, "Anytime." He picked up a picture of the twins from Chloe's dresser, looked at it then placed it back down. "Well, I guess it's time for me to go. Behave yourselves, we'll be in touch. And Kevin, it's not really stalking," Frost teased with a giant grin in Kayn's direction.

"Huh?" Kevin replied, not understanding what he meant.

Frost waved and climbed out of her window, Kayn grinned. *She'd thought he'd just magically appeared. She didn't hear him climbing in her window, she'd been preoccupied by trauma again.*

"He branded me," Kevin commented.

"He was either going to kill you or brand you," she mumbled. *Her hand was glowing. Frost didn't heal Kevin before he left.* "I might be able to fix it," Kayn said, taking Kevin's hand. They heated up and she let go.

Blown away by his healed hand, Kevin whispered, "That was cool."

The bedroom door opened. Her brother stuck his head in and complained, "I told you to come down for dinner five minutes ago."

"Sorry Matty, I'll be right down," Kayn replied. *When I regain my faculties.* He gave them a strange look.

"Kevin, just use the door next time instead of creeping in my sister's window. Are you staying for dinner?" Matt harassed.

"Sure, sounds good," Kevin answered his voice cracking in embarrassment as Matt closed the door.

"Frost was here for a good hour, wasn't he?" Kayn questioned as she looked at her clock.

"At least," Kevin agreed, peering at his watch. Confused, he whispered, "It's only been twenty minutes since I climbed up the tree to your windowsill. That doesn't make sense. Alright, I'm officially a little creeped out by all of this."

"Just a little?" Kayn countered as they sat on her bed, neither one moving a muscle. *I know we need to talk about this but Matt's going to freak out if we don't get down there.*"

"We have a lot to talk about after dinner," Kevin sighed, as he got up and tried to take her hand. Both of their palms began glowing. They let go. "Mental note, no hand holding unless we're wearing gloves," he said as they each grabbed a glove.

16

FOREVER AND EVER, AMEN

*K*ayn took her place at the dinner table as her frazzled mind scrolled through the events of the day. *How was she even supposed to process all of this? Her gym teacher's wife and children must be going through hell tonight. It was her fault. He was just an innocent bystander. It felt like Kevin was avoiding eye contact with her. The hamster wheel between his ears was spinning so fast it was invisible. He'd just given up his life, seventeen was a little young to be thinking in terms of forever.*

Matt kicked her under the table and remarked, "You haven't touched your food."

Mindlessly staring at her plate, Kayn confessed, "I keep thinking about the gym teacher's family."

Kevin looked directly into her eyes and said, "It's not your fault."

Matt squinted at Kevin, commenting, "That was a weird thing to say, Smith?" He addressed Kayn, "I assume you guys are talking about that gym teacher? I got a text from Clay about him getting squished by a tree. How messed up is that? I guess when your numbers up, it's up." He finished another mouthful, adding, "I loved that guy. He was my gym teacher when I went to school there. Kevin, your brother is pretty upset about it. How did a tree end up falling in the centre of the track? It doesn't make sense."

What could she say? Someone tried to kill her again. Kevin probably thought that she was insane when she'd said those words to him at school. She glanced at Kevin. *I bet he doesn't think I'm crazy now. She didn't want her brother to ask questions. He was mortal and therefore completely expendable.* "It was a horrible accident," Kayn said, looking at her plate. Cutting a slice of her cold roast beef, she ate it. *If she didn't eat, she'd draw unwanted attention to herself.* Her brother hadn't heard they'd been standing by the gym teacher. They continued to eat in silence.

After dinner, they went back up to her room. She told Kevin a story about twin sisters who share a soul and other unbelievable revelations far too crazy to be true. He not only believed every word but was a little upset she hadn't told him everything from day one. He, in turn, told her he could see dead people. He said Lily was one of them and that she'd already come to him. The note she'd asked him to read aloud had something to do with having privacy from the spirits and boundaries. She opted out of harassing him for not telling her, they were even. They lay side by side on her bed, staring at each other.

Kevin broke the silence by saying, "You should have seen me outside your window watching you with a shirtless guy. I don't think I've ever been so jealous in my life."

His comment lightened the mood. Kayn chuckled, "Frost's ability turns you on just like Chloe's gift did."

"Your sister turned you on?" Kevin teased, pretending to be shocked.

Punching his arm, she sparred, "You're hilarious."

Kevin laughed, "Kidding, I'm joking. I know what you mean, Lily also has that ability."

"Have you kissed her?" *Why did she just say that? She really didn't want to know the answer, but the train already left the station.* She shifted in bed to meet his gaze. *Absolute truth time goes both ways.*

He lovingly caressed her face as he answered honestly, "I wanted to, but I didn't."

She pulled away as he leaned in, grumbling, "I knew that witch voodoo powered that guy into hitting me with a book."

Playing with her hair, Kevin teased, "In all fairness, you did explode her coffee. That was you, right?"

"She deserved it," Kayn whispered as they inched closer.

As they embraced, he kissed her cheek, saying, "Please give me a chance to explain before you blow things up in my face."

She toyed with his shirt, stipulating, "I promise to refrain from blowing things up in your face until after you've had a chance to explain."

"I'm sure you meant to say you'd never do that," he teased, grinning like a Cheshire cat.

"Never say never," Kayn baited. Her eyes darted around as she changed the subject, "Are there any dead people in my room, right now?"

"Not a one," Kevin vowed, whimsically caressing her hair.

Kayn gave him a playful shove, laughing, "You're bad at lying, you have an easy tell."

Captivated, he probed, "I'll bite, what's this easy tell?"

Kiss me you idiot. She flirtatiously revealed, "If I tell you what it is, you'll change it. I won't know when you're lying."

He clutched her pillow and menacingly threatened, "Tell me or I'll beat you senseless with this green tea scented orthopedic pillow."

Lounging on her bed, she dared, "I'm all for trying something new."

He stopped horsing around, admitting, "I'm sorry it took me so long to see us for what we are."

She placed her gloved hand against his and as they intertwined their fingers, she disclosed, "I thought I was going to have to leave you but now you're coming with me. Can you really tie yourself to me forever at seventeen?"

Kevin lovingly gazed into her eyes as he confessed, "I was tied to you forever at five."

She teared up and let go of his hand to wipe her eyes. Swatting him, Kayn laughed, "You're full of shit, I saw the tell."

With tears of adoration glistening, he whispered, "I knew you were the weirdest, most incredible, completely insane girl I'd ever laid eyes on. I've never regretted giving you that flower, not once. You'll always be my friend no matter what. Nothing can change what will always be the truth." Kevin took her hand again, laced his fingers through hers and brought their hands to his chest, shifting her body closer. His teared-up eyes penetrated hers as he asked, "You can feel my heartbeat against your hand. You know it's the truth."

Deeply moved, with their lips a breath apart, she opted to show him she believed by tenderly pressing her lips against his. As their lips parted, their eyes locked. Their futures had been drastically altered. They had no control over anything. The unknown was terrifying. Everything in their lives was a mess but they were certain. What they wanted was undeniable. Their lips passionately reunited. The G-rating was lost as he boldly seduced her with his tongue. *Where had he learned to kiss like this?* He grazed her bottom lip and she gasped. That was it, the games were done as he rolled on top of her. She pulled up his shirt, wanting his skin against hers, aching to be his. She needed the end of this day to be about more than trauma and pain. She wanted this day to be about something beautiful. She seduced him with her eyes as she removed her shirt and chucked it. His inner dialogue was gloriously epic as she took off her bra making her intentions clear.

Awestruck, Kevin gasped, "Are you sure?"

Nodding, she affirmed, "I've never been so sure of anything." He hastily took off his shirt and tossed it aside. He'd physically changed so much. *His abs were in a league of their own.* Captivated, she caressed his muscular chest as their lips met once again in a beautiful breathless dance. She adored him with every whisper of her being. This was deeper than lust. This wasn't two teens doing something impure. This was the most untainted form of love. It was a passion built on friendship, a devotion built on kissed skinned knees and crying on shoulders. This was a love built on placing brick after brick of trust into its foundation. Their hearts were as intertwined as their fingers. Hers raced as he ignited embers of lust by seductively kissing her neck, chest and continued the titillating journey all the way down to her abdomen causing her to squirm beneath him, laughing. She mischievously pulled his hair. He peered up and grinned as she naughtily bit her lip while beckoning him with a finger to get back up there and kiss her. She gazed deep into her best friend's eyes as she fumbled with the button on her jeans.

From the bottom of the stairs Kayn's brother yelled, "Hey! Don't make me get the hose! Kevin! Your mom says it's time to go home!"

"Oh no, I think he's on to us," Kayn giggled.

Kevin groaned. Tugged his shirt back on, he whispered, "I'm going out that door and climbing back in your window."

She kissed him, teasing, "I have a sneaky suspicion Matt will be checking on me every five seconds tonight."

He chuckled, "I'm glad he didn't barge in here. That would have been awkward."

MATT WAS SEETHING AT THE bottom of the stairs. *What was the appropriate reaction to Kevin and Kayn's changed relationship status?*

Jenkins wandered up and taunted, "What's wrong buttercup?"

"They might be making out, the bed was squeaking," Matt whispered.

Smiling, Jenkins provoked, "I'm sure they are."

"Well, what should I do?" Matt asked helplessly. "I yelled at Kevin and told him to come down. I said his mother wanted him to come home."

"Give the kid a minute to compose himself. If you know what I mean," Jenkins chuckled, patting his shoulder.

"Oh, like hell." Matt hissed. He tried to push past Jenkins to the stairs.

Jenkins assertively seized Matt's arm, saying, "This is Kevin you're talking about, not some schmuck with a sports car who is going to love your sister and leave her. Be happy about this. They may even get married one day." He towed Matt away from the stairs.

"I should at least threaten him," Matt grumbled as he looked back at the stairs.

Jenkins promised, "He's going to stop whatever they were doing and go home. Kevin's a great kid. You'll have the upper hand if you don't overreact."

"She's only seventeen," Matt replied.

"What were you doing at seventeen?" Jenkins asked.

"Oh God, I'll kill him!" Matt panicked.

Jenkins was belly laughing, manoeuvring Matt to the

kitchen, "Let me make you a nice cup of coffee with Baileys in it. It'll calm your nerves."

Sure enough, only a minute went by before Kevin raced down the stairs and waved as he left.

KAYN DIDN'T COME DOWNSTAIRS. Embarrassed, she preferred to avoid lectures. She changed into pyjamas, rested her head on her pillow and thought about her heartbreakingly sad confusingly sexy day.

As she drifted off, Chloe's voice whispered, "That was a little naughty, I'm almost impressed."

Exhausted, she smiled but didn't waken to spar, slipping off into a dreamless slumber.

Stirring, she opened her eyes to a new day. Stretching, Kayn noticed the symbol on her palm, and it all came rushing back. She slipped on the fingerless glove. Stubbing her toe was part of her routine. She was as graceless as a bull in a china shop in the morning. Kevin was already sitting in the kitchen having a coffee with Jenkins when she stumbled in wearing purple pyjamas and a robe with scraggly lion's mane hair. Jenkins was having an awkward chat with Kevin about doing adult deeds elsewhere to preserve Matt's sanity. *Nope, she wasn't doing this. Kevin was a rock star boyfriend. Look at him go. He even admitted they got caught up in the emotion of the day and hadn't thought it through. He was good.* Jenkins gave a mortifying practice safe sex speech as icing on the humiliating conversation cake. She was at the fridge trying not to laugh, looking for something. *She sure as hell didn't want to be involved in this conversation.* Kevin assured Jenkins they'd slow things down, think things through and give Matt time to get with the program. *She agreed a tiny bit. She didn't really want too though.*

Kevin grinned as she went back to the coffee maker, poured herself a giant mug and remembered why she went to the fridge in the first place. She went back for flavoured coffee creamer. *It wasn't there. Ohhh, she wasn't happy about this.* Kevin got up and brought it to her without saying a word. *He knew the drill. Ten or fifteen minutes of peace and she was good to go.* She took her coffee and went back upstairs to get dressed.

A few minutes later she reappeared as her perky happy self. They sat in silence sipping coffee, making faces at each other whenever Jenkins turned around. When he stood up to start making breakfast. They got up to help.

Matthew Brighton was summoned from his slumber by the enticing scent of the sizzling bacon. He walked in and when he saw Kevin standing there, his eyes widened like he was about to throw down. *He totally thought Kevin spent the night.* She pressed her lips together to stifle her laughter. Kevin was obliviously grabbing plates from the cupboard.

Jenkins started giggling. Without turning around, he clarified, "Kevin just got here. He brought us fresh eggs for breakfast."

Her brother's mood instantly shifted from I'll tear your limbs off to awe that's nice as he said, "Thank your mom for us."

After breakfast, they snuggled in fleece blankets on opposite sides of the couch to preserve Matt's sanity as requested. They spent their day watching movies, laughing, and pointedly avoiding conversations involving the day before. They slowly inched closer and held hands beneath the blanket. Eventually, Kevin stopped concentrating on the movie, but he wasn't thinking about naughty stuff like she was. *He was wondering what she could do but she had to take a breather and dial back the drama so she could process everything. She needed to be ordinary* teenagers eating popcorn, cuddling on the couch. She wanted to continue to pretend this was all they were. "Bathroom break. I'll be back," Kayn sang the horror movie watching no-no. Smiling flirtatiously, she provocatively swayed her hips, listening to his musical laughter as she walked away. Realising she was thirsty, she detoured to the kitchen for orange juice. Standing at the sink, she peered out the window and saw a girl in the bushes. The girl met her curious eyes, flashing her a friendly smile. The stranger's wavy hair and natural beauty felt familiar. She was about to open the sliding door to ask if she needed help, assuming she'd lost her dog in the trails. As Kayn touched the handle, instinct prompted her to be wary. She'd been cautioned to listen to instinct. She wasn't overly concerned but still checked to be sure the sliding door was locked before leaving the kitchen. As Kayn passed the front door, she made sure it was locked before wandering into the den. She handed Kevin his orange juice.

"Thanks' Brighton. Why did you lock the door?" he enquired.

"There's a girl in the bushes out back, she probably lost her dog. Better safe than sorry," Kayn answered, sipping her juice. Kevin bolted to the kitchen forcing her to chase after him. *That was a bit of an overreaction.* They looked out the kitchen window and Kayn stated, "She's gone," shrugging. *The warning from last night echoed in her mind.*

"Maybe," Kevin replied. With his arm around her, he kissed her head sweetly as they wandered back to the den. Three aggressively loud knocks on the door rattled them. Kayn reached for the knob.

Kevin asserted, "No. Don't answer it, we don't know enough about any of this. What if it's someone coming for you?"

"They're not going to bother knocking when they come to

kill me," Kayn laughed as she stepped back, gesturing for him to go ahead and open it.

Peering through the peephole, he remarked, "There's nobody there."

That was weird. A shadow passed the curtains in the den. *Was someone in the bushes?* She heard tires in the gravel and looked out the peephole. *Matt was an innocent bystander. She wouldn't be able to live with herself if he got caught up in this.* "Matty's back from the gym," Kayn panicked. "I have to open it." Stepping in front of her, Kevin flung open the door.

Visibly startled, Matt blurted, "If you yell surprise, I'm going to kick your ass."

The fun mix of fear and fury in her brother's expression made her giggle. *Matty was getting sick and tired of feeling like the butt of everyone's jokes.*

Peering out the door, Kevin explained, "Sorry, Kayn saw a girl snooping around outside."

Every car that passed and every unexpected visitor was a threat in the back of her mind now. It felt like she was on borrowed time. It made sense. Her time was already up.

"Maybe, I should see if she's still out there?" Matt suggested, tossing his gym bag on top of everyone's shoes.

He couldn't. Kayn sighed "Don't worry about it. I'm just being paranoid." She changed the subject, "How was your workout?"

Grasping Matt's shoulder, Kevin suggested, "Let's make a fresh pot of coffee. What's new at University? Hook ups worth mentioning?" He not so inconspicuously urged him down the hall.

"Yes, to coffee. University is going well and there's been a few. Why are you acting weird?" Matt answered, understandably confused.

Kayn peeked out the peephole as they walked away.

"You, using the term hook up in a sentence bothers me immensely," Matt commented.

Her brother was touchy and paranoid but how could she blame him? She was all he had left. How was she going to leave him and vanish? He would look for her. He wouldn't just let her disappear. They had coffee, laughed and chatted about random things. Sixty minutes later they were still distracting her brother, whose one-track mind kept circling the conversation back to the girl creeping around outside. Matt left to take a private call.

"There's one of his hook ups now," Kevin whispered.

Deciding now was as good a time as any, she answered his inner dialogue's question about what she could do by showing him. *If you can hear my thoughts, nod.* He nodded and winked. *Lovely. Oh, she could only imagine the weird crap he'd heard listening to her inner dialogue. Awkward.*

He responded without words, '*I already know you're a weirdo it's all good.*'

Kayn stared at the salt and pepper shakers, speaking in her mind, *Watch this.* They shifted a bit. *That was rather anticlimactic, but I can do this. It works better when I'm angry.*

'*Okay, I made out with Lily,*' he thought. The condiments shot across the island, smashing on the floor. "I was joking. Shit," Kevin laughed as they leapt up to clean.

"You better be, I'm getting stronger," she countered as she swept.

"Wow," he commented. '*The ten-year-old in you must be freaking out right now.*' He put a dustpan of shattered glass in the garbage.

Matt walked in joking, "What are we wowing?"

Kayn fessed up, "I accidentally knocked the salt and pepper shakers off the island."

Her brother questioned, "Off the centre of it?" Matt

mumbled something under his breath as he peeked in the trash, looked up and probed, "How?"

"She's always been the accident prone one," Kevin bluntly responded.

They were both bad at lying and Matt wasn't buying it.

"I'm not frigging stupid." Matt said as his inner dialogue took a savagely dark stroll, *'If I catch you trying to have sex with her, I'll tie you naked to a tree in the trails and rub you down with raw meat.'*

Kevin choked, coffee spurted all over the table.

Shooting evil eye daggers with his eyes, Matt coldly stated, "The paper towel dispenser is empty. I'll only be gone for two seconds, don't get any ideas."

Kayn looked out the window and whispered, "This is getting awkward. Want to go for a run?"

"You'll do anything to avoid confrontation, won't you? An hour ago, there was a stranger lurking around out there," Kevin teased.

"True," she replied, feeling trapped within the confines of her house. *She needed to feel free even if it was only a mirage.*

He caressed her arm, vowing, "I promise it won't be like this forever."

She gave him a quick peck on the lips and whispered, "You can't promise me anything anymore, Kevin."

"Call it a feeling but I think we have amazing things ahead of us," he assured, playfully luring her closer.

There would be no college, no white picket fence with the three children playing in the yard as she'd always imagined. They may finish high school, but she wasn't going to hold her breath. How long would it be before they'd be forced to leave with Ankh? Where would they be in five years, in ten? So many questions and no answers. She looked into his eyes and smiled. *He'd been following her thoughts.*

"I will always want to be wherever you are, that much I can

promise. You're stuck with me, Brighton," he vowed, tenderly kissing her forehead.

"I'm sorry you got caught up in this mess," she whispered.

He lovingly teased, "It was my choice to stalk you outside your window last night."

"Yeah, while we're on the subject of stalking." *It was time to fess up about her creative observation before it got out some other way.* She came clean about astral projecting into his bedroom at night and listening in on his most intimate fantasies.

Several shades of scarlet, he chuckled, "I'm surprised you're not running for the hills."

"Why? It was just what you'd expect to hear in a teenage boy's mind," Kayn confessed as heat crept into her cheeks.

He took it to a whole other place by saying, "Do you think about the same things when you're alone?"

"Not even close," she fibbed red-faced.

"You lie," he provoked, enjoying watching her squirm. He whispered in her ear, "I bet your naughty thoughts put mine to shame. Did you hear anything intriguing in my fantasies? Tell me what you heard, don't leave out any details."

Jenkins barged in, announcing, "I ordered pizza and rented scary movies. Let's attempt to take this day back to a PG rating before your poor brother has a mental breakdown. I know it's probably his turn to have one, but I say we skip it."

They looked at each other and silently followed Jenkins back to the living room where they ate pizza and watched movies. It was late. Kevin opted to stay overnight. They secretly planned to sneak away once everyone went to sleep to finish what they'd started. It was the only thing they could control. It was still their choice.

17

BEING PSYCHIC 101

Psychic: From Greek word psukhikos of the soul or life

Sensitive to influences or forces of the nonphysical or supernatural.

(A person) sensitive to forces not recognized by natural laws.

That night Kevin remained on the couch downstairs, even though he wanted to sneak into her room and climb into bed with her, so badly it ached. Matt must have gone to the bathroom eighty times to make sure he was still there. *Maybe he should marry her? It was a crazy idea but what was the difference between being married and what he'd agreed to? He'd consented to be with her forever. Her, and a bunch of partially immortal strangers. He'd met Lily and that shirtless dick Frost. How many others were there? He knew nothing about what he'd signed up for. Nothing but the fact that Kayn had to go and wherever she was is where he wanted to be. They only kept him alive because they thought he had his Granny's gift.*

His physical transformation happened so fast, it was like he went to bed one night scraping the bottom of the gene pool and woke up on top. Out of nowhere, he sprouted up, acne cleared, and muscle appeared. Clay accused him of using steroids which was laughable. Their family doctor did all kinds of tests and in the end confirmed it was a growth spurt. He was a late bloomer. *He might have bought that diagnosis if he also wasn't seeing the dead and hearing other people's thoughts. What if he never got any Psychic abilities? What if he could only ever see the odd confused dead person wandering around in pyjamas and slippers? This Clan he'd joined probably expected him to be able to see the future, or something equally spectacular. At least seeing the dead opened his mind up enough to just go with the insane situation he'd accidentally become a part of. Kayn had done remarkably well, adapting to the craziness.*

He'd been staring at the ceiling tossing around a ball of anxiety for hours. Each time Matt came to check on him, he'd stifled his giggles and pretended to be asleep. He started laughing. *They'd both allowed themselves to be branded by a random shirtless guy in Kayn's bedroom. He'd checked out the meaning of Ankh online, even though he'd overheard Kayn's entire conversation with the overly flirtatious stranger. He'd always known he was meant to be with her. Wherever they ended up, they'd be alright if they were together. He was supposed to pick up Granny around lunchtime tomorrow, but he had lots of questions, and he might need to have a meltdown over the old school supernatural shit he'd accidentally signed up for. He'd go over there first thing, so they had a good chunk of time to talk. Kayn was coming over for dinner, he'd pick her up after that.* His eyelids grew heavy and he drifted off to sleep.

Kevin opened his eyes in a room he didn't recognize. *Where was he? Why was everything covered in plastic? He felt different.* Confused, he looked down. *He had boobs. He was wearing a nightgown. He'd always had strange dreams but never dreamt he was a girl before.* There was a friend mural on corkboard behind the plastic. *He couldn't make out the faces. Dreams usually had figurative meaning. Might as well go with it.* Tearing away the plastic covering the door, he opened it. He was assaulted by an odour so putrid it made him wretch. *What fresh hell was this? Good thing everything is covered in plastic, he was about to toss his cookies. There was another scent, campfire?* Kevin descended a cherry oak staircase. Everything was concealed by plastic but the wooden stairs and fancy railing. *This was a weird dream.* He glanced down to see if he was still a girl and poked a boob. *It felt real, not that he'd had much experience.* He started scrolling through the reasons why a house would be covered in plastic. *He didn't smell paint so that was out. They could be remodelling or fumigating for a rodent or bug infestation? That didn't explain the foul stench of rotting meat with a hint of campfire and egg. Was this a serial murderer's house?* He froze in place. *Maybe he could just go back to bed and avoid finding out?* He opted to go back. There was a solid wall at the top of the staircase. *No choices. Just like real life, avoidance wasn't an option.* A wave of nausea made him clutch the railing and swallow as a barf deterrent. *It was disgusting. So rancid.* He plugged his nose, only taking shallow breaths as he continued down into a plastic covered living room. *The putrid aroma was sickeningly vile.* He was bent over retching as something moved beneath plastic on the couch. *Oh, what in the hell was that? He felt weird. Holy crap. He was floating.* He drifted over to the couch. *There was nothing he could do about it.* Panicking, he tried air swimming away but didn't have a body anymore. *What was this shit?* Hovering above the squirming tarp, praying he was invisible, the plastic removed itself, revealing a decaying, twitching charbroiled cadaver. *Holy crap.* Floating over the body, he went through the wall and moved down a street with every house on fire. He soared higher until clouds surrounded him with white and nothing mattered. *'Kevin, wake up,' he heard through the nothing. It was impossible. There was nothing but white everywhere. No up or down, no left or right, it was just nothing. 'Kevin, wake up!' It was louder this time.* It was like being stuck in a spider web, dangling amidst infinity, unmovable... untouchable. He heard someone whisper, '*Kevin, you need to wake up.*' Feeling the warm moisture of breath through the web in which he dangled, he closed his eyes tightly and opened them again.

A decaying face pushed through the veil and whispered, "You die next."

Jolting awake, Kevin yelled, startling Jenkins reading a paper in the chair beside him.

"Morning sunshine, that was one hell of a nightmare," Jenkins remarked. Flipping the page, he continued reading.

"I should get home. Thanks for letting me stay last night. Tell Kayn I had to take off. I'll text her about dinner later," Kevin hastily commented, collecting his things. He took off. *He needed to see Granny Winnie. He needed to know if he was next.*

The sun was shining so bright it felt like mid-afternoon in the dead of summer. Kevin ran down the gravel path to his car. He got in and the interior was summer hot. *Strange for this time of day. He was going to his granny's house right now. She was always up early.* Driving away, the temperature became icy cold. He reached for the jacket, he'd tossed on the passenger side. Chloe was there. Swerving on the road, he quickly regained his sanity. *Next to him was the bloody deceased version of Chloe he'd found on the bathroom floor.* He took a deep breath of icy air. It had become so cold, he could see breath as he exhaled. He looked straight ahead. *Be cool, Kevin. Be cool. She was your friend.* Pulling over, he turned to her, saying, "Hi, Chloe."

"You can see me. This is an interesting development. Hi, Kevy," Chloe flirted.

It was the same melody filled voice dripping with innuendo, with her in this gruesome state, it didn't have the same effect. "I sure can, Chloe Bear. Is there something you need from me?" Kevin asked as sweetly as he would have if she were alive.

"Not stuttering over your words anymore? You've become a hottie," Chloe seduced, not reaching her target.

They sat together in his car by the side of the road. Kevin tapped his hands nervously on the steering wheel unable to look at her, summoning up courage, he said, "I saw what happened to you that day, I'm so sorry, Chloe."

"You know, I thought about you when I was dying. I'm not sure why, but I just wanted you to know, I did," Chloe confessed.

She'd been his friend. A slightly abusive friend but a friend none the less. Kevin's heart warmed as he turned to her, and there she was, *the captivatingly beautiful version of the girl he'd always been slightly obsessed with. She had not a scratch on her, wearing a white dress that reminded him of something the twins would have worn as children.* "You thought about me because you knew I loved you. I always cared. I was your friend," he quietly disclosed with a freshly aching heart. *She was really sitting beside him.*

"You were always my sister's. I knew you couldn't see past me, but you do now. I'm glad you finally realised it was her," Chloe admitted.

"I think a part of me always knew Kayn was the one, but a piece of me will always miss you, even though you spent most of your time torturing me," he teased and winked.

Touching his face, Chloe confessed, "I understand why you couldn't see her before you lost her. I never really saw you before this happened either. I see you now, Kevin. My sister is a lucky girl. Can I tell you a secret? You are the part of joining with Kayn, I'm looking forward to most."

His crimson face tingled where she'd caressed it. He sneezed three times.

"I'll be damned, that old hag was right," she chuckled, saucily.

"You know you're talking about my grandmother and I'm on my way to her house," Kevin scolded, grinning.

"Don't get pissy with me, Kevy. I'm kidding," Chloe toyed, innocently.

It was like he had her back. Wait, what in the hell am I thinking? Wanting her had been a force of habit for so long. Maybe, she still had the ability to make him want her? A carload of people drove by staring like he was insane. *Yup, I'm talking to an empty seat.* "So, you're coming to Granny's?" Kevin enquired, grinning. *This wasn't going to go well. His grandmother hated Chloe in a ridiculous way.*

"Nothing better to do, my social life has hit pause for obvious reasons," Chloe replied, shooting him a pageant smile.

Smiling, Kevin shook his head as they drove there in silence. Parking in the driveway, he sat for a minute, just breathing. *Was he allowed to talk to his grandmother about any of this?* He looked at the garden encircling her house and for the first time he noticed the stones. She'd been handing him stones his whole life, for every occasion. *It's your birthday, here's a bag of stones. Let me tell you what they're for. He'd pretended to listen most of the time. The next holiday would come, and once again, she'd hand him another bag of colourful stones. She was protecting him. He'd spent his whole life thinking his grandmother was completely insane.* He was still sitting in the car next to his sort of girlfriend's dead sister when his grandmother opened the front door with a solemn expression. *She already knew everything.* He got out and walked towards her. She placed her hand on his shoulder as she guided him inside. Chloe tried to follow but couldn't enter the house.

Granny looked at Chloe and said, "Sorry dear, no ghosts allowed. If I let one of you in, it'll turn into Grand Central Station around here."

That was reasonably polite considering the volatile nature of their relationship when Chloe was alive. She'd acted like it was no big deal that he drove up with the ghost of his girlfriend's dead twin sister in his car. Granny Winnie shut the door in Chloe's face with a giant fake smile. *There it was.* He released the chuckle he'd been holding back. *Those two always had a strange love-hate relation-*

ship. In all honesty it was mostly hate. He snapped back to the conversation he needed to have with his grandmother.

"I've prepared an area for us to speak freely," she explained, signalling him into a circle of stones and what looked like table salt. His grandmother took out a deck of tarot cards and flipped five over as she spoke, "I know everything, let's just cut to the chase. You need to let your abilities guide your actions. In the beginning, it can be difficult to just let go. Being Psychic is like blindly jumping from a plane. You feel like you have a parachute on, but you have no idea if it will open. Usually, a Psychic has years to develop skills, but you don't. You need to surrender to them, or you stand no chance of seeing your next birthday."

She'd always been a little blunt but that was brutal.

Granny removed his glove and turned his hand to look at his symbol. Visibly relieved, she sighed, "Thank God for, Kayn. At least you're protected by a decent Clan." She ran her fingers over his symbol, saying, "Multiple Clan's Oracles have been sniffing around disrupting my Circle's energy." Granny Winnie poured a tea for herself. "If you have something else you need to discuss, best say it. If a grain of salt shifts, we'll have eavesdroppers." Knowledge stirred in his grandmother's eyes.

She knew he had more to say. Kevin explained his dream, "I had a nightmare. A decomposing corpse told me, I die next."

"We are all going to die, Kevin," While stroking his hand, she whispered, "Trust in your Clan. This symbol prohibits you from passing through the hall of souls."

"So, I'm going to die?" He whispered back with his heart racing.

"Hasn't this been explained? Death is a human word, a term that means nothing in the grand scheme of things. Let me clear things up. The brand on your hand is the symbol of Ankh. You are now a Psychic for Ankh, which is why you need your abilities to ripen quickly. You need not fear death for you are now a member of a Clan with Healers. There will be someone to bring you back from whatever fate befalls you. I've known the date of my mortal demise for over thirty years. I even know the graphic details of how I die. I'm not afraid. I go on to do great things after my death. My demise is only the beginning of a new stage in my existence."

He was having a hard time with the confirmation of his death but was open to the possibility that dying wasn't the end. It was strange that out of everything, immortality was the most difficult concept to grasp.

"The gifted rarely make it through childhood without being slated for Correction. The young do not know they need to hide. Power is a seductive playmate for a child. It's an honour to be taken into one of the three Clans. You'll have an opportunity to save many Second-Tier in the future. Third-Tier have been erasing tainted family lines for a thousand years to stop humanity from evolving. If a Second-Tier soul escapes Correction without the protection of Tri-Clan, they can be taken by the Legion of Abaddon."

"What's Abaddon?" Kevin questioned, snatching a cookie.

"Demons," Granny replied, shifting a tray of snacks over.

Meeting his grandmother's eyes, he clarified, "Monsters."

"Monsters works," the elderly woman answered, smiling. "At the age of eighteen, your soul is sealed to your Clan. Until then, avoid being stolen by Abaddon while training for what comes next. Most Tri-Clan don't reach their full potential until Testing. As in all things, there's a test at the end. I know it's a lot to take in."

"That's an understatement," Kevin mumbled.

Smiling, Granny divulged, "Kayn's a special case. Once every thousand years, a spiritual mix-up occurs creating a Conduit. If Kayn successfully merges with her deceased twin, she'll become a receiving vessel for abilities. She must remain with Clan Ankh."

"Won't you get in trouble for telling me this?" Kevin asked.

"We're protected in this circle. Psychics share rules with new physics. If anyone ever asks, I was telling you the rules," Granny answered softly. "There's something else, I'm willing my abilities to you today." Taking off her necklace with multicoloured stones in sterling silver setting, Granny rose from her chair and came over to her grandson, holding the amulet in her outstretched hand. "Never take it off, not even to shower."

"No, I can't. You need your abilities," he rationalized, shaking his head in disbelief. *It felt like she was saying goodbye.* Tearing up, Kevin took the necklace she'd always worn from her trembling hands.

"I keep my gifts. The amulet will make you the receiver of my abilities when I pass," she explained with peaceful acceptance. "Pay attention now, child. You have a lot to learn and I have little time to teach you. A Psychic knows all but tells some. Always hold back, you'll discover people don't really want to know the bad things. If you reveal too much to a mortal, you may cause a Correction. Always keep that in the back of your mind."

"I will," Kevin vowed.

Cupping his chin, forcing him to look into her eyes, Granny whispered, "You are the tether keeping all that is Kayn closer to the surface. I know you don't want to risk losing her, but souls are meant to be whole. They must combine. Kayn will need the strength of both good and evil. The twins are like opposite ends of a battery. Kayn receives good and Chloe receives evil."

"Chloe isn't evil Granny, she's complicated," Kevin defended his lifelong obsession. *She was sitting in the car waiting for him.*

"Evil is a strong word. Chloe's half is particularly dark, whereas Kayn's has always been lighter. You'll understand soon enough. You'll know who to trust. If you end up with even half of my abilities, you'll be an asset to a Clan." They embraced and without further conversation, she kicked the circle aside and strolled out the front door like a badass.

He grinned as he followed. *This was going to be a fun drive.*

"Are you going to make me sit in the backseat young lady?" Granny Winnie asked sweetly.

"Oh, all right," Chloe complained. She appeared in the back seat, pouting.

Kevin glanced in the rear-view mirror as Chloe's fake pout turned upwards into a grin. Smiling, she toyed, "Are we picking up, Kayn?"

"Actually, I'm dropping you two off at my parent's place. You can chat about the afterlife while I go get, Kayn," Kevin revealed, feeling guilty about the emotional conversation he'd had with his girlfriend's deceased sister. *She'd told him she was looking forward to being with him. This situation was so messed up. He didn't want to spring the presence of Chloe on Kayn at a family dinner. He needed to tell her about their conversation, it felt dishonest not to.* "So, I'll drop you guys off."

"I guess so, but only if she promises to be nice to me," Chloe accused, pointing a menacing finger at Granny Winnie.

"Granny, can you please attempt to be nice to Chloe?" Kevin questioned, raising his brows.

"I'm always nice," Granny Winnie curtly responded, glaring at Chloe.

"Like hell you are, old bat," Chloe huffed, folding her arms. She scowled at the feisty elderly lady.

"You are dead. Listen hard, you hussy. Unless you want silent treatment from the one person capable of breaking up your time in limbo, respect the elderly," Granny retaliated, oozing sarcasm.

"Takes one to know one, you menthol reeking, snaggle-toothed, aging cougar," Chloe slammed back.

He had their relationship all wrong. They liked each other. They were both smiling. They'd been apart long enough to miss their verbal warfare. Kevin pulled up at his parents' house and advised, "Granny, you are aware nobody else can see her. I'd simmer the hostility down a notch if you don't feel like being booked into the psych ward." Pointing at Chloe, he warned, "There are ways to make you wait outside if you're incapable of behaving." Getting out, he politely opened granny's door.

"I'll behave" Granny promised, with a far from innocent grin.

Kevin stood there waiting for Chloe to go into the house, but she wasn't budging. "Come on, get out of the car, Chloe. You're not coming with me," he urged.

"Never threaten me, Kevin," Chloe sulked with arms folded, not budging an inch.

Oh, come on. "I'm sorry. Now, please get out of the car," Kevin persisted maintaining his patience.

"Aren't you going to open my door?" Chloe hinted.

"Seriously?" Kevin sighed, opening her door. She got out. He teased, "I'd get in there before Granny Winnie surrounds the house with salt."

With her infamous pageant smile, Chloe exclaimed, "Go get our Candy Kayn. I'm looking forward to this. Even if I only get to watch, it's going to be fun being a fly on the wall for one of these family dinners I was never invited to."

"I never thought you'd come," Kevin stated with a pang of guilt.

Chloe flippantly admitted, "Probably not."

He watched her flounce to his house, walking through the closed door. "Bitch," Kevin chuckled, shaking his head at her for making him open the door. *He'd missed her. It wasn't just Siren Chloe he missed, it was every fake smiling inch of her. She'd always been a constant in his life.* He giggled the entire drive to Kayn's house. *Ghost or not, Chloe would go out of her way to piss off Granny Winnie. So, he was a Psychic now. A dead people seeing, scary dreaming, Psychic. Wonderful.* He parked behind a police car with its engine idling and trudged up the rocky path to the door thinking, *they really should pave this.*

A spiffed-up Jenkins in uniform, answered his first knock, "Hey, Kevy. I'm off to work, take care of our girl." He patted his shoulder as he passed and jogged to his partner's car.

Sure, we're just going to have dinner with my Psychic grandmother and Kayn's dead twin sister, who by the way, looks fantastic. Kevin replied, "Always," as he went in and shut the door. Looking upstairs, he yelled for the Brighton siblings, "Are you guys ready?"

IT WAS AN UNUSUAL AFTERNOON for Kayn. She'd received a few texts from Jesse. *She'd forgotten to clarify the situation. She was in a relationship with Kevin. He wasn't stupid though. He'd seen them together. Boys never bothered to chase her in the past, it was flattering.* Putting on a touch of sparkling lip gloss, she posed in the mirror. *Was it wrong to want to feel desirable? She'd always been strong and funny. Why couldn't she be a little bit of everything?* She heard Kevin calling and hollered, "We're alone! Matt's already at your house!" Beaming, she raced downstairs and leapt into his arms, wrapping her legs around his waist as they kissed.

Cupping her rear, Kevin provoked, "If we didn't have the family dinner from hell waiting for us, I'd throw you over my shoulder and take you upstairs."

She wanted to skip dinner so bad. Releasing her thigh's grip, her feet hit the floor. She locked up and they strolled to his car hand in hand.

Opening her door, Kevin spilled his guts, "Long story short, I had a bad nightmare where a burnt, decomposing guy told me I was going to die next, followed by a strange sexy car ride with your dead sister. She came to Granny Winnie's house where I was given information about being a Psychic and a few warnings. Apparently, you're a Conduit. We'll look it up later. Granny and Chloe were arguing in the car all the way to my parents' house. I dropped them off together. So, I'm sure they're bickering at each other. My family can only hear one side of the conversation. They probably think Granny's gone mad." Kevin took a deep breath, awaiting her response.

Barely flinching during his wild confession, she commented, "You're owning the Psychic thing, congratulations."

"Yayyy, for me," Kevin grumbled. He started the engine and pulled away from the curb.

With a hand on his leg, Kayn probed, "How does she look?"

"At first, she looked like an escapee from, The Night of the Living Dead. When I warmed up to her, she got hot and flirty like she was when she was alive," he divulged.

Grinning, Kayn baited, "Does my dead sister still make you horny, Kevin?"

"Sadly, yes," Kevin chuckled. "Her voodoo powers are less effective when she looks like a corpse. Once she changed into hot Chloe, it was back on."

"Necrophilia is where I draw the line of understanding, just putting that out there," Kayn teased, squeezing his knee.

Pulling up in front of his house, Kevin admitted, "I have a bad feeling about this."

Hearing granny's meltdown as they got out, they sprinted to the door. *Granny was openly arguing with Chloe who no one else could see.*

Granny grabbed a bun off the table and pitched it at an empty seat, "You smelly little wench, you stink like a thousand farts!"

Wow, Kayn thought. Kevin's family was trying to ignore their certifiable grandmother. *She was drinking red wine. Good cover. She was an old drunk lady, instead of just insane.*

Granny shrieked, "Ghosts smell like sulphur, like a foul gassy fart, a gross nasty smelly cheese and feet fart!"

Leaning over, Clay whispered to Kevin, "How drunk was she when you dropped her off? We could have used a heads up."

"Sorry, Bro. She was shit-faced when I got there. I wasn't sure what to do," Kevin innocently replied.

"She hasn't been this drunk in years. She's swearing at people who aren't even there," Kevin's mom whispered, concerned.

Recalling stories of Granny's drunken rants, Kayn grinned. *She'd never been a drunk, only tired of being accosted by spirits.* Kayn glanced at Kevin. *If his family caught on, they'd have to be Corrected just like hers. She could hear Chloe's voice, but couldn't see her.* Standing up, Kayn walked around the table and sat in the empty seat Chloe was occupying.

Kevin whispered in his grandmother's ear, "If you let people think you're wasted, you can say anything you want, smart."

Granny winked and vehemently hissed, "I'm not drunk, I'm being harassed by dead people. Smelly, bitchy, dead people." A bun smoked Granny in the forehead from out of nowhere. She picked up a retaliatory bun as she got up, screeching, "Show yourself, skanky whore bag!"

Eyes widened like saucers as the room erupted with laughter. Clay yelled, "She's over here!" He pointed at Matt.

Granny wound up and rifled a bun right at Matt's head as he looked down at his plate. *Poor Matty was trying to pretend that everyone hadn't gone nutty at the Smith house.*

His sense of humour sparked when the bun hit him, bounced off and knocked over his wine. "That's it, Granny. It's on." Matt declared, winging a bun at the elderly woman.

Snapping back to reality, Granny Winnie ominously stated, "Oh yes, young man. It's on." She picked up a handful of brussel sprouts and threw them across the table at him. Matt ducked and they landed on Kevin's Dad's dinner plate, spilling his wine.

Mr. Smith leapt to his feet to avoid getting it on his lap. He grinned, menacingly vowing, "That is it, Winnie. You spilled my wine. I've been dying to do this for years." Grabbing a handful of the food off his plate, he launched it at his mother-in-law.

Practically cackling, Granny picked up a bowl of peas and hurled them at Kayn, who was almost peeing herself laughing. She ducked, they missed her, and peas rained on Kevin's mom. The table erupted into a laughing drunken food fight.

After the cleanup from their impromptu family food battle, Kevin and Kayn went up to his room. *She hadn't been able to see Chloe, but she'd been able to hear her. Why was that? She'd seen her sister more than once. She'd even touched her in the mirror.* Strolling in, she sat down on his bed as he closed his bedroom door.

Chloe's voice sang, "How much fun was that?"

"Why can't I see her?" Kayn asked in the direction of her twin's voice, longing for a glimpse.

"If I'd known how much fun these family dinners were, I would have come to one years ago," Chloe's voice ribbed.

Looking at Kayn, then at the empty space, Kevin said, "I'm not sure how you're supposed to do this, but you have to join."

Chloe's voice sighed, "I've been trying, it doesn't stick."

Kayn recalled that first kiss. *Even though she'd only been a fly on the wall in her body at the time, she remembered it.* She glanced at Kevin, saying, "When she took my body out for a spin, I was along for the ride."

"I've jumped into her a bunch of times, it never lasts longer than a few minutes," Chloe explained.

Matt stuck his head in, warning, "We're leaving. I want to wash my car before it's too dark."

"Give me a minute," Kayn answered, smiling.

Grinning, her brother harassed, "There's no time for funny business, I'll be waiting in the car." Matt closed the door.

Kayn hugged Kevin, whispering, "I'll see you tomorrow." *It felt weird knowing her sister was there watching her do it.*

"You couldn't keep me away if you tried," Kevin whispered in her ear.

"Are you sure about that? I'm going to be Batman powerful someday," Kayn baited, grinning.

"What if you're only SpongeBob square pants powerful?" Kevin sparred, with his arms around her.

"That is pretty powerful," Kayn gasped, giving him a peck on the lips before stepping away. *She should take off before Matt starts honking.*

Chloe's voice groaned, "You two may very well be the geekiest people on the planet."

Laughing, Kayn teased her invisible twin, "Well, it's always been my long-term goal."

Chloe blurted, "What in the hell is that?"

Kevin started laughing. Shaking his head, staring at his bed. Curious, Kayn asked, "What's she doing?"

Smiling, he replied, "She's lounged on my bed staring at the poster on the ceiling."

Walking her out, they embraced at the door. Kayn kissed his cheek, whispering, "I guess being alone isn't in the cards, is it?"

He nuzzled her neck and assured, "If Matt wasn't waiting in the car and your dead sister wasn't sitting on my bed, you'd be in so much trouble."

Chloe's voice chimed in, "She's hot, even with a moustache. Does my sister know that you're into dudes?"

Kevin spun around, saying, "Your sister did that to my poster. It was a joke, you turkey."

"Well, I prefer turkey over bitch," Chloe taunted.

Wincing, he commented, "Sorry, you heard that."

"I'm sort of a bitch, I can give you that one," her twin's voice admitted.

Beside her, Chloe suggested, "Let's drive grandma home, I think she wants a sleepover tonight."

It was like a tennis match of voices with one invisible player. Shaking her head, Kayn giggled. *She wanted to see her so badly.*

"You can't get into her house," Kevin taunted, grinning.

"Darling, there's no need to go inside. I'm going to ring her phone and set off car alarms in her neighbourhood all night," her devious sibling playfully countered.

Kevin looked at air, commenting, "At least she owns it."

They went downstairs. Grinning, Kayn sang, "Good luck, Smith. See you tomorrow." Matt started honking. She waved and ran to the car.

18

THERE'S SOMETHING ABOUT LILY

*T*he new girl's brother washing his car was distracting enough to forget why she came. *He was bending over, putting on a show. He knew she was there. Brazenly cocky mortal men intrigued her.* Waiting for the sun-bronzed hottie to acknowledge her presence before trying to walk by she saw his face. Lily's heart skipped a beat. *It was him.* Continuing the facade, shirtless Matt drenched himself in water. Mesmerised, the raven-haired seductress, couldn't move. *Here he was again, tormenting her with his existence. It was 1986 the last time she laid eyes on him. His name was Paul. She was wearing a blue satin dress with puffy shoulders. "The Glory of Love" was playing as they danced, and it was nothing less than perfect. Her flings with Sam's reincarnation, always ended in one of two ways, either he'd try to kill her or be killed because of her.*

"Hey," Matt called out. "Are you looking for Kayn?"

"Yes, I am," Lily choked out, unable to breathe. Her heart was always secretly waiting for him. It throbbed with anticipation as she made her way up the gravel driveway towards the karmic joke following her across time. *His brain was probably reeling through memories, trying to figure out how he knew her. This was going to hurt like hell. She wanted to walk away and save herself the pain, but this time it wasn't an option. He was a new Ankh's brother, his days were numbered. Fate was a sick twisted foe.* The smile she adored lured her in. *It was really him after all these years.*

"The door's unlocked, her bedroom is upstairs," he directed, gesturing to the door.

Smiling politely, Lily brushed by him, saying, "Thanks." She opened the door. Went in and took off her shoes. *It's a good thing she wasn't coming to kill her.*

Dropping his sponge in a bucket, Matt followed the insanely gorgeous girl inside. He strolled to the kitchen where Jenkins was reading, saying, "Kayn's new friend is smoking hot."

"Gross," Jenkins replied from behind his newspaper.

Taking an apple from the fruit bowl, Matt clarified, "I'm just saying, she's pretty."

Peering out, Jenkins commented, "Once again, Romeo. So gross."

"I wouldn't try to date her," Matt deflected. Tossing his apple core in the garbage, he wiped his hands on his shorts.

Jenkins laid his newspaper down and laughed, "Now, I'm too curious to keep reading. Are they friends or did you send up a hot stranger?"

"You'll get it when you see her," Matt countered.

"Hot people can be murderers too, Mathew. I'd better make

sure it's a wanted visitor." Walking by with a coffee in each hand, Jenkins warned, "So we're clear, I'll arrest you if she's underage."

Grinning, Matt sparred "I'm only a couple of years older and I'm not a player anymore. She should be so lucky."

Jenkins laughed, "Matthew Brighton, that neon sign on your forehead flashing player is part of your charm." He wandered out, saying, "I'll go check out the girl confusing your morality."

"Age is but a number," Matt called after him.

"Almost four years, my philandering friend," Jenkins replied as he disappeared at the end of the hall.

KAYN WAS ATTEMPTING TO DO HOMEWORK. *Attempting, being the operative word. She wasn't Math's biggest fan. Crap.* She grabbed liquid paper to clean up the mess. Her door opened. Cross-legged on her bed, chewing on a pen, Kayn looked up expecting Jenkins or Matt. *It was that bitch, Lily.*

"Hi," Lily said, closing the door. "You know why I'm here."

Kayn cracked a grin, replying, "I'm flattered but I sort of have a boyfriend."

"Hold that thought," Lily whispered. She took stones out of her backpack and made a circle around the room, then spoke words in another language, "Ας μην υπάρχει σιωπή εκτός του κύκλου."

"What does it mean?" Kayn asked, recognising the language.

"It's Greek for, let there be silence outside of this circle," the gorgeous raven-haired immortal answered as she sat on Chloe's bed, patting the spot beside her. "My ability is like your sister's. If I wanted you to switch teams, you would," Lily toyed, tugging a fingerless glove off, she showed Kayn the symbol of Ankh on her palm.

"If we're on the same side, why have you been such a horrific bitch?" Kayn stated, opting to stay on her own bed.

Caught off guard by her slam, Lily laughed, "I deserved that. Mental sparring matches aside, I'm here to give you a quick refresher. There are three Clans of half-breed immortals on earth, Ankh, Trinity, and Triad. Each Clan contains breeds of Warriors, Healers and Psychics. We train new Tri-Clan for Testing and do dirty work for Third-Tier. Other Clans and soul-eating demons from the Legion of Abaddon will be coming, it's open season on your soul until your eighteenth birthday."

Flopping onto a mountain of stuffed animals, Kayn sighed. *She wasn't a Warrior, a Psychic, or a Healer, this was way too crazy. Wait a minute, did she just say Demons?* Gazing at the stucco hills and mountains on her ceiling, she commented, "Soul-eating demons, seriously?"

Smiling, Lily repeated, "Seriously."

Holding a stuffed animal, Kayn confessed, "I avoid groups of people at school. I'm not big on confrontation. I eat lunch in a bathroom stall to avoid eating in front of anyone. I'm not a spirit world policing kind of girl."

Meeting her eyes, Lily clarified her situation, "No, you used to avoid confrontation. You used to hide in the bathroom stalls to eat your lunch. That's not who you are anymore. We all have the ability to be strong when there is no other choice."

She was about to object when Lily launched a stapler at her. Kayn swung her hand and blocked it, using nothing but instinct. It didn't even come close to touching her.

Smiling, Lily said, "We are always so much stronger than we believe ourselves to be."

Kayn's door opened. Jenkins brought in coffee, announcing, "It's decaffeinated because it's almost eight o'clock. I assumed neither of you wanted to be up all night." He excused himself, closing the bedroom door.

After a pause, Lily continued, "You'll meet more of us at school on Monday. We'll need a few hours afterschool to get started. Don't worry you'll be home before dinner."

"Uh, huh," Kayn mumbled, losing her attitude somewhere around soul-eating demons.

"We're staying at the house behind yours through the trails. It's discreet, yet close enough to get to you quickly," Lily explained.

"What happened to the man living there?" Kayn questioned, remembering how close he was to her that night.

"He's a tad brainwashed," Lily replied, smiling.

"Let me get this straight. You've stolen my neighbour's house with him still inside of it, so you can teach me how to defend myself there. Can't we do it in my room?" Kayn enquired.

The stunning immortal teased, "He has a nice sized basement. I'm guessing your brother may notice a half dozen glowing rose quartz chambers in your bedroom?"

Hesitant, Kayn asked, "What are the tombs for again?"

Giving Kayn's knee a friendly squeeze, Lily said, "They are for healing and travelling purposes. We aren't going to make you sleep in one at night. None of us are Vampires."

None of us are Vampires. Kayn replied, "Right, good to know." *Mental note, no Vampires in Ankh.* "I'll see you at school," she confirmed. *How was this her life?*

"No worries, we're close by. Don't make plans afterschool. See you Monday," Lily chimed, waving as she left her room.

It felt like she was going to find out she was on a hidden camera show. She heard Lily saying goodnight to her brother and Jenkins. The door closed. Putting on pyjamas, Kayn slipped on her fluffy robe and wandered downstairs for a snack. *She felt like eating everything in the house. Scratch that, she planned to eat every-*

thing in the house. Jenkins left a drink on the island. She smelled it, took a swig and spat it out. *Warm pop and alcohol, gross.* Grabbing a box of Triscuits and a tub of cream cheese, she wandered back upstairs. Getting into bed, she turned on the T.V. and began flipping through the channels. A show popped up with an exorcism. She groaned, "Not a chance." She switched the channel. One came on about aliens. She commentated, "Not likely." She farted, releasing one into the wild. Giggling as she flicked channels, she found a superhero show. *The storyline hit a little too close to home. She suspected the Clan's version of immortality wouldn't be glamorous. There wouldn't be jets or fancy cars involved. No bat mobile for her.* Watching reruns of friends, she ate a tub of cream cheese with an entire box of Triscuits while sprawling on her bed. *She felt like a partially sedated moose. She was going to be sick. She had a cream cheese and Triscuit food baby.* Rubbing her overstuffed tummy, she whispered, "I shall name you heartburn." Her phone vibrated. She read Kevin's text. '*I tried astral projection. I just had the chance to see what you do when you are alone. It wasn't as sexy as I imagined it.*' Laughing, she texted back. *You should come over and rub my food baby.*

He texted back, '*My favourite part of your evening was when you farted and laughed at yourself, it was so damn hot.*'

She recalled doing it and laughed harder.

19

TRAINING KAYN

Immortality: the ability to live forever.

Kayn awoke Monday morning with her senses on overload. She could smell coffee brewing downstairs, mixed with the scent of Jenkins' aftershave. He was making bacon for breakfast. She heard the whispering of voices and the ringing of a phone. Kayn could make out parts of their conversation. Her senses had been heightened before, but today it was insanely overwhelming.

It didn't get much better when she arrived at school. *It was too much.* The hustle and bustle of the hallways as her peers pushed past frayed her nerve endings. She watched for unknown faces in the crowd. The hallway was thick with pungent scents. A guy began spraying cologne on himself at his locker; she fought the urge to tackle him and beat him senseless with the aerosol can. It would be easy to attack her while overwhelmed by the sensory confusion caused by this many people in an enclosed space. She scanned the crowd. *It was too public. This other life was a secret. Good or evil, no one could risk being exposed.* Kayn took a deep breath, trying to calm her racing pulse. The intercom screeched. She covered her ears and doubled over. The voice was calling someone to the office.

She felt a hand on her shoulder and heard Kevin's soothing whisper, "You're obviously having the morning, I'm having. Just breathe. Stand up straight and breathe." He slipped his fingers through hers, squeezed her hand and assured, "I'll always have your back. You are not alone in this anymore. We can do this together." He kissed her cheek, laughed and said, "But I do have to leave you. I need to use the bathroom. I'll meet you in class."

The noises in her mind calmed. "Wait a second," Kayn flirted. Wrapping her arms around his neck, she kissed him square on the lips in public. They heard the hushed thoughts of at least ten passing people, *I knew it.* She couldn't help but smile as he raced down the hall away from her. *He had told her she wasn't alone and then taken off. It was kind of cute and so the comic relief she needed.* Kayn remained by the lockers, attempting to pick a posse of immortals out of a crowd. *It was a little funny. Why did she have a feeling this was going to be a total gong show?* Kayn observed the herd of students as they surged down the hall. *Not an out of place Xena warrior princess looking girl in the bunch.* She made her way to her first class, found her desk and bent down to pull out her books. Fumbling with her zipper, she noticed a pair of shoes by her bag.

"Mind if I sit next to you?" The shoes toyed with an all too familiar tone oozing raw sexuality.

Lovely. Kayn looked up, her eyes following the curve of his jeans to his muscular thighs. *It was her half-naked bedroom visitor. The fully clothed version of Frost wasn't less intoxicating.*

"Hi stranger, remember me?" Frost whispered with a dimpled smile as he leaned over to do up her bag. "You should be more careful. If you leave the zipper undone, you might lose something important."

Everything he said sounded naughty. His hand barely grazed hers and an electrifying jolt of pleasure scrambled her common sense. Her throat was so dry, she could barely swallow. *Inconspicuous my ass.* Kayn blinked a few times, gave her sexy pheromone dumb head a shake and sat up in her seat. *Talk about sending in the big guns.* Her eyes were drawn to his tanned muscular arms straining against his shirt. *Logically knowing it was his ability, hadn't altered her reaction a speck.* She stealthily looked around, even her teacher's cheeks were flaming red from his raw sensual vibe. *Great. Every female in a ten-mile radius was totally sidetracked. Scratch that, literally everyone. How in the hell was he passing for a guy in high school? Frost looked like he was in his midtwenties.* She heard his internal dialogue, "*Who is going to call me out frog sticker girl? Certainly, none of these ladies.*"

Lily arrived and chimed in, "So sorry I'm late." She scooted into her seat.

The teacher hadn't even taken attendance. She was as flustered as every other girl and boy in the room. *He was good.*

Kayn heard Lily's voice in her head, '*Tone it down, Frost.*'

'*I'll behave,*' her deviously naughty classmate answered using only his mind.

This was really happening. They didn't need to speak aloud to each other. Her mind scrolled a list of her childhood fears. *Her parents always assured her monsters weren't real and they'd been violently murdered by a mortal monster on a normal afternoon. The monster hadn't come for her during the night as she'd imagined it would when she was very small. Those were the childhood rules. You only ever had to be afraid of monsters in the dark. Now that Kayn was grown up, she understood anyone could be a monster on the inside. Hiding in plain sight would be the easiest thing to do. Would she know a monster if she saw one? She was amped up and more than a little aroused. It was the proximity of the sexy supernatural pool boy seated directly in front of her.* Kayn looked for Kevin. *He hadn't come back from the bathroom.* As she stared at his empty seat, the fear of losing him stifled her reaction to the immortal's ability. The door opened and in walked Kevin. *What had he been up to?*

"Glad you could find the time to join us, Mr. Smith," the teacher piped in.

"Sorry. Running behind this morning," he mumbled, hauling books out of his bag. Noticing the immortals, Kevin shot a welcoming smile in their direction.

He was strangely casual about their appearance. He must have known they would be here too. She looked at her paper and pretended to pay attention until the bell rang at the end of first period. Everyone got up and exited the classroom in a rush except for a pack of girls lingering in the doorway waiting to greet Frost.

"It sucks to be me," Frost sighed. With an arrogant swagger, he sauntered over to his mesmerised groupies.

Lily walked up to Kayn, asking, "Have you met the others yet? Did anyone come and introduce themselves?"

"Besides you two, I haven't even seen anyone new," Kayn answered, watching Frost surrounded by his fawning harem. She scowled as he wandered away with his arms around girls. *What an idiot.* Looking at Lily, Kayn said, "Shouldn't Romeo turn down his mojo if he's trying to fly under the radar?"

"He's having fun. He gets pissy when I mess with his ability to sleep his way through the phone book. Don't even get me started on his naughty behaviour overseas. It's just who he is. We try to ignore it," Lily casually responded.

Kevin walked up, "Hey ladies."

He kissed her on the lips. It made her smile. *He'd kissed her in front of Lily.*

"Let's go find, Lexy. I know where she is," Lily sighed. They made their way to the office. Sure enough, a redhead wearing the most inappropriate outfit ever created was slumped on the bench outside the principal's office picking at her cherry red nails.

"Seriously, you're in trouble already? Thanks for playing nice with the principal by sitting here," The raven-haired temptress teased as they approached.

With a hint of sultry southern accent, Lexy declared, "A bitch mocked my boots. You know how much I love these boots."

Kayn looked at Lexy's mile-long legs and short shorts with fire engine red boots. *Wow. Way to be inconspicuous. She could've picked these three out of a crowd in two minutes flat.*

"Did you forget the conversation we had about lying low and blending in?" Lily ribbed. She turned and assured, "This will only take a second."

After a short conversation with an extremely understanding authority figure, they wanted to point out the Clan member they hadn't met. While searching halls of beige lockers and clicking footsteps, Lily reprimanded the feisty immortal. *Lexy slammed a girl's head into a locker for sarcastically saying, nice boots. Never piss her off.* Skateboarders walked by playfully shoving each other. A blonde guy with unkempt hair grinned and waved.

Smiling Lily declared, "That would be Grey. He's an acquired taste. You'll see him after school. We have it worked out so one of us is in each of your classes. Don't even go to the washroom alone from this moment on," Lily firmly decreed.

No privacy, check. The bell rang, Kayn rushed to her next class with Lexy.

Standing next to her crimson-haired companion's desk, their teacher announced, "For future reference short shorts are only allowed if you're wearing tights."

"I'm sorry, I had leggings on, they ripped. It won't happen again," Lexy vowed. The crimson-maned rage grenade crossed her legs as everyone ogled her.

That was polite. What would it feel like to be jaw-droppingly hot?

Maybe all hot people were mean? She's murdered people. She had a serial killer vibe. Her pencil fell off her desk. She reached to pick it up and it rolled away like someone kicked it. A girl in the next row of desks handed it to her. Smiling, Kayn said, "Thanks." It fell off her desk. *Oh, come on.*

Her teacher picked it up, enquiring, "Having a problem?"

"Sorry, just clumsy," Kayn responded as it was passed to her. *I'm painfully dorky.* Her pencil started rolling, she stopped it and turned around. Her immortal babysitter grinned. *Lexy was messing with her. Oh, crap, her inner commentary had been rolling that whole time. Oh, no. Guess they weren't going to be friends for a while.*

She opted out of running the track at lunch. *There was no point in reviving routines.* Kayn shared fries with Kevin, chatting about normal things while Frost and Lily entertained admirers. Lexy was at the next table playing with her phone, oozing hostility. Whenever anyone attempted to speak to her, Lexy air swatted them away, curtly warning, "Flee."

After a few classes, school ended with the shrill ring of the final bell. Kevin was waiting outside of her classroom. He grabbed her bag and grinned as he chucked it over his shoulder. They walked out to his car passing Jesse and his friends at the main doors. She waved as they strolled by. *She felt guilty about not answering Jesses' message with sorry she was dating Kevin. She'd been side-tracked by craziness. It felt stupid to send it now.* They crossed the street. When they reached his car, Kevin dropped the bags and silenced her conscience with a slow passionate kiss. As their lips parted, Kayn breathlessly baited, "What was that for?" Out of the corner of her eye she noticed Jesse trying not to watch. *Kevin was making the status of their relationship clear.*

"Just for being you," Kevin teased, smiling.

Calling bullshit in her mind, Kayn allowed him to get away with the fib. *He was jealous. It was cute.*

He opened the car door, gallantly announcing, "Your chariot awaits."

Kayn slipped into the front. The backdoor opened, three of the four immortals squeezed in. *She hadn't even seen them coming.*

"Okay chariot driver, you two can make out later. It's training time," Lily declared.

Leaning forward, Lexy explained, "We have to get started. You two have a lot to learn."

"Where are we off to?" Kevin sighed as he put the key in the ignition.

Applying cherry red lipstick in a tiny rhinestone mirror, Lexy replied, "We're going to our house. You're going to love this."

Frost flirted with empty space, "Hope I'm not making you uncomfortable sweetheart. Wow, you two are identical."

Her deceased twin must be sitting there. Kayn turned to her sister's voice, "Hi Chloe. I wish I could see you."

"You two need to combine before something happens. You're not strong enough alone," Lily commented as she rifled through her purse.

"I've been trying," Chloe responded.

"Keep it up. I'm sure you'd rather be a solid person instead of an inconsequential ghost being squished by a stranger in the backseat," Frost taunted.

"It's not like I've never been squished by a stranger in a backseat before," Chloe sexily countered.

Grinning, Frost flirtatiously whispered, "You must be the naughty half, it's certainly a pleasure to meet you."

Kayn rolled her eyes. She glanced back, assuring, "I've already agreed to this. There isn't a choice to be made here, it's done."

Chloe's voice explained, "I've been trying, it only lasts a few minutes. I tried again this morning, but it's not working at all."

Kayn answered her sister's voice, "If I'm stopping you from joining with me, I have no idea how I'm doing it."

They arrived at the porch smoking guy's house, got out and strolled to the door, everyone entered except for Chloe. She was stuck outside. She complained, "Hey, what in the hell?"

Kayn turned back and asked, "Can she come inside with us?"

"Sorry love. No ghosts allowed," Lexy sweetly replied.

Frost stuck his head back out the door and baited, "You're welcome to hang with me anytime sexy vixen. Well, once you jump inside of your sister."

"That sounded so wrong," Kayn laughed. She couldn't help but smile. *Chloe was dead and a boy was shamelessly flirting with her. In another time and place this Frost guy would have been her sister's fantasy man. He would have given her a run for her money.* The house had a unique décor. There was glass shelving spanning the length of the wall with thousands of tiny hand-painted soldiers. The sofa was covered in plastic. *It was a peculiar thing for a middle-aged man to do. There wasn't even a TV in the living room?*

Lily walked up to Kayn and remarked, "If I were to hazard a guess your sister has unfinished business. That's why you haven't merged."

That made sense. Kayn replied, "Of course she has unfinished business. She died at seventeen." She followed the group down to the basement where Lexy and skater boy Grey were waiting.

"What took you guys so long?" Grey asked.

"Nice to see you again Grey," Kevin chuckled.

Kayn questioned, "You've already met?"

Kevin winked as he responded, "There was a conversation a while back about restraining orders and stuff. He's been around."

Grey grinned as he shook both of their hands. He removed a pink stone from his pocket, squeezed it in his palm and chucked it on the ground. A tomb appeared. First as a hologram and then it solidified. *So cool.* All the others did the same with their stones. Kevin and Kayn stared at the ominous coffin-esque chambers lined up across the basement. *This was crazy.*

"Do you like video games kids?" Grey toyed with an Aussie accent and a giant comical grin.

20

TRAINING GAMES

*T*ombs materialized reminiscent of Egyptian tombs she'd seen in an old movie. Lexy placed her hand on the symbol on the lid of the tomb closest to her. Kayn and Kevin glanced at each other, recognizing it immediately as the symbol of Ankh that each of them had branded into their flesh. She took his hand and gave it a squeeze. *Her best friend was nervous. He was probably wondering how far he'd be asked to stray from his comfort zone. He'd never been a fan of confined spaces. There was absolutely no way in hell he was getting into one of these tombs voluntarily.*

Lexy twisted her palm on the symbol, the tombs opened with grinding stone against stone. *There were no more scientific explanations to search for, this was just believing in something bigger than yourself, magic. This was going to irreversibly change her life. She knew it with every fibre of her being.* A magnetic pull was urging her to a tomb in the middle. Kayn let go of Kevin's hand and it was as though her legs had a mind of their own. In the blink of an eye, she was standing before a tomb feeling like her soul made the choice. The tomb had pink stone lining. *Was that rose quartz?* "What are these for again?" Kayn asked with a mix of nervous energy and apprehension. Her pulse raced with adrenaline. Without being given an answer, she climbed into the tomb and laid down. Kayn smiled as she ran her fingers along the pink shiny stone, almost fully encasing her. *She wasn't sure how or why she'd willingly climbed into a stone tomb without any prompting. Yes, it would be a cold day in hell before Kevin willingly got into one of these things.*

Lily sat up in the tomb next to her. With an exasperated eye roll, she commanded, "Get in the tomb, Kevin."

Her best friend answered just as she'd predicted, "Listen, I think I've been pretty easy going with all of this bizarre stuff, but a giant pink coffin may be where I draw the line on my crazy today. I'll stay here to make sure Kayn gets out before dinner."

"If anyone understands how your feeling, it's me. You can stay here just this once, but next time you have to go," Lexy's soothing accent replied.

Peering into Kayn's tomb, Kevin nervously questioned, "Are you sure about this?"

From his perspective, this must be quite a sight. Four specimens of humanity displayed in pink stone lined tombs. They weren't really specimens of humanity at all, were they? They were something more. "It feels right. I don't know what this is about, but I'm certain this is where I'm supposed to be," Kayn assured with blind resolve.

Grey shouted, "Hey Lex, chuck me that iPod!"

Lexy smiled as she grabbed it off the workbench and pitched it into his tomb.

Grey's voice chuckled, "Thanks beautiful. Everything's more fun with theme music. Close us up, Lex."

Kayn's heart thudded vigorously with anticipation, as the lid on her tomb slowly began to close. From the echoed scraping vibration, she suspected they'd all closed in unison. *What in the hell was she doing?*

Frost's sultry voice teased, "Hold onto your pantyhose, love muffin."

Lexy's voice urged, "You might as well learn something if you're staying behind. Help me, Kevin."

Grey's music started. *Eighties rock?* Her tomb jolted sideways with a click, click, click. The rose quartz her body was encased in glowed with luminescent light. *What did she get herself into?* The glare became brighter until she could no longer keep her eyes open. *It was probably too late to back out.* Blinding rays pulsated. She could see the brilliant light each time it strobed with her eyes squeezed shut. The tomb she was in vibrated, and for second, she wondered if that's all there was. Grey started catcalling and hooting. *Oh Shit!* Her tomb shot up into the air with such force, her stomach flip-flopped. Laughing, Kayn squealed with her hands against the sides of the tomb. The mixture of eighties rock and stomach-churning vomit inducing motion reminded her of being on a carnival ride. It stopped moving, and once again, she wondered if the ride was over. Her stomach lurched as the tomb began to fall. *Oh no!* She felt the rippling pressure of wind against her skin. Her hair was whipping around her face. Terrified, Kayn frantically felt for the stone protecting her. *It was gone. Holy crap!* Screaming, and flailing, she plummeted through the moist clouds towards certain death without a tomb. She heard a chorus of laughter through the howling wind.

Frost's voice yelled, "Don't worry!"

Spiralling out of control towards beige land below her rapid stomach-churning descent slowed. Kayn landed simultaneously with the others, squatting in the warm luxurious sand. In shock, she remained bent over, battling the urge to vomit. *Everyone was clapping.*

"At least you didn't scream all the way down. They usually do," Grey announced.

Good to know you bunch of immortal assholes. Somebody could have warned her. She stared at the sand beneath her feet and wiggled her toes. *Why did she have bare feet?* The urge to purge her last meal passed. She stood up and took in her peaceful surroundings. She was standing in what appeared to be a desert. *Had she come here before?* She heard Chloe say her name and spun around. Her heart flooded with joy as she saw her twin. They ran to each other and embraced with tears of joy streaming down their faces. *She could feel her. It was like she was alive.* Stepping back, she squeezed her twin's arms up and down in disbelief. *Chloe was here.* Kayn gasped, "You're here. Wherever we are, you're really here with me."

Grey interrupted their reunion, "This is all beautiful and shit, but it's time to get down to business."

With sun-kissed olive skin and glistening ebony hair, Lily laughed, "Well, this is an unexpected twist. You really are tethered, aren't you? I guess we'll have to train both of you. It's nice to get a chance to meet you in the flesh, Chloe."

As Chloe shook the stunning immortal's hand, Lily caught sight of something astonishing on her palm. She excitedly parted Chloe's fingers and gawked at her Ankh symbol, whispering, "I'll be damned."

Kayn was overjoyed to see her deceased sister shaking Lily's hand. As they noticed the symbol on Chloe's palm, her heart surged with love. She put her arm around her, triggering Chloe's waterworks. *My sister. You're here.*

Frost started to speak, "Today, we'll be learning to trust each other. You'll need blind trust in your Clan to follow through with the questionable things you'll be required to do."

"Questionable is just my style," Chloe dared, eyeing up Frost. Sparks ignited between the pair.

Unable to draw his eyes away, their enticing instructor took Chloe's hand and provocatively kissed it, toying, "It's a pleasure to finally meet you in the flesh."

Biting her bottom lip, Chloe shamelessly scanned his body, taunting, "Likewise."

In this space and time, Chloe was as real as she was. The naughty immortal was totally into her sister.

"This undead situation intrigues me," Frost whispered under his breath.

Grey loudly taunted, "You do realise you're hitting on a ghost? Really Frost?"

Frost defended his actions, "Oh, come on. She's as flesh and bone as you are in this place."

"Get down with your freaky bad-self man. I'm not judging you," Grey chuckled.

"Where are we?" Kayn asked as she slowly spun around. There was nothing but desert as far as she could see in every direction. The clouds she'd passed through on the way down were gone and the breathtaking sky was splotchy vibrant hues of blue. Visually it was like someone just grabbed buckets of blue paint in multiple shades and tossed them into the air.

Smiling, Lily explained, "This is the in-between. This place has many other names, but it's created from our hopes and dreams. Here you see whatever you need to see before you move on. However, we come to train and mess around. This symbol prohibits us from passing through the Hall of Souls. We're not truly dead, just visiting. Trust and ability management is what we'll be focusing on this week."

Kayn's eyes widened as she asserted, "I can't be here for a week."

Lily grinned as she answered, "It will only be a half an hour, maybe a touch more earth time. Trust me, you two have a lot to learn if you're going to stand a chance at surviving this month without being taken. You need to understand your intuition-based abilities and you both could use a crash course in self-defence before being faced with the challenge of fighting someone who knows what they're doing."

A week in the desert learning how to fight. She'd never even been in a fight. Kayn looked at her sister, Chloe was smiling, and it was a real one with not a speck of pageantry, just unencumbered joy. *Her twin felt so alone before she died. She was deliriously happy to be around people like her. She'd read the entries in her sister's diary. She knew what was in her heart.* With meagre abilities compared to her twin, Kayn grabbed Chloe's hand in solidarity, saying, "Okay, what are we going to learn first?"

A gentle breeze blew sand across her feet. *Bare feet.* She was wearing an oddly familiar white dress. The girls wore similar mid-thigh length white sarongs with one shoulder bare. The boy's had material barely concealing their unmentionables. *Why was she wearing something different?* She looked down and her childlike dress had morphed to match the others. *It was disturbingly angelic. Nothing but blind acceptance was going to work here.* She smiled as she thought about Kevin. *He was nowhere near blind acceptance. He'd rather bluntly refused to get into a tomb. Her boyfriend had chickened right out. Boyfriend,* she grinned. *It still felt strange to think about him that way. How were they going to train him when he was claustrophobic?* Kayn was brought back to a memory of searching for him after school. He hadn't shown up at their meeting place. Some jerks shoved him into a locker in the changeroom. He was screaming bloody murder when she rescued him. Chloe started jumping up and down squealing with delight and Kayn stopped daydreaming. *Her sister had a whole week to flirt with a gorgeous immortal boy. She would get to feel what it was like to be alive again. It was only a matter of time before they lost their autonomy forever. What would happen when their souls combined?*

Lily looked directly at Chloe and said, "I am glad you could join us. We aren't sure which of you will be the dominant soul once you've combined. You'll need the same training as your sister."

Chloe answered, "I'm glad too. I felt like I didn't exist anymore until today. Now, I feel like maybe I still do."

Her sister was beaming but Kayn had a mixture of confusing emotions. *A part of her had begun to let her sister go even though she knew what their future would hold. The happiness of being with Chloe again was mixed with the fear that she would be lost when they combined. She was the weaker link. What would happen to her? She'd survived against all odds and her sister died, but it was her identity slipping away like grains of sand in an hourglass.* She felt guilty for her thoughts. *The twin she loved so desperately had been alone for so long. She needed to give her this time. They were both afraid of what came next.*

"Back on track," Lily addressed the identical girls, "I know Kayn loves to run. I can't explain this it's something you have to feel." All smiles, everyone sprinted away from the twins. Ahead of the rest, Lily yelled, "Follow my lead! Remember, we operate with blind trust. Do exactly as we do!"

Without hesitation, Kayn chased after the group. Untamed and free as a pack of wild horses with multicoloured flowing manes, they galloped across the warm inviting sand as it slipped like silken scarves between their toes with each hoofbeat. Kayn's soul leapt to the occasion. The Clan's feet churned up the sand in strange unison, setting it adrift on the breeze in their wake. Chloe caught up with joy sparkling in her eyes.

She didn't feel thirsty or tired and they'd been running for a while. This only made the glorious experience better for her. She always hated it when her body started to scream at her to stop doing what she loved to give it what it needed. She didn't have to worry about that here. The sandy desert was nothing but sky ahead as a cliff appeared out of nowhere. One by one, they leapt over the edge, arms out as if they could fly. Kayn followed fearlessly with her arms raised as wings. *Who wouldn't take the opportunity to experience flight if given a chance? There was one small problem, she couldn't fly.* The rapid descent took her through wispy heavenly clouds. *They'd slowed down last time. She had this.* The clouds altered. *Oh, darn.* Closing her eyes, she descended through a storm. Soaked to the bone as she'd passed through the thundering grey nothingness rain was still angrily pelting. Trying to remain zen, she noticed the rapidly approaching ground. *Oh no!* Adrenaline stole her badass. *They were going to hit.* Frantically looking at the others as the swirling beige grew closer with each passing second, nobody cared. *What in the hell?* Her wet hair thrashed around her. She couldn't remain calm anymore. Waving arms in vain to stop her collision, everyone disappeared. She was falling alone. *Oh! Shit! Help!* The scenery flashed by her peripheral vision. *She couldn't stop! It wasn't working! Shit!* Bracing for impact, she let out a blood-curdling scream just before becoming a splat in the desert.

BACK IN THE BASEMENT, Kevin and Lexy had been chatting about inconsequential things when Kayn's tomb began to pulse out of rhythm from the rest. Lexy calmly strolled over and laid both palms on her tomb. Her Ankh symbol began to glow. She reset the pulse of Kayn's tomb to match the others. "What was that?" Kevin enquired concerned.

"You don't really want to know," Lexy answered, distracting Kevin by offering him a bottled water.

KAYN AWOKE WITH A WICKEDLY painful headache. *Was that sand beneath her?* She twitched her fingers. *It was, good. What happened? Oh, yeah. She went splat in the desert.* Pushing up with her arms, hacking out sand, she peered up, livid. They were standing around her smiling like jerks. "What the hell was that?" Kayn seethed, glaring at the thoroughly entertained immortals. She looked for her sister. *Hmmm, Chloe felt guilty about something.*

"Shall we try that again?" Lily announced.

Let's not.

Lily passive-aggressively pointed out, "At least you did it. Your sister didn't even jump."

Flipping her golden locks, Chloe declared, "I'm not jumping off a cliff without a parachute. I wouldn't even do it with one. Why would I possibly want to jump off a cliff? Do I look insane?"

Frost pressed his lips together to stifle his laughter, but Lily didn't find Chloe's high maintenance shenanigans entertaining, she lost it, "You're dead. For the love of everything holy, you're already dead. You should have jumped without even giving it a second thought."

"I guess that's true. Okay, I'll jump this time," Chloe agreed, rolling her eyes. She winked at Frost. He started laughing.

Lily looked at Kayn and said, "I'm proud of you for jumping. Let's do it again, but this time, try to stop yourself before you hit the ground."

Kayn shot her a strange look and blurted, "How in the hell am I supposed to do that?"

"I threw the stapler at you in your room. You blocked it. It's the same thing, just a larger scale," Lily answered, nodding like what she was saying made perfect sense.

"I've only ever done that with small things," Kayn replied.

Lily patiently walked her away from the group as she explained, "Lesson number two. Adrenaline gives you strength and falling to your death gives you a shitload, harness it. Stop yourself from hitting the ground the same way you moved the stapler."

Once again, they ran through the desert, came to the edge, and jumped off.

WELL, EVERYONE EXCEPT FOR CHLOE, who stopped on a dime. "I just can't!" she shouted over the ledge.

"Did you chicken out again?" Frost provoked.

Chloe whipped around. The sexy immortal was standing inches from her, grinning. "You wouldn't dare," she baited. He gave her a gentle shove. "You Asshole!" Chloe yelled, falling into nothingness.

THE DESCENT WAS FASTER THIS time as everything whooshed past her. Kayn focused on what Lily told her to do. Beneath her the approaching ground was green not beige like sand. *A grassy*

field? They'd changed it up. Nice. Her eyes focused. *A forest. Lovely. I'm sure it won't hurt at all to smoke every branch on the way down. Please. This better work.* Adrenaline coursed through her. She focused through the terror. *This was going to suck.* Goosebumps prickled on the surface of her skin as she rapidly plummeted. *There was a clear patch of grass. Hope.* She imagined the ground was being hurled at her and shoved against impending impact releasing a guttural aggressive wail, slowing her descent. *It was working.* She did it once more with everything she had left and landed in the lush grass with a moderately painful thud.

Everyone else walked out from their hiding spots behind trees around her, clapping, "Almost perfect, Kayn," Lily applauded.

Frost chuckled and suggested, "You should move out of the way."

Chloe was spiralling downwards, thrashing her arms, pitchy shrieking. It looked like nobody was even going to attempt to help her. Kayn turned away as her sister hit the ground with a thunderous pound. In the blink of an eye, they were all standing in the desert.

"Okay, one more time," Lily ordered.

She didn't have the energy to do it again. Lily gave her a playful shove. Kayn toppled over and stayed in the sand, laughing.

Gazing down at her grinning, Lily teased, "Woman up, Brighton." The stunning immortal held out her hand. Kayn took it. Lily yanked her to her feet and teased, "There's no time outs. This isn't preschool."

She wished she was there. Nobody ever tried to murder her in preschool. Heck, hurting yourself was also a big no, no. Her sister groaned, Kayn smiled having just been there.

Getting up, sputtering out a mouthful of sand, Chloe barked, "You Asshole!"

Frost grinned as he replied, "There's no point in denying it.

Suck it up, princess. Time to go again. If Kayn can do it, so can you."

In the days that followed they worked on moving things and pushing objects away. During a brief pause in training her eye was off the ball. *Her sister's emerging love-hate relationship with the incorrigible yet delectable Frost was far too entertaining. It was like watching a soap opera.* Grey launched a giant boulder, Kayn saw it spiralling at her with only enough time to think, *crap.* Her brain exploded like a watermelon dropped off a hotel balcony. She lay on the powdery desert floor with a morbid display of brain matter.

Inhaling air into savagely painful lungs, Kayn faintly groaned as her hazy vision came into focus.

"You are sick in the head," Chloe slammed, kneeling beside her.

Kayn struggled to move only twitching fingers in the sand with an excruciating pitchy echo in her ears.

Lily's face appeared over Chloe's shoulder as she explained Grey's unorthodox move, "This is a dose of reality. Nobody is going to ask for permission to take you out. If you're blindsided, it takes a while to reboot your brain. Nobody would expect to be hit with a giant boulder standing in a desert, but stranger things can and will happen."

Expect the unexpected. Lesson learned. The girls blocked objects for hours never feeling hungry or thirsty, with different places and scenarios each time. *Surprisingly enough, it was Grey she was most drawn to. Perhaps she had the inner workings of a feline? Drawn to the person who didn't appear to like her.* Not trusting his silence, Kayn glanced around. Grey vanished. *Strange?*

Raven hair shimmered in sunlight as Lily clapped her hands to get everyone's attention and announced, "Now, looks like a good time to have a break."

Frost and Chloe vanished leaving Kayn with Lily. Out of sheer curiosity, Kayn enquired, "What's Grey's story?"

Smiling at her, Lily replied, "This isn't how he usually acts. Relationships within the Clan can be tricky. It's not you." She held out her hand and suggested, "Let's go find him."

The scenery flashed, and in the blink of an eye, they were standing in a burnt-out shell of a barn after a fire with squares of unscorched hay. *Peculiar, but everything was now.* "What happened here?" Kayn asked as they sat on a fresh haystack.

"This is one of Grey's places," Lily answered quietly.

A rickety farmhouse appeared in the distance. Black swirling angry clouds formed above as thunder rumbled. *Cool.*

Grey burst out the front door of the farmhouse. "Damn it," Lily stated, "I know where we are."

"What is this?" Kayn exclaimed as the charcoal sky crackled lightning and wind thrashed the barn's fragile blackened frame.

"He made a mistake! He can't let it go!" Lily shouted, barely audible over the howling wind and violent claps of thunder.

Enraged, Grey marched through the field towards them. *This can't be good?*

Over nature's temper tantrum, Lily hollered, "The definition of insanity is doing the same thing over and over, expecting a different result!"

Kayn and Lily stood up as he approached with their hair whipping savagely in the wind. The sky above was swirled with ominous shades of black and grey. *It looked like a tornado was forming.* The barn became solid in the next flash of lightning. The walls shocked her, she stumbled backwards and fell to the dirt floor. *The mortal part of her mind was having a difficult time. She kept reminding herself it wasn't about her, it was Grey's memory.* The stirring of animals, whinnying horses and barking dogs filled her ears as the barn returned to its original state.

Lily began to explain, "It can be hard to comprehend this

truth. There is a reason for everything we're asked to do. The most unthinkable of acts can be the difference between saving one life and thousands. In Grey's case, true evil came in the form of someone he loved."

The barn door swung open in the wind and it felt horrifically familiar. Her heart skipped a beat as her memory flashed back to the night when she came home to a door swinging in the wind. The next flash of lightning revealed Grey's form in the doorway.

He screamed, "Laura!" Wrath silenced the livestock, you could hear a pin drop. "I saved you! I protected you! Why?" He was speaking to nothing but air. He yelled the name again and the hay was ablaze.

Mental note, Grey lights fires with his mind. Kayn whispered, "Who's Laura?"

"She was his younger sister. This night was the result of his mistake," Lily whispered back. Grey continued searching the stalls for the invisible Laura. Lily leaned in and whispered, "Stay out of sight. He's not in control, he'll light us on fire. Trust me, it's a level of unpleasant you'd prefer to avoid."

The barn was stifling, all the oxygen had been sucked out. Panicking, Kayn grasped at her throat. *She couldn't breathe.* Her view from the forest floor as she lay dying flashed through her mind. She saw the branches of the trees above her and recalled feeling like they were alive and somehow mocking her.

Kayn heard Lily's voice say, "You don't need to breath, your body is somewhere else. This isn't real."

As the barn's walls burst into flames, Lily tackled Grey. The barn filled with oxygen and vanished. Kayn took a deep breath. When she looked up, Grey was sobbing in Lily's arms as she stroked his hair lovingly, assuring, "It's all in the past darling, you're in the here and now."

Empathy moistened her eyes. Something dripped on her

brow. She peered up. The burnt frame had reappeared, and the sky was serene. *The storm was over. It was just a leftover droplet of rain.* Kayn sat on the fresh stack of hay that once again felt out of place. An abandoned broken-down farmhouse in the backdrop remained. It was in this moment she understood. *He'd been forced to kill his own sister. Tragedy had created them all.*

21

LOVE, LUST AND THE IN-BETWEEN

*T*he two immortals were sprawled on silken grass gazing at gentle rolling hills of lush greenery speckled with dainty buttercups. Chloe brought Frost to a place from her cherished childhood memories. She picked a tiny golden flower, held it up to her chin and questioned, "So, do I like butter?" She was met with a blank stare. "Come on, don't tell me that you've never heard that old wives' tale." She tossed her flower at Frost.

"I haven't had the privilege. Do tell?" Frost said, grinning at her cute story.

Chloe smiled as she explained, "If you hold a buttercup up to your chin and see a yellow shadow, then you like butter."

Picking a flower, he put it under his chin and tested, "Do I like butter?"

"You do, there's a yellow shadow," she affirmed, winking.

"Oh, I see. Is that the reason we're hanging out in the grass? You were desperate to see if I liked butter? If you asked, I would have just told you," Frost teased sweetly.

Chloe grinned as she picked another and began plucking off the petals with her golden blonde hair flowing delicately into the grass behind her. She heard the buzzing of a bee and excitedly sat up for a better vantage point.

In awe of her, Frost did the same. Reaching out, he touched one of her curls and complimented, "You have beautiful hair."

"I usually straighten it but straightening irons are difficult to come by when you're dead," Chloe commented. She held out her hand and a bumblebee landed on her open palm. It walked with tiny ticklish feet across it as she revealed, "When I was a little girl, bees were the first creatures I knew I could control. I didn't move onto people until I was older."

"I knew I was different when I woke up in a pile of dead bodies at nine-years-old," Frost confessed, watching her.

Chloe stopped playing with the bumblebee. Looking up, she replied, "That's messed up."

Frost grinned and agreed, "It definitely was."

She glanced over with a sultry veil of dark lashes and probed, "I bet you know a lot about life? How old are you?"

Spontaneously laughing, the immortal taunted, "Old enough to know I'm destined to be lying in the grass with you, wondering what I'm doing."

As her tiny buzzing minion flew away, Chloe met his eyes and seductively provoked, "What are you doing?"

He suggestively disclosed, "Wondering if your lips are as soft as your hair," Touching Chloe's bottom lip, Frost confessed, "I want to kiss you so badly it hurts, but it would be stupid to kiss you. It would be ridiculously insane to allow myself to fall in love."

Playing an alluring game of chicken, she cheekily baited, "You only want me because there's no chance in hell of us ever really being together. I know what you are... I am you."

Caressing her hair as he inched closer, Frost whispered, "You know what I am, and you still want this to happen?"

Bewitchingly massaging his earlobe, Chloe lured, "I've never been with a man I couldn't control. It's exciting and dangerous. Honestly, what do I have to lose?" He brushed his thumb on her neck. She gasped as a ripple of pleasure made her shiver. He slid his fingers into the delicate curls on her nape as their lips met with an intoxicating tender caress that intensified into a burning passionate submergence of souls. Frost shifted on top of her.

They leapt apart as Lily sarcastically jabbed, "Excuse me. I believe we're saving sex education training for tomorrow."

In awe, Grey commented, "He never ceases to amaze me. He's like a self-opening piñata of jokes. I don't even know where to start." He began to slow clap and Lily elbowed him. Grey whispered, "Why not sleep with the dead twin? What safer relationship could he possibly find?"

"I'm right here you guys," Kayn sighed. Her sister and Frost got up and brushed themselves off. *Chloe looked happy. Why not have fun with a devastatingly sexy scoundrel?* Kayn grinned and ribbed, "I can't believe it. You're dead and you still have cat nip on you somewhere."

"I found no cat nip anywhere," Frost sparred, his voice laced with innuendo.

"Please Frost, it's getting painful," Kayn groaned, shaking her head. Walking away with Chloe, she caught her gaze and asked, "Are you happy?"

Chloe dreamily replied, "He's amazing."

Kayn hugged her and said, "I'm happy for you." *There was no point in lecturing her. Chloe needed this.*

They spent days learning to defend themselves and enjoying every second they had together. She'd come to rely on beautiful moments with her twin as much as oxygen to breathe. Chloe and Frost took off alone on every break from training. Her sister was falling in love, and unless she was misreading the situation, he reciprocated her feelings. They were always holding hands. Grey warmed up a touch by the time they were ready to go home. Her new friend Lily assured her Grey's indifference wasn't personal. He didn't want to care until he was certain she was staying with Ankh. She could be taken by another Clan, it would hurt more if they were friends. Her sister was getting a chance to experience the great love she'd longed for before she died. It wasn't that absurd. Had Chloe survived and not her, Frost would have been perfect for her sister. She sensed the affair upset Lily. At first, she thought it was jealousy, but after Lily shared the story of Sam, Kayn knew her concerns were based on the fear of knowing her twin's soul was an extension of hers. *It wasn't like she'd be reborn and they'd see each other again.*

Her daydream was interrupted by Lily's voice, "It's time to get back to reality. I think some of us are beginning to lose touch with it. You two had a good start in your training."

Glancing at her sister, Kayn held out her hand needing a last moment, just in case she couldn't see her when they went back to the land of the living. *They'd had the chance to do something most never experience after the loss of a loved one. They were given the opportunity to say the words left unspoken.* There was no ceremony this time or rose quartz carnival rides, just a flash of incapacitating light and she awoke inside a tomb like a butterfly in a cocoon preparing to emerge from a long hibernation. As the tomb slid open revealing Kevin's smiling face it felt like a new life. Kayn took Kevin's hand and he helped her out of her figurative cocoon. *She had a million stories to tell him.* She saw something else in his eyes. *He was wondering if she'd changed. It was true, she'd grown. She felt stronger and less afraid of the unknown. She believed in magic.*

"You have to come next time, it's amazing. Chloe was there. I could touch her and speak to her," Kayn regaled with tears of joy. Their lips met, and as they parted, she whispered, "I missed you."

"You've only been gone for an hour," Kevin laughed as they hugged.

"For us it was a week, but we didn't have to sleep or eat, it was twice that time in training. I need to get up there. I'm hoping I can still see her," Kayn rushed.

Yellow light was emitting from Kayn as she scaled the stairs. Anxious, Kevin jabbed Lexy and said, "Kayn is glowing. Not a happy glow, physically shining."

Lexy chased after her up the stairs, hollering, "Wait Kayn! Stop!"

Pausing on the stairs, Kayn asked, "What?"

Lexy casually touched Kayn's shoulder and the halo of light disappeared.

The crimson-haired Healer grinned and commented, "Good catch."

Curiosity lured her back down the stairs. Looking directly at Kevin, Kayn probed, "What did you catch?"

Her boyfriend whispered, "You were glowing."

Glowing? She'd better stick around for this conversation.

Lexy picked up Grey's earbuds off the floor while enquiring, "What made you feel like telling me about it?"

Kevin shrugged and answered, "She felt unsafe."

Shoving the buds into her pocket, Lexy declared, "Look at you go, you're a viable Psychic after all. That burst of energy after we get out of the tombs is how Abaddon finds unsealed Clan. The halo attracts the Legion like a beacon. All it takes is a touch from a Healer to get rid of it. The veil of light follows the newly claimed. I always see it as a child's halo. To me it's that last touch of mortal innocence and purity."

Smiling, Kevin said, "That's kind of beautiful."

"It is beautiful, isn't it?" Lexy replied. She pointed at Kayn and asserted, "If it happens when we're not around, cut yourselves and get in circle of salt." Lexy raced upstairs.

A circle of salt? They stood there confused for a second before following her.

22

EVIL SOUL SUCKING DEMONS

*C*hloe was nowhere to be found as they stepped outside. Lily told them she'd disappeared into the bushes separating the properties, looking as she had at the time of her death. *They'd seen her that way before, but her new boy toy hadn't.* They wandered across the backyard and made their way into the woods. *She'd been avoiding this place.* Seeing the heart-breaking shrine for her family was like driving a stake into her heart. *She should warn the immortal who cared for her sister.* Touching Frost's shoulder to get his attention, he turned to look at her. Kayn explained, "I should warn you, Chloe's death was excessively brutal."

"I know, I saw you in the hospital," Frost admitted. He read the newspaper clippings on trees aloud, "Local Brighton Family slain. One twin alive in coma." He touched Chloe's picture and remarked, "She was incredibly beautiful."

"Chloe was a force of nature," Kevin affectionately added.

Giving Kevin a playful shove, Kayn taunted, "Should I just leave you boys alone with my sister's pictures?"

Placing his arm around her, Kevin snuggled her against him, lovingly teasing, "I'm not sure you've ever comprehended this, but you guys are identical twins."

"Identical," the immortal show pony confirmed.

Kevin saw Chloe first and whispered, "She's over there." He pointed her out.

As Frost came towards her, Chloe nervously warned, "One more step and the magic will be gone."

"I highly doubt that," Frost replied. "I've seen a rather large number of dead people in my lifetime."

Now that they were back in the land of the living, she couldn't see her sister anymore. Frost froze mid-step, taking in the horror of what Chloe endured in her final moments. His eyes filled with tears as he reached out into nothing but air. With a peculiar expression, he wiped the foreign liquid from his eyes.

Turning to Kevin, Kayn whispered, "I think he's really falling in love with her."

Kevin whispered back, "She loves him. I wasn't sure she was even capable of it."

Old insecurities can be difficult to get rid of. Kayn couldn't help but ask, "Are you a little jealous?"

Gazing into her eyes, Kevin teased, "Do you honestly not know how I feel about you?"

She held her breath sure he was about to confess his love.

Instead of saying the words, he chuckled, "I got branded for you."

He held out his tell-tale gloved hand, she took it. *They had forever.* They left Frost and Chloe alone and headed back to her house. *He dealt with uncomfortable situations by joking around just as she did.* When they unlocked the door and went inside. *Nobody was there. This was exciting.*

"I promised we'd behave," he responded to her thoughts.

Slipping off her shoes, she glanced back, innocently tempting, "Watch a movie and order a pizza?" Kayn scaled the stairs. *He'd be right behind her once he talked himself into misbehaving.* She sprinted down the hall, shoved open her bedroom door and leapt on her bed. Grabbing the remote, she turned on the T.V and began flicking through channels. Kevin entered her bedroom. *He'd taken a while to make his way upstairs.*

He grinned as he strolled over to her bed and announced, "I texted my Dad to tell him I'm staying here until Jenkins gets home." Sitting beside her, Kevin added, "There's a note on the fridge from Jenkins. He won't be back until ten."

She pointed to the flyer on her nightstand. Innocently biting her lip, she toyed, "That's hours from now. We could watch two movies and eat a pizza by ten." *They'd watched a million movies, she didn't want to just platonically watch movies anymore.* She jumped up and said, "I have to run to the bathroom."

Grabbing toothpaste, Kayn squirted some on her finger and rubbed it on her tongue. She drank water, put a dab of perfume on and looked at her reflection. She opened the door to find him standing there.

He cautiously came in and disclosed, "I thought I wouldn't be able to come close to this bathroom without having flash-backs, but all I see is you, just like the day we met." Kevin took a tiny purple flower out of his pocket. He knelt and tucked it into her sock just as he had on that day.

They'd only been five years old when he put that purple flower in her shoe. She could easily picture him on one knee holding an engage-ment ring. For her, remembering that flower meant just as much. As he got up, she confessed, "That was smooth, Smith."

With a giant grin, he flirtatiously sparred, "Brighton, you have no idea how smooth I can be."

He boldly backed her up against the counter, naughtily kissing her neck as happiness surged in her heart. Giggling because it tickled. *She wanted him to kiss her.* She gazed into his eyes as his lips came towards hers.

Pausing with his lips just a breath away, Kevin provocatively teased, "Maybe we should go to my house. I only promised we'd behave here. We can get off on a technicality."

"Get off on a technicality?" She provoked. *She could be naughty too.* Raked her fingers through his hair, Kayn pulled his mouth to hers, ridding him of hesitation. Their tongues intimately danced as hands feverishly explored uncharted territory. He picked her up and she wrapped her legs around his waist as he carried her back down the hall to her bed. The bedroom door opened. He abruptly dropped her, and she landed on her butt with a thud.

Jenkins was busting a gut laughing as he came in, "Seriously? You guys didn't last five minutes."

Cringing, Kayn sighed, "You were never working late, were you?"

"Nah, I was just messing with you," Jenkins chuckled. "I ordered pizza, and here." He tossed a movie at her.

Sitting on the floor, crimson faced, she picked up the DVD and awkwardly replied, "Thanks."

"Oh, don't mention it," he piped in as he left.

They both started laughing. Kayn marched over to lock her door. Just as she reached for the handle, Jenkins opened it and passed her a pizza. Kayn grinned and nodded as she took the box. Painfully embarrassed, she politely said, "Thanks Jenkins." She turned around and declared, "Damn, he's good."

IN THE FOREST BY THE Brighton house, Chloe was back to her

gorgeous self. Hanging out with Frost, reminiscing about days gone by, they were having a wonderful evening even though they couldn't touch physically. They were carnal creatures reaching new levels of intimacy with honest conversation when she reverted to her tragic self. It wasn't just her bloody entrails that shifted the mood. Frogs stopped croaking, the crickets ceased monotonously chirping. Familiar sounds of dusk disappeared as everything became still. Chloe looked away from Frost, her eyes scanned the darkness of the woods. Turning back in her victimized form, she ominously declared, "Something's coming."

A black mist eerily fluidly swirled around trees, methodically flowing in their direction. Frost hollered, "Get out of here, Chloe!" She vanished into thin air as he removed a bag from his pocket and encircled himself with fine white contents. The onyx coloured mist whirled around, unable to enter the ring of safety simple table salt provided. Knowing what this mist would be followed by Frost removed the blade from his pocket and sliced his hand. A thin stream of blood trickled down his palm. He placed the wounded hand on his heart, as his symbol began to glow. He'd learned a long time ago, there were some dark things you never attempt to fight alone.

BACK AT THE HOUSE KAYN and Kevin finished their pizza and were on top of the covers watching a movie like children. They wanted to carry on where they'd left off, but Jenkins kept popping his head in unannounced offering humorous random things. *He'd purposely bought a huge stash of distraction snacks.* Kayn felt her hand warming. She took off her glove, her symbol was glowing. Kevin grabbed her arm, forewarning, "I can't go with you. I'm not sure what this means, but you have to get into the circle as fast as you can."

Whipping her glove back on, Kayn said, "I'll be right back. Run interference with Jenkins."

"Never say I'll be right back. That's how people die in horror movies," Kevin quipped as he slid his glove back on and followed.

They snuck downstairs without a creak. Kevin remained at the door to sidetrack any attempt Jenkins made to go upstairs. The last thing they needed was for a well-meaning parental figure to appear smack dab in the middle of dark immortal shit. With a blinding sense of urgency, there was no time to put on shoes. She quietly opened the door and slipped out. On supernaturally fuelled autopilot, she sprinted down the side of her property in socks to the backyard and didn't hesitate as she bolted into the opening of the woods, she'd run into nearly a year ago. She'd been aware of every sound last time, but tonight, she was aware of the lack of noise. Not a cricket's chirp nor owl's hoot, just the repetitive soft thuds of stocking feet hitting dirt. It was unnaturally silent. There was an ominous presence. *She wasn't afraid.* Her night vision was crystal clear. She saw the Ankh in the distance, surrounded by black mist. Grey, Lily and Lexy were standing in a circle with Frost. *Kevin was right. She had to get into that circle.* She ran directly at her Clan, crossed her arms in front of her face and plunged through the mist. "What's the plan you guys?" Kayn huffed as she tried to balance on wobbly legs, unusually out of breath.

Shaking her head, Lexy explained, "The mist you jumped through stole some of your lifeforce." She touched Kayn, a warm surge of energy flowed through her being as the crimson-haired immortal continued, "If you're injured or killed, I'm the one who repairs your body. Arrianna is our Clan's other active Healer.

Each of us has special talents, but first and foremost, I'm Ankh's strongest warrior. Do what I say."

"Why are we just standing here in a circle of salt?" Kayn asked candidly, concerned after all the bravado in her training that they were cowering in a circle.

"You can't fight mist. It's here to subdue us for something else," Lexy replied.

They seemed far too relaxed. They were all grinning.

"Patience is a virtue," Frost sparred with cocky sarcasm.

"Fools rush in," Lily laughed.

Watching the onyx mist swirl as it circled the group, Kayn had the strongest urge to touch the ring of salt. *What would happen if she threw some at the mist?*

Frost touched her shoulder and sighed, "Please don't. If you touch that salt, we'll all have an incredibly shitty evening."

Mental note: try to remember they can hear your strange inner dialogue. "What comes after the creepy black mist?" Kayn asked, dreading the answer.

Lily grinned and countered, "It's a sensitive area for you."

Oh, Crap. "It's one of those soul-sucking demons you were talking about, isn't it?" Kayn probed as she fought the urge to do the logical thing and run away.

Lexy shook her head slowly from side to side in response to her inner commentary, explaining, "We're going to wait in this circle. When it's close enough, we'll link hands to create a current of energy and blow his ass up. We only have enough to do it once, so we have to wait until its right beside us."

We are going to wait until its right beside us. Great. Kayn whispered, "I pictured us kicking ass not making traps, and for the record, black mist is not what I pictured when you said soul-sucking demons."

"Is that what you pictured?" Lexy enquired, pointing to long curved claws grasping moss-covered bark of a giant fir tree thirty feet from where they were. A black scaly glistening, half reptilian creature slowly moved through the bushes.

"Yes, that's more like it," Kayn mumbled, wishing she hadn't tempted fate. The air became as icy as a winter's night. Each time she exhaled breath rose from her lips in visible panicked bursts. *Oh Shit. This can't be good.*

As the spine-chilling nightmare shuffled closer, Lexy noted, "There is a bright side to this."

"What could that possibly be?" Kayn stammered. *This hideous monster couldn't be real. It was terrifying. Its claws capable of slicing through human flesh like butter. In her worst nightmares there'd been nothing close to this.*

Leaning closer, Lexy whispered, "At least we're here, it could have come into your bedroom and gutted you as you slept."

Well, that wasn't helpful. "Has anyone ever told you Frost isn't the only asshole?" Kayn commented, fighting the urge to flee.

"I'm an asshole with purpose," Lexy remarked, triggering snickers from trapped immortals.

Frost pitched in, "I resent that. It's clearly true, but I resent it nonetheless."

"You're awfully quiet, Grey. Don't you feel like being eaten this evening?" Lily pestered, giving him a gentle shove.

"I hate these friggin' things. For the record, you suck." Grey complained nervously.

"It's super slow. Why don't we throw salt at the mist and walk away?" Kayn asked as it hobbled at a snail's pace.

Skater boy Grey took her hand, whispering, "We've tried and failed. They work as a team. The mist incapacitates you and this giant cuddly guy eats the leftovers and gets rid of evidence."

Lily glanced at Lexy and said, "Stomach or arm?"

"Stomach, I guess. Don't nick my liver," Lexy replied as Lily far too casually stabbed her in the stomach.

Kayn's mouth dropped open. Frost reached for her other

hand and squeezed it, assuring, "She's a Healer. She's fine, that's not even going to wreck her evening." He looked at the others and announced, "Okay, just a few more steps and he'll be close enough to take out."

Once everyone's hands were linked, a current of energy began flowing. It was pleasurable at first, but then, it started to burn. One of her hands felt like it was on fire. Grey's hand had a flame like glow. *She couldn't let go. It was burning.* Conveniently, her energy was fuelled by terror induced adrenaline and there was plenty as she struggled to get away.

Grey tightened his fiery grasp and thought, *'Trust me, you do not want to break this circle.'*

Just when it felt like she couldn't take it anymore, she felt a surge of euphoria unlike anything she'd experienced. A wave of energy rippled away from the circle followed by a burst of flames, disintegrating soul-sucking demons, and igniting the alligator on steroids leaving behind a sizzling charcoal corpse.

"I've got this," Grey announced as he released her hand and kicked the demon's ashes. It dissolved into a cloud of dust that travelled away on a gust of wind.

She gazed at her unharmed flesh. *There wasn't a mark on her. She felt amazing.* "That was kind of awesome," Kayn declared as they all stepped out of the circle.

"Brains before brawn. You don't live this long assuming you can win every battle," Lily replied as they strolled back through the slightly damp but no longer chilly woods to her house. The adrenaline high wavered. *That was a real monster.* A wave of nausea washed over her. *What if one went into the house?* She saw Kevin standing by the edge of the woods, having a conversation with empty air. *Oh, thank God.* "Where's Jenkins?" Kayn called out as she approached.

Kevin closed the space while responding, "He's snoring on the couch. He chuckled, "Chloe ran at Frost like she planned to leap into his arms and stopped at the last second before she sailed right through."

She wished she could see her.

Frost wandered over and sarcastically remarked, "Thanks for picking that one up, Kev."

Lexy gave the show pony a pat on the shoulder and admitted, "He did pick it up. I healed Kayn on the stairs before we left the basement. I thought we caught it in time. Everyone else knew. You took off before I could warn you."

"Good job, Kev," Chloe's voice praised.

Raising a hand to high five her, Kevin said, "Do it tomorrow when you're solid."

Her sister's hand would have flowed through his as nothing more than a chilly breeze.

Glaring at the Clan's Healer, Frost baited, "You stinker, you didn't mention it on purpose. You could have texted me. Hey, Frost. Just so you know, there could be Demons. Keep an eye out."

Lexy winked and sparred, "We don't have a T.V. I was bored stiff, so I rolled the dice. What were the chances?"

"Pretty damn high," Frost countered, laughing.

Lily piped into the conversation, "All joking aside, Abaddon knows we're here now. We have to go back in tomorrow to train."

Kevin nodded, admitting, "I feel like an idiot for not going."

Lily's eyes softened as she looked at Kevin and responded, "No games tomorrow, Abaddon knows she's here. They send one of those things when they aren't sure. Next time, there may be a dozen."

Touching Kayn's shoulder, Frost poorly reassured, "They can't come in your room, that's what the stones are for. Lexy's messing with you, but Lily's telling the truth, they've confirmed you're here. A dozen will show up next time."

Awesome. That's just awesome.

"Afterschool at our place," Lily commanded.

"Yes! This is incredible!" Chloe's voice cheered.

Kayn couldn't see her sister but felt her joy. *She wouldn't have to wait another week to feel alive again. To be honest, she was more than a little stoked. She couldn't wait to show Kevin everything she'd experienced there. Her mind kept scrolling back to, I just helped blow up a real monster. Next time they'll send a dozen of those. Frost confirmed it.* She plastered on Chloe's pageant smile, understanding its purpose. *Fake it till you make it.*

"Chloe, dead or not you're the other half of the Conduit. They're here for you too. It would be beneficial to Abaddon if you never became one. Keep that in mind as you stall for time," Lily warned, walking away.

Kayn looked at where she surmised Chloe must be standing. *The coming week would be their last as separate entities. It was go time if they wanted to protect what was left of their family.*

23

MURDER, RESURRECTION AND MISCELLANEOUS MAYHEM

*L*ily sprawled on her bed recalling each horrific ending to her love story with the mortal reborn under many names. *She was dying to see Kayn's brother again. She could visit him secretly. It was during the week so Matt would be in his college dorm.* Lily concentrated on thoughts of him and she was there.

His room was slightly untidy but not gross. He'd just had a shower and only had a towel around his waist. His torso rippled with toned perfection. This wasn't going to make staying away easier. She remembered his touch like it was yesterday and the feeling of his toned stomach as she ran her hands over those abs. There was no point in getting all hot and bothered over a boy who was off limits. Sitting on his bed, Matt ran his hands through his short damp hair. Reaching for his phone, he picked up a picture of his sisters instead and stared at it. *Kayn's brother had a death sentence and he didn't even know it was coming. The hourglass of his life had started losing sand the moment they met. She'd hoped, if she kept her distance, he'd be spared. Her instincts were telling her that assumption was wrong. History would undoubtedly replay as it always had in the past.* Matt continued his routine and she followed as he went into the bathroom. Watching him brush his teeth, she reminisced his last life.

She recalled every detail down to the song playing as they entered the dance together, "The Glory of Love" by Peter Cetera. It was many decades ago. Lily's dress was poufy shouldered blue satin. Her ebony hair was permed, glistening with sparkles, with curls down only one shoulder. He towed her to the dance floor where she melted against him with her head resting on his shoulder. She swayed to the music in his arms wishing they could stay like this forever but with each steady beat of his heart she heard their inevitable goodbye. Lily ran her hand across his chest as if this action would erase what was destined to happen. As they kissed, it was a moment of blissful perfection in her long, complicated existence. They left the dance early and went back to a hotel where they made love for hours. Afterwards, she lay enraptured in his muscular arms, overflowing with joy. In prior lives, he'd always died before they had a chance to consummate their love. After many reruns of the tragedy, there was a flicker of hope.

He'd kissed her cheek and asked if there was anything she wanted from the store across the street. He wanted butter pecan ice-cream. He kissed her lips tenderly, grabbed his jacket and took off. In what felt like seconds, she heard screeching tires and screaming. An eighteen-wheeler took out her heart right outside of the hotel room where they'd just finished making love. Lily recalled lying in the bed wrapped in the covers, still damp from their union. *Maybe if she didn't move or take a breath?* Despair cascaded down her face as she put her clothes on and raced out into the pouring rain. Drenched to the bone as she saw the truth, she dropped to her knees. *There wasn't even a body left to hold onto as he took his last breath, just blood spatter on the road. He was gone.*

Something hardened inside of her after countless versions of losing her true love. Yet still, in the back of her heart, she waited for him to return as he always had so she could hold him once more. *If nobody intervened, Kayn's brother's death was inevitable.* Her essence returned to her body and Lily awakened with renewed purpose. She would find a way to make Matt an immortal and redesign her destiny to include the man she loved. She just needed a half a dozen miracles and back up. If they left right after school, they could stay under for two hours without suspicion. Two weeks in the in-between might be dangerous for Kevin. He may become lost between reality and fantasy but all three needed to be trained quickly. Lily knocked on Frost's bedroom door.

He bellowed, "What do you want?"

"Can we talk for a minute?" She asked, entering the room without waiting for his answer. Frost patted the bed next to him. Lily strolled around placing stones on his floor and made a circle of salt as she recited the words, "Ας μην υπάρχει σιωπή εκτός του κύκλου."

"If you say it in English instead of Greek, it still works," Frost teased.

Sitting by him, Lily tempted, "Will you help me do something morally questionable if it helps you have more time with Chloe?"

"I'm listening," an intrigued Frost toyed.

"Keeping them in the in-between training for two weeks is dangerous, but if I vow to keep Kevin in touch with reality, it will give you more time with Chloe. When the twins join, maybe you'll have a chance?"

Wincing, Frost probed, "The others will never agree but I'm curious, what do you want in return?"

Scooting closer, Lily proposed, "Help me find a loophole to make the twin's brother immortal."

"I noticed the resemblance. I'm guessing you haven't thought to mention this sick twist of fate to either of the twins?" Frost whispered, grinning.

"I've stayed away, but you know as well as I do, the family's always end up dead," Lily explained her crazy plot.

Frost sighed and whispered back, "A week ago I would have been pissed off about this self-destructive plan, but now, I kind of get it."

"I knew you'd understand," she replied, taking his hand.

Leaning in so close, Lily felt the warmth of his breath on her ear, Frost whispered, "Let's say we attempt to save Matt or Sam, or whoever the hell he is. How would we go about it?"

Lily softly whispered, "Let's mark him, kill him and revive him. If he gains Psychic ability, we can take him with us."

In a hushed voice, he stated, "If he has no Psychic lineage, it won't work."

She whispered, "He's adopted, we have no way of knowing what he's capable of."

Caressing her face, Frost rationalized, "You know how much I want to be with Chloe, but I understand our time is almost up. I've accepted it as fact. I suggest you do the same. You know our wild schemes never work out."

It was usually best to keep the others out of private conversations involving murder, resurrection, and other miscellaneous mayhem so they'd have plausible deniability, but it was too late for that. They had company. Lily opened the door to find Lexy and Grey standing there.

Coming in, Lexy teased, "If you whisper loudly enough, we can hear you, circle or no circle. When someone says anything in Greek, it's hard not to eavesdrop out of curiosity."

Afire with undisguised frustration, Grey instructed, "Make

the circle again, you just walked through it. By not turning you in, we'll get in the same amount of trouble as you two bloody morons. You might as well fill us in."

Lily recreated the circle and the four began arguing about her utterly insane plan. In the end the group agreed to a two-week stint in the in-between but not to the resurrection of Kayn's brother.

24

BEING EATEN REALLY SUCKS

*A*nkh's presence added a touch of reality to the crazy situation, she'd found herself in. Lily strutted down the hall with flawless olive skin, a pearly white smile, naturally rosy lips, and an ebony mane cascading like shimmering silk. The girl was breathtaking. She reminded her of an emotionally jaded Snow White. Grey had grown on her with his boyish good looks and free-spirited ways. He made her grin every time he spoke because she couldn't quite figure out the origin of his accent. She'd originally thought he was a pompous, chauvinistic, idiot but soon realised it was an act meant to keep her at arm's length. His brotherly vibe got him smacked, hugged, or gut punched often, but it was endearing. Spotting Lexy on a bench outside of the principal's office, Kayn grinned. Their Healer had a hint of southern drawl and a kickass punch, which she'd obviously shared with someone again today. *That girl has serious anger management issues.* It was the end of the day. They were supposed to meet in the parking lot. *Lexy might be late.* Gapped out, she nearly got trampled by Frost's flock of admirers as he detoured into the office. *He was the hottest guy she'd ever laid eyes on. He was making her sister happy, so it made him alright in her mind.* She watched Frost smooth talk Lexy out of detention and they walked out to the car. Kevin was bouncing with excitement as they all piled in.

"Meet you there!" Grey shouted, flying by on his skateboard.

"Let's grab a burger before we get started. Waiting in the basement half-starved throws me off my game," Lexy chimed in as they passed Grey.

Grinning, Kevin replied, "You don't have to ask me twice to eat a greasy cheeseburger." He turned into the drive-through.

Once their stomachs were full, Lily mentioned the two-week long stint in the in-between.

"Isn't that too long?" Kayn enquired as they pulled up at the house.

"I thought more than a week was a bad idea?" Kevin asked a little reserved.

"After what happened last night, we have to catch you up to the other two quickly," Lily cautiously responded.

It made sense. Kayn put her hand on Kevin's knee and smiled. *She knew what he was thinking. If he hadn't been afraid to go last time, they'd all be on the same page.* Chloe hadn't uttered a word, but Frost was smiling at an empty space in the backseat. *She was going to see her sister soon.* Sensing omissions in the conversation as everyone got out of the car and disappeared into the house, she waited for Kevin. *You tell yourself that the things that go bump in the night aren't real. That's how you go to sleep and trust you'll be safe until the morning. They were coming for her and always would be. Now that the veil of the spiritual world had been raised, she'd probably never be able to feel that blind sense of security again.*

"Okay let's go," Kevin blurted out.

Shutting off negative thoughts, Kayn opted to focus on the positive. She was going to have the opportunity to hug her sister and Kevin was clearly excited to experience the in-between. Her stomach knotted with apprehension. *If she felt uneasy, there was usually a reason.*

As Kevin passed the empty stoop, he addressed her invisible twin, "How's it going, beautiful?"

Chloe's voice responded, "I'll feel much better in about ten minutes."

"I'm glad," Kevin answered sweetly.

Kayn paused in front of the empty stoop and said, "See you soon."

Her sister's voice replied, "I can't wait."

As Kayn walked in the door it swung shut behind her.

Lexy was the only one standing outside of the tombs as they made their way downstairs, "Hop in with Grey. I wish I could go, but someone has to operate these things."

Kayn watched Kevin pensively walk over to Grey's tomb. He took a deep breath and climbed inside. *Why did she get her own and he had to share?* She climbed into the empty tomb. *This time it felt like she was boarding a carnival ride knowing exactly what she was getting into.* Sensing Kevin's panic as the heavy stone lids began to close, she wished she'd given him a pep talk. *He did have Grey.* The tombs lurched to the side, clicked, and exploded with blinding light.

Eighties rock was playing from Grey's tomb, heightening the exhilaration as they were abruptly catapulted into the air. Grey was hooting with excitement and Kevin was stone silent. Kayn's stomach twisted and churned as her tomb spun. They paused but she knew the ride wasn't over this time as they began to deadfall. She heard squeals of excitement as they descended into the in-between free of tombs. Kevin was freaking out. Fight or flight had taken over as he plummeted into the unknown, flailing and shrieking. Calm this time, Kayn called out his name. Their eyes met and he stopped screaming. *It's okay, calm down,* she spoke to his soul as they descended into the in-between. The group landed gracefully in the desert. Kevin face planted, spitting the sand out of his mouth.

Frost helped him up, teasing, "Bet you were an alto in choir."

Brushing sand off his white Ankh attire without noticing he wasn't wearing pants, Kevin declared, "Actually, I was an alto." Everyone cracked up. Her bestie mocked, "Mature guys, really mature."

They were hysterically laughing, until Lily sighed, "I needed that."

Their weird sense of humour was beginning to rub off on everyone.

Kevin spun around in awe just as she had while taking in his surroundings. He blurted, "Are we staying in the desert for two weeks?"

She'd had the same reaction to the clean slate of the in-between's immortal landing spot.

Lily smiled, gently touched his arm and explained, "This is the in-between. Ankh usually arrives in the desert, but this place is whatever you imagine it to be."

"Anything I want?" Kevin enquired as he gazed up at shades of blue in the sky, shielding his eyes from the sun's glare with a hand.

There were diamonds in the sand sparkling in the sunshine. Kayn knelt to get a closer look, touching the silky sand. *It felt the same.* As she strained the luxuriously fine grains through her fingers, she felt a tug in her heart and knew something was off. Kayn sat in the warmth of the sand examining the sparkling grains. *The diamonds were a hologram.* When she looked up, Kevin was standing above her with a confused expression. *He'd noticed everyone's sparse attire.*

He knelt next to her and whispered, "Where are our clothes?"

While laughing on the inside, Kayn whispered, "Just listen, don't worry about your clothes."

Lily continued to speak, "We arrive on a blank slate and create through our minds what we want our version of the in-between to be. Ankh come to the desert because everyone recognizes it. If you weren't Tri-Clan and you died, you'd arrive to a moment of immeasurable beauty from your life."

"That makes sense," Kevin replied in awe of the glittering sand beneath his feet.

Kayn got up as she watched Kevin wriggling his toes in the sand. *She'd done that too.* The sky altered, swirling sparse white clouds across the azure canvas. Lily was giving Kevin the blind trust speech. *She was dying to show him the miraculous things she'd experienced. She was standing next to Chloe. They were all here. This was her version of heaven even if they were in the desert the entire time.* Kayn squinted as the sun glinted off the diamonds in the sand, creating magical rainbows of light. She was enraptured by the glorious visual spectacle when a past memory filtered through and she recalled when she'd seen diamonds in the sand. After she died, they were glittering beneath the water's surface amidst colourful starfish. Instinct urged her to close off her thought process. *Kevin needed training, not distractions.*

Lily's speech was over, it was time to go for a run. Kayn met Kevin's eyes, whispering, "Do you trust me?"

"Always," he answered as he took her hand.

Not wanting him to feel embarrassed again or discouraged, Kayn quietly assured, "You can't die. We're somewhere filled with beauty and magic. Be free, trust you can never be permanently hurt here."

"Party pooper," Frost teased with a giant grin, shaking his head at her. He leaned over and whispered in Kayn's other ear, "That's cheating love."

"Sometimes cheating is necessary," Kayn whispered back with an innocent smile.

"I'm holding you to that!" Frost shouted as he took off ahead.

Grinning, Kayn raced after him. They sprinted through the exquisitely beautiful desert of diamonds. Approaching the drop off, she slowed so Kevin could catch up and held out her hand. Trusting her, they leapt off the ledge together. *He wasn't going to be able to stop until he knew how.* As they plummeted downwards, Kayn shouted over howling rippling wind, "I have to let go. You have to learn to stop yourself!"

"How?" Kevin yelled, watching.

With her hands out, Kayn hollered, "Use your adrenaline to push your body away from the ground!"

As Kevin rapidly spiralled through the air, Kayn noticed a necklace falling beside him. He grabbed for it and a visible bright yellow haze surrounded him. As he clenched the necklace in the palm of his hand an orange surge of power pulsed around his chest. Kevin placed his hands out, instinctually knowing what to do as energy pulsed forth pushing him away. He slowed to a stop before impact suspended in mid-air. His cheeks curved upwards victoriously. He hovered before allowing his feet to land on the forest floor. Everyone gathered around, shocked.

Frost spoke up, "Wow. I underestimated you, kid."

"Holy crap! How in the hell did you hover like that?" Grey exclaimed, looking at Kevin like he was seeing him clearly for the first time.

Kevin opened his glowing hand to show them the amulet covered in blood in his palm. He'd squeezed the necklace so tightly during his descent into the unknown, it pierced his flesh. Blood trickled down his wrist, christening the sand with his essence. Recognizing the amulet, Kayn hesitantly asked, "Where did that come from?" *She didn't want it to be true. He'd told her the necklace had been willed to him along with his grandmother's power in the event of her death, but he'd left it at her house that day, refusing to take it.*

Unconcerned, Kevin shrugged, commenting, "I guess leaving it behind wasn't optional."

Kayn's eyes filled with tears. *He was still in shock from the fall, overwhelmed by everything. He didn't see it yet, but she did.*

Kevin put on his grandmother's amulet. He started choking, clutching at the necklace, desperately trying to rip it off. He dropped to his knees in the grass, gasping for air in tortured agony. Screaming, he crumpled to his side. Kayn bolted towards him. Frost restrained her as she fought to squirm away, desperate to stop his pain. Kevin was shrieking in pitchy agony like he was being shredded to pieces. Held by Frost, she begged Chloe to help but Grey already had her pinned in the grass. She stopped struggling. Relaxing against Frost, Kayn pled, "He's in too much pain. Please, you have to help him."

Frost whispered in her ear, "He's a Psychic. He's having a violent vision fed to him by the amulet he just put around his neck. Which is never good news but news we need to hear. This is his job now."

Chloe was sobbing and pleading with Grey to help Kevin. Kayn couldn't help but notice Lily's expression. *It looked like she knew a horrible secret.* While Lily was sidetracked, Kevin squirmed over and contacted her flesh, creating a link to his visions. Lily clawed at her chest, dropping to the grass with graphic images of violence and torture flooding her mind, kicking Kevin away in a desperate attempt to free herself before her brain fizzled.

"Do something!" Kayn shouted as they squirmed in anguish.

"I've never seen this happen before. He's passing a vision on by touch. He shouldn't be able to do that. He's not an Oracle," Frost confessed, loosening his hold.

During Frost's confusion, Kayn broke free of his grasp and leapt between the pair, severing the link. Before she could think, the grass surrounding her came alive, rapidly growing, encircling her into a teal mummy. It swallowed her so quickly the others didn't have a chance to react.

BACK IN THE BASEMENT THREE of the tombs were out of sync. *It didn't make sense.* As Lexy touched Kevin's tomb horrific images accosted her. *He'd passed on a Psychic vision via tomb. Impressive. They'd need every second of training they could fit in to have a shot at altering the future she'd just witnessed. The shit was about to hit the fan.* She heard the blaring noise only Tri-Clan could hear and staggered around covering her ears until it ended. That racket meant a battle had begun. The area was sealed off. Bolting upstairs, Lexy rushed to a window. Sure enough, there was a massive amount of Clan fighting in the backyard. They disbanded as swirling black mist joined the party. *They'd be back. It had only been a few minutes since her Clan left to train in the in-between. The house was spiritually blockaded but that didn't mean that there was no way inside, just that it wouldn't be easy.* Sprinting back to the basement, Lexy salted the doorway. Placing a line of stones along the wooden frame, she wedged a shovel under the doorknob, hoping it would hold. *She'd have to wait until the last minute to climb into the protection of her tomb. These kids were going to need every second of their training to even stand a chance. She had to heal them for a few more hours.* Lexy took a knife off the counter, sliced her palm, and placed a dripping hand on the first tomb, sending a current through all. They lit up and pulsated twice with a surge of energy, warning

Ankh something was amiss back in the land of the living. Clutching her head bent over, she willed away the violent, toxic visions repeating in her mind. *It would be extremely helpful if Psychic visions had a time stamp.*

BACK IN THE LAND OF THE deceased, Lily groggily came to in the plush grass and questioned, "How in the hell did you transfer your visions to my mind? That was brutal."

"We have to go home, right now," were the first words out of Kevin's mouth. His voice was raspy, thick with emotion as he explained, "Lexy was torn apart. There was so much blood. You were being torn apart too Grey."

Grey threw his hands up in the air, "Awe shit, not again. I hate bloody dying that way. Just tell me I'm not being ingested by something. Being eaten really sucks."

With only a look, Lily commanded their attention and panic lulled as she solemnly addressed the group, "This is why we have Kevin. Foretold events involving us can be altered. That's what would have happened if we went back now. After a couple of weeks of training, there may be a different outcome." Touching Frost's shoulder, Lily quietly suggested, "Give Chloe whatever she needs to find peace." Cursing like a sexy-accented driver cut off in traffic, Grey paced back and forth. Blocking the irate immortal's hissy fit, Lily vowed, "If something eats you, I'll stab you in the head and heal your sexy body while you have a Pina Colada in the in-between."

"I don't give two shits about my sexy body, it frigging hurts," Grey complained. Smiles erupted in the face of dismemberment. He over-dramatically ranted, "Oh, yeah. Go ahead, have a good laugh at my accent, you bloody idiots. Do you have any words you want me to say today?"

Beaming, Frost provoked, "Say encyclopedia." Grey wrestled him into a chokehold as he laughed hysterically.

"Still funny, asshole?" Grey hissed, out of breath struggling for dominance in his testosterone fuelled tantrum.

"I'm going to pee myself. Stop! It's not funny, I swear," Frost chuckled. Releasing him, Grey shoved him. Frost landed on his butt in the grass.

Lily yelled harshly, "Quit messing around!"

"Where's Kayn?" Kevin questioned.

"I'm going to look for her, come with me. I think I know where she is," Lily answered, "You need to be there too."

"What happens if Lexy dies before she helps us get back?" Kevin enquired, strolling beside her.

Their symbols began to strobe. Lily held up her hand to show Kevin her glowing Ankh symbol, but he was staring at his own. Patiently, she explained, "When tombs strobe out of sync, Lexy knows someone was wounded or killed during training in the in-between. Her job is to make sure our tombs stay in sync. When our symbols go off with long steady flashes versus quick ones, it's her warning us something is wrong in the land of the living. The rest of our Clan is on the way to the house. Lexy is a bad ass. We don't worry about her."

Walking away from the others, Lily pressed, "Understand this one thing, we cannot die. None of us can pass through to the hall of souls to be reborn. If you die, you come here. End of story. Lexy's secured herself in the basement. She'll continue healing us for as long as she can. When she shows up here it means the battle has come into the house. Our mortal shells are safe in the tombs. We just wait here for the rest of our Clan to get us out."

25

THE TRIAD CONNECTION

Kayn was standing in Kevin's grandmother's kitchen. The pots hung above a small island in the centre of the room. The fragrance of lavender still lingered in the air. Herbs grew on the windowsill. Slivered rays of sunshine through vertical blinds, crept across the room making it dim yet cozy. Sensing someone else's presence, she turned and smiled as Kevin's grandmother came across the room with her arms open wide.

With her beloved grin and twinkling eyes Granny welcomed her, "You have no idea how glad I am to see you, dear."

She knew why she was here. "You died," Kayn stated, leaning out of the embrace to see how she felt about it.

The shadow of reality obscured joy as Granny Winnie quirkily replied, "I've known when and how I was going to die for a long time."

Everything was changing too fast. They embraced again. Kayn held on tightly, afraid if she let go, she'd disappear into the hall of souls before Kevin had a chance to say goodbye.

"There's nothing to worry about dear," the elderly woman disclosed, I'll be here for a long time. I couldn't get through to the hall of souls if I tried." Granny opened the top button on her blouse revealing a brand on her flesh by her heart as she told her story, "My family died in a tragic accident when I was a child, only I survived. At sixteen, I fell through ice on a frozen pond and nearly died again. Not long after, a Clan took me from my orphanage. I was naïve but I had survival skills. I'd always known I was different. I saw things other people couldn't. My Clan told me it was a gift. For the first time, it felt like I was part of a family. Triad takes care of business other Clans don't have the stomach for. I had to assimilate to survive. I turned off my emotions to retain my sanity and allowed my soul to go dark. I caught the eye of the Clan's leader and we fell in love. Procreation is illegal under immortal law. When I found out I was pregnant, I knew I had to disappear. I pretended overuse of my Psychic ability fried my brain. A part of me wanted to believe he wouldn't do it but the man I loved desperately left me at a sanitarium and walked away, leaving me to the mercy of dark things. I hadn't been sealed to my Clan. I knew Abaddon may come for me, but it was a chance I had to take. Only one person came to visit, the most exotically beautiful girl, I'd ever seen. She noticed I was expecting. I was sure a Correction was coming but they never came. I named my daughter Lillian, after her."

Kayn's heart warmed, knowing it was probably Lily who came to see her so long ago. *She'd given Granny Winnie's baby a chance to live by saying nothing of its existence.*

Granny continued speaking, "I was a model patient, so they'd see me as emotionally vacant but harmless and let me go. I played nice and made friends with the orderlies. I proved myself to be a gentle, kind spirited person. They released me without a hassle upon the birth of my child. I found a church and told an altered story to a pastor who most likely thought I'd been kidnapped by a cult or something equally macabre. They let me stay in the church basement with my baby girl. That's how I met the man Lillian believed was her father. Paul was a member of the congregation. We got married and moved away for a fresh start. My husband acted like the baby was his to everyone we met. He died in an accident when Lillian was only six months old, leaving me a widow, which was preferable to an unwed mother back in those days. I cared for Paul deeply. He was my best friend, but I always felt guilty for not being able to love him. I allowed him to save me and he did in a million ways. I was devastated when I lost him, but truth be told, I was always carrying a torch for my first love, hoping his powers hadn't driven him mad. Kevin's biological grandfather is Tiberius, the leader of Clan Triad."

Kayn's heart froze in her chest. She'd been following along but hadn't fully absorbed the gravity of the situation until now. "What exactly does that mean for Kevin?" Kayn whispered, afraid if she spoke too loudly someone might hear.

With a reassuring touch, Granny exclaimed, "Your future is a choose your own adventure story. You make decisions and your future will be altered accordingly."

It felt like she'd been holding her breath for five minutes when relief allowed her to exhale. *She couldn't stomach the thought of losing him. Their bond was much more than teenage infatuation. Inseparable since early childhood, almost every beautiful mortal memory she held dear included him. She could close her eyes and be transported back to a million incredible moments in time. She could feel the simple bliss of lying in a field full of buttercups staring at clouds. He'd always been by her side. For so long they'd been untainted by life, with their only complaints being things like his height and her sister's magical voodoo powers. They'd played pranks and envisioned various versions of their futures over their years of friendship.* Kayn came to a silent realization. *The futures they'd imagined had never been theirs to have. Their fates had been set in motion long before they were ever a twinkle in their parents' eyes.* Kayn tilted her head as she questioned, "So, he could be more than Psychic?"

"Nobody knows what he's capable of. Kevin looks like my side of the family but if anyone from Triad sees Clay, they'll catch on quick. Clay looks like his grandfather."

Realising she'd missed the most important fact, Kayn said, "You can get a new body and come back with us."

"I have other plans for my future," Granny Winnie revealed. Beaming, she got up and whispered, "Kevin's here. Don't give him any information. I want to see how much he knows all by himself."

That's why she was fine with being dead. She was Clan, dying was merely an inconvenience. Kevin's bio grandpa was the leader of Triad. Granny knit her brow and shushed her. *Had she always been able to hear her inner dialogue? Awkward.*

Overjoyed, Granny announced, "My sweet boy, you're finally here."

Walking into the room, Kevin replied, "I thought maybe I could sneak up on you."

"You can't sneak up on a Psychic, it's the whole point of being a Psychic. We know things before they happen, silly," Granny chuckled as Kevin came to her with raw emotion in his eyes.

Choked up, he accused, "You're dead. Couldn't you have just changed it?"

Her eyes softened as she explained, "I've known about this for a long time. I was ready. If I'd changed a thing it would have endangered my family." The sweet elderly woman they adored clarified, "If I'd fought back, I would have exposed you."

He hugged his grandmother. She squirmed in his arms. Kevin pulled away, stammering, "What in the hell was that?"

Smiling, Granny answered, "Just a glitch. I willed you my ability. We're connected...Always."

Kevin snatched an apple out of the bowl on the table out of habit, smelled it and took a bite. He smiled as he passed it to Kayn, urging, "Try it."

Hesitantly, Kayn took a bite. *It was the most delicious apple she'd ever tasted.* Beaming, she declared, "This is incredible." She took another bite before passing it back.

Watching their in-between apple experience, Granny Winnie disclosed, "Your futures are altered by the decisions you make. Having a Psychic ability comes in handy. You'll hear this in various languages. Out of devastation comes a greater healing. Out of great pain comes victory. Tri-Clan has a part in everything that happens. You will be asked to do the unthinkable for the greater good. You must decide where that line of right and wrong exists within your soul." She gazed into Kayn's eyes and prodded, "Name one thing you feel you could never do."

"I could never kill a child," Kayn answered as though it were simple fact.

The elderly woman laid out a scenario, "What if you knew a child had a virus destined to kill thousands of people and most were also children? What if that one life could be traded for thousands?" Granny was met by silence as both teens realised, they wouldn't only be fighting other Clans but their own hearts. "Let me show you what I've been through Kevin." She placed her grandson's hands on her temples and urged, "Try to see my memories. It's going to hurt because we're connected but it's important you know everything."

As his hands contacted his grandmother's temples, Kevin shut his eyes and held them there. He yanked them away, looking at his fingertips. Peering up, he asked, "So, I have a monster for a grandfather who is practically Clay's double, and I'm Ankh, so I don't have to be Triad?"

"Yes," Granny replied, "If anyone in Triad lays eyes on your brother, he'll be an insurance policy. He'll be stored as an extra shell for your grandfather or used as leverage to keep you in line. Either way, Clay's soul will be trapped in the in-between."

Mortified, Kevin clarified, "He'd just off his own grandson and steal his body?"

"Without blinking," Granny bluntly answered.

"You can come back with us. You just need a new body," he deduced, curiously touching the lace tablecloth.

Kayn's partially mortal brain was stuck on the details of the identical kitchen too. *How was she holding Granny's tin saltshaker? It even had the banana sticker on the bottom holding it closed. How? Adding real life objects from home was confusing the division in her brain.*

Noticing what they were doing, Granny assured, "I'd rather guide you from afar. If I went back, it would only complicate things."

Trying to keep it together, Kevin whispered, "What will mom and dad think happened to you?"

Granny Winnie cautiously responded, "They'll never know what happened to either of us."

Confused, Kevin panicked, "I'm not ready to leave them."

Sympathetically, Granny whispered, "My dear boy, surely you understand this isn't a choice. The Legion of Abaddon has seen Kayn. It's only a matter of time before they know who you are." She beckoned Kayn with a delicate bony finger.

As Kayn took hold of her fragile hand, her heart clenched, and tears filled her eyes. *It was like fate kept drawing lines in the sand between her and the life she used to have.*

The elderly woman whispered, "There will be time for tears later. We know he has mine, but we need to see if Kevin has access to his grandfather's abilities. This may be disturbing. Don't try to stop it."

Unsure of what she meant, Kayn agreed, "Okay, I won't."

Granny let go of her hands and nodded. Returning the gesture, Kayn got up and went back to her seat.

Summoning her best friend over with eyes reddened by tears, Granny composed herself, apologising, "I'm sorry. I thought if you never knew, you'd be safe. I was wrong." She instructed, "Place your palms on my temples."

"I don't want to do this again," Kevin whispered with misty eyes.

Granny sternly decreed, "If you're more than a Psychic, you'll be valuable. For peace of mind, I need to help you along. See through the connection between us. Go inside of my mind, dig deep. You must stay connected until you've taken everything you can." Kevin tried to pull away. Holding her hands over his, Granny secured his to her scalp, insisting, "You need to do this. Premonitions of the future are helpful but if you can dive into someone's past and see their memories, you'll know what they're afraid of. You'll see if they usually choose to run right or left. Insignificant details give you an advantage in a battle. It's going to hurt like hell, but it's time to grow up, and stop being a chicken shit."

"Did you seriously just call me a chicken shit?" Kevin chuckled.

Kayn muzzled herself with her hands to stop laughing. *This was a serious situation but watching Kevin being called a chicken shit by his elderly grandmother was freaking hilarious.*

Concentrating, nothing happened, Kevin maintained, "I don't understand what you want me to do."

Holding his hands firmly in place, his grandmother persisted, "The information you need is in there. Keep trying until you get it."

"I'll try again," Kevin muttered under his breath.

Something was happening. He's in agony. He's trying to let go. Granny aggressively kept his hands in place as Kayn fought the urge to step in. *He's scared.* Suddenly, his eyes rolled back. He passed out on the kitchen floor.

Lily walked into the room and said, "What happened to him?"

Rushing to his side, Kayn knelt, repeating, "Kevin, wake up," tenderly stroking his hair.

Lily shoved her out of the way, saying, "For heaven's sake, we don't have all day." The gorgeous immortal hauled off and cuffed him across the face.

"What in the hell was that for?" Kevin mumbled, opening his eyes while rubbing a stinging jaw. "Why are you three on top of me?" They continued leering. He stammered, "Which one of you hit me?"

Crouched over him, Lily piped in, "I slapped you. It was me, they were panicking."

"You were out cold," Kayn explained, backing away.

Kevin sat up, looked at his grandmother and said, "Are you sure Triad doesn't know about our family?"

"I can't be certain, it's possible Triad's Psychics have picked it up by now. They were in my house. I have pictures of you boys all over the place. If anyone sees Clay, they'll know."

Listening to their coded conversation, Lily questioned, "What about his brother Clay?"

Granny met his eyes granting her approval. Kevin disclosed, "Clay looks like our grandfather."

"Okay, why is that relevant to me?" Lily toyed sarcastically.

Kevin replied, "Our grandfather is Tiberius, the leader of Triad."

26

I WOULD BEAT YOU TO DEATH WITH MY TIARA

A hush fell over the room. "Shit," Lily cursed. Abruptly getting up, she paced, lapping the kitchen, dangerously close to a mental breakdown. "Shit," she swore. "Damn it, shit."

This wasn't good. Getting up, Kayn blocked her path, asking, "You alright?"

"We are in seriously deep shit. If he knows, he'll be hauling out the big guns," Lily commented, under her breath. "We don't have enough time to get you ready for what could be coming."

Joining their conversation, Kevin rationed, "We'll leave with you. We'll get away from our families, so nobody else gets killed."

Defeated, Lily admitted, "No, you don't get it. It's too late. The fighting has begun, there's no getting away from anything."

Meeting Lily's eyes, Winnie stated, "They were in my house. There are photos of the boys everywhere. If any of his men saw those pictures, Tiberius knows."

With the weight of reality upon her, Lily confessed, "Okay, full disclosure time. Winnie's a Psychic, maybe she can help.

This situation is more complicated than you know, Kayn's brother is Sam's reincarnation. I've stayed away from him, but I don't think it will matter."

"What are you talking about?" Kayn questioned, knitting her brow.

Grey entered the room, recapping, "Let me know if I've mixed anything up. Tiberius was allowed to procreate, and his spawn is Kevin's mom. Kevin's brother looks like Tiberius and Kayn's brother is Lily's great love Sam reincarnated. I couldn't have thought this shit up. It's diabolically brilliant. Fate never ceases to amaze me."

Grey's blunt summation of the shit show triggered unhinged giggling from Kayn. *She couldn't help it. She was going to lose them all. The writing was on the wall. Her brother and Jenkins were probably going to die. Maybe even Kevin's family too.* Cackling, she finally snapped.

Clasping her shoulder, Grey probed, "You okay?"

A few bricks short of a load, Kayn chuckled, "They are all going to die, there's absolutely nothing we can do about it." She howled laughing. *If she didn't keep laughing, she was going to start bawling. She wanted someone to say, no Kayn, you're wrong. They will be fine. We'll find a way to save them all.* She searched faces for a flicker of hope. *Nope. Not a damn thing. Nobody was going to blow sunshine up her ass so she could feel better about this.*

Grandma Winnie assured, "Death is not a permanent state of being."

Her mortal life was about to be throat stomped. Kayn stormed over to the fridge and began rifling through it.

Lily with the perfect body, commented, "That's not going to fix anything."

Grabbing a fudgsicle out of the freezer, Kayn blurted, "I run miles for fun. I can suck back a damn fudgsicle every time I get upset. I don't need well-meaning commentary from the peanut gallery." She lifted her dress to show off her toned abdomen.

Wincing, Lily quietly shared, "Point taken. Just so you know, you're not wearing underwear under your sarong."

With cheeks a lovely shade of burgundy, Kayn covered up embarrassment by biting her frozen treat in half like she didn't care. Swallowing a ridiculous mouthful, she was clutching her head with brain freeze as giggles erupted.

Smiling, Lily suggested, "Rub the roof of your mouth with your tongue, it will go away."

Following instructions, the pain vanished. Impressed, Kayn asked, "Who taught you that trick?"

"Believe it or not, a five-year-old," Lily responded, putting Kayn's wrapper in the garbage.

Grey flirtatiously whispered, "Brilliant I can binge eat anytime I want to speech." Winking, he smacked his abs, toying, "Yours are way better than mine. You have a nice everything else too."

Kevin shook his head at her, teasing, "I got to see your woo ha for the first time with Grey, Lily and my grandmother."

The elderly woman she adored was on her feet coming her way, grinning so widely, Kayn shook her head at herself as she smiled back.

Placing an arm around her, Granny Winnie gushed, "I always get a charge out of you, my dear. You never need to worry about being a bore. Sit down at the table for a cup of tea and do try to keep your clothes on."

Mortified, Kayn obeyed, taking a tea as it was passed, without responding. *Do try to keep your clothes on. That was funny. Well done, Granny. Accidentally flashing everyone took her mind off her mental breakdown.* Granny Winnie poured everyone a piping hot cup of tea.

Gazing across the table, Grey sipped his tea, provoking, "Are you planning to call that satanic nut bar grandpa?"

Too irritated to play nice, Kevin placed his teacup on the lace tablecloth and slammed, "Listen princess, I found this out five-minutes ago, give me a break. I've never met the guy, nor do I want to, after a glimpse of my grandmother's memories."

"Calling me princess, was uncalled for," Grey remarked. He took another sip, grinning at Kevin's rare show of testosterone. Grey sparred, "If I didn't like you, I would beat you to death with my tiara." He took his next sip of tea with a raised a pinkie.

They were sitting at a table with Kevin's recently deceased grand-mother having tea while the shit was hitting the fan back home. She understood their lessons were emotional as well as physical. Granny Winnie was the perfect teacher. They already loved and trusted her. Chloe had loose ends to tie up. They were giving her time alone with Frost. Kevin had taken an, all things Clan catch up course courtesy of Grandma Winnie's memories, and she was finding new creative ways to humiliate herself. Leaning closer, Kayn whispered to Lily, "Can't we at least try to bring my brother and Jenkins to safety?"

"I wish there was something we could do, but everything has already been set in motion," Lily confessed. "I know how unfair this is, I've lived it over and over, for longer than I care to admit."

Grey added his two cents, "I have lived through a thousand karmic lobotomies in my time but this one is rather evil and ingenious."

"Everyone keeps dancing around reality," Kayn stated, meeting the immortal's eyes.

Solemnly, Lily answered, "Reality and afterlife, don't mesh. There are lots of variables in play. If Kevin's grandmother was a Correction, Triad may have gone there first, but the next house on their to-do list is yours. Maybe that nice older guy Jenkins doesn't interrupt anything? If Matt stays at university tonight, they may miss him."

"Matt always comes home on the weekend," Kayn disclosed, letting the impending loss sink in. *Everyone was going to die.* She gapped out, blankly tracing the rim of her cup with a forefinger, running laps in her imagination. Her racing pulse decreased as her breathing levelled out. She tuned back into the conversation.

Granny touched Lily's hand from across the table, assuring, "Someday you'll alter the outcome of this painful circle you've been caught in. Open your heart to change and it will come."

Gazing into Lily's eyes, Grey hinted, "Maybe if you spent less time looking for love in the past?"

Looking directly at Grey, Granny Winnie said, "Maybe you should take your own advice?"

Grey got up from the table, announcing, "I am going to love you and leave you all. Great chat, Winnie. I'll take it under advisement." He abruptly left the kitchen.

She wanted to go back to when she had no fear, with sunshine on her face and joy in her heart.

Shoving over a tray of cookies as she would have on a normal day, Granny caught Kayn's attention, confessing, "At dinner that night, I was dying to stop it but couldn't. I know who you are. I've seen what you are destined to become. All heroes are born out of the embers that linger after the fire of great tragedy."

She'd been reborn that horrible night nearly a year ago, but so had Kevin. She remembered the searing fire of the blade as it sliced through her flesh. She'd held fast to believing it would never happen again. She would have to let that go. She'd signed up for a second chance at life as a sacrificial lamb for the greater good and she was on her way to the slaughter. Violence would always be part of her job description. She could be healed but with sacrifice there would always be pain. They'd come here to learn how to except the premise of immortality. She allowed her heart to succumb to faith. Anger slipped away and in its place was acceptance. Losing everyone she loved, and an afterlife of heroism wasn't how she expected her teen years to play out. Tears surged behind brave resolve. She laced her fingers with Kevin's and closed her eyes, until tears ceased to flow.

He tenderly kissed her hand, vowing, "We'll always have each other."

She was so lucky to have him with her. Trying to ease the tension, Kayn sighed, "So, there was no way for you to come out of the gate with, you're one of us now. You have to leave your family before they get killed."

Smiling, Lily replied, "Someday you'll be sitting where I am wishing it was that easy."

Getting up to refill the cookie tray, Granny said, "It circles back. For every action, the universe has a reaction. This time, Lily was forced to step away from a self-destructive path because of your relationship to Sam, or Matt as we know him. You will give him a chance to save someone he loves before his death as he failed to do in past lives. Jenkins couldn't save his daughter, but he can try to protect you. It must all play out to heal everyone involved. We are all bound together in a circle of souls."

Lily was staring, trying to figure out how she knew Winnie.

Catching her, Granny filled in the blanks, "You'll remember me like this." As Kevin's grandmother spoke, her voice rose an octave. Skin smoothed and freckled. A healthy blush appeared on her cheeks as hair thickened and teeth became pearly white. Skin on her arms tightened as signs of aging vanished revealing a lovely teenage girl.

She'd been innocent too when her life took a turn for the immortal. Watching his grandmother transform before his eyes into the girl she'd been before darkness entered her life, Kevin was sobbing. They rose out of respect as the ebony-haired beauty's lips parted in recognition. Winnie full on bear hugged a stunned

Lily. She'd never seemed like the cuddly type, but she was positively glowing from the thankful embrace.

Winnie acknowledged what Lily did, "You said nothing about my pregnancy after seeing me in the sanitarium. You told no one after what happened to your child, and in doing this, you allowed mine to live. I thought you were the most beautiful girl I'd ever seen in real life. You turned out to be just as beautiful on the inside. I named my daughter Lillian after you."

Tears swelled in Lily's eyes as she responded, "Nobody has ever said those words to me. I've never been called beautiful on the inside, not once."

She felt like she was beautiful on the outside and nothing more. Kayn embraced Lily, whispering, "Somebody should have." *Kevin was only alive because Lily went against the rules to do what was right. She'd often wondered what it would be like to be Lily or Chloe. She may have been clumsy and dorky, but she'd always known she had a good heart. How was it possible that Lily, the most beautiful creature she'd ever seen, didn't know her inner worth? Perhaps, it was so easy to compliment a beautiful thing, nobody had ever chosen to point out wonderful qualities beneath her fancy wrapping. Interwoven lifepaths had come to light on this day. Their souls had been connected long before they met.* Kayn stared at the brand on her palm. *The mark of Ankh had a price, she couldn't go back and make another choice. It would always be an aching reminder of what immortality cost her. She'd see her brother again, he'd find his way back to Lilarah as he had in each lifetime before. Jenkins would fulfil his goal of saving someone he loved. It was going to be horribly devastating and messy, but she'd survive it. Perhaps, once the demons were buried beneath years of healing, she'd be able to look back and see beauty in life's simplicity.*

"Thank you," Kevin whispered in Lily's ear as they hugged.

Winnie didn't know her name was Lilarah, not Lillian. She smiled but chose to remain silent. *Winnie would figure it out.*

27

I WILL LIGHT YOUR ASSES ON FIRE
IF EITHER OF YOU TELLS A SOUL

*L*ily and Winnie were chatting at the table like old friends. Submerged in guilt, Kayn's eyes met with Kevin's. *He was thinking about his family too. There was too much information to process. She was numb.* Emotionally exhausted, Kayn excused herself from the table and left the room. *This house was full of memories preserved in pristine condition but what would it look like when she returned? She probably wouldn't have the opportunity to go to Granny Winnie's house before they left with Ankh. It would be better for her heart to always picture it like this. Peaceful perfection. Would her home still be standing when they came back from the in-between? Would it be full of those dark things? Would Abaddon beat her there? Home is where your family lives. It was a word that would never mean the same thing to her again. Where would her home be now? There were so many things she didn't know. Everything about her future was uncertain.*

Wandering the house, Kayn turned the doorknob to sneak a peek downstairs. It squeaked and she couldn't help but smile. From the creaks in floorboards to the squeaks of hinges, it was exactly as it had been. She descended stairs into the concrete room containing Kevin's red tricycle. She sat on the steps with visions of childhood flickering through her memory. She recalled getting caught playing doctor in the corner beneath the stairs. They'd hidden special treasures all over this basement. *Was everything still where they'd left it?* Kayn crawled under the stairs, brushing away dust bunnies and cobwebs in her path to find a quarter hidden behind a loose board. She crawled back out with the quarter and sat on the stairs. Brushing the dust off her legs, she stared at the coin in her palm. *They flipped this quarter to end arguments.* They'd spent endless hours giving each other pretend speeding tickets riding the tricycle that still sat right where they'd left it when they grew up and got bikes. Kevin always wanted to be a police officer, but she'd never been able to decide. *The choice had never been hers to make. Maybe a part of her knew?* Kayn polished the coin by rubbing it between two fingers. She heard a creak on the stairs and knew it was Kevin.

"Do you want me to call someone who cares?" Kevin taunted as she gazed at the coin between her digits.

Kayn glanced back and questioned, "Call someone?"

"With the quarter in your hand, you turkey," he teased, sitting behind her.

She grinned as she got the reference to the old country song, they'd heard countless times at Granny's house when they were children. Without looking back, Kayn wistfully sighed, "I bet it's a hell of a long-distance charge from here. It would cost way more than this quarter."

"Probably," Kevin stated, lovingly massaging her shoulders.

Turning, she smiled at her best friend and said, "Our life went to hell, didn't it? I guess there's no point in attempting to use this quarter to call for help."

He laughed, replying, "We should totally call 911 when we

get home. That's a fabulous idea. Can you imagine the therapy they'd need afterwards?"

Kayn smirked and decreed, "Nobody would need therapy, they'd all be dead."

Playing with her curly locks, he asked, "Are you okay?"

Half of my family is dead the rest are about to die. I signed up for an afterlife as a sacrificial lamb, boogie man peacekeeper, and murderer. Why wouldn't I be fine? "I thought you were a Psychic, you're sleeping on the job," Kayn baited. She grinned, shifting to face him.

"We're going to be okay, I promise," Kevin softly assured. Cupping her chin, he kissed her softly on the lips.

"I know we will," Kayn whispered back with a weak smile. She turned to look at the basement. *Nobody else will, though.*

"Come back upstairs, Kayn," Kevin requested, kissing the curls on the top of her head. He left her on the stairs to stew for a while longer.

Kayn got up to take look at the basement. She strolled over to the tricycle in the corner. *There were no choices left.* Smiling, she squished her teenage butt onto the tricycle seat and pretzeled her legs, valiantly attempting to operate the pedals. Unsuccessfully recreating a moment from her childhood, she made it five feet before the tricycle fell apart. *Oh Crap. She was stuck.* She heard laughter coming from the stairs. Wincing, she peered towards the giggles. Sitting on the bottom step was a witness.

Grinning, Grey stood up and wandered over, saying, "Hey, I totally understand. I'm not even going to ask what you were thinking. I already know."

This was so embarrassing.

Grey squatted beside her and asked, "Answer one question, was it worth it?"

With a giant grin, she admitted, "Strangely, yes."

Helping her out of the twisted metal, Grey affirmed, "That's all that matters."

He hadn't judged her even though she'd just attempted to do something bizarre to make herself feel better. Trying to ride that ancient tricycle felt oddly inspirational. Kayn smiled, taunting, "Thanks, Grey. You can be nice when you want to."

Chuckling, Grey ribbed, "I should put that in the fine print at the bottom of my friendship contract." He helped her up.

"That cement was damn cold," Kayn complained as she felt her icy behind.

Not so innocently placing his warm hands on her scantily clad butt, Grey confirmed, "It was cold, wasn't it?"

Stepping away from his hands, she remarked, "Hope I don't get hemorrhoids."

The endearingly scruffy-haired blonde immortal knit his brow, saying, "You can't get hemorrhoids from my hands."

She shook her head and clarified, "No silly, from the cold cement floor."

Grinning, Grey probed, "I'm glad you're back to your goofy self again but who in the hell told you that?"

Winnie's voice piped in, "I did and I'm not even going to bother asking you two what you're doing."

Winnie and Kevin were at the top of the stairs. Awkward.

Grey grinned as he bounded up the stairs, apologizing, "Sorry about the touching her butt thing. She got stuck on a tricycle and her bum was cold."

Kevin shook his head, teasing, "You naughty sinner. I was coming to see if you were okay."

"I'm glad to see you in better spirits, however it came about," Granny harassed, smiling.

"I got my ass trapped in a tricycle," Kayn huffed, stomping upstairs.

As she walked towards Grey in the kitchen, he commented, "You totally just let me touch your butt."

"You saved me from an embarrassing situation. Yes, I totally did," Kayn stated.

From behind her, Kevin laughed, "I'm standing right here."

Giving him an enormous hug, Kayn whispered in his ear, "It was all in good fun. I sat on a tricycle and my butt was freezing."

Squeezing her butt with both hands, Kevin flirted, "I would have warmed that up for you. All you had to do was ask."

Grey walked over to the couple, feigning shock, "But Kayn, I thought we had a moment?" Laughing, he vowed, "Next time I have a girlfriend you're allowed to touch her bum once, then we're even." He grinned as he strolled away.

"I'm holding you to that," Kevin shouted after Grey.

Winnie cleared her throat. Kevin respectfully stepped away.

Shaking her head, Winnie sighed, "You need to give me five minutes to get used to seeing you together romantically before you start groping each other in my presence."

"I bet, you always knew we'd end up falling for each other," Kayn responded, wishing she'd embraced her feelings long ago.

With an all-knowing smile, Winnie replied, "I had a hunch."

Kevin provoked, "Does Lily count as Grey's girlfriend?"

Shaking her head, Kayn playfully socked her shit disturbing bestie. *Funny.* Imagining they were really hanging out at Granny Winnie's house, the wall by the sink shimmered and Kayn saw through the mirage her soul created. *This was the calm before the storm. She was already past the end of her mortal life. It wasn't five or ten years down the road. It was already over. It had been over for a whole year even though her heart had been in denial.* She struggled to process everything she'd seen and heard, but her mind refused to accept one more horrible thing. It was too much for her to take so, she chose to laugh in the face of disaster. *Her old life was the mirage, and reality was far too sad. Jenkins and her brother were going to die. When she arrived home, there would be a battle, not over her life, but for her soul.* She stared at the symbol of Ankh. *What would happen if she was taken by another Clan? What if Abaddon took her?* She glanced at Kevin. He looked back at her and smiled. *What if they took him? She couldn't lose him. She couldn't even imagine a day without him. What if she had to spend an eternity without him?*

Kevin leaned closer and whispered in her ear, "You're making me dizzy. I have all of Granny's memories. In every version of my future, I love you. You can't lose me, it's impossible. You're going to make yourself sick, overthinking everything. Once we're safely away from the other Clans and Abaddon, I'll hook you up with stones and elixirs to tone down your easy to hear thoughts."

Smiling, Granny looked at her grandson, saying, "I bet you know things about my life, I can't remember. Do you have any idea how powerful you'll be gaining knowledge and reacting based on others' experiences?"

Tidying a hologram kitchen like it mattered, Lily put the folded tablecloth in a drawer, offering, "I've always been a warrior, he can use my skills. We're obviously not going to have enough time to train him properly before he's chucked into a battle far beyond his experience level."

It was time to forget the things that they could not change and concentrate on the things they could.

Sitting at the dated orange and brown linoleum table, Grey spoke, "He can have mine too. Concentrate on fighting skills, I'd hate to have another guy using my moves with the ladies."

Kevin glanced at his youthful grandmother for guidance, she raised her brows, cautioning, "Nobody knows your limits better that you do. If you're confident you've recovered from reading me, go for it."

Scooting her chair closer, Lily prodded, "Go ahead, read the story of my life."

Placing his hands on Lily's temples, Kevin's eyes rolled back revealing slivers of white. After a minute or two, he slumped in his chair and rolled onto the floor. They gathered around, Kevin opened his eyes, commenting, "You naughty girl."

Grey choked on a burst of laughter as Lily shot Kevin the dirtiest look, thinking, *I will light your ass on fire if you tell a soul.*

"I was messing with you. Don't worry, your secrets are safe with me," Kevin promised, smiling.

"Can we speak privately?" Winnie requested, summoning her.

Following, Kayn gasped as they walked outside, awestruck by crimson and tangerine splashed across the horizon. *It was a sunset so glorious it made her heart sing.* "Time is confusing in this place," Kayn whispered, taking in the splendour of the skyline.

Strolling away from the house, Winnie answered, "Time is something we always feel we need more of. Here, you have all of the time in the world."

Captivated by wonder, lost in the visual majesty of heavenly dusk, Kayn smiled at the youthful version of the grandmother she'd loved as her own. Barefoot in fragrant grass, a light breeze tousled Winnie's locks and the colour of her hair blended with the backdrop of the sky. *It wasn't about surface beauty, it was her graceful self-aware mannerisms. She was more stunning than she'd imagined.*

Amused by Kayn's thoughts, Winnie revealed, "There's a problem with the gift my grandson inherited. Along with good memories, he will store the bad. Trauma prompts our emotions to turn off. I've never loved anyone like I loved Tiberius but whenever he overused his ability, he vanished. Kevin is in urgent need of ability to fight, he's bound to go overboard. Having the knowledge and wisdom of many people is a seductive gift. Our abilities can be like addictions."

Dark clouds wove through the horizon like someone was painting their emotions. "I'll take care of him," Kayn vowed.

Winnie smiled and remarked, "Love is so beautiful when it hasn't been jaded by experience."

Wiggling her toes in the lush grass, embracing the distraction, a hint of lavender in the air reminded her of where she needed to be. *They should make sure he wasn't taking himself out playing with his new ability.*

Elbowed her, Winnie joked, "The grass is actually greener on the other side."

Scenery altered as Kayn giggled and clouds disappeared. *Maybe the surroundings were controlled by their mood?* The air was the perfect temperature with a tingly breeze just as she liked it.

Kevin's grandmother said, "I keep forgetting this is only your second trip to the in-between. It's truly miraculous those first ten times. After that, it's like going home."

"I can't imagine a time when this isn't going to be amazing," Kayn replied. Ripples of pleasure from what she was seeing had given her goosebumps.

Granny agreed, "It is breathtaking but let's get back to the situation at hand. Soon, you'll be back in the land of the living. I don't need to have this conversation with Kevin, he knows what I've seen for your future. No matter what happens, you must remain with Clan Ankh. There is a purpose behind everything, the bad often leads to the good. The only thing that truly matters is your survival."

That was ominous. "I have no plans to change Clans," Kayn responded with questions in her eyes, she knew Granny wouldn't answer.

Embracing her, Winnie whispered, "When the time comes, I hope you remember."

The sweetest girl belonged to the darkest Clan. It showed her strength, but it also proved her ability to be morally flexible. The purpose of their conversation was clear. Kevin's grandmother had done whatever she'd had to do to survive. They would have to do the same.

Promising to return before leaving the in-between, they left Granny's house to continue training.

28

IT WAS ALWAYS GOODBYE

*S*prawled beneath a ceiling of sparkling stars in luxurious grass with perspiration from their glorious union glistening on his skin, Frost teased, "You sure don't waste time, do you?" He turned to his gorgeous counterpart. *They'd made love with a level of intimacy he hadn't allowed himself to feel in a long time. This was going to hurt.*

Rolling onto her stomach with cascading love tousled curls obscuring his view of her chest, Chloe coyly said, "We don't have any to waste."

It felt like she was gazing directly into his soul. She was breathtaking. "You're absolutely right," he agreed, amazed by how easily he'd given his heart away. *It wasn't like him to leave his heart exposed. After eight hundred years of playing the field, leaving himself emotionally vulnerable was one of the only things that scared the shit out of him. Here he was falling for a girl he could never be with.* She rolled onto her back. *Lily told him to give her whatever she needed to feel whole, and in turn, this miraculous girl made him feel complete. He wanted to remember her like this... A vision of exquisite beauty underneath magical stars staring longingly into their light, looking like a magical fairy with the moon's rays creating a glowing halo around her.*

As she lay beneath the heavenly backdrop, Chloe disclosed, "I'd vow to never forget you, but I don't know where I'm going to end up. I've always dreamt of a night like this. You would have been the perfect person for me if I were still alive."

"It's all good, I'm not really a person," he teased, grinning.

"Oh, shut up," Chloe scolded, playfully batting his arm. "You know what I meant."

If he was honest with himself, he'd felt the same way about her ever since he sat on her in Kevin's car.

Lost in his eyes, she disclosed, "I know I'm already dead and we may never see each other again but feeling like this is what I wanted most." With tears glistening in her eyes, she continued, "If we had more time, I'd wait for years but I don't want to disappear forever with anything left unsaid. So, I'm just going to say it, I'm so in love with you. Do you love me back, even just a little?"

To say the words aloud would be like begging for a broken heart, but yes, he'd fallen in love with her and if he didn't tell her right now, he might never get the chance. Gazing into her eyes, he whispered his answer, "Of course I do."

"Do what?" Chloe probed innocently.

"Love you, I love you, Chloe," Frost admitted, hugging her against his chest. He friskily towed her on top of him. Tenderly caressing her face, he kissed her lips. *He hadn't said those words to anyone in a long time. It was what she needed to hear. He couldn't deny it. There was no time for games.*

"I'm sure that was hard to say to a girl that's going to be gone forever, thank you," Chloe whispered.

"We don't know what's going to happen," he soothed.

Resting her head on his chest, Chloe confessed what weighed on her soul, "It always felt like if I kept Kayn at arm's length, I wouldn't pull her into the darkness with me, but I took them all with me, didn't I? I took my whole family with me into hell. If I was the one who survived, I wouldn't be in your arms. I would have ended up with Abaddon. Ankh wouldn't have come for me, I'm not good like she is. I'm the dark and twisty road that leads somewhere horrible, she's the angel on the top of the Christmas tree."

Frost stroked her silky hair, responding, "You really have an inferiority complex, don't you? Give yourself a bloody break. I'm not exactly all rainbows and kittens either. The dirty work needs to be done for both sides." He trailed his finger seductively down her arm. "You're a little flexible with your morals. So am I. Who cares? Your family's expiry date was set in motion a long time ago. It wasn't your fault, the gift we have isn't easy to control. Impossible, if nobody taught you how to manage it. You were meant to join with your sister. You become whole together. Your mother is Ankh, we would have come to claim Freja's child. I was always destined to be with you. You were meant to be here in my arms. I was supposed to love you and you were fated to love me. I will never regret loving you, not for a second. No matter how much it's going to hurt when I lose you. You love me. Believe it or not, that's something I rarely get to hear. I never get to know if it's real either. You've given me a gift to carry with me. I'll always know you loved me back."

Giggling, Chloe provoked, "Wow, you are way mushier than I thought you'd be."

He pinned her down, tickling her in the grass as she laughed. *This was going to hurt like hell.* They spent hours in each other's arms, loving with every breath until Frost sensed they were about to have company. Rushing to get dressed, they tried to look like they were innocently sitting in the grass.

Chloe took his hand, saying, "Promise me something."

"Anything," he pledged, caressing her hand.

"Take care of my sister," she requested, resting her head on his shoulder.

He continued playing with her hand while assuring, "I intend to. You'll be a part of her and even if you never love me like this again, I will always look for you in her. I'll never stop trying to find you."

"I'm counting on it. I'm not afraid anymore," she pledged, kissing him once more.

KEVIN WAITED A DAY BEFORE taking on Grey's memories. After he did, it was like they were old roommates. Once someone knew your darkest secrets from the furthest recesses of your mind, there was no point in being stand-offish. They began training, thinking it would be catch-up time, but every experience he'd soaked up became data in his subconscious. Grey provoked and attacked at every turn. Knowing his every move, Kevin couldn't be done in by flying boulders or surprise attacks. He was a brilliantly skilled fighting machine. *It was wondrous to witness.* The memories he'd absorbed gave him a seasoned response for every action even though the only person he'd ever thrown a punch at was his brother. Granny Winnie's words about the addictive nature of his ability surged forth in Kayn's mind. *His expression made it clear he was suffering.*

Gently touching his shoulder, Lily suggested, "If you physically use up the excess energy it'll be easier to control."

She'd been troubled by his connection to Triad ever since it was revealed, and the conversation with Winnie hadn't helped. What if she lost him? She snapped out of her fear ridden thoughts as Kevin came over, praising, "Way to go, Smith. Cool ability."

"We get a break while they hunt down Frost and your sister," he toyed, smiling.

"Whatever do you want to do?" She baited as he took her in his arms, kissed her and playfully shoved her into the grass. She sprawled laughing, "You're a crazy person. We don't have time for this."

He got down on his knees and crawled towards her, teasing, "It might take them a while to find us."

Giggling nervously, she didn't move away while attempting to be the voice of reason, "We're not alone."

"What do you mean? We're alone," he flirtatiously dared.

She felt the change before she saw it. Looking around in awe, they weren't out in the open anymore, they were alone on a bed in a rustic cabin. *She knew this place.* Rolling off the bed, he took her hand, tugged her up and led her to the picture window. Taking in the beauty with her heart overflowing, Kayn observed, "Your family's cabin at the lake."

Embracing her, swaying back and forth, Kevin kissed her neck, confessing, "We'll be gone long before graduation but I always planned to bring you here so we could be alone."

Staring out the picture window at the wide-open span of the lake, she remarked, "Plotting to sneak me out past the chastity wardens to have your way with me, I'm impressed, Smith. How were we escaping?"

Wrapping his arms around her from behind, he whispered in her ear, "We would have snuck out your bedroom window and left your brother a, *Dear Matt* note. I was prepared to take my lumps when I brought you back home."

A bird swooped and skimmed the water's surface trying to catch a fish. Missing it's intended target. it did another fly by before skimming the surface of the lake again and soaring away with its bounty. "I'm trying to wrap my mind around leaving everyone we love," she disclosed as he nuzzled her neck.

Holding her tighter, Kevin replied, "I've had to accept some pretty insane things in the last year of my life. Leaving town to protect my family is the one thing that actually makes sense."

He chose to omit the other option. What if they were already dead? What if it was always goodbye? She looked into his eyes. *Either her friend was in denial, or so highly evolved it was crazy.* Leaving his side, she strolled over, and sat on the bed. Patting the mattress beside her, Kayn tempted, "Tell me more about these naughty plans of yours."

Sauntering over, he stopped short of joining her, groaning, "I don't have it in me to start something we can't finish. This gift I've inherited has me pharmaceutically enhanced aggressive. Lily mentioned a natural cure for my condition."

Laughing, she teased, "If you're about to say you're in pain and doing it will make you feel better, I may not be able to keep a straight face."

Inching closer, Kevin harassed, "When you put it like that, it sounds like a cheesy line in a video from family planning class."

The cabin was exactly like she'd envisioned in her fantasies. The, me hulk, me need sex speech, wasn't. Acknowledging the sentiment, she pressed, "You knew I fantasized about this, didn't you?"

"I may have tried astral projection a few times," he disclosed. "It's not an even playing field if you know my naughty fantasies and I don't know yours. I was happy to find out you don't ingest a gallon of cream cheese and a box of crackers every night before bed. I knew you were thinking about being with me, as much as I was thinking about being with you."

Studying the familiar curve of his smile, she thought of how his kisses made her heart overflow, replying, "Touché, you have me there." *They were wasting time.* Tugging him to her, their lips met in a delectable dance of desire. In a passionate frenzy, they tried stripping off their in-between attire, but no dice. *Come on.*

She'd accidentally flashed everyone and now, she was sealed in like she was wearing magical chastity protecting underwear. The more they attempted to rid themselves of pesky material, the more difficult it became. It was like trying to create an origami swan with tissue paper while hammered. They ended up laughing and tickling each other.

A few loud thumps on the cabin door was the warning they were given before Frost barged in. He saw their dishevelled state, apologizing, "Whoops, sorry. Carry on, we'll wait outside." He closed the door.

They sprawled flat on their backs, giggling. Kayn rolled over and whispered, "I say we jump up and down on the bed for ten minutes before we go out there."

Grinning, Kevin whispered, "We'll wait five minutes and then walk out together. You look mortified, I'll act confused. Now, that would be realistic."

She loved him so much. She smoked him in the face with a pillow.

Swatting her back with one, Kevin sparred, "Oh, is that how you want it?"

They got lost in a savage no holds barred pillow fight for a few minutes before remembering they were waiting. Thinking of the aggressive sound effects, they met each other's wide eyes and burst out laughing. Opting to own it, they strolled out holding hands. Kevin plucked a feather out of her hair.

Frost announced, "Are you ready to learn something cool?"

Kevin sparred, "Had you given me five more minutes, maybe I would have."

Instead of responding to his smart assed commentary, Frost leaned closer and whispered in Kayn's ear, "It obviously wasn't supposed to happen." He handed her a sword.

Old timey sword fighting, really? "You can't be serious," Kayn countered, hesitantly accepting the sword. *It was too heavy.* She tipped over and it sunk into the ground. Trying to pull the sword out, it wouldn't budge. *What in the hell? Why would he give her this?*

Watching her making a spectacle of herself trying to tug it out of the sand, Frost teased, "You get to watch." He tossed Grey a sword, prompting, "Let's show them how it's done."

Catching the sword in mid-air like it was as light as a feather, Grey provoked, "Bring it on, buttercup. You haven't beaten me once in forty years."

They fluidly clinked swords just as she'd seen in the movies. Their sword play was so perfect it looked choreographed. Kayn watched, her lips slightly parted with unhidden admiration. *Now, this was awesome.* When she was sure nobody was watching, she tried to dislodge her sword from the sand. *They make it look so easy.* Their swords clashed and clicked together with the expertise of countless years of training.

Watching intently before walking over, Kevin yanked Kayn's weapon out like taking a marshmallow off a stick. He gave her a funny look, toying, "Having trouble with your sword?"

Glaring while attempting to hold her sword upright, it was like it weighed a hundred pounds but only for her. *Maybe Kevin was strong now?*

"My turn," Kevin declared, raising his sword.

"Bring it on little man," Frost jested, grinning as he raised his.

Kayn scowled at Frost's pleased grin. *He always knew just what to say to piss someone off.* Their swords clashed with momentum altering from casual play to furious competition. Noticing Chloe standing beside her, Kayn extended her hand, wrapping identical fingers around her sister's, feeling warmth as mutual adoration filled her with peace. Lovingly squeezing her sister's hand, she smiled at her, and went back to watching the testosterone-fuelled sword fight. *Kevin might beat Frost. He'd copied Lily and Grey's memories. He had the information inside of his brain from every battle they'd fought. His gift was so cool.* Frost's confusion over how he was getting his ass kicked by someone who'd never used a sword was priceless. Everyone's attention was drawn to their comical sword play. A seventeen-year-old was handing the immortal his ass on a platter. Chloe tightened her grip, luring her attention away from the fight. Grinning at her twin, she went back to watching Kevin.

Making eye contact with Lily, Chloe mouthed, "Goodbye."

Without a peep, Lily mouthed, "Goodbye," smiling as she vanished. Expecting fireworks or mystical glowing light when they merged, everyone's eyes were glued on the comical action as the sword fight morphed into a pissing contest. The raven-haired seductress stepped between Frost and Kevin, gushing, "Amazing."

"How in the hell did you guys teach him to do that?" Frost stammered.

Grinning, Lily replied, "You were otherwise occupied. You missed out on the conversation with Winnie." She gave Frost a rundown of the revelations he'd missed during his break with Chloe. When she was done explaining afterlife bombs in Kevin's genetic line, Frost was understandably stunned.

"Well, at least now it makes sense," Frost mumbled.

Kevin wandered over and draped his arm around her. Kayn snuggled against him, whispering, "That was hot."

"Really, hot?" Kevin knit his brow, questioning. "Since when do you use the word hot?"

Kayn flirtatiously tempted, "Am I not allowed to think you're hot?" Shifting her golden locks out of the way, Kevin stealthily surveying the crescent birthmark behind her ear as he planted a kiss there. *He'd double-checked her identity, she was a little offended.* Her sense of humour being what it was, she pensively bit her lip, met his gaze, and went all in seductively kissing him. Wrapped up in each other, they forgot there were witnesses.

Laughing, Grey taunted, "Don't make me think up a bucket of water to chuck at you."

She wasn't sure what happened. Public make out sessions weren't usually her thing. Her senses were humming as she endeavoured to calm her raging hormones by taking a deep breath. *In all honesty, she'd never had the opportunity to find that out what her things were. She felt like being reckless.*

"Alright, naughty vixen, it's your turn to learn new things from me," Frost announced.

Was he talking to her? She spun to face him.

The deviously attractive immortal pointed to the ground and instructed, "First you have to pick up your sword, make sure you have a good grip on it. This will be a great way to get rid of some of that excess energy."

What an ass. Kayn lifted the incredibly heavy sword out in front of her. Frost swung his and knocked it out of her hands. It dropped, creating a cloud of dust. *Yes, she sucked at this.*

He smirked, strutting around like a peacock, scolding, "I said, get a good grip on it."

It's frigging heavy you douche bag. Kayn picked it up again. *It was even heavier.* Struggling to keep it upright, she asked, "Is this a joke?"

Knocking the sword out of her hand again, Frost baited, "All right love, this is getting a bit ridiculous."

Oh, she wanted to kick him. Kayn fought to pick up her sword.

Frost turned his attention to Kevin, disclosing, "I've had the joy of being tortured by Tiberius on multiple occasions. I've experienced his frustration when things don't go as planned. The last time I had the thrill of spending alone time with my brother, it was a lovely afternoon of excruciating disembowelment. For the record, that's an extremely unpleasant way to die."

Kevin's eyes widened as he clarified, "Your brother."

"Yes kid, we're related," Frost replied. Raising his arms, he announced, "Take a look at the glorious genes you've inherited. Your grandfather Tiberius is the leader of Triad. Thorne, our older brother is the leader of Trinity."

Kevin enquired, "Are you the leader of Ankh?"

Frost smirked and explained, "I started out as the leader but for personal reasons, I opted out."

Taking advantage of Frost's attention elsewhere, Kayn ran at him attempting a surprise attack, swinging her sword at the cocky immortal with a vengeance. He gently tapped it out of her grasp. She lost her balance, landing on her knees. *That was dumb.*

He directed the next spar at Kevin, "Do me a favour, spend one on one time with your girlfriend, teach her how to handle a sword."

She caught the multiple meaning of his barb. *What a jerk.*

Towing Frost away from their new Ankh, Lily hissed, "That's enough. You're being a complete ass. I get it, you're panicking about what Tiberius is going to do when he finds out. Yes, this situation has the potential to be one hell of a shit show, but at this point we have no choice, so let's own it."

"Who's panicking?" Frost coldly replied.

In a hushed voice, Lily reprimanded, "You are supposed to be training, not browbeating her."

Crouched by Kayn, Kevin whispered, "Ignore that idiot."

She barely had the strength to move. Peering up, Kayn whispered, "I can't get up." Fighting to lift her weight with her arms, she couldn't. Looking up at a clearly frustrated Frost, she whispered, "Something's wrong." Her vision wavered as she crumpled into a ball. Instantly, Kevin was trying to revive her.

Rolling his eyes, Frost sighed, "Oh, for heaven's sake, what now?"

Lily gave him a shove, explaining, "While you were fighting, Chloe disappeared. We have to wait and see if it takes."

Stunned, Frost stepped back. Shaking his head in denial, he whispered, "Are you sure?"

Grey gave his shoulder a brotherly squeeze, confirming, "I saw it happen. I didn't want to jinx it."

Frost stormed away. Grey attempted to follow. Lily stopped him, asserting, "Give him time alone, he knew this was coming."

"He really cared for her," Grey whispered, watching Frost disintegrate into the air.

As he vanished to one of his special places in the in-between, Lily whispered, "Chloe missed her chance at anything real by losing herself in her Siren ability during her mortal life. Frost knew she needed somebody to love her because they chose to. He allowed his heart to go for a jog. He'll get over it. He always does."

29

THE END OF THE FANTASY

They had been sitting in the grass for nearly an hour waiting for Kayn to come to when Frost solidified out of thin air. Sitting with the concerned immortals, he enquired, "Has she opened her eyes?"

With a warm smile, Lily responded, "Not yet."

Looking past Lily at Kevin, Frost said, "I guess this is a golden opportunity to get to know my surprise nephew. Tell me, what can you do?"

Waiting in uneasy silence for a while when Frost blurted a random question, Kevin snapped out of his stupor, "Huh?"

"Not speech writing, then," Frost ribbed, peering over at Kayn's lifeless body.

Gently stroking Kayn's hair, hoping wherever she was, she felt his presence, Kevin stated, "I'm not in the mood for games."

His blood relation, prodded, "Kayn's fine, Lexy's got this. I'd like to run you through scenarios to see what you're capable of."

With no intention of leaving her, Kevin responded, "I see dead people. I noticed an aura around Kayn after her first trip to the in-between. When our symbols flashed that night, a voice warned me not to go and I knew Kayn had to get into the circle. It was basic Psychic stuff until my grandmother died and willed me her powers. During our visit here, I figured out how to see and retain other people's memories."

Impressed, Frost urged, "Stick to absorbing memories, never erase any if you can help it. Memories are all we have. Losing them is a fate worse than death." Frost glanced at Lily.

Noticing his gaze, Lily said, "Huh? What did I do?"

"My point exactly," Frost grinned, taunting, "Remind me to get you guys a dictionary so you can learn to start your sentences with something other than, huh."

IN A LAND ALL THEIR own, Kayn and Chloe wandered hand in hand through a breathtaking field of buttercups in search of bumblebees. With joyous hearts the duo frolicked in the glorious magical meadow of intoxicating scents and visual splendour. There was not one fuzzy bee collecting pollen on the millions of delicate sunshine coloured flowers. Neither spoke, trying to hear familiar humming. Chloe sat down, tugging Kayn with her onto plush, vibrant foliage. They each picked a flower. Chloe plucked the petals off immediately but Kayn didn't want to damage hers. She felt guilty for removing it from the earth. They understood these things about each other. Kayn aspired to heal and Chloe's first impulse had always been to destroy.

Chloe spoke first, "Promise me one thing. Keep living your life in the light, never allow me to draw you into the dark."

Peering up from the dainty yellow flower, Kayn said, "We can find the middle ground together." They turned towards echoing voices coming from beyond the horizon.

Kayn took her sister's hand as Chloe whispered, "I think it's almost time for us to go."

"I don't want to lose you again," Kayn whispered.

Chloe quietly vowed, "You will never lose me."

With those final words, Chloe's essence absorbed into Kayn's hands followed by a burst of glorious light. She felt warmth as her sister's soul came to rest in her heart. Unusually alert as the voices grew louder, everything went black. She'd always been uncomfortable in the dark, but something calmed her this time, and she found it intriguing. *There could be anything or anyone beside her, she would have no way of knowing.* She attempted to open her eyes, but they wouldn't budge so she decided to see with her other senses.

Inhaling the invigorating scent of the ocean, she successfully opened her eyes and found herself thigh deep in liquid heaven. There was nothing but water for as far as the eye could see in every direction. Vibrant coloured shells and starfish adorned the ocean floor of shimmering ivory sand. *She needed to choose a direction and start walking. Which way took her to shore?* Stubbornly in place, flashes of white light whooshed past her feet in the water. She leapt out of the way and lost her balance, tumbling backwards into the shallows. Gleaming orbs encircled her. With a racing heart, she knew there was nothing to fear. The spheres of iridescent light were out of reach. Wanting to touch one, she squinted in the glare reflecting off the water, slowly inching her hand towards the circular beings. It tickled as they circled her fingertips and scattered in every direction across the surface of the water in a burst of light, leaving her in the centre of a star. Shielded her eyes with dripping salty fingers, she laughed. As she uncovered her eyes, her breath caught in her chest. A stunning golden stallion was making its way through the shimmering water towards her. *She didn't know much about horses but didn't want to be in the path of hooves.* Kayn slowly rose. The stallion stopped advancing. Closing the space between her and the regal being, she assured, "I'm not going to hurt you." Light breeze rippled his majestic mane like a cape of gold. *She'd never laid eyes on anything so wondrously free.* Aching to touch it, Kayn inched closer to the exotic creature, whispering, "Who are you? What are you doing out here with me?" Kayn was almost able to touch him when beneath her feet thousands of white lights sped past in the same direction. The stallion reared, whinnied, and galloped away following the lights. Kayn turned to see what they were running from. Coming at her was a wall of water as large as a mountain. All she had time to say was, "Shit!"

She awoke gasping for breath recalling her last moment of consciousness. *The wall of blinding pain. She received the lesson loud and clear. Always look behind you. Especially if there is something unusual distracting you. She felt like an idiot.* She saw Kevin and Frost. Her heart warmed to both giving her an inkling of how complicated joining with Chloe could become if she allowed her heart to lead the way. *She had to hold on to the person she'd always been. Kevin was her future. He'd given up his life, without a hint of hesitation.* Keeping her gaze on Kevin, Kayn mumbled, "That was unpleasant." She sat up, shook off the trauma and explained, "I just got hit by a tidal wave the size of a mountain because I was busy watching a horse in the water."

Frost sarcastically baited, "You seriously didn't see that one coming? I bet it didn't seem strange at all that a horse was just randomly there to entertain you in the water?"

She muttered under her breath, "You are such an asshole."

The gorgeous immortal, provoked, "Thank you for noticing. I do try hard at it."

Feeling the strength of the pull towards Frost, she had to look away. *Yes, her sister's love for him was going to be a problem.*

Grey comically pointed out, "You will find Frost much less of an asshole when there are no stupid people around."

Frost patted Grey on the shoulder and said, "Thank you, I'm touched buddy."

"Trust me, pretend you didn't hear it," Lily advised. Rolling her eyes, she added, "You'll inadvertently start asshole love fest. Frost thinks being called an asshole is a compliment."

"Thanks for the heads up," Kayn whispered, wishing she hadn't said a word to him. *Frost was looking at her like a dog with a savoury bone.*

Hugging her, Kevin whispered, "Is it still you?"

She squeezed him extra tightly, replying, "It's me." Inhaling his familiar scent, her heart surged with adoration. Her chin was resting on Kevin's shoulder as Frost's defeated eyes met hers. *He'd heard their conversation.* She kissed Kevin's cheek and let him go feeling horrible. *It wasn't necessary to rub it in.*

Quickly snapping out of it, Frost began schooling Kevin on Tiberius's capabilities, "Your grandpa can procure information from people and turn off the ability to feel pain. Being the sadistic sociopath, we all know and openly despise, he usually opts out of using it, even to help his own Clan. He's one of those take it like a champ leaders." He finished with, Doctor Evil finger air quotes.

She pursed her lips so she wouldn't giggle.

"Turning off pain sounds useful," Kevin acknowledged. He turned and winked at her.

Even though she was trying to keep her eyes focused on Kevin they kept drifting to Frost.

Frost caught her staring but didn't call her out, he stayed on task, "You have your grandmother's memories. I'm certain that feisty old broad was paying attention to how Tiberius did things. A Healer's gifts are usually compassion based. Your grandfather's abilities are rage based. You don't look like a guy with rage issues. You come across as a gentle and meek little guy. Will you be able to summon up enough rage to fight for the people you love when it counts?"

Frost was trying to provoke him. He'd used the word little. It was on.

Kevin fired back, "Are you serious? You think I can't summon up enough rage? From what I understand our only option seems to be running to lead the other Clans and demons away from our families, so they won't be brutally murdered. If the other Clans have figured out my part in this, we're shit out of luck. Everyone we love dies and my brother Clay gets to become a skin coat for my grandpa. My mom is a sitting duck. My dad is dead the second he walks through the door. What's left of Kayn's family is going to die, and then there's Kayn. The thought of someone hurting her makes my blood boil. We've been enlisted into a Clan where we get the privilege of being supernatural chew toys. My grandpa has the personality of Satan, my grandmother was just ripped into pieces. Have I missed anything?"

"Nope, I think you got the gist of it kid," Frost quietly replied as his asshole juju gradually sunk into the emotional quicksand of empathy. He opted for a courteous tone, "I think we should try to test for pain removal abilities. Sit here and sift through your grandmother's memories, Tiberius may have shown her how they worked." Nodding, Kevin closed his eyes, trying to locate what Frost asked him to find.

Hugging her knees to her chest, Kayn was resisting the urge to sooth herself by rocking back and forth with Kevin's speech about how they were all going to die repeating in her head. *She'd absorbed her twin's soul, Kevin was sifting through his dead grandmother's memories, this was insanity. None of this is possible. She was stretching her boundaries too far. With each revelation he'd listed, her heart became heavier until it felt like dead weight within her chest.* A voice in her mind, whispered, '*Shut it off. You have to shut off your emotions if you're going to have a chance.'* She was rocking, even though she didn't intend to. *This whole ordeal would be a lot easier if she succumbed to the insanity. She needed to permit herself to go a little crazy. Not skin coat wearing, dancing around wearing someone's scalp as a hat certifiable but just mad enough to have someone ask her to do something nuts and she'd be able to say, hey let's do it, without requiring a rational reason.* A hand squeezed her shoulder. She peered down at the delicate fingers and knew it was Lily.

The gorgeous immortal with glistening midnight hair whispered, "Right now it feels impossible but someday all of this crazy stuff will be normal. There are no accidents in our lives just horrible lessons and excruciatingly painful moments. Every event has its own special purpose in the development of your soul. I was told something years ago and it's gotten me through everything I've faced so far. I whisper it to myself whenever it doesn't feel like there's a way through something. Do you want to hear it?"

Her eyes were pressed shut and her arms were coiled around her knees as Kayn nodded.

Lily replied, "Breathe in, breathe out and put one foot in front of the other until it gets easier."

Focusing on breathing, Kayn loosened her grip on her knees and turned to look at Lily. *She was smiling, not a fake one, a genuine one.*

The stunning immortal remarked, "It works, doesn't it? From now on, concentrate on the basics. Try to follow orders without taking it on as your own. It's all inevitable in the grand scheme of things. Everything that happens was always going to occur, with or without your involvement. If we weren't here, it would be a random accident. Death is only an opportunity to rise again. It's not the conclusion to someone's story. There is no end, once you comprehend it, everything is clear. We are all immortal. The only difference between us and them is we get to keep the boxes we came in."

She felt better. Clasping Lily's hand in hers, she said, "Thank you."

"No problem, that's what friends are for," Lily answered.

She'd never expected Lily to become her friend. Kayn looked for Kevin. He was still sitting there with his eyes closed. *She wanted to shake him out of it and tell him what Lily just told her. She had a new perspective. Her best friend needed to hear this, but they'd have time to talk later, he was busy rifling through Granny Winnie's memories.* Standing, Kayn took a deep breath and everything seemed brighter. She walked towards the others with a smile on her face as her mind whispered, *breathe in, breathe out, left foot, then your right foot. You are doing great.*

Grey was speaking, "Maybe we shouldn't be training without knowing if Lexy is still outside of her tomb able to heal us?"

Frost grinned as a giant boulder materialized in his hands.

"Bloody hell," Grey stammered, sprinting out of the clearing towards the woods.

After giving his buddy a sporting shot at fleeing, Frost wound up and pitched the boulder. In the distance, Grey went down in a splash of blood and meat. He winked at Kayn and said, "Don't say I've never done anything sweet for you."

Frost thought murdering Grey in the same way he'd killed her during training was sweet. It was a little funny.

Encircling her with his arms from behind, Kevin kissed her neck, saying, "You're going to ask me to slay someone to prove my love to you now, aren't you?"

Smiling, she answered, "I think I'm all good with a flower in my shoe or a zombie pen holder."

They far too casually strolled over to Grey's bloody carcass. *She'd never been on the other end of this moment. She'd always been the victim.* She watched in wonder as his broken bones shifted back to their original placement and his flesh healed.

"Question answered. Lexy's running the tombs, it's all good," Frost declared, chuckling.

Facedown in soil, Grey moaned and complained, "Don't you think it would have been a good idea to try out Kevin's pain dulling ability before giving me a backwoods lobotomy, you jackass?" He thrust himself up with his sun-kissed muscular arms and glared at Frost.

"Sorry, I jumped the gun. We'll have to do this again. Kevin, try to get rid of Grey's ability to feel pain first, we'll even let Kayn throw it," Frost instructed.

Glaring at Frost, Grey vehemently hissed, "No, we will not kill me again. You run away, Kayn can throw your boulder."

Laughing aloud, Frost agreed, "Sounds like a plan. We don't need to test Kevin's ability first. Our Kayn can't even manage to swing a sword."

He was such an ass. Kayn looked at Grey and declared, "Fine. Let's do this." She stared at her hands as she thought of holding a giant boulder, one appeared. *It wasn't as heavy as she'd thought it'd be.*

Walking in the opposite direction, bouncing from side to side, Frost provoked, "Let me know when I should start running, froggy."

She scowled at his ignorant little nickname. *Oh, he was going to get it.* Kayn yelled, "I'd start running!"

He jogged away in slow motion, chuckling. Lily signalled for Kayn to pass the boulder to her. Grinning, Kayn did, with no qualms whatsoever. *Frost didn't seem to value the idea of fair play while dealing with other people when he was the one holding the weapon. If anyone deserved an attitude adjustment it was him.* Lily wound up and hurled it, flawlessly recreating Grey's demise by boulder. They were all laughing as they made their way to Frost's body.

Grey snickered, "Won't we feel like a bunch of douches, if he didn't heal and Lexy shows up." They circled him waiting for the process to begin, it took longer than expected. Just as they were all becoming nervous, it began.

Lily whispered, "Let him think Kayn did it. He was in dire need of an afterlife lesson."

They smiled at each other as Frost pushed himself up onto his knees. Turning to Kayn, he declared, "I didn't even see that one coming, good job." Jumping up, he made his way towards her, toying, "Glad I could help you release some of that pent-up aggression, you're welcome. Now that you have your strength back, let's see how you handle a sword."

Groaning from the overabundance of innuendo, Kayn said, "You never give it a rest, do you?"

"No rest for the wicked.," Frost sparred as a sword appeared in his grasp. Sauntering her way, dragging his weapon, dust rose.

Thinking of a sword, one appeared in her hand. *It wasn't heavy.* Kayn provoked, "You haven't said a word about my sister. Are you so old you've forgotten her already?"

Frost smirked and toyed, "Miss Brighton, was that trash talk? I'm honoured, get your halo dirty. It must be difficult wearing that nun habit all the time. Does it get hot under there?"

Her pulse raced in reaction to his naughty commentary. She elevated her sword with no issue, taunting, "I adore black. The lame innuendo is becoming painful. You've had no reaction to losing her. It's just an observation, there's no need to get touchy about it."

His eyes glinted with humour as he sparred, "Sweetheart, in a real battle nobody is going to put down their weapon until you get your emotions in check." He swung his sword, she blocked his blade with her own.

For a split second, Kayn thought she'd done something right, until he looped his arm around hers and tugged her against him. She exhaled, attempting to have no reaction to the length of his lean body pressed against hers.

He spoke softly into her ear, "Chloe's right here, she hasn't gone anywhere. She's inside of you. I won't lose you to another Clan. Do me a favour, stop pissing around and learn something."

His breath tickled tendrils of hair on her neck. Swallowing a lump of emotion, Kayn taunted, "Fine, quit messing around and instruct me." She elbowed him away. He laughed, stumbling backwards. She swung her sword, striking his arm. It looked like even give and take as they fought but she was fully aware he was taking it easy on her. Kayn lost her footing, landing with an ungraceful thud in the grass. Frost held his hand out as a peace offering. Hesitating, because she knew he was up to something, she couldn't resist. As her hand slid perfectly into his masculine grip, he pulled her up into his arms.

His husky voice was filled with innuendo, "Let me tell you a secret darling. Emotions can make you strong as a lion or weak as a kitten. If you know what buttons to push, you can take anyone down." He whispered in her ear, "You're an open book."

She might be in trouble. Her body had a mind of its own, her response to his touch was instinctual. He didn't miss her racing heart as she melted against him. His eyes lit up with the knowledge that Chloe was there in some capacity. Frost bit his lip pensively as he let her go. *She had to do a better job of hiding her sister's feelings.* Avoiding his eyes, she made an inward effort to regain control. *Kevin was who she loved. She was in charge.* Kayn stepped away from Frost's magnetic pull.

Irritated, Kevin called him out, "Are you almost done flirting with my girlfriend or do you need a few more minutes, Frost?"

Grey came to Frost's defence, "Don't get your panties in a twist. He's just trying to get to his point, creatively."

"Right, creatively," Kevin repeated, rolling his eyes. He raised his brows at Kayn, making it clear he saw her reaction. *It was the first time he'd called her his girlfriend.* She felt her heart close off to Frost as she shoved the unwanted feelings deep down where they belonged. *She'd explain things to Kevin later. He'd understand if she blamed it on Frost's voodoo powers.*

Frost gave the rest of his speech from a respectable distance, "Sadness makes you feel weak. Deal with grief when we're done fighting. Bravery, duty and anger are powerful. There's a fight ahead if you want to remain with Ankh. Concentrate on how angry you are. Channel rage into strength. You can't afford to waste time anguishing over things."

He was trying to prepare her for the inevitable. Everyone might already be dead.

Lily's eyes softened, saying, "Nothing we've done in training makes sense yet. Jumping off a cliff helps you understand death isn't permanent, it builds trust and conquers fear. All we have time for is the basics, death isn't permanent. If you find yourself afraid, use it to your advantage. Fear can either make you more powerful or be crippling. What makes you strong one day can incapacitate you the next. That's why you must force yourself to do the things that terrify you. Once you've empowered yourself, fear becomes a weapon in your arsenal. Decades from now, pain will be the only thing you fear. We feel the pain, every second of it."

"I know what pain feels like," Kayn answered coldly.

Breaking the invisible barrier required for ration, Frost took Kayn's hands in his, clarifying, "After you've been captured by Abaddon, you'll understand. Gratuitous torture is a trauma beast. I'll do everything within my power to make sure it never happens to you, but contrary to popular belief, we aren't superheroes. We're just people with no expiration date, required to take one for the team in the grand scheme of things. Yes, you've stared evil in the eye and spent an hour or two with it. Imagine what happened to you lasting for weeks. We destroy each other by crippling minds. Well, we have Siren, so we rarely have the need for it. Triad and Abaddon are experts. We can't die because we cannot pass through the hall of souls to be reborn. If we've gone crazy because we've been tortured for too long, the only way out is to have our memories wiped. I've lived this long without being wiped by learning to turn my emotions off when it counts."

"Rage out," Grey provoked. "Allow yourself to feel the fury for all you've lost and may lose. Embrace it as soon as you step out of that tomb. If you're afraid, channel it into energy. Fighting through fear gives you strength."

Kevin stated the obvious, "What are we fighting for if there's no hope to save the people we love?"

Meeting their eyes, Lily stressed, "We have to fight to keep Kayn. If all three Clans and Abaddon have shown up, everyone's Psychics know about her. A Conduit is a rare ability."

"If Psychics know about an ability that doesn't exist yet, what if Triad knows about Kevin's connection to their leader?" Kayn enquired. *She couldn't lose him.*

Lily's eyes softened as she responded, "It's only been an hour in the land of the living. We learned about his background in the in-between. It is possible Triad saw pictures at Winnie's house. If we keep Kevin with us until he's eighteen, he'll belong to us."

"Long story short, we're competing against the other Clans and the Legion of Abaddon for your souls," Frost concurred, ending the speech.

30

HOW TO TAME A DRAGON

*M*aterializing out of thin air, Lexy declared, "The game has officially changed." Embracing Grey, she whispered, "I behaved myself." Grinning at the others, she filled them in, "We are so far up shit creek, not even a motor could save us now. I counted ten Triad outside. When Trinity showed up, left them duking it out and came here before they breached the house."

How were they going to fight their way through that many people? Meeting Kevin's eyes, she knew he was thinking the same thing.

The crimson-haired Healer of Ankh explained, "You never send more than six Clan members, it's an unspoken rule. This event is stacked in Triad's favour. It doesn't make sense. Why would they send this many Triad for a girl who hasn't been Enlightened yet?"

As weight settled on her heart, Kayn sat in the grass, blankly disclosing, "They may not be here for me."

Visibly confused, Lexy sat next to her, questioning, "Why would they send ten Triad for a Psychic?"

Remaining standing, Frost decreed, "He knows."

Lexy exclaimed, "Quit talking in code. What's going on?"

Joining them on the lush greenery, Grey put his arm around Lexy, explaining, "They'd send ten Triad for Tiberius' grandson and a Conduit."

Looking at Kevin, Lexy sighed, "I hate being the only Healer onsite, I miss out on the good stuff." She gawked at the teen, commenting, "You poor thing."

She didn't know how to fight. She couldn't make things magically appear in the real world. Kayn peered up at Frost and questioned, "How do we get back if Lexy's with us again?"

Lexy took it upon herself to reply, "We're stuck here until the rest of Ankh arrives and fights their way into that house. On the bright side, I get to play a part in training, that's going to be fun." Shimmying closer to Kayn, Lexy whispered, "Unwinnable battles have been won throughout history for love. You have two Ankh in love with you, it's possible."

Kayn shook her head at the flame haired badass beside her and whispered, "Frost's in love with Chloe. We've joined, she's gone."

Yanking a dandelion from the ground, Lexy squashed it in her palm, leaving behind a stain as she casually remarked, "Good, you're going to need all of the mojo you can get, it's a gong show back at the house."

She felt his eyes on her. *Do not look at him.* Her heart raced. *Do not react.* Kayn couldn't help it, she turned. Frost was grinning. *Damn it.*

Frost sat in the grass behind her, teasing, "You keep telling yourself that frog sticker girl." Running a curly strand of her hair between his fingertips, he whispered, "It feels the same."

She looked at Kevin. *Why was he allowing Frost to mess with her? He knew she got the shivers if anyone touched her hair. It felt like they were both testing her.* Staking claim by sitting and placing an arm around her, Kevin glared at Frost, shaking his head. *She'd seen that look in his eyes before. Frost was dancing on his last nerve.* Lacing her fingers with Kevin's, she raised his hand to her lips, kissing it. *She needed him to know he'd always be her choice.*

Reciprocating by kissing hers, Kevin gazed into her eyes. Leaning in, he tenderly kissed her temple, whispering, "You're sure your feelings for me haven't changed?"

She glanced back at Frost, responding, "One hundred percent sure."

Frost flirtatiously baited, "Really? One hundred percent?"

"You heard her," Kevin bluntly stated, squeezing her hand.

Chuckling, the love of her sister's life provoked, "Did I?"

She wasn't impressed by their territorial game, and honestly, the bounty of unrestrained testosterone in the air was concerning. They were acting like dogs repeatedly peeing to mark their territory and she was the tree.

Lexy stood up, shook her head at the boys and sighed, "Miss Brighton has the strangest inner dialogue. I'm going to find Lily. Boys, please refrain from marking your territory."

Kayn awkwardly stared at the grass in front of her. *They heard everything she was thinking. Awesome. She was the supreme master of dorkdom.* She peeked to see their reaction to Lexy's slam, they all started to howl. *It was time for a subject change.* She looked at Grey and enquired, "Is Lexy your girlfriend?"

Grey grinned at her avoidance tactic and replied, "No, she's my best friend and sort of my job. We aren't allowed to sleep together. It's against the rules. It's hard to have a relationship without the best part."

That caught her attention. She repeated, "Your job?"

Relaxing in fragrant grass, Frost suggested, "They should know who they're dealing with before they have their asses handed to them for saying the wrong thing."

Chuckling, Grey scooted closer, saying, "Four decades ago, when I first joined Ankh, everyone was chasing this infamous Dragon Tri-Clan told horror stories about. Dragon is slang for a warrior with the ability to shut off emotions. Lexy survived a dozen Abaddon attacks and fought off every Clan who tried to claim her. Our Oracle told us I was the only one who'd be able to bring her in. I was sent into the wilderness alone. I'd been walking for a day with no sign of her when I got caught in a trap. I knew she'd check to see if she caught anything. I was just hoping a bear didn't eat me first. When she came, it was obvious she'd been alone in the woods for a long time. She hadn't bathed, her hair was matted. I was pretty sure she was planning to eat me."

Thinking Grey was joking, Kevin chuckled.

Dead serious, Frost confirmed, "No, she was really going to eat him."

Kevin glanced at Kayn. She widened her eyes.

Grey continued his tale about catching Dragons, "We had an immediate connection. I needed to help her. She let me out of the trap and took off, leaving me with a severely injured leg. I followed her to a cabin. I remember standing on the porch, contemplating the stupidity of following her inside. When I went in, she seemed alright with my presence. She healed my broken leg and made me eat a squirrel. I got her drunk. It's a touching story. I told her about Ankh being my family and asked her to come with me. I told her we had to go. I wasn't eighteen yet and feared ending up in Triad. Of course, that's when they showed up. We fought Triad off together, but they captured me. Lexy escaped, tracked Triad through the forest and saved me. While I was unconscious, she tied up Tiberius, hung him in a tree and slit his throat, leaving witnesses."

Lexy was awesome.

Grinning like he'd heard her thought, Grey continued, "We found out she'd been living in that cabin with a pack of dogs for years with no human contact. Her canine companions vanished, she'd been alone for the last six months. Our Testing group was Arrianna, Lexy and I. We helped Lexy regain her humanity and she brought us out of Testing in record time. We save each other. I'm Lexy's Handler. If her sanity strolls off the deep end, it's my duty to bring her back. My ability is pyrokinesis but starting fires was never my calling, I put out Dragon's flames. Lexy's so much more than just our Clan's Dragon. She's a gifted Healer and the best friend anyone could have." Lexy appeared with Lily. Grey hopped up and jogged over to talk to them.

Chuckling, Frost whispered, "I've known her for forty years. The moral of this story is, don't piss Lexy off, she's a Dragon. You'll see her in action. She's a slightly psychotic superhero."

It was in Grey's eyes even though he'd denied it. He wasn't allowed to be with her, but he loved her. He was the ying to her yang. For four decades, he'd been putting her first. It sounded like a marriage.

Leaning in, Frost whispered, "If they hook up, Handlers are spelled to forget intimacy as they sleep."

If they fell in love, he'd never be able to remember his feelings for her or what happened between them the night before. Picking a buttercup, Kayn whispered, "That sounds like a messed-up fairy tale storyline."

Frost shifted her hair, so it trickled over her shoulder, toying, "This is not a fairy tale. This is a nightmare. I've been living it for a thousand years." He got up and left.

She didn't turn to watch him go. Unclenching her fist, she'd squashed a buttercup in her palm. Hiding it, Kayn focused on what mattered. Kevin was picking grass and tossing it over his shoulder like it was a normal day. Sitting in the meadow, Lexy re-joined their discussion. *Don't think about Lexy, she can read your mind.*

"Grey told you the story of how we met," Lexy commented.

Squatting beside her, Grey teased, "It's the most interesting story I know."

Rolling her eyes, Lexy prompted, "Any questions?"

She had so many. Curious, Kayn tossed one out there, "What's the least painful way to die?"

"Drowning," Lexy disclosed with a grin.

Plunking herself in the grass, Lily said, "Same."

Grey tucked a flower behind Lexy's ear, saying, "Falling is a quick explosion of pain. Healing after multiple falls hurts like a son of a bitch."

Kevin questioned, "Healing hurts?"

Chuckling, Grey explained, "There's a training exercise where you fall and go splat repetitively until your brain refuses to allow you to get back up. That sucks."

Peacefully weaving dandelions, Lily confirmed, "Agreed."

Trying to weave, Kayn braided stems. Without directing her question, she enquired, "What's the worst way?"

They echoed Grey's response like smart assed siblings, as he blurted out, "Being eaten really sucks." He chucked a handful of grass at Lily and Lexy, adding, "Lava also sucks."

Lexy tossed a fistful of grass back, sparring, "No, starvation is the worst. It's a drawn out excruciating process."

Grey changed his answer, "Scratch eaten and starvation. Hell, I'd find being slowly dipped in lava preferable to Tiberius torture week. Seven fun filled days of creative torment. The psychopath kept healing us. I was stabbed and skinned alive. He removed my intestines, playing morbid games, keeping me alert to watch. I was incapacitated and locked in a room with buzzards picking at my flesh. There were spiders, snakes, rodents, and he went full Godfather on me with power tools.

Day seven, Lexy and the others busted us out. Frost had it much worse. He spent a week feeding Princess Lily grapes."

With midnight tresses shimmering in sunshine, Lily revealed, "He watched me bathe in rose petals. We chatted, he rubbed my feet for hours."

"No rush to call for help," Grey pointed out.

Lily tossed a handful of grass his way, arguing, "I was in a room with a Tri-Clan block. I thought he'd only taken me. When I escaped, I cut my hand. That's how they found us. You were blocked too. I'm not the only one with a symbol on my damn hand, Grey."

She had to ask. Kayn looked at Lexy, enquiring, "What did you do to Tiberius for hurting Grey?"

Grinning like a happy memory crossed her mind, Lexy far too casually responded, "I tied him up, gagged him and fixed him. I may have also released the rodents, spiders, snakes and buzzards before closing the door."

Raising his eyebrows, Kevin probed, "Fixed him?"

"Let it sink in," Grey hinted, smiling.

She neutered Tiberius. Hardcore.

Mortified, her boyfriend plucked a fistful of grass and tossed it over his shoulder, whispering, "Remind me to never get on her bad side."

A ladybug cruised over one of Kayn's bare feet. *Where did that come from?*

Tossing a woven flower crown at Grey, Lily sang, "Here you go, Princess."

Smirking, Grey bantered, "Hilarious." Placing the crown on his head, he baited, "Call me King, Master or whatever floats your boat."

Lily crossed her tanned legs, daring, "Feel free to wear that crown while you hold your breath and wait."

Their constant sparring reminded her of kids kicking sand at each other in a playground. Seeing Kevin in a halo of eternal sunshine, Kayn imagined, she was a normal girl with a boy she adored on a sunny afternoon. Caressing his face, she kissed him, gazing into his eyes as their lips parted.

Lily threw a bucket of metaphorical ice water, "Heartbreak is worse than any version death."

"I've had my ego wounded, plenty of times," Grey sparred.

Shooting him a look, Lily slammed, "That's not heartbreak you whiny man child. It's not my fault you can't comprehend friends with benefits."

"Arrianna broke Grey's heart," Lexy reminded, backing up her Handler.

Grey took Lexy's hand, replying, "I appreciate the gesture, but I cheated on Arrianna and she dumped me. It doesn't count as a broken heart if you do it to yourself."

These were the days of our afterlives. Frost appeared, strolling over to where they were hanging out in the heavenly meadow. *She felt guilty. A touch of Chloe's feelings lingered, but she wasn't going to admit it.* Remembering her easy to hear inner dialogue, Kayn was relieved to see Kevin and Grey walking away.

Without saying anything, Lexy scrambled to her feet and held out her hand. Helping Kayn up, Lexy said, "Kevin seems like a great guy."

"He is," Kayn replied, smiling.

Lexy urged, "Let's go." They ran to catch up to the others.

As they joined the pack, Frost teased, "Hi Froggy."

Idiot.

Keeping pace with the rest, Lexy gave them a dose of reality, "You'll be training until Ankh releases us from the tombs. Triad are brutal bastards, fighting them is a bar brawl, anything goes. Trinity takes you down with poison arrows from a distance. You'll be drugged if you're hit. A mortal nicked by an arrow will die within an hour. Large battles have a three hour time limit with a shield disguising energy. Mortals in a five-mile radius lose time. Mortals inside the shield must be Corrected. Compulsion is unreliable, rules are set in stone."

"Once Abaddon arrives at a two or three Clan conflict there is always a shield," Frost clarified. "When the battle's over, they'll incapacitate us with a noise. We gather our deceased, clean up evidence and have twenty-four hours to get as far away as we can. We aren't allowed to pursue each other during that window of time, Third-Tier will be monitoring us. This is a battle for souls, most of us will be dead by the end of it. Once again, we do not stay dead. When the fight times out, they'll collect our bodies and revive us. Our Oracle has given us instructions. We need to get Kayn from the house with our tombs, through the trails, and into to her spiritually protected room. She stays there until the battle times out. It sounds simple but I promise it won't be. They don't have to enter the room to get you to come out."

He didn't mention Kevin. Kayn asked, "What about Kevin?"

Frost's eyes softened, replying, "We don't know how much the other Clan's know. Mortals can be in your protected area, but your room is setup to protect one Second-Tier. If two are inside, it may weaken the barrier enough to allow Abaddon in. You both have unfinished mortal business. Kevin needs to deal with his. There are emotional hoops you must jump through on your way to Enlightenment. If you haven't dealt with this part properly, you'll never make it out of the Testing."

Closure was the true purpose of their return to the small island town. With no need for sustenance, they trained for six days, less than an hour Earth time. Ignoring their fears, they endeavoured to learn all they could, running from arrows and practicing with swords. When they reached the end of rushed training, Kevin was holding his own against his instructors, but she was going to die five seconds into the fight. They visited Winnie as promised, hoping she'd shed light on whether anyone knew about Kevin, but she wasn't there. Kevin struggled to see if they'd altered future events, but his Psychic gift had been stifled by the ability to absorb memories.

To lift their spirits, they gave them time alone. One would expect teenagers in love to finish what they started at the cabin, but thinking of something just as magical, they were transported back to the day they met. Chloe and Kayn lay in the grass with tiny chins propped up by dainty hands, watching furry bees moving from buttercup to buttercup, humming a song. A four-year-old version of Kayn with grass stains on her white dress and a streak of mud across her cheek tried to blow curls out of her eyes with a puff of air. Sighing, she glanced at her sister.

A tiny perfectly coiffed Chloe, scolded, "Be quiet or they won't come close enough to touch."

Out of the corner of her eye, she saw a boy with a mass of dark wavy hair coming over. He got down in the grass and quietly observed. He asked what they were doing, Chloe explained. He told her his name. He thought it was weird they were trying to touch bees but seemed satisfied with the explanation. Randomly, Chloe flounced away, leaving her with a boy. Unsure of what to say, Kayn got up and tried to go.

Stopping her, Kevin insisted, "This is for you." He passed her a purple clover.

Furrowing her brow, Kayn gave him a giant toothless grin and replied, "Thanks." Smiling, she walked away staring at the flower.

Miniature Kevin trotted up beside her, asking, "Do you know what you are supposed to do with that flower?"

Pausing, Kayn turned to him, saying, "No, I don't."

He held out his hand and she gave it back. He pulled out one of the tiny straight purple petals, announcing, "Taste it."

She hesitated, so he did it first. When she tried it, Kayn's cheeks cracked a wide smile as her squeaky voice said, "It tastes sweet." Sitting at a picnic table with their moms becoming fast friends, she plucked the last petal and popped it in her mouth.

Kayn's mom reprimanded, "Sweetie, no. Dogs pee on those."

Returning from the playground, her duplicate grimaced at the mention of dog pee and smiled at the boy holding Kayn's hand. Smart, even as a child, Kevin held his other hand out to her twin. Thinking about it, Chloe took it. This was how Kevin became friends with the twins. By the time their mothers packed up to go home, they were making plans to meet up the following day. Matt came bounding up with Kevin's brother Clay. The messes of freckled mischief already knew each other from school. Kevin secretly tucked a clover in Kayn's shoe when Chloe wasn't watching because she didn't have a pocket and they smiled at each other.

Brilliant light flashed, and when they opened their eyes, they were grown up, lying in that same school yard together amidst a sea of buttercups and bees.

Kevin plucked one lone purple clover from the ground and questioned, "Do you know what this did?"

Kayn leaned in, kissed him gently on the lips and replied, "It got you a best friend."

His eyes flashed as he flirted, "What would it get me now?"

"One of these," Kayn teased as she socked him in the side. He groaned and tossed a handful of grass in her face. Plucking fistfuls of grass and buttercups out of the ground, she pinned him by straddling his chest and face-washed him with it, leaving his skin comically stained yellow and green. He was laughing as he fought back and did the same to her. They were giggling and rolling around in the grass just as they would have before the madness stole their mortality.

With epically perfect comic timing, Lexy's voice said, "I won. I guessed you'd be doing something weird and here you are, painting each other's faces yellow and green. That is pretty damn weird."

They froze with Kayn straddling Kevin, mid buttercup grass face mash. She emptied her hands. He spat the grass out of his mouth.

"Way too vague, Lex. It doesn't count," Frost chuckled.

Grey shrugged and declared, "It does look like fun though." He turned to Lily.

Lily's ebony mane of hair lifted in the slight breeze as she hissed, "Don't even think about it, I'll kill you."

Flame-haired wild hearted Lexy apologised, "I'm sorry, it's time to go. I guess you'll have to go green."

Her Handler chuckled, "That was adorable. On the bright side, maybe it'll look like you have something funky and the demons won't want to eat you. Nobody likes an upset tummy."

With her arm around Grey, Lexy praised, "You are adorable."

Grey ducked out from under her arm, grabbed a handful of grass and passed it to Lexy, provoking, "Do me. You never know."

"I think that might be the most romantic thing you've ever said," Lexy commented, shaking her head.

"Fine. I'll do it to myself," Grey declared, grinning.

Smearing a handful of grass on Grey's face, Lexy whispered, "Stop speaking, you're only making it worse."

Scowling at Kevin and Kayn, Frost ordered, "Get up, you two. Your weird behaviour is contagious." Grey smeared grass on Lexy's face and laughed. He tried to do the same to Frost who asserted, "No buddy, I'm okay with looking moderately sane today." They strolled away barefoot in the grass together, most with green and yellow streaks on their faces and arms.

Grey leaned over, whispering, "Pay no attention to those two party-poopers. This will be our tribal warpaint as we own the insanity of this day." He raised a hand triumphantly above his head, shouting, "We shall not go quietly into our padded rooms! We must bounce off the walls finger painting everything green, yellow and red!"

Kayn glanced at her goofy Clan member, asking, "Why red?"

"There's always a crazy amount of blood," Grey confessed.

Scowling, Kevin said, "That was almost a great motivational speech, until it got creepy."

United in silence, each emotionally prepared for the battle ahead in their own way. Kayn's thoughts were too scattered to concentrate so she opted out of thinking about anything but the glorious feeling of her bare feet in silky warm sand. She wriggled her toes in the velvety grains, smiling at Kevin as they shared a quick flash of a memory from their childhood. The sand was glittering in the sun with diamonds. The others kept their mouths shut allowing them a final moment of joy. They knew what it meant so did the newest members of Ankh. *There was no need to say the words aloud. Was this the secret of the afterlife? Learning to ignore an impending painful end by embracing the simple moments?*

With no warning, they were thrust upwards so harshly their spines were curved to the point of excruciating pain. *This wasn't how she left the in-between last time.* Stomachs churned and twisted in a vomit-inducing dance until they were falling inside tombs. *This time, no music was playing. There was no excitement, just apprehension. She wasn't strong like the others. Kevin acquired strength and catlike reflexes born from his ability to retain memories. Kayn gained Chloe without her ability.* They plummeted and spiralled downwards blinded by the strobing light, coming to an abrupt halt. Flashing light ceased. Kayn kept her eyes shut for a moment. *Her chest felt like it was on fire.* She gasped for breath inside of the tomb and opened her eyes.

31

BRAINS BEFORE BRAWN

*K*ayn felt the tombs being shifted apart, and as they opened, her heart palpitated nervously. *Only her own Clan could open the Ankh tombs.* With that thought, her demeanour restored. As her tomb opened, she laid eyes upon four new Ankh faces.

Lily gasped, "Daddy, you shouldn't be here." Grasping his hand, a man who didn't appear much older assisted her out of a tomb. All six climbed out as Markus introduced himself to Kayn and Kevin. The others in the room were Arrianna, Flora and Orin. Arrianna looked her age. The others appeared to be in their mid to late twenties.

"Skipping this wasn't one of my options," Markus replied, hugging his daughter. Arrianna, Lexy and Grey embraced. *She remembered the story. The went into Testing together. Their special bond was obvious.* Sensing Kevin beside her, Kayn reached for his hand.

"What's going on outside?" Frost directed his question at Markus.

Markus grinned as he answered, "Not much, honestly." In silent solidarity, they scaled the stairs trusting his words.

Cautiously peering through the blinds, Lexy asked, "Where did they go?"

Arrianna shrugged and replied, "There was nobody blocking our entrance to the house when we got here."

"I had a feeling we were being watched. How many were outside when you left?" Markus questioned.

"I counted ten Triad fighting a bunch of Trinity. Abaddon showed up so I went downstairs. When I heard someone walking around upstairs, I knew you wanted me to behave so I got into a tomb," Lexy explained.

A petite blonde with straight hair named Arrianna exclaimed, "Triad wouldn't be able to stand in a circle of salt to do the usual Abaddon disposal method, Trinity would have picked them off with arrows from the tree line. Maybe they all went to the next location?"

Taking her father aside, Lily whispered, "Did you know about Kevin?"

Addressing his daughter's concerns, Markus whispered, "I've always had my suspicions regarding the Smith family tree. As soon as I begin reading a story, I attempt to guess the plot twist. This was foreshadowed on the first page. I knew the Brothers of Prophecy when they were children. I played a part in raising them. When I saw young Clay, I knew this was going to be a page turner."

Lily questioned, "Do you think Tiberius knows?"

Her father replied, "Judging by the hoard of Triad Lexy saw, I'm guessing he does. We don't have time for this conversation. The Clans may have been chased away from our tombs, but they know where we're headed when we leave this house. They'll be waiting for us."

Leaning in, Lily whispered, "Do you think they've already killed what's left of Kayn's family?"

Smiling knowingly at his daughter, Markus quietly answered, "No, I wouldn't. I'd leave them alive as bait."

Pretending she couldn't hear their messed-up father daughter conversation, Kayn couldn't take it anymore. *Her family was going to be used as bait. Now that she was back in the land of the living, she couldn't shove her desperation aside. She needed to know if they were alive.* She felt her pocket. *It was heavy.* Cheering on the inside when she discovered she had her phone. She sent her brother a text, "Matt, are you okay?"

"I'm fine?" He instantly replied.

She had to hear Matt's voice. She needed to know it was him. Kayn dialled her brother.

Matt answered, "Hey, Candy Kayn."

With no time for small talk, Kayn questioned, "Are you at home?"

"I just pulled up the driveway," Matt calmly responded.

Willing her brother to understand the urgency of his situation, Kayn asserted, "Get away from the house. You need to leave."

Matt stammered, "Someone just pulled up and blocked me in the driveway. Who is this clown?"

Panicking, she made eye contact with Lily. Frazzled by fear, Kayn shouted, "Drive over the lawn! Do whatever you have to do! Get the hell out of there!"

Kayn heard a crash, then another. Matt yelled into the phone, "He's frigging smiling while he's ramming me!"

Her eyes clouded with tears. She spoke as calmly as she could manage, "Listen carefully, Matty. Get into the house and lock the door. Run up to my room, place the stones in the bag on the windowsill in front of the doorway. Circle the room with salt. Bring Jenkins with you if he's home. We'll be there in a minute."

Matt joked to dispel fear, "Rocks, salt, seriously? Who is we?"

Enough of this bullshit "Get the hell out of the car! Run! They're going to kill you!" Kayn screamed at the top of her lungs. She heard the car door slam and the rattle of gravel followed by the slamming of the front door. Her brother's voice shouted for Jenkins to get upstairs. There was the creaking of the stairs and thudding of his footsteps as he sprinted down the hall, then shuffling.

Out of breath, Matt demanded answers, "What in the hell is going on, Kayn? Who was that?"

Where to start? Kayn blurted out, "I'm in a Clan of immortals with Kevin and Lily. I'll explain when we get there. Don't leave the bedroom."

"Sure, you are. Is that it?" Matt replied with a mix of sarcasm and disbelief.

Not even close. Kayn instructed, "Make sure you salt the door, demons are coming. I'm hanging up. I'll be there soon." Kevin was on his phone pleading with his mother to leave the house. His mom must have hung up. He stared at his cell for a second before dialling another number. *At least Matt played along.* She heard Kevin leaving a message for Clay. His voice cracked with desperation, "Don't go home. Do not go home after work today, no matter what."

How long would they wait outside before they forced their way into her house? Kayn saw an open path to the door and bolted for it. She was roughly obstructed by Frost.

Holding Kayn, as she struggled, Frost reprimanded, "Don't be ridiculous you'll never make it past Abaddon. You have a better chance in a group. If you run out there half-cocked, it'll be game over."

That made sense but logic was clouded by the overwhelming desperation to keep her brother and Jenkins from suffering the brutality she'd faced.

Frost released her. Lily blocked Kayn's path, clarifying, "This house is spiritually protected, Abaddon can't get in. This is an obvious trap. They permitted Markus and the others to come in to get us out of the tombs. Why settle for an appetizer when you can have a full meal?"

Guarding the door, Lexy offered another option, "Your only alternative is to go downstairs and get into a tomb. We'll close you in and let you out when it's over."

Knowing she couldn't save them, a small part of her wanted to take Lexy up on the offer of an easy way out. Matty and Jenkins had loose ends to tie up, this wasn't only about her.

"Kayn understands how things need to play out. She won't try to leave again," Markus responded with unhidden empathy.

He was the one in charge, for even the bad ass Lexy didn't attempt to assert her opinion once Markus had spoken.

Commanding the room, Markus addressed to the two newest Ankh, "There's only one feasible reason why this house hasn't been breached by other Clans, we're surrounded by Abaddon. I know you've seen one, but can you imagine the blood bath from ten or twenty?"

Bloodbath. Awesome. Kayn stated the obvious, "How could ten or twenty of those giant clawed monsters be roaming around without being seen?"

Their unassuming leader, teased, "It's been taken care of, stop trying to skip chapter's young lady."

Leaning closer, Frost whispered in her ear, "I already told you about the shield."

In a fatherly authoritarian tone, Markus said, "There's a clear path through everything using brains over brawn. When we try to leave this house, they'll show themselves. The mist feeds on spiritual energy. It will slow us down, but it can't kill us. That's where those clawed beasts come in."

"Being eaten really sucks," Grey mumbled, leaning against the creepy plastic covered couch.

Amused, their leader directed his next question to his daughter, "Lilarah, how much salt is in the kitchen?"

Lily answered from the hall, "At least ten bags, maybe more. Why?"

Markus grinned as he answered, "I have either a brilliant idea or a completely suicidal plan. It really depends on how you look at it."

Oh, wonderful. Kayn's eyes kept darting to the door fighting to use logic over emotion.

"I'm listening," Grey baited. Ankh's resident daredevil was always up for a mission with no rational shot at success.

Markus let them in on his certifiably brilliant idea, "Everyone who just came back from the in-between will go with Kevin and Kayn. But first, I'm going to need you to get in the shower fully clothed. Soak your clothes and cover yourselves in salt. We'll create the distraction, the six of you run for the tree line. You're going to need to outrun Abaddon until you've taken down a few Trinity and Triad. Don't kill them, they're going to be alternative snacks. If this works, the salt will make you the less appetizing option. Abaddon will pass you by and clear your path to the house. Frost, you're in charge. Get Kayn to what's left of her family. Keep Kevin with you and stay inside the house. Get Kayn into the secured room and keep her there until it's over." Meeting Kevin's gaze with his own, Markus explained, "I'll be blunt, kid. This area is spiritually blocked off. Once people are in, they can't get out. There's no way to get to your house until after this is over. If you stay inside Kayn's house the others will fight to keep everyone away from it and outside. Once the fight has timed out, I promise we'll go check on your family." Kevin nodded without speaking.

Their leader continued instructing, "Grey and Lily take the

front yard. Keep them out of that house for as long as you can. Lexy, guard the backdoor. Kill everything that moves." Gently tilting Kayn's face upwards with a hand so their eyes met, Markus solemnly disclosed, "They won't attempt to get into the house until you're in there. Your brother and Jenkins are leverage. If you keep them in the bedroom with you, they'll have nothing to hold over you. Everything is going to happen quickly. Use logic. Do not make rash decisions."

Searching his eyes, she knew there was a lot being left unsaid, Kayn whispered, "I wish I could say I understand, but I don't."

Entertained by her honesty, their fatherly leader affirmed, "You will. Now, go upstairs with the others and cover yourself in salt or you won't even make it out of the yard."

Got it. Get upstairs. Demons are going to be everywhere. Quickly scaling the stairs, Kayn heard voices, making it easy to determine which room they were in. They'd already begun soaking clothes and dousing themselves with salt. *It didn't seem fair. She had a chance to get to her family and he didn't.* Kevin was on the phone begging his mother to listen. They froze as the tone of the conversation changed.

With tears in his eyes, Kevin pled, "Mom, please go. Get out of the house, right now. I know I left Clay a crazy message." Kevin became quiet. "I'm not on steroids. I'm not doing drugs. I need you to get out of the damn house." There was a pause in the conversation. Kevin whispered, "I'm sorry, I didn't mean to swear." He warned, "When Clay comes home, it might not be Clay." He dropped the phone. Clutching his head, he sunk to his knees, crying out in agony.

Blocking her path, Frost grabbed Kayn's wrist, calming her down, "He's a Psychic, I know you remember what happened to you the last time you tried to interrupt."

IN THE TIME IT TOOK to blink, Kevin was in the foyer of the house he'd grown up in. He climbed the stairs to his room. His mother was rifling through his drawers, cursing under her breath, "Not doing drugs my ass!"

This was a vision. She didn't believe him. How was he going to get her to leave the house?

Watching her frantically searching through dressers, he urged, "Mom, you have to leave." *She couldn't hear him.* Giving it his all, Kevin screamed, "You have to leave!"

She flinched, looked behind her and shook her head. It was possible her reaction was a well-timed random act, but instinct told him otherwise. *She had to open-up enough to believe what she was hearing was real. Frost said something about a door being left open. How had he worded that?* Kevin tried to remember Frost's speech from the day they were marked Ankh. *Maybe it was just left open on that night? He had to make her listen. Both of her biological parents had abilities. She had the genetics.* Searching for his grandmother's visions, he filtered through the surplus of immortal information stored in his brain. *When Chloe's voice reached out from the other side, she must have been there in spirit form screaming for her twin to run. He might be able to get through to his mother.* He peered out his bedroom window as vehicles pulled up on the lawn. *Oh, his mother wasn't going to like that. What were the chances she was going to be quiet about it, so she didn't make her situation worse?*

His mom walked right through him, opened the window and bellowed, "Clayton Harold Smith! Your father will have a shit fit when he gets home! Get those cars off the lawn!" She closed the window, muttering to herself, "I'm not making food for all of those people." She marched out of the room to give Clay hell.

There was no time to figure this out. Frantically trying to rifle objects at her, his hands passed through everything. *In this form, he was helpless. Her time was up. There was nothing he could do.* As she reached the stairs, Kevin screamed with everything he had to reach her subconscious, "No! That's not Clay! Get out of here! Go! Run! Lock yourself in the bathroom!" *She couldn't hear him.* Defeated, his eyes filled with tears, pleading, "Mom, please go. It's not Clay." Hesitating, she looked back. *He was getting through.* Halfway down the stairs someone came in and closed the door.

She didn't move a muscle, saying, "Clay is that you?"

Willing her to hear him, Kevin pled, "Run mom. Get upstairs. Climb out a window and run. It's not Clay. Go, before he sees you. That's not your son." She wasn't moving, it was as though she'd heard his warning but couldn't allow herself to believe the voices in her head. Kevin continued trying to get through, "This is Kevin. You need to trust me, that's not Clay. Hide, those men are there to hurt you." Clay appeared at the bottom of the stairs and she smiled. He smiled back and that's all it took for her to feel at ease. *She was going to ignore her intuition. Most people do.*

Mom walked down the stairs, gave his older brother's look-alike an enormous hug, then pulled away. She gave him a once over, asserting, "Get those vehicles off the lawn. Your father is going to lose his marbles."

If she was used to ignoring voices, she'd never allowed herself to believe.

His brother's look-alike leaned out the door, yelling, "Move those cars off the lawn." A grinning Clay double closed the door and turned to face his mother.

Concerned, she confessed, "I was on the phone with Kevin.

You're right, he must be having a breakdown. I don't know what to do."

Clay cocked his head, questioning, "Where is, Kevin?"

Come on mom. His mannerisms are off. You must see it.

His mother replied, "I think he's with Kayn."

The Clay look-alike suspiciously paced back and forth as he stated, "Well, that's convenient."

Her expression changed. Visually inspecting Clay, his mom replied, "What does that mean?"

Hope leapt in his heart. That's right Tiberius show her who you are. Clay wouldn't have used the word convenient.

"You hugged me all stiff like a robot," his mom commented, slowly catching on. "What's wrong with you?"

Chuckling, his brother's mirror image shook his head, toying, "I've never had anyone complain about the quality of my hugs before." Looking at family pictures in the hall like it was the first time he'd seen them, he snatched the picture of young Granny Winnie off the wall, cracking, "That bitch never even told me about you."

"You know I don't like it when you use that kind of language, Clayton," his mother scolded.

Grinning, Clay's duplicate peered up from the photo, baiting, "I guess Winnie never told you anything about your father?"

Stepping away, she enquired, "What's gotten into you today?"

Clay's duplicate instructed, "Hand me your cell... Mother."

The word mother hit a nerve. He saw it in her eyes, instinct was screaming at her. She passed her phone to Clay's look-alike.

Grinning, the imposter re-dialled the last number, pressing speakerphone. It rang once and went straight to messaging. He smirked, announcing, "He's not answering. I'll leave a message. Hi Kevin, it's Grandpa Tiberius. We're having a family reunion, you should join us. Scratch that, I've changed my mind. Meet me at the Conduit's house. I'll bring mom and leave a note for your brother to meet us there."

His mom whispered, "You're not my son, are you?"

Staring at a family picture on the wall, Tiberius replied, "Do try to follow along, dear. I'm your father."

Puzzled, his mother said, "That's impossible, you'd be old."

The shifty immortal chuckled, "Wow, your oldest could pass for my identical twin. Good-looking kid. I just realised I don't even know my own daughter's name. That was awfully rude of her."

"It's Lillian," she whispered, inching away.

Tiberius shook his head, pointing out, "That bland name is probably why you turned out so homely."

Planning to run for it, his mom kept glancing at the kitchen, making her intentions painfully obvious. *Yes, Mom. Run.*

Taking a step closer, Tiberius admitted, "I'm pissed at your mom. Had I known this information earlier, I would have made her death a little more personal."

Stunned, she whispered, "What? You killed my mom?"

"Save time sweetheart, call me daddy. I did kill her, and it was fun, but I didn't know who she was at the time in all fairness to me," Tiberius disclosed as grief washed over her.

His mother's eyes darkened. Her expression changed to one he'd only seen on rare occasions. Bubbling over with rage, Lillian Smith yelled, "You son of a bitch!" Throwing pictures at the twisted stranger half her age claiming to be her father.

The voices in her head might come in loud and clear now. Frantically waving his hands, Kevin shouted, "Mom if you can hear this you have the gift! It's real, I have it too! He's here to kill your family, run!"

Giggling as she rifled everything within reach at him, Tiberius redirecting each item with a swipe of his hand. Lillian threatened, "I don't know who you are, or what you are, but I'll tear you to pieces with my bare hands before I let you touch my children."

She heard his pleas. She knew this man was here to destroy her family. For an instant Kevin was proud. *He didn't know his mom had this fire inside of her.* In a swift movement, the immortal wrapped his fingers around his mother's neck and squeezed. She flailed and clawed at his hands, trying to scream as he choked the life out of her. When she'd calmed down a touch, he released her. Gasping for breath, she fell to her knees.

Laughing at Lillian's spunk, Tiberius chuckled, "Oh, I like you so much more now. You have giant balls. You must get that from me. You probably think I shouldn't kill you because you're my daughter. Well, you're not how I imagined you either, but I can fix that. I'll find you a younger prettier shell. I can't have a homely daughter, what will all of the other immortal fathers say?"

"You're insane," his mother stammered. "You can't be my father, I'm over fifty."

"You must have been ancient when you had children," he ignorantly ridiculed.

Tired of immature insults, she slammed, "You insignificant asshole, I ran a successful company. I'm a powerful woman!" His mother picked up a ceramic owl from the hearth and pitched it at Tiberius's head. He didn't even attempt to duck, and she smoked him a good one.

Rubbing his noggin, Tiberius praised, "Good shot, sweetie." He pointed at the wall and said, "So, the scrawny kid with acne is the only one with powers?"

His mother glanced in the direction of the kitchen, inching away from Clay's duplicate. Fury rippled through Kevin's soul as Tiberius stepped towards his mother. With unbridled rage, unlike anything he'd ever felt, he blocked the immortal's path, swinging his fists, hissing, "I will kill you if you lay a finger on her."

Ecstatic, Tiberius waved his hands through the air, laughing, "Wow, you are a talented kid, so scary. I'm looking forward to meeting you in the flesh. I'll be at the Conduit's house in say fifteen minutes. Are you planning to stick around for the show?"

Helpless in this state, all he could do was watch.

The Clay look-alike strode towards his middle-aged offspring, saying, "Listen sweetheart, daddy needs to brand you so when I break your neck, you won't really die."

His mother spoke under her breath, "You are a stark raving lunatic if you think I'm going to allow you to brand me. What kind of sick bastard are you?"

"My name's Tiberius, if you're more comfortable calling me that, but I'm not feeling sick bastard as a pet name. Dad or father is another welcome alternative. Unfortunately, I must brand you. There's no way around it. We can do this the easy way or the hard way. I can let you have the control over this part of our introduction." His mother grabbed a vase off the counter to use as a weapon and his grandfather chuckled, "Hard way it is." He punched her in the face, knocking her out cold, then knelt beside her, branded her chest, and unceremoniously snapped her neck. There was a noise. Tiberius noticed his double standing there.

Clay just witnessed himself murder his mother. *His sibling was in shock and rightfully so.* Watching colour fade from Clay's face, rage drained from Kevin's soul until he felt empty. *He couldn't do a thing to stop it. It sounded like Tiberius was planning to keep his mother. If he kept his brother, they had a chance. He still had an opportunity to save them.*

Traumatized, gawking at his doppelganger, Clay stammered, "Did you? Is she dead? What are you?"

In awe of his duplicate, Tiberius bantered, "In the wise

words of late Grandma Winnie, you're not the sharpest knife in the drawer. I get it, all my genes went into creating those stunning good looks. There's a remarkable likeness."

Stunned, Clay didn't move a muscle with his mouth agape as his evil twin placed an arm around him, apologising, "I'm afraid I've used up my patience dealing with my daughter and the clock is ticking. I have other places to be and people to kidnap. Hi, I'm your grandpa." Tiberius socked Clay in the face, knocking him out cold. He branded his brother Triad and broke his neck.

Kevin lost his connection. His vision wavered and everything exploded with light before it went black.

OPENING THE DOOR, TIBERIUS BELLOWED, "Zachariah, put these in a tomb in the back of the truck!" The immortal watched young Zach struggling to drag bodies of his deceased family members through the grass out to the truck. *He'd have better luck moulding his grandson to his likeness. He liked the kid, but Zach was better suited for Trinity. He'd never been emotionally compatible with Triad. He wasn't eighteen yet, he'd do the kid a favour and leave him behind for one of the other Clans. He didn't have viable abilities, the last thing he needed was a weak link. One weak link and the whole group wouldn't make it out of immortal Testing.* Tiberius instructed, "Chuck those in the same tomb, we need to save space." Casually sauntering back into the house, whistling a tune, Tiberius wandered to the kitchen. He collected household cleaners from under the sink, putting metal cannisters into the microwave for shits and giggles. *There was something he needed first.* He couldn't help but grin as he walked out of the kitchen and saw Zach evacuating cats. *That softy.* Picking up the photo of young Winnie off the floor, Tiberius cracked the frame and took out the picture. *Her hands would have touched this before it went into the frame. He'd cared about her as much as he was capable of and she'd hidden his child. He'd keep Lillian entombed for twenty years, just to make a point. After he revived her, he'd wipe her memory and make her think he'd always been her father. If she adored him, he might even learn to care about her. Time to finish this up.* Removing a lighter from his pocket, he went back to the kitchen and lit the curtains on fire. *You'd think inflammable kitchen curtains would be a thing.* Setting the microwave for three minutes, the immortal danced out of the house. Standing by the truck with the engine running, Tiberius kissed Winnie's picture, vowing, "I'm going to turn our Kevin as dark as I am. You can watch from wherever you ended up, my love." Tucking the picture under his shirt, he got into the truck. As they drove away, there was a small explosion as the Smith house went up in flames.

KAYN HAD BEEN PRACTICALLY HOLDING her breath waiting for Kevin to awaken. He came to, wildly thrashing around the bathroom. In a show of testosterone, he got up and punched a hole in the wall.

"Feel better?" Frost chuckled. Roughly gripping his arms, he provoked, "That anger you're feeling, embrace it."

"Embrace it. Really? My grandfather just branded my mother, snapped her neck and did the same to my brother," Kevin raged.

Frost shoved Kevin into the shower stall. "That's good, they're still alive. He'll chuck them in a tomb. I bet he leaves them in there until after the next Testing. Salt yourself down so we can go kick his ass."

Her family was next. Nobody was going to keep her family alive though. Nauseous, Kayn watched as they soaked Kevin and doused him in salt. Lexy helped him out of the shower, and with only a touch, his bleeding knuckles were healed. The fury in his eyes spoke volumes as they descended the stairs. She took his hand, assuring, "They're still alive." He squeezed her hand but didn't say a word. The group made their way into the living room where they all placed their hands together. Without hesitation, Kevin walked forward and placed his hand with the others. *He'd come a long way in only a short period of time.* She joined in.

Markus saluted the group, "May you run so fast the wind feels you. Fight hard enough for your heart to heal. Be good but never blind."

They chanted Ankh three times like they were at a sports event. Their symbols glowed. Riding a wave of intense solidarity, unlike anything she'd experienced, it felt like they were still joined as she stepped away. Kevin took her hand, intimately kissing her palm, he closed her fingers around it so she could save the kiss for later. *It was from a favourite book.* A tear trickled down her cheek. *They'd help each other come back from this.*

Kissing her face, stopping the tear in its tracks with his lips, Kevin whispered, "No crying, it will make you weak. Be angry. Be strong. I'm not letting anyone get up those stairs to take you, I promise."

He was acting like she was more important. She wasn't.

Interrupting their moment, Markus assured, "Kayn, if you get upstairs into the safe room and deal with your goodbyes, you'll be doing something equally important."

Kayn pled, "Can't he come with me?"

Their wise leader replied, "He needs to face Tiberius."

No. Kayn spun around to look for Kevin. He was standing by a window, determined and unafraid. Frost motioned for her to come stand with him at another window. *This was an experiment in ingenuity. Blind faith. The salt was going to work as a deterrent. It had to.*

Markus addressed the group, "Orin and Arrianna are staying here so they can heal us when the battle times out. We're not pre-opening windows. You're all going to jump through the glass and make a break for the woods during the chaos."

"I certainly hope they're not double-paned," Kevin joked.

Comic hearted Grey chuckled, "It will be double the pain."

"That wasn't even funny," Lily complained as Markus handed everyone knives.

Kayn whispered, "Why aren't we using swords?"

"Long distance running with swords is never a good idea," Frost whispered back.

That made sense. Markus began to count. *Wait. What was he counting to? He didn't say what he was counting to?*

The front and back doors opened, mp3 players with speakers blasting heavy metal were tossed out. Black mist descended as the speakers hit the grass. Markus and Flora raced out, luring the mist away from the house to the road. They tossed a circle of salt around where they stopped. Markus shouted, "Now!"

The remaining six simultaneously crashed through windows with glass shards flying, rolling as they hit the grass. Scrambling to their feet, they booked it for the woods. Dark fog followed as they sprinted across the lawn. They burst into the trails with mist in pursuit swirling through the trees. *They had to slow down. They weren't supposed to outrun the mist. It needed to be right behind them. They didn't have the numbers to win this fight but they sure as hell had the brainpower.* Mist floated hauntingly along the forest floor triggering fragments of that fated night. Fuelled with the fire of survival, Kayn led the way down the winding path.

Sprinting past her family's shrine, slivers of things best left buried invaded her mind. *The vile man's shadow, the smell of his breath, the stickiness of his skin.* Fighting the urge to vomit, she ran faster.

Pre-emptively tuned into Kayn's thoughts, Lexy shouted, "If that creep shows up! I'll personally rip him a new asshole!"

"Slow down!" Frost hollered. "That mist is going to save our asses!"

Insanity or genius? The next five seconds would decide. They raced around a curve in the trails, directly into four unsuspecting Triad.

Raising his hands, Frost yelled, "Stop!" They all froze as Triad cockily wandered over.

"Those are cute little knives," one of the Triad mocked.

Eying up her adversaries, Lexy declared, "Honey, you know I don't need a knife."

"Holy crap it's her," a Triad panicked, backing up.

"I'm not going to touch you," Lexy vowed, innocently batting her eyelashes as things went according to plan. The mist swirled around the Ankh to avoid the salt and went for the Triad.

"Shit!" they screamed as they tried to scatter but not a one made it five feet before being subdued by the mist.

Part one of the plan was complete. The mist would signal to the demons keeping guard over their friends that it was lunchtime.

As THE SHARP CLAWED DEMONS moved away from the salt circles and writhed their way towards the forest, Markus and Flora quietly cheered. "I'm frigging brilliant," Markus whispered, watching his symbol. When nothing happened, he waved to the others. Dying to jump up and down, they couldn't draw unwanted attention. The demons were Ankh's backup.

They'd just finished packing up Ankh's personal items when Markus and Flora sprinted back into the house. Grinning, Orin high-fived Markus, commenting, "Pure genius using demons to even out the playing field. I'm almost excited to come back to work next year."

Putting his arm around him, Markus replied, "We'll be glad to have you back. Thanks for coming to help today. Keeping Lexy behind during this big a job would have been a crying shame. She scares the crap out of Triad."

Arianna walked into the room, saying, "I changed the tombs back." She placed five small rose quartz stones in Markus's hand. He shoved them in his pocket.

Tossing a backpack on the sofa, Orin stated, "On principal alone I need to remove the plastic and dump a pot of coffee on this guy's couch."

32

LOOSE ENDS

A Triad was pleading for mercy as Grey stepped over his body. He grimaced and apologized, "Sorry, man. This is going to suck, so bad." Whistling for others to wait, he put him out of his misery but couldn't get the blade out of his skull. It wasn't going to budge so he ended up leaving it there.

Lexy tossed her Handler a new weapon, teasing, "You're such a softie."

Grey defended his actions as they continued running through the bushes, "Maybe one day he'll do me a favour. It's generally traumatizing to be eaten alive."

Her brain was struggling to rationalize everything she was seeing. It'd be an emotionally scarring ordeal to be coherent as your limbs were being torn from your body while something scarier than the devil ingested you. This kind of thing becoming normal seemed just as far-fetched as everything else in this new life. They emerged from the bushes. *There it was... home.* The back route to the house was clear. Shrieks of anguish came from the incapacitated Triad. Seeing Jenkins in the kitchen window, Kayn frantically waved for him to open the door as they sprinted across the backyard.

The last one in, Grey closed the door, announcing, "See, one less Triad is screaming because I was nice enough to stab him in the head."

With a wet dishcloth in his hand, Jenkins hadn't missed the inhuman shrieking in the bushes. Panicking, he tried shoving his way past the immortals. Frost blocked the door. Jenkins asserted, "Someone's screaming!"

Why was he still downstairs? Kayn took Jenkins arm, instructing, "You need to go upstairs." She ushered her confused mortal protector down the hall.

As they reached the landing, he whispered, "Did that kid just say he stabbed someone in the head?"

Grey comically hollered after Jenkins, "I stabbed a Triad in the head because he was going to be eaten by a scary demon with giant fangs and claws!"

Struggling free of Kayn's grasp, Jenkins grabbed his gun from his holster and ran back to the kitchen.

Grey blocked him before he got there, saying, "Dude, trust me, what's going on out there is way out of your jurisdiction."

"I have a gun," Jenkins courageously stated, raising it.

An enormous tar black glistening scaly demon with beastly penetrating yellow eyes hobbled out of the brush with a squirming disembowelled Triad hanging from its fangs.

Frozen in place, Jenkins mumbled, "What in the hell is that?"

Grey held up his hands, rationalizing, "You are brave. I see that, but the gun in your hand won't even slow that thing down. We're immortal, we've got this. Go upstairs and check on Matt. Kayn will be right behind you. She'll explain everything. It's your job to keep her safe. Make her stay in that room by whatever means necessary."

As the nightmare inducing monster devoured someone in

the backyard, another beast emerged from the forest. Jenkins blankly left the kitchen. Kayn took his arm as she led him to the stairs, whispering, "You are going to have to blindly trust me for a few more minutes. I'll be right behind you. There's something I need to do first." When Jenkins reached the top of the stairs, Kayn went back to the kitchen. Approaching the others, there were two monsters now and people armed with bows in the yard. *This must be Trinity.* Throwing salt around themselves, they waited in the circle luring the demons close enough for disposal. Kevin noticed her there and she walked into his arms.

"Get upstairs. I'll be alright," Kevin whispered in her ear.

Holding him tighter, Kayn implored, "Come get me as soon as you can." She kissed his cheek, and as she went to leave, he pulled her back into his embrace.

With tears in his eyes, he lovingly kissed her on the lips once more, asserting, "No matter what happens. Stay in that room."

Her heart tightened, she hesitated. *She couldn't lose him.*

Patiently, Frost urged, "Get upstairs. Don't worry about the kid. Ankh will be outside guarding entrances, holding them off for as long as they can. With any luck, we'll keep everyone away until this fight times out."

She felt the surge of energy created by the Trinity. Her eyes darted to the kitchen window as two clawed demons caught fire and turned to ash.

Ankh's crimson-haired Dragon, announced, "I should get out there and kill people before Trinity casually strolls in the door."

She felt better knowing Lexy was on their side. Kayn chose that moment to go.

Frost called after her, "Don't even think about coming out of that room, Kayn!"

Grey and Lily were about to walk out the front door when

Kayn grabbed Lily, offering, "You stayed away from him for me, but I know you need to say goodbye."

Rolling his eyes at Lily, Grey said, "You've got five minutes." He marched out with his weapon and sprinted at the immortals accumulating on the front lawn.

The two girls raced upstairs passing pictures of the family that was no longer. *She couldn't think about any of that now.* As they burst into the room Jenkins grilled, "What in the hell is going on? What was that thing? Who are these people?"

For a second, she was speechless. *This was it.* Staring at her purple bedspread and posters on the walls. Kayn told the story of her death, and the choices she made to come home. Quickly explaining, when she finished, they were looking at her like she'd lost her mind. *She didn't care.* She persisted, "I love you both so much. I need you to know that. I wouldn't believe this either. Shit is about to get so weird, you won't have a choice but to see the truth."

"We're far past weird. I just saw a monster eating someone. I need a rational explanation," Jenkins muttered with his hand pressed against the window.

There were none. Defeated, Kayn picked up a raggedy stuffed dog off her bed. Holding her childhood plaything, she confessed, "I wish I had one to give you." *She didn't have the time to walk them through the stages of acceptance. How could she when a large part of her was still in denial?* Matt was sitting on her bed.

Glaring at her brother, Jenkins prompted, "Don't you have anything to say? Someone needs to be the voice of reason."

He'd just turned to her brother as the voice of reason. These must be desperate times.

Matt solemnly peered up at her and said, "You forgot to hang up the phone."

Oh shit. Kayn took her cell out of her pocket. *She'd been on with Matt the entire time. That wasn't good.*

Her last living sibling, proclaimed, "Unless my sister managed to pull off a fifty-person prank involving strangers and monsters. I'd say we're screwed."

They all were. She looked out the window as Grey went flying. He was getting his ass handed to him by someone twice his size. His assailant was shot in the back by an arrow and they went down. *Was the shooter in the trees?* Kayn looked at Lily, warning, "You'd better make it quick, Grey's getting his ass kicked."

Peering out the window, Lily shrugged, as she replied, "Grey always looks like he's getting his ass kicked. He's fine. He's a durable guy."

Grey was laughing while dodging each arrow soaring his way. *It looked like he was having fun.*

With love in her eyes, Lily approached Matt, disclosing, "You don't know me in this life. We've loved each other for hundreds of years, I need to do this at least once." Lily hugged him.

Seeing her brother's heart burst with joy as they embraced, she knew their connection was real. *It felt like words in a story until she saw the magic between them. Lily belonged right where she was, with her head on her brother's heart.*

Matt whispered in Lily's ear, "I'm not sure how any of this is possible but if what I overheard is the truth, I'm going to die. I'm not ready to go, I just found you."

With breathy angst, Lily whispered, "I thought if I stayed away, you'd have a chance. We'll meet again in your next life, true love always finds a way."

Matt gazed into Lily's eyes like she was the most miraculous thing he'd ever seen, confessing, "I haven't been able to stop fantasizing about you. I thought there was something wrong with me."

"The whole lot of you are certifiably insane," Jenkins

declared as he began to pace, not wanting to entertain the idea that any of this was real.

Forcing herself to let go of Matt, Lily explained, "I need to get out there. Grey needs me, but this might be easier to swallow with proof." Lily tugged off her fingerless glove and revealed her symbol of Ankh. She nodded at Kayn.

Guess this was happening. Removing her glove, Kayn showed off her matching symbol.

"Wow, I'm guardian of the year. You got branded. That's why you've been wearing that weird glove. Did Kevin get branded too?" Jenkins stammered, just mystified.

He needed more proof. Kayn placed her hand against Lily's, their symbols softly glimmered. Jenkins and Matt swallowed back the disbelief. As their hands parted, glorious light vanished.

Attempting to wrap his mind around glowing symbols on hands, Jenkins questioned, "Are you aliens, because I'm way too far away from the kitchen to make a tin foil hat."

Raising an eyebrow, Kayn remarked, "Seriously? Aliens you can rationalize but not demons?"

In unfiltered shock, Jenkins revealed, "Honestly, you kids lost me at, 'I stabbed him in the head.' I saw a half-eaten corpse in a monster's mouth and my mind fried. I heard blah, blah, demons are coming to eat us. Blah, blah, we're all going to die."

Strangers were having an actual sword fight on their front lawn. One of them yanked the cherry tree right out of the ground like it was nothing and smoked someone else with it, sending them soaring through the sky. They cleared the grass and landed at the end of the gravel driveway.

Matt backed away from the window. He sat down on Kayn's bed and quietly said, "Somebody just hit someone else with our cherry tree."

Pausing his nervous pacing, Jenkins looked outside. A man

was playing baseball with people, using the cherry tree as his bat. He blurted out, "Shit, we really are going to die, aren't we?"

The man she'd grown to think of as a father, sat on her bed next to Matt. *How was she supposed to say goodbye? She understood the premise behind the in-between. She was secure in the fact that she'd see them again, but it didn't help in these final moments when the instinct to protect the ones she loved was breaking her heart. Logic was the only thing stopping her from telling them to run and hide. Leaving the room would be pointless, there was nowhere to go.* Kayn's vision blurred with tears as she said, "Maybe if I'd died that night things would be different?"

Her brother's eyes flooded as he whispered, "Don't you dare say that. Don't even think it."

They embraced. *He didn't understand. How could he?* Burying her face into her brother's shoulder, she whispered, "I'm so sorry."

"If it is my time to die, so be it," Jenkins stated, "Thank you for allowing me to be a part of your family." He hugged Kayn, then patted Matt on the shoulder. Matt pulled him in for a hug and it pushed him over the edge. Their emotional goodbye was interrupted by something hurled against the bedroom window. The glass cracked and it drew their attention back to the situation at hand. A second object was thrown, the glass shattered and sprayed across the room. They reacted by cowering and covering their eyes.

In true immortal form, Lily addressed the group, "We get to choose how we live not when we die. Our objective is to keep Kayn with Ankh. Other Clans are here for her, those demons that ate the guy in your backyard also came for her. Even if the fight ends up in the house, Kayn stays protected if she remains in this room. We're trying to buy time. There's an invisible clock when the alarm goes off this craziness disappears. Kayn, don't get suckered into leaving this bedroom, for anything or anyone."

Passionately kissing Matt, Lily strutted away, leaving her stunned brother sitting there. She used Kayn's stuffed animal to brush away jagged glass on the window frame. "I love you. I'll see you again in two or three decades," Lily called out, heroically leaping out her bedroom window landing on the Triad swinging the tree. Pinning him with her knees, the fearless onyx-haired immortal stabbed him in the chest with her dagger.

They were watching the battle in awe as Matthew Brighton confessed, "Is it wrong to be this turned on right now?"

"Officially the grossest moment of my life, thanks for that," Kayn teased, watching Lily kicking ass like a warrior princess on the front lawn.

"Ditto," Jenkins added, placing his arm around her. "That girl is the same age as your sister."

"Don't quote me, but I think she's two hundred years old," Kayn clarified, smiling at Matt.

"That's not better," Jenkins commented, grinning.

Matt took action, "Stay away from the window. Let's block the door with furniture."

Blocking the door with furniture, that's cute. Kayn laughed, "I have a feeling that's not going to work. You saw that guy swinging a cherry tree around like it was nothing, right?"

"Point taken," Matt replied.

Lily was swinging the tree now and it looked like she just got a home run as a girl went soaring into the bushes. *It wasn't about what she needed. It was about what they needed. This wasn't the end of her life, it was the end of theirs.* Kayn swallowed the mushy sentiments threatening to spill from her lips. Instead, she chose to agree with her brother, "You're probably right. We should try and block the door, even if it only gives us a few more minutes. A wise person once told me even a few minutes can change the game." *Was it wrong to give them hope?* Kayn made eye contact with one of the men on the lawn who grinned back at her and pointed, showing his friends where she was. Kayn stepped away from the window as a half a dozen arrows came soaring in. She yelled, "Down!" They all dove beside the bed. Kayn stammered, "Did anyone get hit?"

Showing her at a scratch on his arm, Matt answered, "One grazed me but I'm alright."

She knew what that meant. Her brother had less than an hour to live. Her heart ached as she glanced at the clock on the wall and gave him a sliver of truth, "Those arrows are drugged, Matty. How do you feel?"

Her brother replied, "Meh, it stings a little. It's just a scratch."

Kayn kept a straight face as she suggested, "Let's block this window." *Don't cry. It's better if he doesn't know.* Crouching together, they shoved her dresser across the room until it was flush against the window, leaving only the top half unblocked.

More arrows came whirling with expert precision through the small opening. Matt yelled, "Get down!"

They dove on the floor as arrows struck the wall narrowly missing her. *That was too close.* Kayn closed her eyes with her cheek against the carpet. *How were they supposed to feel like they'd saved her if she died first?* They congregated in the corner.

Jenkins suggested, "Let's stay away from the window. One of us will get hit for sure if we try to stack something on top of the dresser." Arrows whizzed through the opening from a different angle. One was stuck into the wall inches from Jenkin' head, he gasped, "Shit, that was close."

How was Trinity aiming without being able to see them? If she didn't block the rest of that window, they wouldn't have a chance to find peace. Adrenaline released, Kayn shivered as her pulse raced. Led by instinct, she bolted across the room, flipped her desk, and easily smashed it into manageable pieces with her fist.

Matt's jaw dropped as he whispered, "She's like a superhero or something."

"Or something," Kayn muttered under her breath, tossing jagged wood at the open top half of the window with accurate precision.

"Blocking the door seems dumb now," Matt chuckled.

He was slurring words. Knowing they were going to die any which way this played out didn't make accepting it any easier. Her only duty on this earth was to protect them until they had a chance to save her. She'd already failed her brother. Kayn enquired, "Matty, can I look at your arm?" *It was an insignificant looking cut.* Running to the bathroom, she returned with antiseptic and a cloth. Soaking it, she pressed it on his arm. *She wasn't sure what she was trying to do. Maybe tending to his wound would give her heart what it needed?*

As Matt stroked the carpet, Jenkins whispered, "What's on those bloody arrows, rhino tranquilizers?"

"They're meant to take down an immortal," Kayn whispered, blinking back tears.

Waving his hand in front of his face, Matt sighed, "There are pretty rainbows on my fingers."

Jenkins looked at Kayn, whispering, "Well, he doesn't care about dying anymore."

Wanting to make sure he was comfortable, Kayn crouched by her brother, suggesting, "Matty, let's go to the washroom." She helped him get there, sat Matt on the closed toilet like a chair and handed him a magazine. Smiling, he opened it, amazed by the contents. Closing the door on her obliviously happy brother, Kayn came back, saying, "He's all good." *She chose to leave the Matt will be dead soon part out.* Remembering the brains before brawn speech, she gave it to Jenkins as they searched for objects they could use as weapons with glass crunching beneath their shoes on rose-coloured carpet. *She needed to keep Jenkins busy. He had to believe he could save her.* She listened to him spouting off brilliant ideas. He brought up the metal towel rack in the bathroom. She vetoed the idea, knowing Chloe used it as a weapon on the night she died. *It felt like bad luck, not that luck mattered anymore.*

Jenkins was optimistic about their chances of survival even after what he'd been told and everything he'd seen. Mortality was such a beautiful thing. She wanted to hope for their survival but knew better. She was already dead and suspected she'd be dead again before this day was through. They would all be dead.

DOWNSTAIRS, THEY WERE PREPARED TO protect the interior of the Brighton house. It hadn't been breached because Ankh was doing a kickass job of keeping everyone away. Peering out the living room curtains at the epic brawl, Frost sent Kevin to the kitchen, knowing Ankh's Dragon was guarding the sliding doors.

Watching Lexy kicking everyone's ass in the backyard, Kevin was thoroughly entertained. *She was awesome. He'd never seen someone fight like this before.* Each time she was hit by an arrow, Lexy yanked it out, broke it in half and screamed with fury. *She needed music. What had Jenkins been washing dishes to?* Kevin turned on his middle-aged friend's iPod and cranked the volume, thinking it might confuse the fighters outside. 'Achy Breaky Heart' blared through the kitchen and patio speakers. The entire fight paused. Everyone stared into the kitchen.

Lexy mouthed the words, "Do not make me die to Billy Ray."

Kevin smiled as he turned it up louder. Lexy shook her head, grinning. He was laughing so hard, he couldn't breathe when Frost stormed down the hall.

Furious, Frost scolded, "Glad you're taking this seriously, you little shit. Turn down the music." Glancing out the window, he had a hard time containing his laughter when he realised Kevin was messing with their Dragon. Lexy tore arrows out of her shoulder and thigh like they were merely an annoyance, healing instantly. Patting Kevin's shoulder, Frost cautioned, "I enjoy this song. I once won a bet by listening to it on repeat for a week, but I think we agree it isn't the kickass motivational battle anthem she needs. Trust me, you do not want to piss Lexy off."

Kevin pressed the screen and changed the background music to 'Domino' by Kiss.

As the crimson-haired warrior tore another arrow out of her stomach, she looked at Kevin and smiled. *How many arrows could she take? She wasn't even trying to avoid them.*

"Much better. She may not seriously wound you now," Frost teased, motioning for Kevin. They dashed down the hallway to the living room. Frost pulled back the curtains, revealing Lily mid Triad toss.

Kevin whispered, "It feels like we should be helping?"

Closing the curtain, Frost explained, "Our orders were to stay in the house. Our time's coming. Lily's been avoiding arrows but she's exhausted. Lexy will keep fighting until she has fifty arrows in her. It may be the strength of her Healing ability, but I think it's sheer determination."

"You dodged my question," Kevin exclaimed.

"No, I didn't. I told you, our time is coming. All they're doing outside is buying us time. They're the first line of defence, we're the second. There's a blackout bubble over the area. When this battle times out, we'll be incapacitated by a noise. All Kayn has to do is stay in that room without allowing humanity to cloud her judgement."

"What creates a blackout bubble? How long does it last?" Kevin asked, fascinated. He shifted the curtain to watch.

Frost replied, "That is a story for another place and time."

Turning, Kevin panicked, "Lily just went down." Their palms glowed and pulsed three times.

Exhaling, Frost stepped away, calmly saying, "Don't freak out. They're all dead. Healers never stay dead long, Lexy will be back to help. It's our turn, we just have to keep them downstairs for as long as we can."

UPSTAIRS IN THE BATHROOM, THEY were wrestling with Matt to stop him from eating toothpaste. It took a minute to realise they were being ridiculous. *If Matt wanted to spend the last moments of his life eating toothpaste, they should say go to town and leave him in his happy place.* Kayn's heart started beating faster, skin prickled as blood raced through her veins. Her hand warmed, pulsing with light. *She knew what it meant. The Ankh protecting the house were down for the count. The fight was about to come inside. Kevin was downstairs.* Kayn stared at her bedroom door. *She wanted to go to him but understood this wasn't about her. Her brother was dying, but did Jenkins really have to die too? She could find somewhere for him to hide.* She checked on Matt, he was off in his own world, sitting in the empty bathtub singing a childhood tune about diarrhea. Opening a bottle of shampoo, he squeezed it all over his head as he sang off key. *The attic above her bedroom was the best hiding spot.*

Squinting, rubbing his eyes, Matty complained, "It's in my eyes, help! Help me!" Comically slipping in the tub.

There was no way he'd be capable of climbing up into the attic. Jenkins wouldn't go anywhere without them. Grabbing a towel, Kayn flashed back to Chloe's demise, ignoring the urge to knock her brother out with the rack and haul him up to the attic. *The poison would kill him, it wouldn't matter where he was.* Wiping shampoo out of Matt's eyes, she tenderly touched his sticky cheek. Kayn turned away, with tears streaming down her cheeks. *Jenkins was standing there.* She plastered on a smile, blinking away tears.

Touching Kayn's shoulder, Jenkins pressed, "You don't need to protect me. What's the real deal here?"

With everything out of her control, she gave it to him, "The countdown to Matt's death started as soon as he was grazed by that arrow. We're all going to die today, it's an inevitable fact."

Jenkins teared up, whispering, "Not you though. Not if you stay in this room."

DOWNSTAIRS, THEIR FIGHT WAS JUST beginning. Kevin was a mess of unfiltered inner dialogue. *His brother and mother had been taken by Triad. Someone would have to be there to stand up for them and make sure they were treated properly. Why was he even considering something that could be the most epically stupid mistake of his life?*

Contemplating biting his tongue, allowing idiots to fall where they may, Frost listened to the kid beating himself up. In a show of conscience, he asserted, "Don't even think about going with Triad like a naive idiot, not even to save your family. They'll wipe your memories."

"Quit listening to my thoughts," Kevin complained, gazing longingly up the stairs.

Smirking, Frost countered, "Quit having stupid ones and I won't feel compelled to speak out against the insanity." They startled as something large crashed against the front door. A brief eerie silence was followed by a rhythmic knock. Strolled over to the entrance, Frost sarcastically provoked, "We don't want any." With his fingers, he simulated a countdown. The door exploded into wood fragments.

His brother's look-alike was standing in the doorway. *How had his mother been fooled by this idiot? He would have been able to tell this wasn't Clay for dozens of reasons. This guy wasn't wearing gym clothes or ripped jeans. His older brother's grand entrances usually involved a beer can crushing into his forehead or a well-timed burp, not busting through a door. They were identical in looks but worlds apart in mannerisms.*

Coolly leaning against the railing, Frost sparred, "Seriously? There's this thing called a doorknob, it wasn't even locked."

Opening his arms, Tiberius chuckled, "Kidding, no cuddles for you brother." Surveying his surroundings, he reminisced, "I get all nostalgic and shit when I think of our week together. That look on your face as I removed your intestines has proven to be rather inspirational for me." Triad's leader picked up a picture off the shelf and circled the twins with his finger, intimidating Kevin without saying a word.

"Glad I could brighten your week. It's too bad you never got what you were looking for," Frost answered, smiling.

In a disturbingly sweet tone, Tiberius revealed, "Oh, I wasn't looking for anything. It was just an excuse to have one on one time with my bro. Well, I also wanted to try to bed your fiancée, wife, convenient plaything, what was her final title? Sorry, I know that's a touchy subject."

"Her final title is, friend," Frost corrected. "Don't you have new material? It's been the same pathetic you stole my girlfriend crap for a thousand years. There's this crazy thing called moving on. You should try it, I have."

Tiberius pointed at Kevin like he was an object in the room, saying, "Thanks for fixing up the kid. That's one less thing I have to do when I take him off your hands."

Kevin raised his weapon, heroically declaring, "Let's go, old man."

Howling laughing, Tiberius teased, "With that knife. Really? Should I get Uncle Frost to tie my hands behind my back to make it fair? I'm sure he has plenty of bondage experience."

Frost groaned, "How were you allowed to breed?" Saucily wandering over to a muscular ogre obediently waiting in the doorway, he harassed, "You get to pick any shell you want. Why in the hell would you choose the missing link? You look like an example of Neanderthal man on an evolution chart."

"Authentic Neanderthal, isn't he?" Tiberius proudly replied.

The brutish Triad growled. Frost dramatically jumped back. He enquired, "I'm curious, does having the intelligence of a can of spam aid in the mental recovery time after being eaten by a demon?"

Tiberius openly laughed before declaring, "Tell you what, I'll just take this kid and the Conduit. I'll trade you for three partially digested under eighteens. You can find out for yourself."

Frost sighed and countered, "Yeah, I'm sorry, that's not going to work for us, there's an intelligence clause in the fine print to join our Clan."

Tiberius held out his hand to Frost, saying, "It's always fun chatting with you brother but I have places to go and people to kill. Till next time, Zoolander."

Puzzled by his brother's handshake offer, Frost said, "What?" He looked up and Tiberius sucker punched him.

You've got to be kidding me. Laughing nervously, Kevin nudged the immortal with his foot and sighed, "What in the hell?" *Where was the fight? One sneaky punch and the great Frost was dead to the world.*

With a forced smile, Tiberius admitted, "Kid, I honestly don't give two shits about you at this point. I'd rather just kill you, chuck you in a coffin and chat later. It's been a long day. I heard you have my abilities. That makes me warm and fuzzy enough to say, come willingly, it'll be less traumatic for you."

"You really are a shithead, aren't you?" Kevin taunted as he grabbed the landline off the end table and rifled it at Tiberius.

"Really? You're the one throwing things at your grandfather, show some maturity," Tiberius chuckled as Kevin began pitching everything within arm's reach at him. "You have an enormous set of balls like your mother," the immortal provoked, fending off flying mementos with waves of his hand.

"How do you like me now?" Kevin announced as he picked up the end table, swinging it at his grandfather.

Chuckling, blocking his mini attack, Tiberius retorted, "Okay, I love a good battle of wits, but you appear to be unarmed. No song lyrics or cheesy movie lines during a fight. It's wrong for so many reasons." Kevin swung the table again. Tiberius took it away, snapped it in two and smiled as he crushed a piece into dust. He cockily blew it off his palm, patiently urging, "You're wasting my time, kid. I already have your mother and brother. Your father's still alive but he won't be if he shows up here. The faster we do this the better his odds are."

With those words Kevin was defeated. *It was true. This was the first place his dad would look.*

Tiberius took advantage of Kevin's split second of indecision by pinning him against the wall and branding his chest Triad. He unceremoniously broke his neck. Kevin's body crumpled to the floor. Turning to instruct his Neanderthal, his backup was lying in a pool of blood on the floor with his throat slit. Frost was gone. Ready for a surprise attack, Triad's leader hissed, "I knew you went down too easily, you sneaky bastard!" Searching for his sibling, Tiberius took an arrow to the heart and another in his head courtesy of Trinity.

STROLLING BACK INTO THE HOUSE behind Trinity warriors, Frost kicked his brother, chuckling, "I owe you one." *He'd lost count of his dalliances, but he'd serviced the curly dark-haired one multiple times at Aries Group events. She was fun. He couldn't remember her name.*

Baffled, Glory lowered her bow, toying, "Would saving you make us even in your mind?"

"Totally even, beautiful," Frost flirted, opting out of a name attempt. *She didn't seem happy to see him. It felt like he was missing something.* The last time they were together leapt to mind, *Oh, crap!* Trinity shot him with an arrow, another followed, penetrating his lower spine rendering him defenceless.

"You bitch!" Frost groaned from the ground.

The dark-haired immortal warrior sparred, "Karma's a bitch."

She hated his guts and rightfully so. They hooked up in the woods when they were supposed to be fighting. Black mist came. He'd sort of accidentally tripped her while fleeing the scene and left her to be devoured by demons.

A few Trinity grabbed his arms as Glory whispered, "We're going to drag you and your frenemy outside. If leftover demons are wandering around, you'll get what's coming to you, then we'll call it even." They dragged Frost out and left him on the lawn.

They tugged Tiberius out and were just about to do the same

to Kevin when a newbie named Melody whispered, "Let's leave the kid inside." Shutting his vacant eyes, she tidied his hair.

One addressed the group, "We have shooters in the trees, they'll take out anyone who tries to come through the front door. We can buy you ten minutes. Get the girl to come out of that room. Mark her, kill her, and carry her out the back. We have the rest covered. Thorne and the others are almost here for clean-up." They raced down the hallway towards the kitchen.

MEANWHILE UPSTAIRS WACKY DRUGGED MATT wrestled past Kayn and Jenkins, sprinting out of the bedroom, yelling, "I'm freeeee!"

Jenkins blocked Kayn's exit, reasoning with her, "Frost and Kevin will look out for Matt. Listen, your brother is dying and he's deliriously happy. Hell, I wish I'd been shot by an arrow."

This was their final act, none of the mortals would be allowed to live. Her heart clenched in her chest as Lily's words replayed in her mind. *We are all immortal.* Jenkins agreed to climb up into the attic if she went first. *He knew she'd go after Matt.* Kayn wrapped an arrow in a towel and took it with her. She scaled shelves into the attic, then helped Jenkins.

Closing the slab of lumber, he sat on top of the opening and implored, "Please, stay here with me. They said I could protect you by keeping you in the room."

Theoretically, they weren't in the room anymore. She smiled.

WHILE TRINITY WAS FIGURING OUT a plan, Matt appeared at the top of the stairs, foaming at the mouth because he'd been eating toothpaste. Excited, he shouted, "Is it Halloween? You're the girl from Flash Dance!"

"I think he just insulted you, Mel," Glory whispered.

"I never noticed it before, you look like her," Melody teased. "Were we expecting the crazy guy to be here?"

Glory took a step upstairs towards Matt, explaining, "It's an eighties party. We're just waiting for your sister."

Higher than a kite Matt innocently replied, "Kayn can't go to a party today. People are fighting on the lawn. Hey, is the front door gone?"

Smiling warmly, Melody enquired, "Honey, did somebody nick you with an arrow today?"

"Yes, one of those suckers scratched me," the boy complained, showing her his boo, boo.

Melody questioned, "And the white stuff on your face?"

Matt licked his lips and replied, "Tastes minty." He squinted, pointed at the lifeless body in the doorway and asked, "Is that Kevin?"

"The lightweight passed out already. Go get your sister and tell her it's time to go," Melody instructed, feeling guilty.

Burly Triad raced through the missing door. They'd been hit by arrows, but it hadn't slowed them down. Glory commented, "Sharpshooters my ass."

They rushed at the girls. One launched Melody across the room into the closet door with inhuman strength. With the wind was knocked out of her, she caught her breath, groaning, "Shit that hurt. What in the hell do they feed you guys?" A Healer, it took a lot more to subdue her, Melody leapt to her feet. He tossed her again. The heat in her spine let her know he'd done damage as she peered up, dazed. Glory was being strangled against the wall.

Higher than a kite, Matthew Brighton still had the instinct to try to save Glory. He raced down the stairs and launched his mortal toothpaste covered self at the giant ogre's back and hung on like he was riding a bull at a rodeo. He bit his shoulder. The man ripped Matt off and launched him against the wall with so much force he was killed instantly.

Racing for the Triad in triumphant testosterone fuelled bliss, Mel slashed his jugular. A fine mist of blood sprayed everywhere. He staggered and went down. She froze after the violent act for a heartbeat. That's all it took for the other Triad to grab her shirt, yank her to him, and stab her repeatedly in the stomach. Trinity came to her aid, shooting a half dozen arrows into her assailant's back. He'd dropped but wasn't dead. She had to heal quickly. Placing her hands on the Triad's chest, Melody screamed with rage as she absorbed what was left of his energy to heal herself.

A Trinity remained in the doorway. Derek apologized, "Sorry Mel, we need to up the dosage. They aren't going down fast enough."

Reigning in the energy she'd stolen, Melody declared, "No Shit, Sherlock. I'm the only Healer on site. If I go down the jobs over."

Grinning, Derek winked and teased, "Don't die then."

"Shoot them with fifty frigging arrows if you have to, just keep those mutants away from the front door," Mel asserted.

"That was the last of Triad, they're dead," Derek replied.

Melody took a deep breath as he disappeared, that's when she saw Glory's body. *When did she die? This fight was a shit show.* Placing her hands-on Glory's chest, she began healing her, knowing she may not have the strength to heal her completely. With Triad out of the picture, she didn't need to.

Groggily opening her eyes, Glory whispered, "You didn't come back to the room last night. Tell me everything."

Her best friend had been dead and the first words out of her mouth were in search of gossip. She was hilarious. Melody cleverly bartered, "We should dispose of the bodies before chatting about my sex life. It's just a thought."

Ruffling Matthew's hair, Glory exclaimed, "Toothpaste boy tried to save me." They dragged Matt to the closet and shoved him inside. Glory smiled and said, "Thanks toothpaste boy" as she closed the door.

Matthew Brighton's corpse lay in the closet that once held his mother's body, his eyes staring into the unknown. As further proof fate weaves a tangled web. Melody stared at the boy on the floor by the doorway. *Toothpaste boy called him Kevin. It was a name powerful enough to alter her perception of the situation. Kevin was her little brother's name. He was dead, all their families were. Was he the Conduit's brother or boyfriend?* She deduced it must be her boyfriend. *There was a picture of toothpaste boy on the wall.*

From the top of the stairs, Glory announced, "The room is spiritually protected. We have to get her to come out, and we're running out of time. What did the guy in the closet say the kid on the floors name was?"

"His name is Kevin," Melody replied with an aching heart.

Grinning, Glory declared, "Good, we have a name. Kevin was probably her boyfriend. This should be easy."

Melody wasn't even eighteen yet, and in her heart, the death of her family was far too fresh to be flippant about the demise of someone else's. She couldn't stop staring at the boy with her brother's name. *She knew a boy who loved her enough to give his life for her, once upon a time. She'd started adding, once upon a time to stories of her mortal life so she could look back and pretend it was just a beautiful story. The immortality that followed had become more of a nightmare.* She thought of Glory's words. *This should be easy.*

She looked up as Glory warned, "Don't get all sentimental

because he has the same name as your brother. That's going to happen a lot. Get a grip. Push those feelings down, Mel."

The boy's lifeless eyes seemed to be looking directly at her. Accusing her. "You were already dead when I got here," Mel whispered.

Glory piped in, "Please don't talk to the dead bodies, it creeps me out."

33

REDEMPTION AND SACRIFICE

"*K*ayn! We have Kevin! Come downstairs!" Glory yelled from the hall. There was no reply. They were pressed for time. Glory looked at her friend and instructed, "Do me a favour? Check that guy's pocket for a phone."

Melody tossed it to Glory. She caught it and sighed, "Kids now a days. There's always a cellphone." She opened his text messages, scrolled down to Kayn's name and as she texted, she spoke the words aloud, "This is Trinity. We have Kevin. We are going to burn the house down. Come downstairs, the clock is ticking."

"That is not how you make friends," Melody sighed, shaking her head.

IN THE ATTIC, KAYN'S POCKET vibrated. *Who would be texting*

her now? She took out her phone and read the text without registering her reaction. *She was going to lose him. Kevin was about to be taken by Trinity.* She had to stop her hands from shaking to reply. She texted, "Be right there." She took a deep breath in and out to calm her racing pulse. *This was what she'd been warned about. This was how they were going to lure her out and they were going to succeed. She had to go. She wasn't going to do this without him.* Kayn closed her eyes and took more cleansing breaths before peering up at Jenkins. *He was deliberately blocking the exit. For someone without powers, he was good at reading minds.*

Securing his position, Jenkins enquired, "I take it that wasn't a good message?"

There was no point in beating around the bush, Kayn replied, "Trinity has Kevin. They are going to take him and burn the house down if I don't come down there."

"They could be bluffing. What if they don't even have him? You were warned about leaving for anything or anyone. That includes Kevin," Jenkins reasoned with her.

What if they weren't bluffing? She was far too mentally exhausted for ration. It was all too much. Tears of frustration surged forth. *Her brother would be dead by now. She'd already broken the rules by leaving the safety of the bedroom to get Jenkins up into the attic and there were no consequences.* She'd half expected an immortal being to burst through the roof like the Kool-Aid man and yank her out, but here she was in the untouched attic full of treasured relics from her childhood. *Did she feel like being burned alive and allowing Jenkins to suffer the same excruciating fate? Not so much.* She looked into Jenkins' eyes as she explained, "I don't care if I'm with Trinity or Ankh. I only care about staying with Kevin."

His eyes clouded over with tears as he moved out of her way. As they embraced, Kayn whispered, "Thank you for everything. I love you."

Jenkins whispered in her ear, "Back atcha kid."

They both knew this was goodbye. They wouldn't allow him to live. She knew the rules. You kill the mortals that know too much.

She was climbing down the bathroom shelves when Jenkins popped his head out and disclosed, "I'm not sure you're thinking straight. Heck, I know I'm not. Maybe you should listen to Lily and stay in the bedroom?"

Meeting concern with certainty, Kayn questioned, "Haven't you ever risked everything for love?"

Winking at her Jenkins grinned as he disclosed, "Yes, right now." He smiled at her one last time and closed the hatch to the attic.

Leaving the bathroom, she took the final stroll through her bedroom, wistfully touching Chloe's comforter as she passed by. *Her mind had lost the ability to reason with her heart.* Fully aware she was making a mistake, she opened her bedroom door. *She had to get to him. The coast was clear, there was not a soul between her and the top of the stairs.* Her heart ached as she passed the family photos in the hall. *All they were now was a gut-wrenching reminder of a life that was no longer.* A vivid memory flashed through her mind. All three Brighton kids with freckles and curls racing down the hallway squealing as their father chased them, pretending to be a monster. They would always run into their parents' room and hide under the covers for that was always the safest place to be. *There was no safe place for her now, was there?* She paused in front of a toothless picture of her brother as a child. *Matt stayed strong for her when she had no strength left to give him in return.* She covered her mouth with her hands to stifle the noise from a sob. *Her brother was probably dead, but with no mark of a Clan to keep him from his destination, he'd be reborn. Maybe he'd already passed through the hall of souls? He could be taking his first breath as a newborn. Imagining the beautiful music of his first crackling cries filled her broken heart with hope.* With a shuddering breath, she kissed the palm of her hand, willing it to follow him into his next life as a soft kiss upon his newborn skin. She placed her palm on his picture as she recalled the words that would always stay with her and bring her strength. *We are all immortal.*

Her brain valiantly fought to reason with her heart. *Go back to the bedroom. You are making a mistake.* As Kayn took her last private steps down the hall, it felt like she was walking down the length of a plank unprepared to take that leap into the unknown. *It was ironic that these plush carpeted stairs, a monumentally happy thing in her mortal life would be the endpoint of her journey. These stairs held so many glorious memories. She'd grown up running down them so she could jump into the arms of her father as he came home from work. She slid down them with her siblings for fun. Strange things cross your mind when you are terrified and pretty sure you're doing the wrong thing. At this point, it was go big or go home.* She thought about what she'd been told about changing fear into fury and her brain attempted a rage inducing pep talk. *Her family was dead. All of them were dead now, and these assholes were planning to take the only person she had left. They would believe she was strong because she'd show them nothing but courage. 'Fake it till you make it,'* her mother's voice echoed in her mind. She stepped out at the top of the stairs, showing herself, with plans to be revered as a beacon of vengeance. Her expression changed as she saw Kevin's lifeless body at the Trinity's feet. Taken over by panicked desperation she couldn't disguise, Kayn was just a girl in love with a boy who died. She bled emotion so raw and powerful it rendered the Trinity speechless. Too much humanity survived behind her exquisitely tortured eyes.

Moved by her devastation, Melody of Trinity explained, "We didn't kill him, he was already like this when we got here."

Kayn stepped down a stair with tears in her eyes and declared, "If you've made him Trinity. I'll go with you willingly."

Confused, Glory knelt to check Kevin's hand. The symbol of

Ankh was no longer, but as she exposed his chest, there was a fresh brand of Triad. There was still fighting going on outside. Someone staggered through the doorway and passed out with an arrow in his back.

Melody commented, "Seriously?"

Looking at Melody, Glory ordered, "There's no time. You're not strong enough to brand, kill and heal both. Leave the kid marked Triad. Thorne will lose it if you don't come back. You know what to do. I'll make sure they're still waiting," With that, the Trinity bolted out the missing door.

Coming down to the second stair, Kayn questioned, "Kevin was marked Triad, where are they? Did they just leave him?"

"We were told they were all dead," Melody replied.

She wasn't sure why, but she trusted this stranger from another Clan. Kayn ran past Melody and knelt by Kevin. Seeing the mark of Triad scalded into his chest, she pulled him to her lap, cradling his lifeless body in her arms. With teary eyes, Kayn pled, "Bring him back. You don't have to worry about me. You can kill me later." *They hadn't had enough time. They were supposed to do this together. Ankh was written across Kayn's soul. Triad was written across Kevin's.*

Melody shook her head and whispered, "I was given a direct order. I'm a new Healer. If I bring him back to life and mark him Trinity, it's going to take more than the two minutes we have left. You'll be Ankh. You'll still be separated."

An incapacitating noise dropped both girls to the floor. They covered their ears, screaming in unison until the excruciating sound abruptly stopped.

With empathy in her eyes, Melody whispered, "It's over, I'm sorry. That was the line in the sand. I'm not allowed to alter anything now."

Blinded by tears, Kayn cradled Kevin's lifeless body in her arms. Stroking his hair, she kissed his lips, tasting her own salty tears. With an aching heart, she sobbed, "I can't lose him too."

Those were the magic words that reached in and seized the Trinity girl's heart. She latched on to what humanity she had left, and whispered, "Screw the rules." Melody grasped Kayn's arms, disclosing, "You have no idea what I'm giving up."

Kayn's lifeforce travelled a warm sedating path up her arms and luxurious warmth filled her heart. The love she felt exploded in the core of her being as the euphoric sensation travelled down her arms and out of her body. She collapsed on the floor.

Overwhelmed by the intensity of the love she'd absorbed, Trinity's Healer embraced the boy. Warmth of Kayn's essence flowed through her as though she were an extension cord for the transfer of Kayn's being into Kevin's empty shell. *She'd given them the chance to say goodbye.* Melody crumpled to the floor. White light hovered like afterglow of a lightbulb, as two partially immortal girls drifted off to dream in the land of the in-between.

Healed by Kayn's essence, Kevin gasped for air as three Triad walked through the doorway to gather their Clan's bodies.

Winded from the action, a rough-looking girl addressed him by name, "Hi, Kevin. There's no point in wasting my breath with pleasantries. You won't remember any of this after Tiberius gets through with you."

"What happened here?" A curious burly Triad exclaimed.

Confused, Kevin noticed a girl with shoulder length chestnut hair he didn't recognize and Kayn lying next to him. *They were breathing, it looked like they were asleep.*

"Nobody cares. Grab the boy and chuck him in a tomb, he belongs to us," a Triad commanded.

One of Triad's henchmen swung Kevin over his shoulder. Heels clicked over to his dangling head. Squatting, a girl roughly tilting his face towards her, questioning, "Which one of these ladies is the Conduit?"

"They're both Trinity," Kevin incoherently mumbled, limply hanging over his captor's shoulder. A Triad booted the girl with the chestnut hair in the stomach.

As he tried to speak, the blonde blurted, "Oh, shut up. I'm not the one you need to impress." She snapped Kevin's neck, silencing him.

Waking, Kayn groggily attempted to stop them from taking him, "No, don't..." A Triad coldly stomped on her face, killing her.

THIS WAS A TIME WHEN the lines were drawn, and the game had been played. There was usually a victor and a loser but today it was a strange tie. The leader of Ankh beamed as he strolled into the Brighton house. The girl they'd lost was lying next to Kayn. They'd been about to claim Melody when she was stolen by Trinity.

As fate would have it, Orin was standing beside Markus. His eyes lit up as he urged, "Trinity is gone, we can take her."

Glancing around, Markus answered, "They wouldn't leave a Healer behind."

Arrianna sauntered in and backed up Orin's claim, "Trinity's gone, if we don't take her, Triad will."

"If you're certain Trinity's gone, it shouldn't be an issue. Take the Conduit first. She's dead, put her in a tomb," Markus ordered, pointing at the mashed face of an unrecognizable girl. "Take your time waking her, Triad has Kevin."

As they lugged Kayn's dead weight across the lawn, Arrianna whispered, "Tell me why I just lied to my boyfriend. Trinity's in the trails."

"She's my daughter," Orin explained.

Helping Orin haul Kayn's body up the ramp into the back of the rig, Arrianna looked into his eyes, replying, "That's a good enough reason for me, I never officially saw Trinity."

They placed Kayn inside a tomb. Orin put his hand on the side, and it ground shut. Rushing down the ramp back to the house because of their time sensitive fib, Arrianna declared, "When you come back to work next year, Ankh will have three Healers."

Grinning, Orin corrected, "You mean four. My offspring is a Healer." Appearing to be nowhere near old enough to have sired a teenage daughter, he was one of the seventeen original Children of Ankh. They entered the house in time to witness the moment Melody switched Clans.

TAKING THE TEEN'S HAND AS she came to, Markus explained, "We meet again, Miss Melody. Trinity left you behind and you're not fully sealed. The decision is yours, Ankh or Triad?"

The girl with the chestnut hair, whispered, "Ankh."

Smiling at her immediate response, Markus apologised, "Sorry, you know the drill. This is going to sting." He turned his ring and rebranded the palm of her hand with the symbol of Ankh. Crying out in agony, Melody was instantly wide awake.

"In case you've forgotten, my name's Markus. Welcome to Clan Ankh," he announced in a fatherly tone.

"Just do it," Melody urged, wincing while squeezing her eyes shut, knowing what came next.

Committing murder in the civilized way, he swiftly snapped her neck. Signalling for the others to take her, Markus excused himself as he scaled the stairs, heading for the safe zone their newbie opted out of. Half expecting to find members of Kayn's family in the spiritually protected room, it was trashed and empty. *There was a mortal somewhere. He could sense it.* Hearing something move above him, Markus smiled as he realised, she'd tried to hide someone in the attic. *Mortals.* It took him moments to find the entrance. With Jenkins' weight on top of it, he pushed it open like it was nothing. A middle-aged mortal was flung across the room. Markus climbed through the opening and closed it for privacy. He sat on top of the escape hatch, smiling.

Prepared for the worst, Jenkins said, "You're here to kill me."

"I'll be blunt. Burning this house is the most efficient way to dispose of evidence. If you try to flee, and another Clan catches you, it's going to be brutal. We aren't allowed to leave witnesses. I promise it will be fast, and I think she's waiting for you."

"Who?" Jenkins asked, looking around the darkened attic.

Pointing to a corner of the room, Markus disclosed, "There's a little girl over there, she's soaking wet."

Jenkins' heart leapt. His eyes overflowed with tears as he whispered, "My little girl drowned, a long time ago."

The leader of Ankh's eyes softened as he spoke, "Often spirits show themselves in their last mortal form. Sometimes, when it's time for a soul to pass on, the people they love are in so much pain, they can't bring themselves to leave. Once they've missed the opportunity to move on, they forget how."

Jenkins shuddered, sobbing, "She's really here with me?"

"If you go now, she may leave with you. You can go home

together," the leader offered, peacefully. She was sitting in the corner of the attic, trembling, afraid for her father. The leader of Ankh spoke to the small water nymph with an upturned nose, "Come, you can fall asleep tonight in your father's arms."

The ghostly entity cautiously came towards her father. When she was close enough, the child reached out and tenderly stroked her father's face. As her tiny hand moved through him, Jenkins sneezed. Feeling her presence, love filled his heart to the point of rupturing. He whispered, "Come home with me, sweetheart. I've got you."

Making eye contact with the tiny cherub-faced child, Markus promised, "Hug your daddy and you can be together." The child melted against her father. Jenkins felt his child in his arms and his heart surged with love as the immortal swiftly snapped his neck. The immortal looked at the middle-aged man slumped in the corner. On his face, he wore a smile, for in his last moment he'd felt his little girl in his embrace. Crawling back to the opening of the attic, Markus leapt down. He set fire to the bedding in each room, then jogged downstairs to the kitchen. He turned on the burners without lighting them, set the drapes in the living room ablaze and looked in the closet on his way out. The glazed eyes of Kayn's brother stared back. The leader of Ankh assured, "Rest in peace, Matthew. I'll care for your sister as though she were my own. I promise." With that, Markus walked out of the Brighton house.

With most of Ankh healing in tombs in the trucks, they drove away. In the distance, gas from the burners ignited an explosion, lighting up the night sky with dancing flames as a symbol of redemption and sacrifice. The Brighton family was gone. Only two bodies were found in the rubble. It was a blessing it burned to ash and debris. The people of the sleepy town could begin to forget about the horror that occurred within its walls. On the same night, the Smith home burned. No bodies were recovered. The family vanished without a trace. Kevin's father would never learn of his family's mysterious disappearance. He'd never know the pain of their loss nor would they grieve his. Mr. Smith died of an aneurism, passing on as he placed his key into the ignition. He was discovered the next day in his vehicle, looking like he'd peacefully drifted off into a sweet sleep. *This signified the ending to a story. The spiritual would grasp it was only the beginning of another.*

34

DON'T WAKE ME. I DON'T WANT TO LEAVE THIS DREAM

*M*atthew Brighton vaguely recalled the moment of his death. There was a blur of movement, then nothing but silence and isolating darkness. *He'd grown accustomed to waking up in strange places. This had been the story of his life. So, why would it be any different after his death?* There was no heavenly glow as one would expect, and for a second, he feared his mortal shenanigans had caused him to end up in a bad place. Wearing something constricting and itchy, he was standing on a firm surface, but there was no light. *Well, shit. This wasn't good.* There was a loud hollow click and a song began to play. He recognized it from his childhood, 'The Glory of Love' by Peter Cetera. *His mother played this song in the car when he was a child. He'd always loved it.* Matt's head began brutally pounding as it spun through his experiences. The pain ceased. Squinting as lights blinded him, he took in his surroundings. He was at a dance with cheesy gold and silver decorations. *Maybe, this was hell?* He wandered over to a punch bowl on a long table, hoping it was spiked. *He needed a drink.*

Grabbing the scoop, Matt helped himself, chuckling, "Yes, it's spiked."

The lights began to whirl around. *He recognized this place, it was an old roller-skating rink. It felt like he should be skating around in a circle holding someone's hand. Lily's hand. He wanted to be holding her hand.* Memories shuffled in his head. *He danced to this song with her.* The old song ended and began playing again. He doubled over as many lifetimes flooded his brain with information. *The strobe lights weren't doing him any favours.* As lights flashed and changed their timing, he had a vision of crossing the street to get ice-cream. He glanced back at the hotel where he'd left her, when he turned back, he saw the headlights of a big rig. *It was unpleasant but over in a heartbeat.* Closing his eyes, he recalled loving Lily repeatedly to the point of desperation as they danced their way through time together.

His heart brought him back to the first time he laid eyes on her. He was walking home as a vision in white galloped past, bareback on a horse with bare feet, and midnight hair streaming behind her in a wave of shimmering silk. *Back then, it was a peculiar thing for a lady to do.* He was awestruck by her exotic beauty as she galloped the span of the field over the hill. He went that direction instead of going home out of sheer curiosity. Eventually, he came across her black stallion wandering by the riverbank. She was swimming with her undergarments on the shore. Their eyes met. He couldn't bring himself to move. *A respectable woman would never swim naked in a river. They just did not do these things.* She didn't get mad at him for staring. Instead, she strolled out of the water and stood before him nude. Without the smallest attempt at modesty, she retrieved her clothes. As she put on her undergarments, she asked for his name.

He'd almost forgotten it. He replied, "Samuel Roberts."

Extending her hand, she reciprocated, "Lilarah."

They sat on the riverbank and talked until dawn with their

toes dangling beneath the surface of the water. He kissed her lips to the explosion of morning's first rays and fell in love with a kiss. In an instant, he belonged to her. They spent the summer making love under twinkling stars and made a pact to be with each other forever. There was only one problem with their plan, he was betrothed to somebody else. When he went to his family, they agreed to meet her. She charmed his father and brothers, but his mother saw her as a threat to her social standing. Lily was too free-spirited for polite society. They refused to release him from engagement, so they planned to run away together. He was supposed to meet her by the river, but he was foolish enough to tell his brother. His family locked him in the cellar, holding him captive for weeks, telling him he'd been enchanted by a witch. He escaped and ran to where Lilarah and her father were staying. They were gone. When he arrived home, his family had been slain. His fiancé swore she'd seen Lilarah. He didn't believe her until he discovered a note saying he'd pay for breaking her heart. During his family's memorial, he saw Lily in the distance beneath a willow tree. Overcome by grief, believing she'd bewitched him and murdered his family, he stifled heartache with alcohol. By morning, every able-bodied man was hunting her down.

When they returned with her body, he discovered the girl he'd loved beyond reason and sentenced to death was pregnant with his child. The all-encompassing devastation as he placed his hand on her rounded belly was seared into his soul. Enraged her rival was with child, his betrothed confessed to writing the note and convincing the town to hunt a witch in his name. Unable to take another breath, Samuel Roberts leapt off a cliff to his death.

He'd been responsible for her death the first time. Perhaps, that was why he died, in every version of his life that followed. The agonizing emotions made him long for her. This was how they'd become stuck in a never-ending circle of pain. He could love her for a thousand lifetimes and never be able to repay what he'd stolen. How had she found the strength to forgive him? He was grateful for every second she'd given him. He remembered everything now, but still wasn't sure if he was in heaven or hell. The doors flew open and Lily walked into the dance. She was breathtaking even with a bad perm and a puffy shouldered blue satin dress. Her eyes lit up as she saw Matt and they walked towards each other. *Heaven,* he thought as music restarted, growing louder on cue. Matthew Brighton was in heaven.

Moments earlier the Brighton house was an epic gong show.

Yanking an arrow out of his shoulder, Grey proceeded with his drugged, testosterone fuelled hissy fit, "Come out of the trees and fight me!" He was hurling objects at the branches trying to knock Trinity's shooters out. One nosedived from his safe spot in the tree and ran. Cheering, Grey pursued him into the woods.

Grey was too drugged to be much help. The archers were trying to subdue their Dragon guarding the backdoor. Nobody wanted to get up close and personal with Lexy in a fight, she had no fear and recovered so quickly it felt next too impossible to keep her down. Dealing with Triad, Lily's hand lit up. *Either Lexy or Grey took a terminal hit.* Envisioning Lexy with fifty arrows in her heaving Clan away from the backdoor, Lily brandished the tree, smoking a Triad into the woods, shouting, "Fore!" They were coming back for more, faster than she could do it, like a bunch of enormous ogre children lining up for airplane rides. Pivoting to boot a Triad in the head, the raven-haired Siren felt the searing of an arrow through her thigh. Snapping off the end, Lily winced, tugging it out. *Archers and relentless Triad, she was the last one standing.* With intuition formed by centuries of Tri-Clan squabbles, she sensed an arrow's path as it whistled through the air and ducked. Lily heard Tiberius' voice. Distracted for a millisecond, a Triad knifed her in the back. Woozy, she kicked an assailant's shin, and took another arrow while snapping a Triad's neck. *She was tired, drugged and bleeding out. She could barely stand.* With one card left to play, Lily primally screamed, releasing a burst of pheromones. Trinity fell out of the trees on the outskirts of the yard. Those approaching with bows drawn, dropped into the grass. As fate would have it, an arrow released, plunging into her heart. *She'd become accustomed to dying. The lights would go out and when they returned, they would be brighter than the sun.*

The darkness went away and the in-between burst forth with blinding light. Standing alone outside a school gymnasium, Lily looked down at her blue dress and felt her permed hair. *She was in one of her most treasured moments.* Fighting the urge to squeal like a thirteen-year-old, she stared at blue double gymnasium doors, knowing Matt was waiting for her. She took a deep breath and pushed open the doors. Their song was playing, perfectly timed to take her breath away. Lily's eyes teared up. *Matt didn't look confused or frightened. He was patiently waiting.* He strolled towards her. She began walking, and they met in the centre of the gym. She'd replayed this in dreams a thousand times often awakening in this exact moment, with her heart dangling precariously on the edge of the glorious memory.

With a spotlight on him, Matt teased, "So, you're obviously dead too?"

Lily gazed into his deep pools of blue, enquiring, "How much do you remember?" He responded by holding out a hand. Lacing her fingers with his, they fit perfectly as always. Tugging her to him as the intensity of the lyrics heightened, he kissed her with such passion it took all her strength to not shove him down and have her way with him on the dancefloor in the floodlight.

When their lips parted, Matt spun her and drew her close, whispering, "I remember everything." She swayed in his arms as he whispered against her hair, "Take care of my sister."

They stopped moving. Meeting his eyes, she replied, "It's sort of my job." *There was no way to guarantee Kayn's safety in life or death but she would be standing beside her.* They danced with their hearts so full they might spontaneously combust until the song finished and began again. There was strange symbolism as the scenery altered and they found themselves in the motel room where they'd spent their final moments together before his death during his last life.

"I've dreamt of this, I thought it was a fantasy," he confessed, skillfully unhooking clasps on her dress, revealing her exquisite shoulders to curvaceous hips like he was unveiling a masterpiece.

It looked like someone kicked him in the gut. Her heart swelled into an orb of adoration as she questioned, "Are you okay?"

"I've never been this okay," Matt vowed, gazing into her eyes. Lily began to glow, dissolving into gleaming dust, she vanished. Squinting in light, he stared at his palm as it disintegrated into nothing. Matthew Brighton was recycled into the hall of souls.

BACK IN THE LAND OF the living, Lily stirred within her tomb. The lid ground open to a grinning Frost. She seethed, "You jerk, I was five seconds from..." She left the rest to his imagination.

Grinning from ear to ear, Frost chuckled, "That sucks. Shitty deal, my friend."

"Asshole," Lily complained as she held out her elegant hand to her immortal counterpart.

Frost declined and teased, "Sorry honey, I don't know where your hands have been."

Lily got out of her tomb herself and huffed, "My hands didn't have the time to be anywhere inappropriate. You make me want to bang my head on one of these tombs."

Frost whispered in Lily's ear, "You're obviously feeling a little frustrated. It's not my fault. There's no need to take it out on me... Unless you want to. You know I am always willing to take one for the team."

"You've taken one for literally everyone's team," Lily sparred.

Markus strolled around the side of the truck, saying, "I really don't want to hear this kind of talk coming out of my daughter's mouth, it's disturbing."

"That ship sailed long ago dad," Lily teased as she hugged her father.

"You're always my little girl, no matter what," Markus replied, kissing Lily's forehead.

They opened the next tomb. Lexy was still cursing at whoever killed her last. Their Dragon decreed, "The next time I see that Triad kid, I'm going to rip his arms and legs off with my bare hands."

Always amused by Lexy's lack of verbal filter, Frost announced, "In other disturbing events, we lost Kevin to Triad." Sort of a gentleman on occasion, he helped her out of her tomb.

"Does Kayn know?" Lexy asked, concerned.

Frost gave her hand a squeeze as he replied, "We were told to give her extra time in the in-between." Standing hand in hand in front of the next tomb. Frost casually enquired, "What's a Zoolander?"

Laughing, Lexy said, "I'll find it on YouTube and show you later." She started giggling again because he totally had that over-posed underwear model look. They moved on to the next tomb. It opened, revealing a confused new girl and boy. Ankh's newest acquisitions said an awkward hello. Lexy cursed and stormed away at the sight of the boy.

Frost greeted the two newest Ankh, "Welcome to Ankh. I'll be your tour guide because one of you was stupid enough to piss off Lexy. I remember dimples. You're one of the girls who shot me. Don't worry, I don't hold grudges."

Melody took Frost's hand. As he helped her out, she replied, "You slept with my best friend and fed her to demons."

"I guess you have me there," Frost chuckled.

Climbing out of the tomb by himself, Zach said, "I ran that girl over with a truck. Tell me she's not the Dragon Tiberius tells horror stories about."

"You are in so much trouble," Frost decreed.

Terrified, Zach blurted out, "Aren't you supposed to protect me?"

Leading the pair away from the tombs, Frost taunted, "I'd suggest flowers, but she'll probably just chew them up and spit at you."

Markus appeared at the bottom of the ramp. Standing beside him was a furious Lexy. Ankh's leader grinned at the two newbie Ankh, suggesting, "Come with me." He escorted them away.

Glaring as Zach inched past, Lexy went to assist Frost.

"If it makes you feel better the new girl killed me," Frost disclosed, smiling.

Grinning, Lexy commented, "Markus says I can do whatever I want to him after he's fully sealed to our Clan. I can be nice for a couple of months."

Frost probed, "Can you be nice for a few months?"

She wandered up to Grey's tomb without even attempting to answer Frost's question. Opening his eyes as his tomb opened, Grey stretched, grinning like he'd just done something naughty.

"Why are you smiling like a cat who just ate a canary?" Frost toyed, leaning against the wall.

Climbing out, Grey confessed, "I had the naughtiest dream."

Catching him up on what he's missed, they told Grey they lost Kevin to Triad but gained two new members of their Clan. Knowing how to make him feel better, Frost told Grey about how he'd woken up Lily before she had a chance to consummate her relationship with the mortal. They howled. Giving his friend a pat on the shoulder, Frost whispered, "That's what friends are for." The group strolled down the ramp. As they went around the corner of the truck, Grey bumped into Melody. Their eyes met. It was easy to read between the lines.

Lexy placed her arm around Melody and sighed, "Let's go anywhere else." She shot a disapproving look at Grey as she led her away.

Frost shook his head at his friend, teasing, "Even a cat knows that you should never pee where you sleep."

35

PLEASE REMEMBER ME

*K*ayn's body lay healing in a tomb, but only her body. *Her soul was elsewhere.*

She awoke in a field of buttercups identical to where she'd played as a child. Fuzzy bumblebees were darting from flower to flower. Calmed by their gentle buzzing song, Kayn looked at her hand. *She was a child.* Giggling, she got up and danced barefoot in a sea of bumblebees not the least bit concerned about being stung. *She remembered why she was here. She'd lost Kevin. She needed to find him.*

Blinding light exploded around her, and when she opened her eyes, the field was a forest. The bees humming song was silenced, replaced by a cricket and frog serenade. Sensing something had changed, Kayn looked at her hand again. No longer a child, she leapt as a garden snake slithered across the trail. *She wasn't afraid of snakes.* Walking barefoot the roots, stones and pinecones caused her no pain. She stopped at a tree surrounded by flowers. *It was the memorial for her family. A picture of her still hung on the tree even though she'd survived.* She removed the picture and sat to look at it. *It felt like a dream.* A dark-haired child was playing in the distance. His hair was scruffy and just a little too long. He disappeared into the trees. Certain it was Kevin, she chased after him, but no matter how fast she ran, he was always just out of reach. Somehow, she ended up back at her family's shrine in the forest. She saw a note with a bumblebee sticker, she hadn't noticed before. It was a journal entry of Kevin's from second grade, written in green crayon. *I saw a bumblebee today. I love bees, even more after they fly away.* Kayn's heart tightened. It would have meant nothing to most, but to Kevin, Chloe, and Kayn, it was a magical poem about their unspoken love for the simple things. Kayn recalled relating to its secret meaning when she was only in second grade. She was so touched he'd chosen this to place on her memorial, her eyes clouded with tears. For in a strange way, it foretold the future.

Gazing up at the cerulean sky, Kayn pled, "Please, you've taken everything from me, can't you let me say goodbye?" She heard Kevin shouting her name as though the in-between granted him the ability to hear her plea. She walked in the direction of his voice.

Kayn froze in place as giant transparent intricately interlaced webs blanketed in spiders the size of her hand appeared on either side and across the path above her head. Her heart was palpitating with sensory incapacitating panic uniquely reserved for the most terrifying moments in life. She couldn't swallow. She was so afraid she couldn't even will her legs to take a step. The spiders above her were descending rapidly from their lace-works, soon they'd be close enough to bind her in silk. She had to walk through the tunnel of webbing to get to his voice. Kayn turned, but her escape was blocked by spiders frantically building webs behind her. It was all legs and enormous furry bodies. Had she spun around without thought and bolted in terror, she would have been caught in it. *She had to move.* Kayn took a cautious step and then another. They were building at a furious pace behind her. She was so panicked her brain didn't want to cooperate. Something touched her head. *No, no.* Hesitant to look, she did. A spider stroked her hair, taunting her. Shrieking, she ran through, ducking under webs as swarming depravities sealed off the pathway in front of her. The webbing closed ahead. Squealing, she plunged through sticky silk covered in writhing furry bodies. Free, she tore off hideous arachnids and webbing, jumping, shrieking an ungodly pitch. When she ceased screeching, everything she feared vanished. They were gone but she was still bouncing around with heebie jeebies. She persuaded herself to breathe. *She was starting to understand. She wasn't supposed to be able to find him. He was Triad. She was Ankh. The in-between itself was trying to prevent them from reuniting. Stay centered, you need to find him.*

Kevin's call echoed in the horizon. She sprinted for his voice again and arrived back at her family's memorial. She didn't allow this to fluster her as she kept running in the direction of his call. *This wasn't working. They told her this place could be whatever she imagined it to be.* She pictured his smile and the sensation of being wrapped in his warm loving arms. The scenery altered and she was now standing alone in an open meadow. She felt like cheering but kept it inside. *She'd changed the scenery. Maybe, it was the first step to finding him.* He was calling her name. She took off in the direction of his voice as the landscape changed to the place where they watched clouds after class. *This was beginning to feel like a game.* As Kayn trudged through high grass, it came alive and wrapped around her ankles. She tumbled flat on her face with a soft thud as the grass tightened it's grasp on her legs. It felt like human arms as it began dragging her backwards. She stopped herself by clawing at the grass and digging fingers into soil, but only for a second before greenery bound her hands. Struggling, she fought to wriggle free, as it stretched her body in either direction. When she thought it was going to tear her in two, the grass slackened and she surmised the in-between was only trying to frighten her to distract her from her mission. *She had to find him. Whatever the cost.* She tore her hands free. Seemingly alive greenery wrapped around her throat. She struggled as it squeezed so tightly it began slicing through flesh. Feeling a warm stream of blood trickling down her throat, Kayn clawed at the braids of grass constricting her airway, writhing. *It wasn't killing her it was just wasting her time. Training. What had they taught her? She'd only had to think about a giant rock, and it appeared in her arms. She needed a knife.* One appeared on the ground before her. She let go of the grass and allowed it to wrap tighter around her throat to grab for the blade. Before she could reach it, the grass wrapped around the blade and pulled it into the soil. *Are you trying to stop me from finding him? Is that what you are trying to do? Enough!* The grass loosened. *Vocal commands didn't work here.* Kayn tore grass from her throat, half expecting it to continue to fight back but it didn't.

That Healer did something to connect them and it was against the rules. The Clans were not supposed to be able to meet up in the in-between. It was easy to read between the lines. A voice in her mind kept whispering, *keep trying. You can find him Kayn.* She could still hear him calling out to her. Kayn began calling back with everything she had left inside of her. As she raced for the sound of his voice, the scenery flashed with brilliant blinding light and she skidded out onto a frozen lake. *You are not supposed to find him.* Her breath rose, her bare feet ached. Goosebumps formed on every inch of her skin. The temperature was dropping drastically. Shivering, barefoot on a sheet of ice, it was torturously painful. She was afraid if she moved, she'd fall through into the freezing water. A flash of skin tone in green caught her eye. *Kevin was across the lake.* She called out for him but all that came out was air. *Her voice wasn't working.* He disappeared into the brush. Her feet were so agonizingly painful, she had to move. She began walking as fast as she could across the icy surface of the lake towards the shore where she'd seen him last. Halfway across the frozen water, the ice began to crack in a thin line. *Go back*, self-preservation whispered. Her heart screamed, *you must go forward. You can find him. This is your last chance. Keep going.* It was insane to continue walking in the direction of the rupture, but she followed the instinct to keep going. She'd almost made it to the other side when it crumbled around her. She fell through ice into glacial water. Torturously submerged, time slowed to the ticking of a clock as her mind whispered, *it's all in your head. This is not real.* Floating in the wasteland of the icy beneath, bubbles left her lips and travelled to the surface, blocked by the ceiling of ice. She didn't struggle, nor did she try to swim for the surface to escape the excruciating pain. Her heart said, *release the need for salvation. Fight past the pain. Do not allow it in. See where you want to go. Believe Kayn. Let go and believe it's possible to find him.* She allowed her body to float as she saw herself safe and warm, in Kevin's loving arms. Light flashed and in an instant, she'd been granted salvation from the icy beneath.

On the shore with the temperature back to normal, it was like it never happened. Kayn raked her fingertips through her wild mane of curls, she touched her dry dress. Faintly hearing a Rascal Flatts' song her mother loved, she sprinted towards the music. As she ran scenery in her peripheral vision flashed highlights of her mortal life. Tears formed in Kayn's eyes as her childhood played. *The visions confused her purpose with the allure of the moment. He was a part of every exquisite memory.* Watching heartwarming images with wonder, she snapped out of it as she heard Kevin call her name. *That was sneaky. The in-between was supposed to take her where she wanted to go and her desired destination was Kevin. She had to focus on what she wanted without being tempted by distractions.* Dropping to her knees, Kayn closed her eyes, and concentrated on the feeling of his lips as they met hers. *Their first kiss left her breathless in the aftermath, but the second kiss, it was all her. She allowed her heart to drift to each one.* Submerged in warmth, she whispered, "I love him. Let me say goodbye." As the ache in her heart grew unbearable, she stifled a sob as she was blinded by radiant light. The heavenly glare caused her to close her eyes. Before they opened, she felt the silkiness of sand beneath her fingertips. *She knew where she was. She was on her knees in the desert of diamonds.* Kayn smiled as she opened her eyes. In the horizon, the sun was sinking beneath sand as skyline swirled with vibrant orange and crimson pastels. She saw him, standing beneath the backdrop of the setting sun. It was like someone allowed her oxygen to breathe, her heart overflowed joy. Across the wide-open span of silken sand, they raced towards each other as music grew louder. Like magnets, they drew closer and closer until Kayn leapt into her best friend's arms. They spun around barefoot in the warmth of the sand. Their lips melted together in a breathtaking dance of lust, love and everything in between. *These were their final moments.* He touched her hair, feathering kisses on her eyes, cheeks, and forehead. She felt their hearts beating as one as they embraced. *There was no time for tears.* Squeezing his eyes shut to stop himself from crying, he gently kissed her lips, wiping salty tears from her eyes with his thumb.

Tenderly touching her face, Kevin whispered, "I'm so stupid. What have I done?"

Her eyes flooded with devastation as she whispered, "Don't forget me. We'll find a way to fix this." Running his finger over her birthmark, he touched the freckles on her face and one on her shoulder. *He was trying to make sure he'd remember her. She* had so much left to say but forming the words felt impossible. *It was done. Their fate had been sealed. No words could fix this. A chain of events had been started and it would change everything between them. There was nothing they could do.* The symbol on Kevin's chest lit up. Kayn's hand began to glow. *No, she wasn't ready to leave him! Please! Not yet!* Their time together was coming to an end.

Pulling out of the embrace, wanting nothing to be left unsaid, Kevin vowed, "I will remember you. I promise."

About to say she loved him, his lips met hers in a desperate attempt to claim a final kiss. A kiss snatched away by destiny as separate Clans claimed them. They began to glow so brightly they were compelled to back away from each other, covering their eyes with their hands. They closed their eyes and thought the same words of love as they dissolved into dust and blew away on a gentle breeze flowing through the desert of the in-between. *Kevin went back to Triad where he would have his memory erased and Kayn to Ankh where she would never be able to forget.*

Kayn awoke inside her tomb, shuddering as her eyes clouded with tears. She inhaled her first breath in the land of flesh and blood. *She'd never had to face a moment without knowing he'd be right by her side. The notion of a tomorrow without him was utterly terrifying. He was the needle on her inner compass, constantly influencing her in the right direction. They would find each other again. She pledged her heart this one thing.* Grinding of stone on stone made Kayn flinch as her tomb opened. Rays of glorious sunlight blinded her momentarily, she was forced to shut her eyes once again, and when she did, tears streamed down her cheeks. *She wanted to keep them closed forever.* She took a deep breath as she attempted to buy her heart one more second before having to face her new life. She willed her eyes to open and then to focus through the blurry film of tears. As she looked at the concerned faces of the Ankh surrounding her tomb, she understood she would never be alone. Her story was nowhere near its end. She had to focus on who she was and what she was meant to become. This was only the first chapter of her story. The next chapter had yet to be written.

The Beginning

THE CHILDREN OF ANKH SERIES UNIVERSE

There are many books in this universe to keep you occupied while you await the next one. Read on Dragon lovers.

KAYN'S SERIES

Sweet Sleep
Enlightenment
Let There Be Dragons
Handlers Of Dragons
Tragic Fools

LEXY'S SERIES

Wild Thing
Wicked Thing
Deplorable Me

OWEN'S MIDDLE GRADE SERIES

Bring Out Your Dead (A short novella)

Subscribe to The Children of Ankh Universe website and be the first to get updates, contests, and series release info. Hope to hear from you on social media. *"She's a batshit feral hitwoman for a Clan of immortals, and sometimes just a girl in love with a boy destined to be her Handler. The only thing standing in their way is cannibalism and intimacy induced amnesia.*

Jump into Lexy's part of the universe. BUY IT HERE:
    www.childrenofankh.com

A NOTE FROM THE AUTHOR

I began writing this series shortly after my MS diagnosis. I had many reasons to fight, incredible children, a wonderful family and amazing friends. This series gave me a purpose. Whenever things become dark, I use my imagination to find the light within myself. No matter what life throws your way, you are stronger than you believe. I hope my character's strength becomes an inner voice for the readers who need it. Stand back up, and if you can't stand, rise within yourself. *We are beautiful, just as we are. We are all immortal.*

She had never coveted the role of princess. She'd always wanted to be the hero.

Any time after book two, Enlightenment, you can jump into an epic side series with Lexy as the main character without spoilers. Find out how Dragons are created. She's a certifiably insane feral hitwoman for a Clan of immortals. Her Handler has intimacy induced amnesia. What could go wrong? A dark paranormal fantasy thrill ride.

No matter how far she ventured from this farm, she would always be the monster created within its walls of timber and shame. They would see what she really was. She was a murderer, a psychopath and a victim. She was all three of those things.

Children Of Ankh titles can be purchased retail wholesale through Ingram distribution and online sources. Once you've finished Kayn's series, there's more Children Of Ankh Universe books ready to go. Stop by childrenofankh.com for giveaways and release dates. Please post a review of Sweet Sleep. Thank you for being awesome. XO

Book two, Enlightenment is next. Enjoy the ride.

BIOGRAPHY

Kim Cormack is the comedic author of an epic dark sci-fi fantasy universe, "The Children Of Ankh." She worked as an Early Childhood educator in preschool, daycare, and as an aid. She has spent most of her life on Vancouver Island in beautiful British Columbia, Canada. She currently lives in the gorgeous little town of Port Alberni. She's a single mom with two awesome offspring. If you see her back away slowly and toss packages of hot sauce at her until you escape.

Made in the USA
Middletown, DE
09 March 2021